THE MOUNT

For my girl, Rachel.

From the first chat about this story in a little coffee house in Stratford, to now.

Enjoy.

THE MOUNT

THOMAS ANTHONY ELLIS

First published 2018 by DB Publishing, an imprint of JMD Media Ltd, Nottingham, United Kingdom.

ISBN 978-1-78091-554-8

Printed in the UK

Also from Thomas Anthony Ellis:

REUNION

Grace Darby has her life designed and decided for her. Michael Alpin has nothing to give to love than his life itself. Whilst Michael offers Grace the escape and adventure her heart craves, Grace in turn offers him his sole reason to be. As their love endures the tests of the First World War, the Irish War of Independence, and the deeply rooted designs of their families, Reunion delivers a romantic triumph in what could also be regarded as an utter tragedy.

Author Bio:

Thomas Anthony Ellis was born in Birmingham, UK, and is technically one of the world's oldest millennials, although he feels much older. Having studied Criminology in Sheffield University, and being awarded GE Star Student of Europe for his work in English Literature, he went on to write his first novel Reunion which was nominated for Best Novel at the 2011 Brit Writers Awards. Thomas now lives in Solihull with his partner Rachel and their two doodle dogs Barney and Lilly. Thomas and Rachel are currently expecting their first child, a little girl, in October this year, although they are yet to decide on a name. But they know it starts with E, or B, maybe.

Acknowledgements:

A huge thank you is due to everyone at DB Publishing for their tireless support, especially Steve Caron and Dan Coxon who have given me the creative licence to tell this story my way. With another three books mapped out, the future is extremely exciting. Thank you for believing in me.

I must also say thank you and sorry to Rachel who had the patience to live alongside me throughout this caffeine fueled journey, filled with countless nightshifts of typing, and endless pacing. Just so much pacing. I love you. Your excitement on hearing this story is the sole reason I wrote it.

One Year Ago

He stroked the mask.

It looked just like her. The dimple in her chin, the button nose, the thin puncture where they'd put the knife. The coldness of the clay reminded him of how her body had felt that day. Smiling, he rolled his thick finger across the small lump that sat just above her lip.

She had a mole. A pretty one.

His task was simple. He needn't have brought the mask with him, but it felt right. After all, she had belonged here once. Maybe this could be her final message to the world she had known before her transformation.

The night was warm, and the air felt close. The thick noise from the crickets cut through the whispering breeze as the tired wind tickled the long, longing grass. Pausing, he knew he had to choose his spot wisely.

Can't let them separate. The number's important.

He had climbed to the summit of the mount and looked out across the small village in front of him. An idle river ran through the middle, choking the ancient church that rested to the north. Beneath it, scattered rooftops sat like small stepping-stones across the lazing landscape. Small pockets of light glowed from the few households that had remained awake. The scene, glittering between the sky's cold canvas and the white light of the moon, reminded him of the night before Christmas. His excitement was almost unbearable.

Restraining himself, he adjusted the sack that hung over his shoulder. It wasn't heavy. There were only three small items resting inside.

These presents are to be presented for all to find. Those were the instructions.

He took a moment to compose himself. Finding a nearby bench, he sat down, placing the mask carefully by his side. Her closed eyes faced out towards her old hometown.

Many will be looking for her soon. But she'll never look back.

He was certain that her lips were pursed into a small smile. He mirrored the expression, his lips slithering across his crooked clenched cheeks. She looked peaceful. He hadn't seen her suffer much. Her fear was misplaced as her dying breath had revealed her true beauty, like a fresh flower taking full bloom. There was no trace of her agony captured within the clay. Now, she felt no pain. And she never would.

A small trail of moonlight stroked the ground at the mount's summit. Hell-bent on hiding, he held the darkness close to him. His orders were clear; he wasn't to be seen.

Tracing the sharp sliver of moonlight that scratched at the soil, he saw a small army of red ants scurrying over to an abandoned piece of apple core. Before long, the rotting fruit vibrated violently within the moon's soft spotlight, as the ants devoured what little flesh remained.

He watched intently until there was nothing left.

Masked by darkness, he waited patiently for the last house light to go out. He paused to look at her face, smiling. Once all was lifeless below, he removed the gifts from his small sack. Holding them within his fat hands, he could feel their feathers come to life within the soothing breeze.

Carefully, he began placing them next to one another. One by one.

One for sorrow…

'Hello Mr Magpie. Where's your friend?' His voice was trapped between a whisper and feverish giggle. Excited, he looked at the mask through the corner of his eye. He was certain she was still smiling at him. Feeling his thick heart thump against his chest, he picked out the next gift.

Two for joy…

Excitedly, he grabbed the mask and kissed it. It didn't matter how still they felt – how utterly devoid of life they were – he was certain her cold closed lips kissed him back. Lost for breath, he placed her back on the bench and continued his task.

The final gift was now within his trembling hands.

Three for a girl…

He stood back.

Finished, he examined his generous offering. They had been preserved and presented perfectly. As ordered, he had bound the dead bird's feet with a small piece of string. Noting the footpath that had been trodden into the earth by countless hordes of human traffic, he was certain they would be found by someone. After all, they had already gathered the fierce attention of the insatiable army of ants. He watched as a small bead of single-filed fire crawled towards the three dead birds. He didn't attempt to stop them from their duty. They had their right to take whatever life offered them. As had he.

He examined a small metallic plaque that rested on a stand in front of the bench where the mask lay. On it was a map of the village before them. Smiling, he looked from the mask to the map before taking out a knife and scratching out the location of where the young girl's house would rest.

'Your home is not here anymore.'

He sniggered as he looked at the sleepy village that rested beneath them. A village that would soon come to life through the death that it had suffered.

Checking his offering one last time, he was now sure that his task was complete. He had delivered the gift. They would be satisfied. And yet, a fear cradled him. It was a feeling he had felt before. A feeling that always came before a punishment. He had never meant to hurt anyone. He didn't ever mean to get things wrong. But he knew he had taken a huge risk tonight. Maybe he had made a mistake.

He had done something wrong.

He knew he shouldn't have taken her.

Chapter 1

'Fucking scum!'

The punch hurt more than the words. His right eye closed up. His outstretched hands were now attempting to steady himself on the ground.

'What's the matter... are we too old for you?'

The boot shattered his ribs on impact.

He turned to face upwards. His back warmed the cold floor of his cell. Sunlight masked his sight.

A silhouette swung towards him.

'She was just a kid!'

The shadow packed a punch. It flattened his nose completely. Cartilage cracked between the knuckles of his attacker's fist. Blood began to stream into his gaping mouth.

'Come on pussy... fight back.'

What was the point? He had little fight left in him. And after all, he was guilty.

That's what the police had claimed. That's what the press had said. That was what the jury had decided, unanimously. Forget about evidence. Forget about the cracks in the case. Nothing outweighed the allegation.

Child-killer.

He had no defence at all.

'Where the hell is she?'

Pain exploded across his jaw.

Even if he had wanted to, he could no longer answer. His jaw was dislocated. Pain poured into his screaming mind. Teetering on the narrow edge of consciousness, he wondered whether darkness was now the better option for him. At least then he wouldn't feel anything; he wouldn't feel what was coming next. And then – when silence came – he wouldn't have to listen to the countless, endless accusations.

But he knew his fate. He knew that if he chose the darkness – if he allowed himself to lose consciousness – then he would never wake up. His attackers would undoubtedly kill him. For the rest of his life he knew that he would always have to be the last one to fall asleep, and the very first one to wake. Being sentenced to life in prison, he may as well have been sentenced to death. He knew that if he closed his eyes before anyone else, then everybody that surrounded him would do whatever they could to keep them shut.

He took a deep breath. Blood choked him, clogging up his airways. Spluttering, he tried to get to his feet.

'Don't you dare get up!'

His arm was swept from under him. His swollen face crashed into the floor. Pain punctured his entire body. Quickly, the cell became a hot haze of stench and anger. He could hear at least three different voices hurling insults at him. And he knew who they belonged to. He knew the voices well. He'd heard this exact acidic pitch almost every day since he had arrived.

'Pervert!'

'Paedo!'

'Nonce!'

He'd heard it all before.

Yet, he couldn't tell which voice was hitting him. But it no longer mattered. They'd all get their turn. And they would all take it.

They always did.

Although today felt different.

Despite the overused insults, and reopened cuts that hadn't had time to fully heal, there was an air of calmness that unnerved him. A sense of delay, or savouring.

Before now, the attacks had been executed quickly, and they had been more public.

This attack was private, slow and methodical. There was no furious flourish, or frantic swinging of fists and feet before a sharp exit. He had come to learn how they attacked.

He had entered the prison expectant and braced for the beatings. He knew the punches would be coming. He knew that his judgement was not reserved for the courtroom only. His judgement was far-reaching, and far from over. It had been made quite clear that the guards were not protecting him. He'd noticed that there was always a slight delay between the attacks and their intervention. The guards openly hated him as much as the other inmates did. They showed it through their lack of urgency. Their delay in dealing with any attacks was their way of hitting him, their way of hurting what they couldn't hit themselves. Yet despite all that, right now, he prayed that the guards were simply having their fill, that their absence was through delay rather than unknowing.

However, the voices of the guards could not be heard. There was no sign of intervention, no sign of salvation. The attacker's punches were not punctuated by orders to 'stop' or 'back away'. Today, they were taking their time. Today, they were calculated. There was no sense of panic in their insults, no urgency in their act. Every punch was clean and measured. It was clear that nobody was going to stop them.

He knew then that they would kill him. Strangled by fear, only his mind could cry out.

Prove I did it. Prove my guilt!

But it was worthless. The call for proof hadn't worked in court. Nobody had felt the need to prove what they had already come to accept. He was guilty. From the first day that the young girl had disappeared, he knew he was a marked man. He was the only suspect, and his arrest was enough to convince the public that the demon amongst them had been swiftly snared. It didn't matter that her body was never found. It didn't matter that his conviction was solely based on conjecture and circumstance. The fact remained... a girl was missing, presumed dead. And he had been arrested, assumed guilty.

All sense of innocence was lost that day. One life stolen, another completely spoilt. Forever.

Regaining his focus, he felt fingers take hold of his blood-soaked hair, yanking his head backwards and arching his neck to its limit. He then felt the full force of his attacker as he thrust his head forwards, towards the ground.

And then, he felt nothing at all.

Chapter 2

The water beat down upon Addison's sunken shoulders.

The frosty blast felt like shards of glass scratching against his shivering skin. He couldn't stand any heat. Not anymore. His trembling body tensed as the ice-cold water banged at his back. Goosebumps rose to their peak, threatening to tear right through his thick forearms.

The cold shower was only meant to distract him. It was never meant to punish him for what he had done. He just needed it to help him focus on something else. Anything else. Addison knew that he'd never wash away what he'd done; he was forever stained by the death that he'd caused. Fighting the increasing urge to blink, he let the water wash over his open eyes. He had grown fearful of closing them. No matter how tired he became. No matter how much he wanted to. He always knew what image would greet him in the dark. Beneath the murky waters that drowned his memories, strong tides waited to drag him under. Every blink brought with it a wave of the face he'd missed, and each night delivered a sleepless slumber that he could never be able to alter, which set stage to a squalid scene that had been etched into his strained, sunken sanity.

It had been three weeks since he had last slept, and every waking thought felt like a fog surrounded it.

Turning the shower off, Addison grabbed a towel and began to dry himself. Due to the cold water, no steam had gathered in the small bathroom, so the long mirror in front of him was not curtained with condensation. Instead, he was greeted by a clear reflection of the man he now was.

Exhausted. Washed up. Spent.

His partner was dead. And many blamed him for it.

So did she.

Facing his image, Addison assessed the man who looked back at him. The once sharp grey eyes had dulled, no longer holding any trace of the spark that had shone within them. Lined by strands of silver hair, his thick beard had grown out longer than he'd ever worn it before. And his once hulking shoulders now sulked as if weighted down by the world itself. Teetering on the brink of breaking, he stood and stared at the stained shadow of his former self.

Tracing his image, he noticed a bead of water that danced down from his sunken shoulder. He watched as it writhed and wriggled through the marbled skin that wrapped his left forearm. Fierce scars, some surgical, some not, danced from his wrist towards his elbow. Still watching the bead of water, Addison half expected to see it pool within the banks of ridged skin. His body had been torn apart that day. The rocks had tried their hardest to rip her away from him. But he'd refused to let go. And now it wouldn't let go of him. For almost a year he'd been faced with picking up the pieces of everything that he'd broken on that single afternoon. He'd broken bones, procedures, promises. It had been his biggest mistake.

A fatal mistake.

Fully aware that he'd be held accountable, Addison knew he had made new enemies from old friends. But none of them mattered anymore. Many were just the distant collective who only unite to holiday in the misery of others. The grief did not belong to them. They didn't know his partner like Addison did. All they had lost was a name, and in turn gained a cause to hide their own failings behind. They hadn't lost someone they loved. They hadn't lost their best friend. Addison had. And, following weeks of scrutiny and an exhaustive internal investigation, today Addison was set to discover what little hope remained within the fallen ashes of his once bright career.

Sizing up what he should wear, Addison gathered that his uniform was no longer needed. He wasn't even sure if he'd ever get to wear one again. The last one he had ever worn had been on the day when everything had altered. Following the incident at the lake, his uniform itself had been seized for evidential purposes. Although, Addison wasn't sure what they expected to find.

I couldn't reach him. Why did he follow me?

All washed up, Addison felt like he was choosing his own funeral suit. He opted for a more modest look, with a simple pair of dark jeans and a navy blue shirt. He was too tired to bother with anything too fancy. If he was facing the firing squad, he wanted to make it clean and simple. No point muddying the ceremony with questionable attire. And after all, he wasn't sure if he'd ever be accepted in uniform again.

He knew that killing one of your own was unforgiveable; the damage... irreversible. Consequently, Addison had been stripped of his anonymity, removed of his collective identity. He no longer belonged to the *uniform.* Those who wore it would always reject him, casting him out from the biggest gang around. His brothers would banish him. His sisters would shun him. Exiled, and with foes forged from friends, Addison belonged to nothing he had ever known before.

Having worked as a police officer for nearly ten years, Addison had only once had a stint in a 'non-uniform' role, and only briefly. Having passed his exams to become a detective, Addison joined the local investigation team before working his way into Warwickshire's CID unit. Thorough, stubborn, and not the usual clock-watcher, Addison quickly gathered a solid reputation as a dedicated detective. But he always missed the *uniform*. Outside of it, he felt somewhat exposed to internal scrutiny. As a true team-player, Addison had enjoyed the collective concealment the uniform offered him. He had fully embraced the mantra that all uniformed officers worked to: 'We are the same'.

With this in mind, Addison was more than aware of how a quick costume change could give the impression of an entirely new character. People accepted appearances. They welcomed them, encouraged them. As much as it was denounced, prejudice was pivotal in identifying deviants, those few souls that stood outside the many simply served to identify what they no longer were. Evil defined good. Disorder defined law. And the deviant defined the group. And so, the uniform was key to gaining access to an accepted collective. Addison knew that the clothes didn't just make the man... they masked them. His faults were forgiven, his demons lost, because the main appeal about a uniform was that people didn't always examine who was wearing it. They just accepted what it presented, a representative of the many.

Once Addison had made detective, the dropping of the uniform was taken by some as an abandonment of where he'd come from. It didn't matter that Addison had no real option. It didn't matter that his role required him to dress another way. He was now somewhat different, separate from his peers. And he hated it. Addison hated being apart from his friends. Fashioned through countless acts of joint courage and support, his team had become a family to him. A family that he would never abandon. Not intentionally.

It wasn't just the new clothing that didn't suit Addison. The role itself wasn't as cerebral as he had first hoped. Addison soon learned that there was a strict process to investigations that anyone could be trained to follow. Instinct was ignored. Intuition abandoned. And only the facts that were presented were now acknowledged. It made him feel limited. After three years out of uniform, at his own request, Addison had been transferred back into a Response Unit. He craved the excitement, the allure of reacting to the unknown.

Yet, it was the unknown that had brought Addison to where he was now. Like any officer at the start of their tour of duty, Addison had no idea what that day would hold for him. He could never have predicted the events that unfolded that afternoon. But the day was now done. A man was dead. A woman was widowed. And a father was lost.

It should have been me.

Looking at his empty bed, he could see how only half lay dishevelled and disturbed. The other half was tidy, tucked in, cold. It had been that way ever since she had left him. Addison understood how hard it had been for her. Having to cope with the death of her brother would have tested anyone to their limits. The fact that his death was caused by her boyfriend took her to a place where forgiveness wasn't only forgotten, it was impossible.

Addison had been living with Rosie for a year before the incident. It was her brother, Joe, Addison's partner, who had introduced them in the first place.

There was nothing Addison didn't love about Rosie. Her drive, her beauty, her exceptional normality, were just small parts of what now summed up his world. She was everything. Or had been. She was now gone. And there was no going back. He'd witnessed grief a thousand times on the faces of countless victims, but he could always switch off from it. He could remain cold. The pain didn't belong to him, so he didn't need to own it. Once his shift was done he could return to the warmth of his home, to his reality. He'd never had to truly cope with the anguish before. The pain that remains once everyone has gone. The hurt that hums in the silence after all the supporting faces and sincere smiles have returned to their real lives. It was only until he was on the inside that he could see the truth in the agony. To see how impossible it was to bind the bonds that had been torn apart. Especially when you were the one that had caused the tear.

Heading downstairs, Addison could hear the sound of four feet charging down after him. Like some form of morning ceremony, Addison's chocolate brown Labrador – Marshall – would always see him off. Perched in front of the door, and completely blocking Addison's exit, Marshall waited.

Addison was no stranger to this ritual. Holding out two closed hands, Addison presented his fists to his smiling ally. Marshall knew his part, but always played it out like it was the first time he'd seen it. After a sniff and a sideways glance, Marshall placed his dark, heavy paw on the hand that he knew held no treat. Invariably, Addison would open up his empty hand before acting disappointed.

Finally, Marshall – excited and expectant – placed his paw on the remaining fist. And to script, Marshall wagged his tail proudly as Addison presented his reward, a chunky golden marrowbone biscuit.

'That's my boy,' said Addison with a warm smile. He ruffled the dog's head as he passed.

Outside, the bright morning carried a crisp, refreshing chill. Spears of soft sunlight broke through the small set of trees that faced Addison's mid-terraced house, pressing against the small lawn on his driveway. Pausing, Addison greeted the stillness of the scene. No doubt his future would be full of enforced changes. He knew his path had been altered. But right now, within the motionless midsummer morning, Addison allowed himself to fade away. For just a moment, the entire day appeared to be set on pause. Only the supple sound of a morning breeze brushing through the grass punctured the air.

Addison cut short his respite.

It would take him ten minutes to drive to the station, where his fate would inevitably be sealed. Taking a deep breath, he prepared himself for what decisions lay ahead.

His damned day was back in play.

Chapter 3

DI Banks lit a cigarette. She knew she wasn't supposed to be smoking on site, especially in the office, but today warranted it. She was stressed. Seriously stressed. It wasn't even half ten in the morning and already she had seen four reports of burglary, two minor assaults, and a domestic incident which left a man with an 'accidental', yet in her opinion well-earned, stab wound to his shoulder.

The strain of the job seemed to stretch out the skin on her forehead. Her face felt tight.

But it wasn't the police to-do list that was stressing her out. Today, DI Banks was having to reshape the future of a once rising star in the force. Having led the Response Unit for almost five years, she was well versed on what made a great cop. And in her opinion, Addison Clarke was it. Or at least, he had been.

She knew more than most what had happened that day. She had even been the first to call him a hero for what he had done. But a foolish one at that. And – as she knew all too well – how often the foolish fell. And Addison hadn't just stumbled. He'd fallen hard. And fast.

Now he just needed to be picked up, and pushed.

In front of her, taking up most of her tiny desk, was DC Clarke's impressive career file. Not that she needed it. To her, it didn't really matter what it said in there. Not anymore. The records were irrelevant. She knew his merits. She had seen him work. Nobody had ever had a bad word to say about the man. Not until that afternoon. Now everything was different. Now, there was nothing but negativity. His reputation had suffered beyond repair. That was all that mattered now... reputation. And she wasn't going to allow an individual's reputation to tarnish that of the collective.

Taking a moment to adjust herself, DI Banks felt a wave of nerves wash over her. Sipping her now stone-cold coffee, she took a seat and waited.

It wasn't for long. Addison was always on time.

'Morning Ma'am.' Addison peeked his head around the door. 'You wanted to see me?'

Addison didn't wait for an invitation. Walking into the small office, he could see his old beat through the panoramic windows that ran along the entire wall. Outside, it looked a lot quieter than he remembered. But then, it was 10:30 a.m. By now, the honest would be occupied, the lazy would be distracted by daytime trash TV, and the junkies would be sleeping off their morning buzz. Every one of them had a focus, and for years Addison's focus had been every one of them. Hoping not to appear preoccupied by the past, Addison took a quick look at his inspector. He noted that she seemed a little more groomed than usual. Her lank hair was down, which was against her own strict ruling, and he could smell a faint whiff of perfume muddled up with the usual blend of tobacco and cheap coffee. She had clearly made some small effort on her part to appear more presentable, pleasing even.

Her approach was obvious.

He knew she had bad news.

'Good morning Addison.' She felt bad calling it good. If anything, it was a pretty crappy morning so far. And it wasn't going to get any nicer. 'Please, take a seat.'

She pointed her arm in the general direction of the only other chair in the office. She was trying her best to remain casual, almost engaging.

Addison picked up on it.

'Now Addison,' she shifted in her chair a little. 'You know how much we at the Warwickshire Police Service truly value our workforce. And you are no exception to this. We've seen great things from you.'

'Thanks. But with all due respect Ma'am, try pitching that to the masses. I don't think you'd get many supporters.'

Despite skipping breakfast, Addison didn't have much of an appetite for a shit-sandwich. He knew what was coming. He'd seen it dished out countless times. Regardless of the ingredients, the recipe was always the same. Offer the chump an initial compliment to soften the blow, layer it with the crucial criticism that was cause for the whole conversation in the first place, and then end on a soft piece of praise, but not too much so that the lasting flavour is anything but the crap-tasting *constructive* filler.

Looking at his inspector, he knew what she was thinking. Her whole body language reeked of awkward guilt. But she didn't need to feel it. It wasn't her fault. She was just a messenger who was positioned close enough to make the decision seem more warm and personal than the cold clinical one it really was. The decision was made by the institution, not the individual. Her smile said it all.

'DC Clarke, well done for being on time today. Nevertheless... you killed a cop, everybody hates you, and we all wish that it was you that had died that day. Did you get a haircut? It suits you.'

Well, that's the type of tripe he was expecting to hear her say anyway.

But she didn't.

Instead, she plated up a whole new proposal that Addison never considered to have ever been on the menu, let alone the table. Watching her lips move, and hearing the words she had to say, Addison felt like dog-dirt. There he was projecting his own sense of guilt onto somebody who had no real personal duty to look out for him. She didn't need to do all that she could in an attempt to save his career. It would have been easier, even understandable, if she were to advise that he leave the police force immediately. But instead, she sat there smiling.

Smiling, and offering Addison a lifeline.

'So, Addison...' she paused to gauge his reaction. 'What do you say?'

The proposal was a peculiar one, one that, if offered a year ago, Addison would have flat-out refused, almost insulted by the idea. But right now, it felt like morphine to a wounded soldier. Though it may not save him, it would sure as hell help with the pain.

'The department is new... kind of,' DI Banks continued. Addison hadn't said anything for a while, so she still felt like she needed to convince him of the position.

'Officially it's called the "Tasking Team". Primarily, it was set up to review old, cold cases. The exaggerated internal pitch would say that it's an exciting area wherein to ensure that the police aren't missing opportunities to catch criminals. Whereas the negative slant would see it as a waiting room for retiring officers, accompanied by a few of the sick, lame and lazy ones as well. Granted, it's not the most exciting of roles but...'. She looked her most sincere. 'Addison... it does give them something to come to work for. They have purpose. And occasionally, they even pick up on any appeal cases that come along the way. You see, we also have to ensure we don't open ourselves up for any public scrutiny when these cases get reviewed. In these instances, all you'll be doing is making sure we didn't cut any corners during the investigation.'

'Wait, you want me to rat out officers that may have messed up?'

Addison was back in the room, although he wanted to run out of it. Here he was, sat accused of causing the death of a fellow officer, and now they wanted him to poke about into other people's investigations with a highlighter pen and a direct line to the Chief Inspector. Not a chance. The Professional Standards department, who had a reputation of culling officers just so they could clean their computer screens of a complaint, were already doing a stellar job at pissing police officers off.

Addison loathed them. He knew first-hand that everybody was a genius with retrospect. Professional hindsight was a hindrance to all good officers just trying to do an honest job. But hindsight was a callous bitch, often favouring the unknown, untested result, and siding with hypothesis rather than actualities. And, most of all, it screwed cops over. When an officer – overworked, underpaid, and exhausted – had to make a split-second decision down a poorly lit alleyway on a bleak Saturday night, you could always rely on the Monday morning jury – well rested and sat comfortably in their air-conditioned offices – to come up with a more favourable course of action. Every scenario played out perfectly on paper; there were no variables to consider. The textbook was gospel. If a man was angry, politeness cured his woes. It didn't matter that he was drunk, holding hair freshly torn out from the scalp of his beaten wife, whilst his bloodstream pumped half a gram of cocaine around his steroid-inflated body. Words were enough. Professional behaviour bred professional results. On paper at least. On patrol, however, it was nothing but variables. Addison knew that more than most. And although Addison knew his reputation was dead, he was in no rush to bury others with him.

'It's not like that at all Addison. Not... at... all. All you'll be doing is a paper exercise. Just a tick-box audit to make sure that all basic enquiries are accounted for. Nothing sexy. Nothing scandalous. We just don't want to leave ourselves vulnerable.'

DI Banks looked flustered. 'Forgive me. I know this isn't what you wanted to hear, and I appreciate it's a little below your skill set, but it is an option. I'm sorry that you're having to be moved in the first place. Yet the truth is, we needed to find you a role where you could... well... work alone.'

'Oh,' Addison sunk in his chair. He knew she was right. Who would partner up with somebody who killed their last one?

'Addison...' She looked serious for a moment. More stern than sincere. 'You were not found to be responsible for PC Foster's death. No matter what people continue to say. No matter what looks they give you, or the comments you may hear. You are innocent. But that said, the facts remain. What happened that day, it altered everything. Your home soil has shifted. Maybe a change would be good for you after all.'

Addison knew what she was saying. *Sod off and make my life easier.* God knows he agreed with her.

'Okay.' Addison made sure he smiled sincerely. He meant it. 'I'll take the job boss. Thank you.'

'Great news.' DI Banks looked relieved. She thought that there would have at least been an objection of sorts. Technically, DC Clarke didn't have to do anything. But she knew it would make things run a lot smoother if he left.

'You start in three days. That should give you plenty of time to get adjusted to your new surroundings.'

'New surroundings?' Addison looked confused.

'Oh... did I not mention?' DI Banks tried to act casual. She was too close now to scupper this masterstroke. She'd played it perfectly so far. The best result for all was just inches away. That is, inches that equated to around fifty miles away, when looking at a map of the entire county. 'You'll be based on the outskirts of the force area. In a little village called Claymore. It's quite lovely.'

Pretending to busy herself with already open mail, she gave Addison a look that simply said 'We're done here'.

Shrugging off the shock, Addison took the hint. Getting to his feet, he thanked DI Banks again, and then – with little fuss – left the office. Outside, nobody was waiting to say goodbye to him as he pulled out of the station. His once second home.

He didn't realise that he would never return.

Chapter 4

The bed was more comfortable than his usual one. Which only meant one thing: his body was in a bad way. Having been in prison for little over a year, Benjamin had been sent to the outpatient ward no fewer than nine times. Usually it was for minor cuts and bruises, small-time injuries that simply needed documenting. Not that the records were always accurate. With departments having to perform a balancing act between funding and threat levels, the sickness records were stitched up almost as frequently as the inmates were. Often, the visit to the ward was more a matter of process than any true provision of care. Injuries always had a cause, and a cause created blame. As long as the prison wasn't to blame, then the warden was happy to go on record and have the patient treated. But never before had Benjamin felt the luxury of a soft mattress on his back.

So far during his stay, from the more accommodating inmates, Benjamin had been treated to a towel in the mouth, a face in the pillow, and even a sock around the throat. It seemed that all that was left to offer him from the hostile-hospitality board was the cold, sharp shank in the side. However, today he was given a comfort he was not expecting. The sweet touch of a soft mattress was an indulgence he hadn't felt since he'd lost the luxury of being able to call himself a free man.

Nevertheless, what little comfort the bed offered had been almost completely lost on Benjamin. On a colossal cocktail of medication, he had spent the last day between a swirl of stained white light and deep darkness. And though he'd been barely able to remain awake long enough to take a mouthful of water, Benjamin did remember a face. A lurking shadow that stayed by his side, watching him. His vision had been veiled by a mixture of bandages and powerful painkillers, but one face seemed to stay firm within the shaded memory. Trying to focus on his surroundings, Benjamin struggled to open his right eye. His left eye was completely swollen over. As the medication began to wear off, pain crawled across his body. His limbs now throbbed with an angered ache which left his bones feeling so brittle they seemed to be on the brink of breaking. It took all of his strength just to stop himself from shaking. Clenched, and tensed, his fractured frame fought the surging pain that came with such traumatic recovery.

If Benjamin was at all happy to still be alive, then his body wasn't celebrating it.

'Well... good morning, Mr Farrow.' The nurse's soft voice didn't mirror her actions. Despite Benjamin's obvious injuries, the nurse pushed and pulled at her patient until she could release the pillow from beneath his heavy head. Beside him, Benjamin could hear the dull popping of the pillow as she plumped it up. When his head finally came to rest upon it, it felt as though his mind was melting into a soft marvellous cradle of morphine. Instantly, endorphins crashed through his tenderised flesh, urging him to sleep. Feeling the weight of recuperation draw his good eye closed, Benjamin saw the face again. It appeared to smile through a gnarled, garish grin. Its fixed feverish eyes froze upon his own burning brow. Fearful, Benjamin tried to fight the urge to sleep, but he was exhausted. Reluctantly he granted slumber his full surrender. But the face followed him, deep into his restless siesta.

Several hours later, Benjamin woke startled and panicked. It had felt like only a moment had lapsed since he had fallen asleep, and there had been no rest within it. The corridor outside the prison ward was now dark and gloomy. Menacing murmurings swayed through the humid night air like the prison's own simmering, sinister breath. Trying to ignore it all, Benjamin felt the soft press of water against his cracked lips. The nurse, now tired from her long shift, was back at his side.

'Thank you,' croaked Benjamin. His dry throat felt scratched by the first words he had said in over a day.

'You're welcome,' smiled the nurse. Though her eyes contradicted her. Her cold gaze was indifferent. Her care more obligatory than earnest.

'Who was he?' Benjamin tried to sit up. Pain clamped his back to the bed.

'Who was who?' Feigning interest, the nurse carried on with her general duties as she spoke. She was already late off, and was in no mood to start a conversation.

'The man who was with me earlier. He had a scar across his lips.' Benjamin could see the face clearly. It felt as familiar as it was unknown. Like a forgotten friend.

'Oh... *him.*' The nurse paused. The thought of the man made her shudder. His entrance was always announced by the stench that preceded him. A dank, mouldy mixture of sweat and dry blood. 'You'll be best staying away from that one.'

'Really?' Benjamin's head felt heavy.

'But then again, credit where it's due. He did bring you here.' The nurse looked at Benjamin as if she was assessing him. Clearly his lack of memory offered some measure of the attack on him.

'Where is he?' Benjamin nodded for some water. It smoothed his throat as he swallowed.

'Don't you worry about that maniac. He'll be in isolation by now.' The nurse almost laughed as she continued. 'Especially after what he did.' The nurse nodded to the bed next to Benjamin's. Straining to turn his neck, he saw that he wasn't alone. Lying just a few feet away from him was a man that Benjamin knew well. He owned one of the voices that had accompanied the punches back in Benjamin's cell.

'Paedo' was his usual condemning contribution. Benjamin had heard it spat at him before. And though he wasn't entirely sure which injury the man had inflicted on him, it was clear that he had been made to pay for it. Thick bruises masked his eyes. His left wrist was supported by a makeshift sling, and his neck bracketed by a thick brace. Two porters were now preparing to take the man to hospital. Clearly, the small ward wasn't equipped to deal with the level of injury he'd sustained.

It had never occurred to Benjamin that maybe he needed to go to hospital as well. But then he'd never experienced any preferential treatment since he'd arrived almost a year ago. That was... not until now.

Benjamin felt confused. Nobody had helped him before. Not like this. Benjamin's enemies had always been allies to one another. He was the preferred prey to the caged crowd. Never once had someone stood forward and protected him.

'Did he do that?'

'Apparently so. By all accounts, he's even confessed to it. Way before the warden had even caught wind of the fight taking place, he'd walked straight to his office and coughed up to everything. If you ask me, it seems that he wanted people to know what he'd done.' The nurse almost looked impressed for a moment, before continuing.

'For what it's worth, it seems your friend got to you just in time. Our man here – and a couple more like him – were punching your ticket, and there was to be no return journey, trust me. Based on the bruises to your body, they were using your face to knock at death's own door for you. And – believe me – he was mighty close to answering. Those men, they'd have killed you, happily, no question. But then the cavalry arrived. Two of your playmates left just before your knight in grimy armour could get his hands on them. But this poor chap here, well, he didn't get the chance to run away. After running out of bones to break in this sorry sack of a man, your friend dropped him like a discarded toy and then dragged your battered body here. I hate to say it, but I'd say you owe him your life.'

Benjamin remembered now. He remembered ceiling lights pulse above him. He recalled how the cold floor dragged beneath him. And he remembered the face flashing in front of his.

'It's all coming back to me.' Benjamin's cloud of confusion began to clear. 'He was talking to me. Asking me questions.'

Don't worry.

Tell me what happened.

I'm here for you now.

'Probably just making sure you stayed awake.' The nurse checked her watch. It was getting late. Her double shift had ended over an hour ago, and she'd already given this creep the main fill of her day. The truth be told, she was cold when it came to giving people like him care. She had to be. Many of her friends had often questioned how she was able to look after people in prison; how she could tend to those that had caused so much pain to others. Especially those that had hurt children. She always tried to tell herself that they were more misunderstood than monsters. But she'd seen otherwise. Most of the inmates were wired differently to the masses outside. Their parts were the same, but they housed them in different places. Their sense of sympathy seemed reserved only for themselves, each one of them pleading that they were the victims of their own lives. None of them appeared to offer it to those that warranted it. And yet, their anger was available to all. Not just for those that deserved it.

Stood assessing her patient, she saw what she saw in all of them: pain. A pain she knew he probably deserved.

'I need to know who that man is,' said Benjamin. He could see the nurse was readying herself to leave. 'Please. I believe you... I think my life rests on it.'

'Sorry, I have no idea who he is.' Her interest in him had clocked out sometime ago, and she herself should have clocked out hours before then. 'I'm sure he'll make himself known to you eventually.'

Turning, she flicked off the light as she left the small ward. She was certain that the monster she'd seen that day would surface soon enough. It was clear he wasn't done with Mr Farrow just yet.

Chapter 5

The small Anglo-Saxon village of Claymore, divided by the now dried out River Cane, sat at the gateway to the county of Warwickshire. Overlooking the village were the ruins of the 1,000-year-old Abraham's Castle. Shaped by warfare, Castle Abraham was now just a shell of its 11th-century craftsmanship. Torn down through battles and internal divide, what was left of the castle now fell between two opposing churches. The east side was occupied by the grand Catholic Church of St Thomas More, whilst the west was home to the imposing Anglican Church of St Augustine. Abandoned and undisturbed for decades, the landscape had quietly moved into the castle, long after the warring families had moved out. Trees had entwined themselves with the remains of the gatehouse, and a mosaic of moss blanketed the stone walls. But one of the churches remained alive with people. Beneath the scornful gaze of the summer sun, the splendid stained-glass windows that draped the ever-open oak doors of St Thomas More cast a colourful eye upon the church's close community. A community that had been unsettled for over a year since its number had been dramatically reduced by one.

Elizabeth Silver was six years old when she had gone missing. She was last seen by her mother Beverly, having tucked the young girl safely into bed around 8 p.m. However, in the morning, the girl was gone. There had been no sign of a break-in; no evidence of a struggle. She had simply vanished. The police search had lasted for nearly two weeks, assisted by countless community meetings, local press coverage, and volunteers travelling from nearby towns to help in any way they could. But Elizabeth was never found.

Yet her killer was.

Benjamin Farrow, a part-time teacher, had been working at Claymore's local primary school when he was arrested for Elizabeth's murder. Police reports stated that several witnesses could place Farrow near to the Silver residence during the early hours of that morning.

Also, a local boy, out for no known sensible reason, had seen a young man walking alongside the River Cane, just south of the Oakland Woods. The boy stated that this man was holding the hand of a young girl wearing light blue pyjamas. Sadly, he was too concerned about the drugs in his pocket to report the matter at the time, instead deciding to smoke his whole supply, blindly unaware that he was the last person to see the young girl alive. Further police enquiries had identified CCTV which showed a figure, loosely matching Farrow's appearance, riding a bicycle in the direction of Elizabeth Silver's house half an hour before the sighting by the river. A non-driver, Farrow was known to travel to work on his trusted one-speed bicycle. And to all the community concerned, that was enough.

Benjamin Farrow was guilty.

The press had agreed. After a month of speculation and community-led conjecture, the media finally had their monster. Too plain to demonise through photographs, the press painted a picture of a fiendish Benjamin Farrow through vitriolic adjectives and bold suggestions of bad character. They deemed him a 'loner', an 'outsider', and 'unusually quiet'. Soon, a shadow of doubt shaded Farrow's social profile, making it seem as if nobody in Claymore ever truly knew the man. A fact entirely planted, cultivated and then harvested by the press. The 'unknown' was the key to it all. Fear now sat in the shadows, and doubt clouded everyone's judgement. To those in fear, doubt was enough. And the media were the puppet-masters of fear.

Before long, they were pulling at every string.

Moving between the lines, the newspapers manipulated what wasn't known about Benjamin Farrow to make the absence of any known home life to appear abnormal, and by walking the razor-thin line between suggestion and slander, the tabloids sharpened and fashioned the people's fear against him. But there was no novelty in it. The formula was simple. They started with what was known. A child was missing. A community was disturbed, in need of answers. Then they suggested a solution. Benjamin Farrow, through allusive allegations and sly subjectivity, was offered up as the only viable option. And everybody took it.

On the day of his arrest, flanked by almost every officer from Claymore's local police unit, Benjamin Farrow had simply smiled and said... 'She's not here.'

Throughout the police interviews and proceeding court case, Benjamin Farrow denied knowing where Elizabeth Silver was. But he wasn't believed. Following a surprisingly short trial, Farrow was found guilty of the young girl's murder, and sentenced to life imprisonment. And though his guilt offered the masses an answer, Farrow's refusal to accept the blame kept the mystery alive. His silence had offered no circumstance or closure.

Elizabeth's body was never found.

She remained missing. A child lost to all that loved her. Now all that remained was a community which would never forget what they would never know.

*

Addison's directions had been vague at best.

Pass the church on your left.

They failed to mention this place had two of them.

Keep the river to your right.

Given the fact that the river ran around the churches like a dried-out piece of old rope, the directions didn't offer him much hope of finding his new station on time. Waiting for him there would be his new shift Sergeant and a complete new team of strangers. Which wasn't such a bad thing. Addison knew that anonymity came with benefits. With it, he would be able to carve out a new career path for himself, achieve new goals, however limited they may now be. And – more importantly – he would have the chance at beginning to forget the guilt that defined him back home. Ambiguity certainly had its advantages.

Eventually, having chosen to entirely ignore the directions offered to him by DI Banks, Addison tossed the scribbled-down guidelines onto the passenger seat of his force-provided, unmarked Vauxhall Astra, and followed the local signs to the station.

He was there within minutes. Having reluctantly travelled the entire circumference of Claymore for the best part of half an hour – passing field after field, and navigating countless tight rural roads – it occurred to Addison just how small the village was when you knew the layout. Local stores appeared squashed together as they lined the cramped high street that stretched through the centre of the village. The local houses seemed scattered amongst high hedgerows and far-reaching land, littered with bulging apples trees and wild flowers. It was clear that the village enjoyed the spoils of the wild, rural countryside, but there was an air of grooming to the landscape that told Addison that this was a proud place. And he knew its public would reflect this sense of solidarity fiercely. Feeling a wave of anxiety wash over him for the first time since arriving, Addison realised that he was not at home in this situation. A proud community often policed itself, and Addison didn't like feeling unnecessary. He needed to feel needed. Although, it was clear he was no longer needed back home.

Passing through a row of regimented scarlet oak trees, Addison pulled into the police station's car park. The small building was placed on the very edge of vast ancient woodlands, carpeted by English bluebells. Looking back from where he'd come, Addison couldn't help but feel isolated from the community he was set to serve. This wasn't a station that sat at the centre of the village. Access was not easy, and he imagined that they didn't have to deal with wave after wave of human traffic. If someone wanted to visit the station, they could only access it by the small, single-lane road, framed by the fierce row of trees, whose leaves were turning a soft shade of red, in clear defiance of the season. Still, a little sunlight broke through. Looking around him, Addison reasoned that if someone wished to report something in person, getting here alone was a solid testament to the conviction in their complaint. Nature had been tailored to test everyone intending to attend the station. Any sense of doubt, in either the purpose or importance of the report, would have built up by the time they had arrived at the station's door.

Addison knew that many would have turned back. The distance left no avenue for impulsive reporting, and filtered out those less committed to the cause. In person, anyway. There was always the phone.

Entering the only door at the front, Addison could hear a ringtone being interrupted.

'Good afternoon, Claymore division, how can we help?'

Addison saw a middle-aged man sat at the reception desk. He held the phone in one hand, and a small fork in the other. A large slab of cheesecake rested on his desk. Looking at him, Addison noted that his skin was a little pocked, and his face was the greyer side of pale. Strange, given the miniature heatwave the town was enjoying. Entertaining his caller, the cop seemed deflated by what he was hearing, as if the call had somehow interrupted his day. Ignoring professionalism, he attempted to answer with a mouthful of food.

'Yes, Mrs Martin,' sighed the officer who acknowledged Addison with a wave of his fork. He flicked it towards the single chair in the small reception area. A splatter of buttery biscuit beat Addison to it, so he decided to stand instead.

'But of course Mrs Martin... we are well aware that the hedge is overgrown. But this a civil matter. Please, call your solicitor.' He hung up.

Addison smiled.

'People will always bloody moan won't they?' He took another mouthful of food. 'Forgive me, where are my manners.' He stood up, dusting his creamy hands onto the bottom of his blue jacket. 'I'm Sergeant Derek Parker.' He held out a hand. Crumbs of blended biscuit and jam flecked his fingers.

'Pleasure to meet you Sarge,' Addison stood up and shook Sergeant Parker's sticky hand. 'I'm Addison Clarke.'

'Oh, I knew that already.' He shifted a lump of cheesecake to the side of his mouth as he smiled. 'I know all about you son.' His smile didn't wane. His eyes said it all. He knew.

So much for new beginnings. It was clear that Addison's past had been shared by his old force, and now he felt a fool for having let himself believe that he could start afresh.

'Come now, don't look like that. We all have a story.' Thankfully, Sergeant Parker had found a cloth and began to clean his hands.

'True. But some stories don't have a happy ending.'

'Don't be so daft. I read the report. You're fine. That guy – Foster was it? He caused his own death, not you. Shake it off. Move on. To me, and everyone else here, you're completely innocent. And trust me... that's all that matters to the people of Claymore.' He tossed the last piece of cake into his mouth. 'You'll soon learn that here... we care for the innocent. It's only the guilty we go after.'

His laugh was surprisingly high-pitched.

'And another thing, forget all this "Sarge" nonsense. Just call me Duke.'

He slapped Addison on the shoulder and ushered him into the station. There was a sense of real strength in the man, born through brutal honesty and optimism.

Addison liked him already.

Chapter 6

Sergeant Derek Parker had given Addison the whistle-stop tour of the station. Taking into account the size of the building, anything more would have been excessive and a little awkward. Aside from the reception area, there was a small team-room, consisting of four tables with a computer and telephone on each. Next to this was a tiny kitchen leaving little option other than to cook at home or microwave at work. And lastly was the locker room, offering one toilet cubicle and a single shower cubicle which, if the crime scene tape that was being used to hold it together was anything to go by, was broken. Walking back through the team-room, Addison was offered the last remaining desk. Various framed photographs and miniature mascots of various forms decorated the other three.

'Welcome to the Tasking Team.'

Duke had explained that the team was established to offer roles mainly for officers on restricted duties. That way they could join a team and fill their days until they were fit to go back outside to play with the real cops. Most of their time was whittled away on dead-end enquiries and keeping the public up-to-speed with where their investigations were at. After all, like the few force issued posters that sat Blu-tacked to the wall declared, 'Communication Breeds Community'. Not quite the sell DI Banks had offered back home.

If not only through selfish pride, Addison found himself starting to simmer over. He'd clearly been played. Back on the force, he had done his time. He'd passed the psychological tests. He was no longer injured, and occupational health had had no choice but to rule him fully fit. Even the internal investigation was over. There was no reason for him to be restricted. Unless they wanted to keep him hidden.

'To be honest…' smiled Duke, about to confirm Addison's suspicions, 'there's never any real reason to leave the station.' He shrugged as he opened his second chocolate bar of the day. Ignoring his frustration for a moment, Addison wondered how the human dustbin stood before him managed to maintain his thin frame.

'Is there a gym nearby?'

'Not that I know of,' mumbled Duke. 'But the road and the fields are free to use. Think of it as a rural sports centre.' Duke enjoyed his own joke more than Addison did, slapping him on the back as his hearty laugh took a sharp turn and quickly descended into a small coughing fit. Seeing Duke's grey face begin to turn a darker shade of blue, Addison returned the favour and slapped his Sergeant firmly on the back. A small lump of phlegm-covered Mars bar thumped the floor.

'Talk about death by chocolate,' smiled Addison. 'Not a bad way to go, I suppose.'

'Ha! I wish.'

Unfazed, Duke dried his eyes as he ushered Addison outside. 'We've arranged some small lodgings for you above the old Fallen Oak public house. Trust me, you'll love it there. They do a cracking Sunday roast – the barmaid has a fair set of Yorkshire puddings of her own – and they often keep the pints pouring way into the early hours of the morning as well. You'll be happy there. And don't worry, I've checked and they allow dogs, so your Labrador will be right at home in no time.'

'Cheers. That's very kind of you. As for the boy, well, he'll be staying at home with Rosie. But credit where it's due... you've certainly done your homework on me.' Addison knew he shouldn't have been surprised at the level of research his supervisor had done on him. These days, with social media and the online press, it wasn't difficult to see who someone was. Especially one as hot off the press as him. Addison doubted that many transferred officers came with a kill count.

'Believe me son, every detail is considered around here. Don't be shocked that we looked you up. We're not interested in all that drama you left behind. We just wanted to put a face to a name. And see where that face best sat. That's all. Claymore is a new beginning for you... a chance to reinvent yourself. We've all been in need of that at some point.'

Before long, the orientation was complete and Addison had been given the rest of the afternoon off to get settled and move his belongings into his new lodgings. He'd been surprised at the size of the space that he'd been given. The flat above the public house had opened up into a small two-bedroom apartment area, although he was advised to keep the spare bedroom empty. The landlord had explained that the extra room was often used by him or any other intoxicated publican who was unfit to drive home.

'Better to have them crash here then out there,' he'd said. Given the rehearsed delivery of the joke, he'd clearly used it before, not that it mattered to the half-cut gnarled-nosed publican who laughed like it was the first time he'd heard it. Knowing his audience, Addison had laughed politely. After all, the man's generosity was unexpected and massively welcome.

Inside the apartment Addison set up his laptop, found a socket for his phone charger, and filled the wardrobe with the few items of clothing he'd brought with him. Despite having never considered his move to be a permanent one, Addison did see the sense in setting up home here. That way he could quickly immerse himself into the community, get to know the people around him, and assess their expectations. Back home, Rosie had agreed to move back into their house, but she was actively looking for a place of her own. Nevertheless, the idea of her being there soothed him somewhat. Being able to picture her in their home – in a space he had shared with her – offered him a glimmer of hope that the past would be strong enough to somehow save them. He knew that what they had, before her brother's death, was something worth fighting for. He just wasn't sure how much fight they both had left in them.

With the little he had brought with him now all in its place, Addison decided to go for a run.

The afternoon was held within a relaxed summer breeze. Clear skies had coloured the land with a soft smooth shine, and the residents had all begun to settle into their early evening routines. Setting his iPod onto shuffle, Addison filled his lungs, feigned a couple of default, defunct stretches and then headed into town.

It felt good to be out. Brushing past the small shops and market stalls, he noticed that everything around him seemed still and static. Traffic had stalled into a standoff along the single-lane roads that snaked away from the main high street and out towards the many side roads and country lanes. He chose to follow one at random. Within minutes, Addison found himself on the outside of the village. Pavement was replaced by the solid, stiff soil of sun-drenched marshland, and the long dry grass jabbed at his legs as he continued to run through the fields and towards the woods that crowned the small town.

Oakland Woods, with its vast shape and size, was bordering on a forest. Huge, hulking trees hung from the clouds above and stamped into the earth below them. Enjoying his surroundings, Addison pressed on. He didn't care that his legs were pricked and torn by the countless nettles and thorns that graced the emerald bushes cloaking the woodlands. Further inside, sheltered by the grand curtain of the oak leaves overhead, he found a corridor of shade that cut deep into the woods. Undeterred, he carried on. Darkness greeted him. Shaded from the sun, shadows merged, obscuring the route ahead. And yet, despite the complete lack of light, his feet were welcomed by a beaten path. People clearly used this path often. Deep inside the darkness, Addison was easily able to find his footing, and before long, through the canopy of leaves and branches, light greeted him. Now outside of the woods, sunlight shone upon a thick trench of dry dirt that had once been flowing with fresh spring water. Addison recalled the brief history lesson that Duke had offered earlier that day.

The once pulsating River Cane had since been dried out as part of the investigation into Elizabeth Silver's disappearance. The community had refused to leave any stone unturned and, given that there had been a suggestion that the young girl's body had been concealed within the river's waters, the river was completely drained. Completely in vain. Elizabeth wasn't found within the waters, or buried beneath it. Now, dry and desiccated, the river served as a dreary reminder of an unnatural abstraction. And with it, the life it had once held was lost.

Gathering his bearings, as he passed over a small wooden bridge, and into a neighbouring field, Addison moved with the village behind him. Soon, the land began to steepen. Music poured into his ears as the sun crawled closer towards him on his approach to the top of the small mount. The darkening skies remained clear of any clouds, offering up a ceiling of deep endless blue which shared the horizon with a blanket of arid angered earth. Sat there, between the soil and skies, the mount served as a perfect mantle to the setting sun. Pausing, Addison admired the view. Beneath him sat the entire village of Claymore, settled and quiet. Turning, he noticed a small stand that stood by his side. It held a metallic map of the town it watched over. Inspecting it, Addison took time to learn the lay of the land. The map was dated 1887, and looked every bit its age. Tracing his finger along the line that represented the river, Addison noticed how the village appeared untouched since the map's design. The high street was hidden from view, and the residences appeared too sporadic to ever dent the true natural detail of the landscape. Feeling somewhat omnipotent, he continued to read the map like a blind man would read braille. Surveying the land, his eyes traced the scene mapped out by his finger. Curious, Addison paused as his fingertip settled on a ragged marking within the metal. He could feel that a part of the map had been viciously scratched, almost rubbed out entirely. Looking out to where his finger rested, he saw a small detached property. It was nothing unusual; rather ordinary compared to the sites surrounding it. In the garden a child's swing rested beside a large wooden shed with a damaged roof. It was startlingly ordinary.

Watching the sun set, Addison wondered what lay ahead for him in this town. A reinvention? A new beginning?

The future appeared nothing more than a mystery to him.

Chapter 7

He didn't risk yawning.

The nurse had reset his dislocated jaw as best she could, warning him that it would be several weeks before he would be able to fully open his mouth to its limit. Even with his mouth tightly closed, he could feel the bones sag within his clenched cheeks. The bones were still brittle, and even a simple sneeze could pop them out of place. Again, suppressing the urge to yawn, Benjamin arched his back and held his hands against his jaw. His whole face felt tenderised; the gentlest of touches felt like gritted teeth tearing into his flesh. The swelling had softened, but now thick bruises blooded his eyes. And yet, despite him still sporting the trophies from his last attack, Benjamin had something of a milestone to celebrate. It had now been nearly two weeks since the assault. This was a record in his books. Never had so much time passed without any form of beating. Solitude had provided a sense of security; nothing could get close enough to hurt him. But he knew it wouldn't last. He knew that the inmates would again grow angry. He knew that incarceration carried with it a feverish frustration. Frustration fuelled by pent-up resentment and anger. The psychological barrier – placed by the man who had saved his life – would soon fade.

Nevertheless, it had been the first time that attacking Benjamin had any repercussions of any sort, let alone ones as brutal as those dished out that day. And they were noted. Forget the ripple effect, this sent shockwaves throughout the entire prison. Inmates and guards alike felt the force of it. Something had shifted. The initial reaction within the prison to somebody siding with Benjamin had been an awkward balance between repulsion and surprise. When the news spread that one of the attackers had been hospitalised, repulsion turned to hatred, and surprise turned to fear. Emotions that, when mixed together, promised nothing but bloodshed.

Benjamin was yet to know his saviour's name, and he wouldn't brave asking anybody for it. Despite his jaw feeling like it would pour out of his mouth if he were to open his lips to talk, inmates had only ever acknowledged Benjamin's presence with kicks and punches. He quickly knew that if he was to ever survive this ordeal, he would have to do it alone. An irony highlighted by the fact his only protection now sat in solitary confinement. Benjamin's sole ally was isolated, controlled, distant. Even the guards were now avoiding him. But that had its benefits. It had been a few days since Benjamin last flinched at any noise that came from outside of his cell door. Too often it had been followed by the delivery of his latest penance. Yet, for two weeks and counting, this hadn't been the case. For two whole weeks, Benjamin had almost found a peace in what had otherwise been his hell.

*

HMP Fordbridge was a Category A prison facility, and had been Benjamin Farrow's residence for over a year. Housing nearly 400 of the UK's most dangerous and violent offenders, the prison had the tough task of not only separating these offenders from the public, but also from each other. Murderers and rapists neighboured armed robbers and paedophiles. And none of them were prepared to get along. Recently, Fordbridge's most infamous inmate – James Jenkins – had made national headlines for plotting to butcher and eat a fellow inmate. Fortunately, the guards had reached Jenkins' cell just in time to stop him from dragging his home-made blade across the entire length of his victim's throat. But Jenkins had managed to gather a taster. When the guards found him, he was already drinking the man's blood as it burst from his severed neck. It took three guards to wrestle him from his prey, costing one of them their index finger when they pointed it too close to Jenkins' face. Tearing it from the knuckle between gritted teeth, Jenkins swallowed the finger whole, before collapsing on the ground in a fit of hysterics.

The story was sensational, and a sure hit for the press. But the public were divided. The inmate Jenkins targeted was an ageing sex offender with an unquenchable appetite for pre-pubescent schoolboys. Many wanted to see him die, and painfully. But few felt comfortable celebrating the actions of a man as abhorrent as James Jenkins. The public were confused, unable to accept the roles played by both men. The victim was a depraved predator, whilst justice was delivered by a madman. The victim – who had somehow survived the attack – was subsequently transferred. But Jenkins wasn't. Initially sentenced to life imprisonment for the murder of his father, Jenkins had received three more life sentences whilst inside. With no other means of controlling the man other than incarceration, it had long been decided that James Jenkins would die in prison.

But then, so would many others.

With no threat of ever being free, Jenkins saw other inmates as fair game. The state could do nothing more to him. There was no psychological illness. They couldn't simply diagnose him and then dispatch him out to a mental institution. His impulses were instinctive and intentional. His every action was rationalised. He was where he was meant to be. And he loved it.

Benjamin knew that Jenkins had set his sights on him. Killing a child-killer was one of the finest prizes for any 'lifer'. There were few gruesome acts that trumped killing a child, and Benjamin was aware that he was considered to be something more than just a killer. His so-called crime had been made even worse because of the beauty of his victim. Just because Elizabeth Silver was a pretty young girl, it was always assumed that her abduction had a sexual element to it. The collective mindset could not accept that the act of child abduction would hold no additional angle or agenda. The act itself was not enough for them to accept. People acted out of purpose. Nobody would just kill a child for the sake of ending a life. There had to be a reason. And because the act was one that no sober-minded person could ever consider – its purpose should follow suit. The motive needed to be monstrous. Many stressed that there were more carnal means of removing innocence. The murder was simply a cover-up for the cause; a mere disposal of the one person who held the truth to the horrors that had happened that night. And so – to all – Benjamin was more than a murderer. He was guilty of every act that cowered within the darkest corners of the human mind. He was guilty of what everybody feared within themselves. And he would pay for it.

Given the fact that he had made no attempt to kill himself – despite the constant advice by the guards on how best to do it – Benjamin was finally trusted with a pencil. He considered writing something to somebody... anybody. What he had recently been told excited him. There was to be some big news ahead. But he was more than aware of the risk posed by sharing secrets. He was also aware of the threat found through association. His solicitor had strictly advised him to be careful of the links he created whilst in prison. Especially now. Since the recent development, he was under stern instruction to pick his friends wisely. The wrong ally could be as damning as any enemy. Particularly now that Benjamin was planning his escape. More than ever, he didn't want to be connected to the wrong people. The truth was simple. If he was to have any chance of appealing his case, he needed to gain the people's sympathy. His solicitor had stated that it would be easier for people to deny his guilt if his plea came from an angle of suffering and agony rather than one of judicial failings. And so, it was clear. Benjamin's salvation depended on the mercy of others. His sole purpose was to convince people that it was unjust to rob a man of his freedom for a crime they could not prove had occurred. And once this was understood, his punishment was unjustifiable.

Elizabeth's body had never been found. It had been over a year since her disappearance, and still there was no sign or clue as to what really happened that night. And yet Benjamin was ordered to accept the guilt for her death. The only thing he could accept was that she was most certainly dead. Surely the family would have heard something by now if this wasn't the case. And many agreed with him. Including the police. But even they hadn't found anything to prove that she had been murdered. It was clear that everybody's focus was altered by the sensitivity of the case. Judgments became blurred and confused. It became reasonable to presume that Elizabeth was dead because there was no proof to suggest that she was still alive. There had been no dramatic return or reunion. There had been nothing at all. No communication; no noise. And it was this silence, this muted rebuke of any tragedy having actually occurred, which proved deafening to Benjamin's plea of innocence. Stolen from her family, Elizabeth Silver would be forever framed by the sadness found within a lost youth, leaving Benjamin the task of convincing people of his innocence for a crime that could never be confirmed. A girl was dead because there was no proof of life. And a man was guilty because there was no proof of innocence. All innocence had been lost that night. Including his.

Thinking back to the day of his arrest, Benjamin had started it like any other. Apart from one minor daily detail. Having reported his bicycle as stolen a few nights before, Benjamin was unable to take his morning bike ride down to the local store. Often, he would stock up on local produce, be it milk, honey or bread. And often he would throw most of it away as it had gone off before he'd ever get the chance to make full use of it. Never having any friends or guests to his house didn't deter Benjamin from buying fresh food and drink almost every day. For him it had become more of a social occasion than a chore born from necessity. It gave him a chance to learn the life that lived around him. Benjamin also loved being outside. Most of his childhood had been spent inside cold, uncaring walls. In places where hatred was housed. As a child he had dreamed of running away, he used to pray for a time when those that hurt him could no longer reach him. Once old enough, he made a life for himself. A life that had been removed from him. Now, he would spend the rest of his adult life trapped in surroundings that mirrored his earliest memories. That was, unless he could find a crack in the case. Any crack or oversight that offered him leverage. All he required was a small doorway of doubt, and he could walk free.

And so, he plotted his escape.

Every night he recounted the events of that day. Every spare moment was spent dragging himself through the countless questions at court. In his mind, he had heard the evidence a hundred times. But the outcome was always the same.

Guilty.

Remembering his return from the store on the morning of his arrest, Benjamin recalled how the police arrived without any warning at all. Given the gated community that surrounded him, it would have been clear to everyone that Benjamin was going to be arrested. Yet nobody warned him. Nobody thought it best to tell him. And that told him everything. Benjamin was going to be found guilty, because to them, he already was. Surprisingly, the police had been borderline courteous, greeting his arrest with a pained smile, as if the act was one that merely inconvenienced him. But nobody was being themselves. Nobody was being true to who they really were. They were scared, in desperate need of balance once more. It didn't matter what tipped it back, so long as it went back, back to normal. Benjamin was the same. He wanted what everybody else wanted. In that moment, all he wanted was the truth to be told. He wanted her body to be found. At least then the misery would be over. Closure could be had. And those guilty would be known.

*

Dressed by darkness, he listened for signs of life behind the door. Thoughts of violence echoed within his clouded conscience. An agony gripped his mind so tightly that it was brought to the very brink of breaking beyond repair. Recently, a side of him had emerged that he'd never known before. A side of dark desires and dreams. A capacity to know anguish he prayed no other would feel. Pain had become a passion; a relentless reminder that he was still alive. Pain was all that he felt. Fuelled by a shaded side of himself, he tirelessly fought the urge to succumb to his grave yearnings. Seduced by self-destruction, he was now dedicated to learning parts of the mind that he could never have comprehended before. He needed to know what made a man do what he did. But his purpose had poisoned him. As unimaginable acts streamed seamlessly within his every waking thought, countless possibilities presented themselves. He no longer feared the unknown. He despised it.

Driven by his decline, the walls seemed closer to him now, holding him in place. Almost comforting in their closure.

Clawing sense from the sheer madness that gripped him, he knew he would never be truly free until he fully understood the urges he fought so hard to resist. More than anything, he needed to realise their motivation. He needed to know how a man could be his worst.

Was he capable?

Alone in darkness, all he had for company were the questions that plagued him. Questions he was convinced could be answered. All he needed was the opportunity to ask them.

I need to ask him.

I need to cope.

I need death.

Chapter 8

Cold sweat clothed him.

The dream was always the same. The outcome no different. This rare rest greeted like it always was. By death. Pausing his racing mind, he'd almost become able to manage the anxiety that ensued. Almost.

Deep breaths. Think of nothing. Stay still.

A surge of panic pulsed through his body. The weight of guilt pinned him in place, as if an anvil had been rested on his sinking chest. It always felt the same. The side of his conscience which now despised him never extended the courtesy of letting Addison realise that he was dreaming. Instead, he would fall into a state of unconsciousness which tricked him into feeling that he was still wide awake in his own bed. His room appeared normal. His mind lucid; as if his brain had taken a snapshot of his surroundings. And in that restful moment, nothing was different. Nothing, that is... apart from the feeling, and its vile introduction. The first time he had felt it, the pressure had been so hard that Addison truly believed that he was going to die. He could feel the blood rush through his skull, his slowing pulse began to beat at the very base of his unbending bones. His lungs held no breath at all. Screaming didn't help. His cries were muffled. His body remained motionless. But it always passed.

The whole painful process was now an accepted, if not unwelcome, acquaintance to his nights. Feeling the anxiety finally wash over him, Addison sat up. Thankfully, the attacks were growing increasingly calmer, and less frequent, but only because first you had to be asleep for them to occur. For months Addison had existed between a blend of night terrors and insomnia. Often the insomnia won the battle, keeping Addison up for weeks at a time. Days blurred with nights, seconds felt like hours, and every conscious thought felt heavy and laboured. The attacks no longer bothered him. He saw them as more of a kickstart, like his battery had run flat and needed a jolt. And there was nothing like pure panic to get the pulse racing.

Sitting up, Addison steadied his breathing. He knew that he wouldn't be able to get back to sleep. Not now. He never could. Outside, the early autumn sun skulked from its deep slumber. Dawn coloured all. Soft streams of light kissed the land as streams of shade crawled across the far-reaching fields. Stretching out towards the street beneath Addison's apartment window, the sunlight shone through the windows of the cottages that lined the small road. As the light flickered upon the glass, shadows drew out a shaded memory.

The water was dark. I couldn't see him.

Frozen by thought, Addison could see the silhouette of his friend swimming beneath the shadow's surface. Small lines of light framed his screaming face. Death had him by throat. Shadows smothered him, dragging him away from the light, deeper into the shrinking darkness. Until he was gone. Trying to reject the recollection, Addison forced himself to think of her. He forced his mind to focus on the face that he had saved that day. But even she was crying. A sense of complete loss still swirled within him. But he never felt he had the right to gain any sympathy for his situation. Addison had survived that day. His best friend – Rosie's brother – had not.

The morning light leaned against the land. Watching the world wake up around him, he pondered his plans for the day. He was pretty sure he could do as he pleased at work. The Tasking Team wasn't the dynamic role he was hoping for. But at least he was left to his own devices. That way he was certain he would somehow benefit this small town. He knew that there was always work to be done.

He just didn't know what Sergeant Parker had waiting for him.

*

Billy Jackson was the local neighbourhood nuisance. A small fish in an even smaller pond, he'd soon grown bored of his quaint, somewhat dull, surroundings. And despite his tedium, Billy had never been brave enough to ever leave. The world outside would have swallowed him whole, and he knew it. A single child to a single middle-aged mother, he had the complete run of his little empire. And without boundaries, or any pressure to ever achieve anything, Billy saw no need to move on with his life. Soiled by a lifetime of being spoilt, Billy had mastered the art of emotional blackmail. His mother, Catherine, had little else left in her life to call her own. Her husband had followed his ambitions and pursued work in the city, and had soon become seduced by the bright lights and liberated lifestyle. Not to mention his young, nubile secretary. Infatuated by what was soon discovered to be a fad, Billy's father had chosen to abandon his family for a young skirt, who had left him the moment he had asked for a bigger commitment. But the man's embarrassment was no match for the heartbreak Catherine had suffered. And continued to suffer. Seizing his mother's grief as a free pass to live a lifestyle of lost promises and abandoned potential, Billy ignored his intellect and wasted his time – and his mother's small salary – on fruitless hobbies and low-level drugs.

Billy was determined to go nowhere, and quickly.

His latest misdemeanour was a minor case of criminal damage. Bored, and with a can of spray-paint for company, Billy had begun using Claymore as his canvas. His most recent tag was an open eye with a single blood-red tear falling from it. The local officers linked this to the fact that Billy had played a significant part in solving the Elizabeth Silver case. Left to his own usual devious devices, Billy had been walking the streets on the night of Elizabeth's abduction. And it was his testimony that had allowed the police to put Benjamin Farrow firmly in the frame. Although seemingly reluctant at first, Billy had eventually provided a statement which had put Benjamin's hand tightly in Elizabeth's on the night she was taken.

The boy had been crucial. And he felt it. Suddenly, he had a purpose. People were finally interested in what he had to say. The prosecution pounced on it. It showed that Elizabeth had been led away by Benjamin. It was their smoking gun. And it blasted any alibi to pieces. It was the kill shot. Straight to the head.

Meanwhile, Billy – for the first time in years – had been trusted by the police to do the right thing. And, because of his assistance, and as a sign of gratitude for his contribution to the biggest case in Claymore's history, the police had been a little lenient on Billy's nocturnal activities.

Until now.

'He's more witless than key witness,' laughed Duke as he took a mouthful of his stem ginger and honey ice cream. It was an unusual snack for such a cold morning, but he'd insisted on showing Addison the local ice cream parlour before starting on their rounds. Duke was adamant that the ice cream in Claymore was world-renowned, serving people who had travelled miles just to take a taste of tradition. Given the mixture of regional accents in the place – ranging from every angle of the compass – Addison thought Duke might just be telling the truth. The parlour was unusually popular given the season, and a solid queue had formed. A queue completely ignored by Duke.

'It's amazing what a reputation can get you,' smiled Duke. 'Take Billy *big-bollocks* Jackson for instance. Here we have the local scrote being treated like royalty, all because he told the truth for once. Fuck me.

What next, an OBE for not mugging the little old lady when you help her cross the street?'

Addison wasn't fully up to speed on the Elizabeth Silver case, but he'd soon catch up. What was crystal clear so far was that the case had set the people's pulse onto an almost united beat. Tragedy often did. He'd seen friends side with strangers because of what he'd done. Reputations were replaced in an instant when enough people were willing to accept the new common truth. He'd seen those he loved chose sides with the loss that he'd created rather than stand by him. Death was a bond like no other. It wrapped people up with a bitterness that could only be broken by having something – or usually someone – to blame for it. And blame was a toxin to all of those obsessed with establishing it. Even him.

Finished with their mini tour, Addison was now driving through a labyrinth of side roads that eventually led to the back of the local churchyard. His supervisor was a self-proclaimed specialist on the trends of the townspeople, and Billy Jackson was known to be a creature of dishonest habits.

'If I know Billy, and sadly I do…' said Duke. He directed Addison to park up just behind the groundsman's house. 'Then he'll be looking to have his afternoon smoke around about now. The groundskeeper here has been complaining about a strange, sweet smell for the last few days. So, I'm pretty certain that young Billy-boy has found a new place to weed out some of his loose time. If you know what I mean.' He feigned smoking what appeared to be an imaginary cigarette. Though the fact he was rolling his eyes suggested something a little more potent.

Pulling the car over, Addison smiled as he watched Duke's mind at work. His Sergeant seemed to have the attitude of a toughened city cop, but the approach of a laidback local. He knew how the rules worked, and he knew how to work them.

'There's the little ball-bag now.'

Before Addison could react, Duke was already out of the car and heading towards a small spiral of smoke that streamed from behind a nearby tree. Eager for some excitement, Addison had caught up with Duke before they reached it.

On the very edge of unwinding, the young boy became startled when he saw the two men appear from separate sides of the tree. Neither were wearing uniforms but he could smell cop a mile off. Fearing they'd find what he was hiding, Billy reached for the small bag of pills within his jacket pocket, and chucked them into his mouth.

'Quick…' shouted Duke, almost laughing from the audacity he was witnessing. 'The little sod's trying to swallow his whole supply.'

Addison could only stand and watch as Duke placed Billy in a headlock and proceeded to punch him through the stomach.

'So, you fancied popping, did you? Well, let me give you a hand with that!'

The young man's legs left the floor on impact, as Duke forced his fist up through his gut, under his ribs and past the lungs.

'Addison, quick. He can't swallow if he's winded.'

Duke laughed as he landed the final punch that brought Billy to his knees. But he wasn't finished with him. Seeing the young man gasping for air, Duke took hold of his hair and forced two fingers firmly down Billy's throat. Vomit soon followed, and Billy fell to a heap on the floor. Both his stomach and lungs completely emptied.

'Ha! Check out Superdrug here.' Duke nodded to Billy. 'On its arse. Just like the store.'

Eventually, the drugs had been bagged by Duke and handed to Addison. But that was as far as the usual police procedure went. Instead of putting Billy under caution and escorting him into custody, Duke directed Addison to drive to a nearby public house, just on the southern border of the town. It was a quiet little drinking hole where only locals strayed towards during the day, and staggered home from at night. It had a warm home-from-home feel. And it was a great place to have a nice chat.

'Come on then, shit face... spill your guts.' Duke was eyeing the laminated dessert menu as he spoke to Billy, who seemed a little too at ease with this process than Addison was comfortable with.

'I ain't saying nothing.' Billy was sat back in his chair, arms crossed. His skin was beginning to gather its natural tone again, moving away from the green nauseous shade he'd been wearing for the last ten minutes.

'Utter fucktard. Ever heard of a double negative?' Duke pointed out the sticky toffee pudding to the waitress as she passed. 'But saying that, you do have a habit of making two wrongs work for you. Don't you?' Billy shifted awkwardly in his seat. Addison remained silent. He knew his role was to play the passive member of the audience this time. Although, he wasn't exactly sure what it was he was meant to be witnessing.

'I know my rights.' Billy leaned forward, locking eyes with Duke. 'And I've done enough *rights* recently to last me a lifetime.'

'Oh, of course... where are my manners? On behalf of the people of Claymore, we are sincerely grateful for your assistance in the case of... blah, blah, bloody bollocks blah.' Duke waved his hands dismissively, then looked his most serious. 'Cut the crap, Billy. You can't dine out on your involvement in the Silver case forever. You've had your fill and more. But if you're still feeling a little peckish... you playful little prick... then let's see what I can dish up for you. For starters, my colleague here has a bag full of serious prison time boiling away in his pocket, and he's happy to serve it up. That is... unless you start talking. Who's your dealer?'

Billy flinched a little. He looked at Addison. He didn't know him, so he didn't trust him. That's how things worked around here.

'Talking to you guys makes me sick. No pun intended.' Billy's face offered a smartarse smirk. 'I've talked enough. I've said all that you wanted to hear, so, leave me alone.'

'Oh... I wish I could Billy... honestly, I do.' Duke leaned forward. 'Do you think that I take a shower every morning just so that I can go outside and roll around with pieces of shit like you all day?'

'Don't blame me for your stink, Sergeant.' Billy gave a wry smile. 'You're dirty enough without me.'

Addison saw a flash of anger cross over Duke's eyes. It was as swift as a blink, but it was there. As if the curtain had been pulled back slightly. Peering in, Addison had caught a glimpse of what burned beneath the surface of his sweet-toothed Sergeant. There was a restrained aggression burning backstage, an anger Addison had seen a thousand times over. It was a hatred buried and bound by guilt. A hatred born from weakness. A weakness often defended by attack. Like a cornered animal, those feeling this weakness always felt forced to tackle those putting them there. In a flash, Duke's weakness was clear.

Billy had something on him.

Chapter 9

Her body had never been found.

Frozen forever at the tender age of six years old, Elizabeth Silver had become the girl-ghost that now haunted her hometown. Many had accepted that she would certainly be dead. But nobody accepted that anyone could truly be capable of killing her. An unassuming child, Elizabeth often blended into the background of her busy classroom. Not one to quiz, or warrant any extra attention from her teacher, there was never a reason for Elizabeth to ever really stand out from her peers.

But she had done, to someone, however briefly. And now she was gone.

Whoever had taken her from her home must have done so for a reason. There must have been some purpose to her disappearance beyond just the need for her death. Many reasoned that an appalling cause must exist if only to justify the devastating effect that her death had caused. The result itself was not enough. It was too much without a reason. The effect caused by the child's removal – the fracturing of a family, the cracking of an entire community – was never considered to have been the motive behind the act. Quite the contrary, in fact. The courts dismissed any notion that the act was anything personal towards the Silver family. The family lived rather modestly and had no known enemies. Acting as a small, private unit, the Silvers went about their business beneath the radar of the local gossip and scandal merchants. In truth, before the event, they weren't really considered by many at all. It wasn't until they'd lost everything that they were then seen for who they really were, and for the parts they played.

The courts also concluded that it appeared that nobody was set to gain from this murder. There was no clear motive. But there was a murder. The courts were certain of that. In fact, there were only two facts that they were certain of. They were certain on both the act and the actor. Elizabeth Silver was killed. And Benjamin Farrow was the killer.

But why she'd been murdered was another mystery entirely.

The man deemed guilty of killing her had always contested that he had not. And though sorrowful for the family's loss, Benjamin Farrow had never offered them the closure that they deserved. Instead, he left them tormented by the depths of their own torturous imaginations.

Sat on her daughter's bed, Beverly Silver fought back the images that shot into her mind like poisoned bullets. Flashes of her daughter, frightened and alone, fired through her unguarded thoughts. But they eventually passed. They had to.

Beverly had found distraction to be her favoured ointment. Preoccupation offered her the strength she needed to face the day alone. As soon as the investigation into Elizabeth's disappearance had found a chief suspect, Beverly had been left to deal with her own grief in her own way. On the morning of Benjamin's conviction, Beverly's husband had disappeared.

As Elizabeth's father, Steven Silver, had loved both his wife and daughter entirely. Loyal, committed, and infatuated by his family, Steven had proven to be the perfect husband to Beverly. But the incident changed him, and soon his infatuation with their loss had forced them to part. Unable to cope with their grief together, Steven and Beverly eventually agreed to deal with their demons separately. It was clear that they were united in their grief, but individual in their methods of coping with it. Whilst Beverly surrounded herself with memories for comfort, Steven stripped away his identity. His only way of coping was to remove any association with what defined him, and tackle what haunted him on his own. He had always promised to contact Beverly once he had done what he needed to do. But she had not heard a word from him since that day. She hated how selfish he was. But had to admire his devotion. The morning that Steven had left, he had simply told her that he acted out of love alone, before leaving her for what they both knew was likely to be a lifetime. Steven was hell-bent on locking himself away from the world until his closure was complete. So, whilst his wife faced each day without him, Steven chose to hide his face away. Until it all ended, at least.

But Beverly couldn't hide. She didn't have the option of escaping what surrounded her. She knew her role was to remain in Claymore and represent all the values that had made Elizabeth the precious child they'd both cherished. And now her daughter's potential would never be fulfilled. There was no means of building any more memories with her. The man that had taken Elizabeth that day had already robbed Beverly of her future with her daughter, and so she would never be ready to abandon the past they'd shared as well.

Looking out from her daughter's window, Beverly saw the small swing on which she'd forever pestered her parents to push her higher towards the heavens. But Steven used to toy with her, stopping her before she got as high as she could. Once, he'd stopped the young girl and simply whispered, 'The heavens can wait for an angel like you.'

The memory of it no longer brought tears. Instead, Beverly smiled as she allowed the warmth of the past to encase her from the chill held within her future. Like the lazy allure of warm blankets on a cold winter morning, tempting people to shun the toil of their working day, Beverly's comfort blanket was woven by the fabric of her forever-family. A family lost to the future, but sewn tightly to her past. Plucked from the present, Beverly allowed her thoughts to carry her to a time where she had all that she'd needed. A time which could never be altered by the actions of others. A time where Elizabeth would always be with her.

Strengthened by the life she'd known, Beverly whispered a small prayer for Steven. She asked for his security. For his safety. And above all, his salvation. Deep down, she knew she would never see him again.

Taking the time to straighten her daughter's duvet, Beverly stood and pondered the day ahead of her. Routine had become a fond friend, and today was when she'd take a stroll into the village and collect a few fresh groceries. She would always buy more than she needed, but none of it went uncooked. Fixed as a wife and mother, Beverly would always cater to those that were no longer there. At mealtimes she would often set a place for both Steven and Elizabeth, though she would never plate anything up for them. Steven liked his food fresh from the pot, and Elizabeth would always follow suit. The young girl was stitched to her father's side so tightly that he'd taken to calling her his shadow. Though he would always stress that she was not the darkness but the light that surrounded him, casting out her soft silhouette so that he would always have by his side.

The kettle clicked. Hot steam spiralled from the spout. Her soft hands cradled the mug she always chose. It had been a gift from Steven. The outside was wrapped by her favourite photo of her daughter that he'd sorted through some cheap online store. The young girl was smiling widely in the photo, which was framed by a caption which simply read 'World's Best Mum'. Elizabeth was four years old when the picture was taken. They were on holiday in Devon, and it was the first time the young girl had ever seen the sea. It was also the last. Wrapped within the memory, Beverly poured herself a cup of tea. She added two teaspoons of honey for sweetness. It was how Steven used to make it. He hated unnatural sugars. He was always so bloody health-conscious. It used to drive Beverly mad how he'd constantly monitor what foods he was eating, and it made her feel guilty for the small treats she allowed herself. For him, a biscuit was broken down into the exact amount of press-ups it would take to work them off, or how many miles a bag of crisps would cost him. She smiled at the memory of her man as she added forty press-ups and a few dozen sit-ups to her saucer.

Taking her sweet treat into the small living room, Beverly turned on the TV and sat on her favourite chair. The room was only big enough for an armchair and a two-seater sofa. But it was all they'd ever needed. Steven had always chosen the single seated, well-worn chesterfield armchair, and he'd been welcome to it. Beverly thought that it looked too rigid to ever be comfortable. Instead, she was happy in her snug, cosy sofa, with its plumped-up pillows and additional – Steven would say unnecessary – scatter cushions. And tucked in snuggly at her side would be Elizabeth.

Elizabeth would always hold one of the cushions close to her. She had felt protected within this room. She had felt safe. Sinking into her chair, Beverly shook the image that blotched the memory. Her imagination often did that. Whenever Beverly sought security and comfort within a sweetened recollection, her imagination had a knack of souring it, replacing what had been with the twisted and sharp reality of what must have been.

Beverly didn't know her daughter's end. She didn't know her pain. But she knew her daughter would have been frightened.

Why didn't she scream?

Beverly was never keen to forget the memory of her daughter; she would always cherish the blessing that was her only child. But she did pray for the day that she could forget what happened to her. A feeling riddled by guilt and a sense of selfish preservation. She hated it. Who was she to ignore, neglect, or to even overlook what happened to Elizabeth? Who was she to ask if there could be a moment that she wasn't pained by the absolute agony with which her daughter had endured? This wish, this rejection of acceptance, was one that made Beverly feel her utter worst. It was one that made her question her true value as a mother. One that made her wonder whether she ever deserved such a delight as her daughter in the first place. Maybe her murder had been a punishment for Beverly's self-absorbed enjoyment of the small universe that she'd surrounded herself with. Maybe it was a result of how short-sighted she had been to only focus on what was the centre of her entire world – her family. She never took the time to spot the asteroid that was hurtling towards them. Maybe her right to raise a child as precious as Elizabeth was removed because she could not protect her daughter from the very world that surrounded her. After all, if she could see beyond the small fort that was her family, then maybe she would have spotted the man that had taken her that night. Maybe she would have seen her daughter's killer before it was too late.

But she could not let her loss poison her. That's what the family liaison officer had said to her anyway. She knew that it was too late for Steven. The venom had struck almost instantly, and he was now fuelled by nothing else. However, Beverly had to find a balance. She had to find a place where she could cope with the pain brought on by the loss that she had suffered. And yet, this was the easiest part of the process for her. The memories were by no means the hardest thing she had had to face. Instead, they served as wholesome distractions from what she would never truly realise. Beverly had never known the facts behind her daughter's disappearance. There had never been any closure other than that of the decision of one man's guilt and the punishment he now faced. And still, Beverly would never realise what really happened to her daughter. She would never know what it truly was that she needed to come to terms with. There was no confirmed diagnosis for her anguish. And it was this that had plagued both her and her husband. The unknown had made them both question everything that was around them: their lives, their love, their connection. But there were no answers. Only questions that promised no peace.

Turning on the TV, Beverly froze. Fear forced her to sit still, and fixed her in her place. There, on the large flat-screen TV that they had spent countless hours as a family watching was the face of Benjamin Farrow. In full High Definition, the cold eyes of her daughter's killer stared back at her. It made her blood drop to freezing point. The man who had murdered Elizabeth now peered into her home with a menace that defied motion. After what felt like a lifetime, the still image faded, and revealed a young journalist stood outside the Warwickshire Crown Court. Beverly couldn't focus enough to listen to what the journalist was saying. The sound of a cherished mug smashing upon the cold wooden floors rattled beneath her, the sound bouncing around the walls that now crept in on her. Tears watered her cheeks as the only semblance of closure that had allowed her to endure each day had now been obliterated by six simple words that stomped across the bottom of the screen.

Elizabeth Silver Case: Set For Review.

Benjamin Farrow had been given a second chance.

Chapter 10

'So, did you do it?'

He decided to be honest.

'Of course.'

Benjamin tried to get comfortable on the seat. No matter how many of these crappy meetings he'd been forced to attend, he could never relax. He was certain that the prison had ordered these rigid plastic chairs just to piss him off. They reminded him of his early school days. He had always hated school. The rules, the constant reminders of how inadequate you were, the bullies with no purpose other than to make your most precious years feel like your worst. But then, school was heaven compared to what he'd once called home.

'Good.' The woman smiled. 'These exercises are for your own benefit. I'm sure there's no better killer of time than a distraction.'

'Oh, believe me. There are other killers in here that concern me more than your little tasks.' Benjamin felt bad for being blunt. The woman was only doing her job. And if the truth be known, he didn't mind being in the company of someone who didn't want to pull his throat out and feed it to him.

'I'm sure there are. Forgive my poor choice of words.' She blushed slightly.

Her name was Monica Dawkins. She had worked at the prison before as part of her university course to become a forensic psychologist. Now that she was fully qualified, and Benjamin was working towards a review of his case, it had been decided that Monica and Benjamin would meet up every two weeks for an assessment of his mental state. That was it. No hidden agenda; no traps. Benjamin knew that there was every chance that Monica would be called upon to offer evidence against him during his trial. But there was no real need for confidentiality. He wasn't going to plead any form of insanity. He wouldn't wear that mask. He had always pleaded his innocence. And that was what he would only allow Monica to see. Nothing more.

'You look nice today.' Benjamin tried a smile. His jaws still ached from the attack a month ago. 'I like it when you wear your hair like that.' He was lying. Her clownish make-up looked as if she'd used the leftovers from a fancy-dress store, whilst her frazzled hair suggested that her commute to work had involved a cannon.

Careful, she's part of this whole circus show. Don't be the freak.

Monica squirmed. Her hand instinctively flashed up towards a strand of her soft brown ringlets. She tucked it behind her ear.

'Sorry for being inappropriate.' Benjamin meant it. 'I didn't mean to make you feel... uncomfortable.'

'No... it's fine.' Monica pretended to be writing something down on her notepad. A single squiggly line sat between two doodles that she'd drawn during the meeting with her previous client. Her last patient had been the usual self-pitying piece of scum who was declaring suicidal thoughts just so he could sit in an office and look down her blouse for half an hour. She'd seen a thousand like him. But not many like Benjamin. Not on the inside anyway.

Purposefully, she made eye contact with her patient. He was staring straight at her. 'I'm happy you're being honest with me Benjamin. I did encourage that from the start. So... honestly... don't feel like you can't tell me what you're thinking. Within reason of course.'

'Of course,' he said. 'There's always reason.' Benjamin fidgeted again. His left ass-cheek was beginning to fall asleep as the plastic chair continued to bite at his buttocks.

'Tell me,' Monica continued, 'you say you completed the task that I set at the end of our last meeting. How did you find it?'

'Easy. You didn't ask much.'

'It's not my role to ask much. I'm here to listen. I'm sure you can appreciate that some people require a little probing before they open up about themselves.'

'True. I've been told that I'm a little closed off. I don't really let people see me; who I really am.' Benjamin laughed. 'Not that a single person believes a word that I say anyway. Killer. Rapist. Paedophile. These aren't words that I would ever use to define who I am. But that's what people choose to see. The monster that they've branded.'

'Is that how you feel you're seen?' Monica scanned Benjamin for a reaction but nothing showed on the surface. In fact, she had to admit that on the surface Benjamin was an attractive man. His light blond hair accentuated his hazel eyes. And despite approaching thirty-five, his face held a hint of boyish charm.

In truth, Monica didn't recognise him from the portrait the press had painted. He was more man than an animal. More beauty than beast.

'Miss Dawkins,' Benjamin had felt her eyes on him. 'I can't help what they see. Their perception of me says as much about them as it does of me. How do you see me?'

He didn't need to be a scientist to recognise the chemistry between them. Granted, today she looked like Coco the clown's younger, less groomed, sister, but he had to accept that she exuded a subtle scent of sexuality. Her soft tone. Her nervous nature. It appealed to him.

'Well, I'm not here to answer that. I wanted to see how you view yourself, and that's exactly what my task was looking to achieve. As you know, I asked you to recall a happy memory from your childhood. I think we could learn a lot if we focused on exactly where memory lane takes you. Somewhere safe? Somewhere scary? A lost time now unforgotten? You see, the past often seems so sure to us. It's where most of us believe we were at our happiest. No matter how confused we were at the time, what has been is a solid state, unalterable if not slightly edited. It's what lies ahead that often causes us anxiety, stress, fear. The future is a constant variable where all possibilities exist. But the past is fixed. It's done. Benjamin, I appreciate that your head might be in a confused state at present, especially with your case review, but there must be some feelings of excitement in the mix, possibly even hope?'

'Nope. Not if I'm guilty.' Benjamin noted the positive stance his doctor had taken on the case review. Did she believe him? Was she one of the few that had felt he'd be thrown to the lions without a question answered truthfully? He wanted to test her a little.

'Mr Farrow,' she tried to sound professional. Almost sterile. 'Let me assure you these meetings aren't set up for me to assess your part in the crime that has brought you here. You know as well as I do that I can be called upon to give evidence in court, and I must remind you that what you say could be used against you.'

'Or *for* me.' Benjamin smiled. She mirrored it. 'I like our chats Doc. I do. I'm sorry that I get so negative during what is one of the few highlights of my prison-day diary. It's just, I can't help feeling... I don't know... apprehensive. I got chucked in here like some stranded scapegoat that got scooped up and served as an easy sacrifice to the occasional God-fearing public. So, why won't this process be the same? It failed me then. And there's every chance it will fail me again. My blood has been spilt, and nobody wants to wear it on their hands. All they get is a chance to take a second bite out of me. They left me wounded, and now they want to go for the kill.'

He looked at her. He wanted to see how she reacted to him.

Monica fought the urge to rest her hand on his knee. Whilst other inmates would rip her hand off just so they had something fresh to jerk off into, she felt safe with him. But that could be even more dangerous.

She knew there was a line that she should never cross with one of her patients. She should never trust them. Not fully. No matter how they appeared to her.

'The truth will come out, Benjamin. Justice... believe in that.'

'Who knows,' replied Benjamin after a pause. 'Maybe nobody will ever know what happened to that girl. The fact is... she's gone. And with me out of the picture, nobody needs to be reminded about the fact that she's not around anymore. If I'm out there... amongst them... then they can't forget. A lost youth refuses to leave you. It just stays with you forever. Screaming at you. Trust me on that one.'

'Benjamin...' Monica spoke softly. She'd noticed how he always reacted to the slight change in the tone of her voice. 'I really want to know. What was the memory that you came up with?'

'Friends.' His smile sat beneath the saddest eyes she had ever seen. 'That's where memory lane took me... to a couple of friends I spent my youth with. Who knows where they are now. The police didn't bother to look for them to gather a character reference. Not that they'd want to anyway. Why the hell would they? Never associate yourself with a monster. Sound advice really.'

'Those friends, in the memory...' Monica sat back. 'Were you doing anything together?'

'Running. Playing. Hiding. Just being kids. One was an oaf of a lad. Dumb, but kind... kind of. He always followed us around... the other friend and me. We made our days better when we were all together. We helped each other forget the times that upset us. And, believe me, there were so many sad times. That's why we were inseparable whenever we got the chance to be together. We felt like a family. Almost looked like one. How times change.'

'The times you shared with these friends. They meant a lot to you?'

'Oh, they were everything. Truly treasured moments. We used to hide in the local woods, make dens, little traps that weren't any good. I was a little older than them, maybe by a year or two. The youngest had an old head of their shoulders... pretty much ran the show. The other was the opposite. He was closer to my age, but he had the brain of an infant. It made him temperamental at times. But it always came from a good place. He just needed love. We all did.'

'Is that what you felt when you were together: love?'

'I guess so. But it was more than that. We'd been through a lot together... and even worse things apart. But we coped better when we were together. Nobody allowed us to be ourselves when we were alone.' Benjamin looked up from his lap. She was staring at him intently. Her pen rested on the arm of her chair. 'Call me stupid, but I suppose I'll never feel that way again.'

'And what way is that?' Monica could see that Benjamin was becoming upset. A flash of fear fired behind his dampened eyes. 'What will you never feel again?'

'Safety.' He looked to the floor. 'It truly is a numbers game, Doc. The monsters that come for you at night, they're not shadows with devilish eyes. Or ghosts that scream as they bang at your windows. They're men like I am now. Made of flesh, bone and hatred. They're real. Not figments of your imagination. They're not made up reasons to make sense of why we feel afraid. They're not the bogeyman, or the big bad wolf. They are real people. And they're the real reason that fear exists. And yet, they do have something in common with the make-believe monsters.'

Monica shuffled forward on her chair.

'What's that?'

His face was his most serious.

'They all come out at night. They all wait until you're alone.'

Chapter 11

She hoped they would like it. Her teacher seemed really pleased, so much so that she'd even allowed them to take their work home. Her friend Amy had stolen all the good crayons, so she had to make use of the little stubby waxy ones that had flecks of other colours rubbed into them. But she didn't mind, she was a better drawer than Amy anyway. She was happy with her picture. So much so that she hadn't even shown it to anyone at home. Not yet. She wanted it to be a surprise.

So, she waited until night-time.

The toilet flushed from the bathroom on the landing. She could hear them finally getting ready for bed. It had taken almost all of her strength to stay awake. They'd never let her stay up this late before, and they'd be pretty mad if they found her up at this hour. So, she chose to wait. For hours. And hours. Until it was way past her bedtime. But she knew that it would all be worth it. She was sure of it.

Her plan was simple.

Creep downstairs. Stick the picture onto the fridge. Sneak back to bed. Wait for the reaction tomorrow.

They'll love it!

Especially him.

She stood by the window so that she could look at her drawing. Only the faint white light of the moon split the darkness of her bedroom in two. She hadn't risked leaving the light on. They'd have come and checked in on her if all didn't seem like normal, and then all her hard work would be ruined. And she definitely didn't want to spoil the surprise.

She was so excited. Outside, the noises that the night brings had come out to play. Heavy rain began to rap against the window.

A floorboard creaked.

He was outside her room.

Quickly, she sprinted to her bed and leapt beneath the covers. She closed her eyes just in time to miss the stripe of stale yellow light that crept around the door from the landing. A silhouette briefly leaned in and then out, as if swallowed by the closing mouth of the door.

He was gone.

She gave it a minute. Across the landing, distant murmurs met one another momentarily, before the shuffling of a bed quilt signalled the start of complete silence. Until he started snoring.

She knew they were sleeping. Scared to open both of her eyes, she let one creep open slightly. Strained light scrawled out across the ceiling from outside. The small dotted shadows of the rainfall pebbled its soft white canvas.

That's when the storm broke.

Quickly, the room began to darken. Outside, thick, heavy rainclouds heaved across the rolling skies. The thunder that they brought with them sounded like stones being dragged along the road that ran beneath her bedroom window. Streams of water tumbled down the narrow footpath, and deep into the nearby woodlands. Howling winds began to whistle against the windows. The night's chilling chorus grumbled on.

Eventually, she braved herself for her little adventure. She didn't mind the noise. It set the scene, and she had a great sense of the dramatic.

Dropping one leg at a time out of her bed, she scampered across her plush pink carpet until she was stood by her bedroom door. Tentatively, she placed an ear against the cold thick wood, hoping to hear any sign of life from across the way. But there was no way of telling anymore. The volume from outside had increased, gently rocking the house within its tight, icy grip. The door pulsed beneath her ear. Strong winds followed. She could feel it creeping through the small gap she had left open in her window. It tickled at her feet as it rushed out beneath the door and onto the landing.

She followed it.

Excited, she opened the door and was greeted by blinding darkness. Not even the outstretched moonlight could reach into the thick fog of night that blanketed the stairwell. It took a few moments for her eyes to adjust. Darkness swirled in front of her, casting out monstrous shapes just inches from her face. A ghost. A devil. A hand. She knew it was only her imagination at work. She had a very good one. The teacher had told her that.

So did they.

She hadn't known them for long. She was five years old when they first met almost twelve months ago, and the last year that she had spent with them had been the happiest time of her life. To all around them it was obvious that they were in love... and now so was she. But it hadn't always been that way. When they had first visited, she was suspicious of them. She'd been let down before, by people smiling and talking just like they did. They all said the same things, made the same noises. Mostly it was couples feigning interest like they had walked into viewing a property that didn't look anything like the advert, before overlooking her just because she looked a little 'different'. But then *they* were also different, different from the rest of them. Mainly because they had come back. They had promised that they would, and they had kept their promise. It didn't matter to them that her appearance was different to theirs. It didn't matter that she stood out. They didn't want her to blend in anyway. It didn't matter to them that she didn't resemble of mixture of them both, or even just one of them. They were proud to call her their daughter.

Smiling at the thought of her new parents, she shuffled through the shadows until she could feel the beginning of the bannister. Blindness folded in front of her. Her eyes still hadn't adjusted to the darkness. It was deeper, thicker, more alive than she had ever known it. Clutching at the bannister, she let it guide her downstairs. Step by step, tiptoe after tiptoe, she slowly made her way down the stairs until finally she landed at the bottom. The hallway pulsated in front of her. Beats of light scurried across the wooden floor.

Three taps knocked at the door.

She paused. It must have been a branch being beaten against the house.

Then it tapped again. With purpose.

She stood frozen to her spot whilst the winds continued to whirl outside. Trees danced menacingly within it. The rain spun and turned, bending to its will. The solitary streetlamp that faced the front of the house was barely strong enough to shed a hint of light upon the small frosted windows that lined the front door.

It's all in my head. Nobody's out there.

She was frightened. They didn't have many visitors, and she was frightened that if he came down now to answer the door, he'd catch her stood there. Then all would be lost.

But he didn't come. Maybe the noise was lost amongst nature's chaotic chorus. A howling choir that could muffle any scream or cry. After all, the noise she had heard wasn't that loud, just more deliberate. It didn't have the constant tapping that the rain brought with it. It lacked the bass brought by the thunderous clouds. And it paled in comparison to the pitch of the lightning that punched at the earth. It was different to all the other noises that she had stayed well hidden within. It didn't sound natural. The wind and the rain was constant. But the tapping was only for a moment. It sounded calm, intentional, purposeful. She reasoned it was nothing to worry herself about. Just her mind playing tricks on her.

Then it happened again.

And again.

Three taps rapped on the door. She felt cold. A sickly sweat clung to her skin.

Was that a hand?

A clump of darkness passed by one of the windows. She couldn't breathe. The image was obscured by the frosted glass. Terror froze her feet to the floor. She wanted to run. She needed to scream. She needed them. But then they may get upset. They may think that she was crazy, that she was more trouble than she was worth. Why had they taken a risk on this unknown entity? Like the lost, or abandoned puppies raised in a shelter, she was too old to come without any issues. She was troubled. She *was* trouble. They'd send her back.

It had happened to others. She'd seen them return like broken toys in their original packaging. She didn't want to go back. She liked it here.

So, she stayed completely still. She didn't want to wake the house. She didn't want to let them down. They trusted her; they believed in her. She was only trying to do something nice.

Then the fear passed.

Creeping closer to the door, she knelt down and slowly lifted the lid to the letter box, only to be greeted by the bristled teeth of the brushes beneath. Her hand was shaking as she pushed the brushes apart. Cold air spat back at her. She couldn't see a thing. But that was good. It was what she had hoped for. Nothing wasn't a bad thing. It meant no thing; no witch, no ghoul, no monster. It meant there was nothing there. There was nothing standing by the door. There was nothing to fear.

Ignorant to the young girl's relief, the storm raged on. She could hear the rainfall thump at the ground. It was almost soothing. It gave a rhythm to distract her. Allowing herself to calm a little, she smiled as she felt the wind that wavered through the trees. Standing firmly, a few feet from her front lawn, she could see the light of the streetlamp leaning towards her doorway. The light was clean, unbroken, not splintered by shadows.

Somewhere in the distance, lightning struck. A flash of light took a snapshot of the world outside. For the swiftest second, the forest was bathed in light. Trees were illuminated from root to crooked tip in an instant. There was nobody there.

Remembering the lesson they had taught her, she counted out the seconds until she could hear the thunder. One... two... three... four...

The skies purred as the thunder roared into life. She had almost managed to count to five. That meant the lightning was far away. She was safe. Forgetting fear for a moment, she remembered her mission. Thankfully, the racket hadn't wakened them upstairs. This made her happy. Hopefully they'd love what she'd done for them. And after all they had done for her, it was the least she could do. They'd given her a home. They'd shown her love. And they'd let her dream of a life not haunted by her past.

Hurrying along the hallway, she finally reached the kitchen. The large fridge-freezer was a hulking slab of metal that sat between two custom-fit cupboards. They'd used colourful magnets to pin small reminders to the fridge's front door: shopping lists, memos, bills. It served as a daily aide-memoir to all that was important to them. And they needed to know just how important they were to her.

She had the perfect way to show them.

Unrolling the paper, she tried to fold it in the opposite direction to straighten it out, but the corners kinked in a little. However, it was fine. The picture she had drawn was still clear and the title of it wasn't covered by the kinked corners. She had decided not to use their names. She'd done this on purpose. Of course, she knew them. In fact, until now, she'd always used them. Sometimes… too much. She knew that it was something that they'd even picked up on. Especially him. It was something significant to them. As if acceptance was found in some other label or title. All they had ever wanted was a child… specifically a daughter. And now – in her – they had one to call their own. One to adore and love completely. And in time the love they had shown had made her proud to be who she had become.

Theirs.

Until now, when talking about them, she would only ever use their actual names. Others at school said 'Mum' and 'Dad'. But she didn't. She was different. She said Lisa and David.

But not anymore.

Finding a couple of magnets, she placed her picture centre-stage, amongst all that was important to them. She smiled as she saw the drawing of a young girl with big fuzzy hair holding hands with a man and a woman, both of which would have had bright red hair if it wasn't for selfish Amy stealing all the good colours. But that wasn't important anymore. It was the message that mattered the most. For her, what it said above the young family was what it had all been about.

'My mummy and daddy and me. Our family.'

Mission complete.

Quickly, she sneaked back upstairs, dashed across the landing, and climbed into bed. She was so excited. She just couldn't sleep. Not now. She knew that they would absolutely love the picture. Especially him; her daddy. She didn't want to hurt them before, but she could only bring herself to commit to seeing them as her parents once she felt safe with them. And now she did. They weren't ever going to leave her. Not now. Not like the others.

As she settled somewhere between suspense and slumber, the lightning began to work its magic on the room. The night applauded thunderously, and the clouds twirled and bowed within the swirling moonlight. She felt colder than before. Distracted by the storm, she failed to notice that her window had been opened wide, letting all the cold air in.

As well as the monsters.

As the lightning flashed she could see all kinds of ghosts and ghouls projected onto the walls. The branches of trees tossed amongst the breeze became the long reaching hands of witches and goblins. The shadow of a cloud formed the outline of a ghost that leaped onto the walls with every flash of light. The demonic display was almost hypnotic. And it was beginning to scare her. She reminded herself that it was all in her imagination. Her daddy had told her how doubts came out to play at night, that the dark was just the day taking a nap, that it didn't bring any danger.

But then every flash of light brought with it a new monster for her to face.

Lightning flashed.

A huge dragon sprawled across the walls, before disappearing into the dark.

Lightning flashed.

Small spiders dotted the ceiling, melting away as the rain dragged them down the windowpanes.

Lightning flashed.

A ghost pulled itself from under her bed, until it was swallowed by shadow.

Lightning flashed.

The shadow of a man stood at her side.

His hand covered her mouth.

Chapter 12

‘Complete parasites. The lot of them.’

Duke pushed through the door that led into the small office where the Tasking Team operated. If you could call it that – operational. Granted, they were all in, but they were either sick, injured, or had a story to tell.

Maggie McAndrew was sat in front of her desk that looked more like a shrine to the Mother Mary than a workstation. A portly woman, putting it politely, she looked out of breath even when she was sitting, which she often was. In front of her was Darren Hoggit, a man taking up residence on the very brink of a breakdown. His weathered face suggested that it took all his strength just to maintain his once cheery smile. He was pleasant enough. But clinically depressed. Two divorces and a lost custody battle had caused him to burst into tears at one-too-many domestic incidents, leaving him unable to work outside of the station and housed firmly in the ‘too difficult to deal with’ box.

Stood at the back of the room, and seemingly making a constant round of hot drinks, was Geoff Talbot. Geoff was still recovering from major stomach surgery which had made him non-operational for almost two years. A former officer from the response unit, he had gone stir-crazy after just two months cooped up in the tiny, unairconditioned office. Now, after another twenty-two months, he had become more of the bat-dropping brand of crazy.

‘They still out there then?’ Geoff spoke through a face fixed in fury.

‘Unfortunately, yeah...’ Duke mumbled as he stuffed the first finger of a Twix into his face. ‘Clicking away like a right bunch of bastards. They’ll hardly get a picture worth printing around here... not with Hoggit’s miserable mug anyway.’ He sat down. Geoff brought over his coffee.

Lots of milk and six sugars. It was almost grey in colour. Just how he liked it.

'Thanks,' Duke washed another mouthful of chocolate down. 'Did any of them speak to you? Any of you?' He looked around the small room.

'No Sarge,' Hoggit took a swig of his tea. It didn't have the sweeteners in that he'd asked Geoff for, but he didn't want to trouble anyone, so he continued to drink it regardless.

'Excuse my language, but one of those friggin' blighters asked me a few questions.' Maggie's accent switched from Midlands to Irish, and then back again. 'They recognised me from the original case. Even knew my name. Sodding heathens, the lot of them.'

'What did they ask you?' Duke had almost drained his coffee. The working day was not even ten minutes old and already his head was banging.

'Just the usual...' Maggie's face turned from white snow to scarlet red. 'Is the retrial down to a lack of evidence? Are there any other suspects? Do we regret arresting Farrow?'

'Hell no.' Geoff was still standing. He was too angry to relax. He rarely did.

'Too right,' Duke stood up. 'We all know Benjamin did what he did. This whole review is just some sodding cluster-fuck that will only serve to screw this town. There was little else that we could have done at the time, and there's even less that we can do now. We got our man. End of story.'

'So, why have they reopened it?' Maggie looked flustered. She'd worked the case the first time around, so much so that she'd grown very close to Beverly Silver. And although she'd only felt a fraction of what that poor woman had felt at the time, the impact of the loss still haunted her to this day. 'God knows what her poor mother would be feeling right now.'

'I know,' Duke opened up a Yorkie bar. Two blocks of the chocolate bulked out his cheeks as he spoke. 'Maggie, when Addison comes in I want you two to head over to visit Beverly Silver. See how she's doing. Okay?'

'No problem.' Maggie was keen to get over and see her friend. If not only to appear more interesting through association. She was known to prattle to her church group, which was half the reason she was on the team. The other half was a chronic case of hypochondria, buried snuggly under a layer of biscuit-based blubber. 'Any idea what time the young lad will be in?'

'Who, Addison?' Duke sat down. 'He shouldn't be long. I've sent him on a little errand this morning. The second I saw that news break last night, I knew we'd be in the sodding firing line. So, I've sent Addison to collect all the papers from the original case. He didn't work on it, so I thought it would look a lot better – and cleaner – if we had an objective review of it all. Once Addison shows that we're squeaky clean and we didn't cut any corners, then that whole pack of bottom-feeders outside can be sent packing.'

It was half an hour before Addison arrived back at the station. And despite the morning traffic and the mob of reporters blocking his access to the front of the building, he was happy with the time he'd made. He was well aware of why the press had gathered. Duke, by means of a midnight rant, had briefed him fully.

The press had turned.

At the time of the original case, a lot of the media were happy with the swift justice served on Benjamin Farrow. Because of the stellar work of Claymore's finest, it wasn't too long before the public could sleep safely in their beds having banished the demon that once moved amongst them. And the press were onboard with it. Even celebrated it. Initially, anyway. Inevitably, the nationals soon moved on to another tragedy with which to spoon-feed the waking world; some fresh tasting morsel of moral panic with which to unease the public. But that was just the nationals. The local press were different. The case remained relevant to the regionals. Long after the conviction, it still resided within the small column inches that they failed to fill with anything else of local importance. It was only after the dust started to settle, and the public didn't hold the same appetite for re-hashed narratives, that the slight murmurings of an unfair trial began to surface. Some people always liked to appear differently minded to the majority, laying the boot into the authorities and getting their kicks out of conspiracies. And that's exactly what the case of Elizabeth Silver became – one big blend of mystery and theory. Soon, fact matched fiction, and lies became the truth. Nobody focused on what was known. Nobody focused on what had been found. Instead they searched for theories within the shadows. Theories that focused solely on what was unknown. They were always harder to disprove that way. Nobody truly knew what it was that hid in the dark. And seldom would the truth be as interesting as the unimaginable. The truth was final, complete. The unknown, however, had no ending at all.

And so, the stories continued. Poisonous theories persisted.

Why had her father left?

Who was Benjamin Farrow, really?

Did the police know something?

Was she even dead at all?

These were the questions Addison had anticipated being asked. But it wasn't his place to answer them. His role was clerical. Having not touched the original enquiry, he was the most sterile option Claymore had to a fair review of the police investigation. For him, it was just basic admin. A formality.

He hoped.

Carrying a large cardboard box full of tired old police papers, Addison avoided the sharpened eyes of the camera-carrying harpies that swarmed around the station by sneaking through the small fire escape at the back. Duke had told him that he'd leave it open so that Addison could bring in the paperwork safely. Duke made it clear that he despised the press, and was in no rush to feed the beast by accidentally handing them a glance at an original witness statement or crime scene photograph.

Dumping the box onto his desk, Addison couldn't help but think that the whole process would have been a lot easier if Claymore had moved with the times a little. Back on his old patch, Addison's paperwork was scanned onto a computer system, and the papers were stored only for when – and if – they were ever needed in court. But the way Claymore operated felt different, almost rustic. Everything was analogue, outdated. But maybe a little more authentic. Having the original papers, with their original coffee stains and creases, made Addison feel a little more connected to the case. He liked it. It was novel to him.

'Good, you're finally here,' said Duke as he offered Addison a Rolo – but not his last one. 'At some point today, I need you and Maggie to go and visit Beverly Silver at her home. Local gossip tells me that this poor lady rarely leaves the home anymore. So, I'm sure you'll find her in.' Duke turned to face Maggie who was already growing excited at the thought of her little venture outside. 'Now Maggie, this is just a courtesy call. Nothing more. We don't want a fishing expedition. And we certainly don't want it looking like we're covering our tracks. The case is closed as far as we're concerned. That's the official line. Did everyone hear that?'

Duke looked around the office to see if they were paying attention. Darren was scribbling down notes in case he needed reminding of the simple messaging. He needn't have bothered. Duke made it crystal clear.

'We're not investigating anything. As far we're concerned... we're done. The last thing I want is for that baby-snatching scrap of crap Benjamin Farrow to reap the rewards of any cock-ups on our part. So, Maggie... Addison. It's a welfare visit only. Nothing else. Understood?'

'Loud and clear,' Maggie smiled.

'Are you sure you want me to get involved?' Addison looked at Duke, unsure what he could really offer. 'I thought it was best if I just stayed out of it. Kept a distance.'

'True...' Duke offered Addison another Rolo. He always felt less guilty of gluttony if he offered his sweets around. Seeing Addison shake his head, Duke stuffed one in his mouth, guilt free. His speech was muffled by chewed caramel. 'There'll come a point where you may have to ask some people a few questions. Just to gather a little clarity. I reckon Beverly will trust you more if she'd met you beforehand. She's going to get asked a lot of questions soon, so she needs to know who her friends are.' Duke nodded to Maggie who took this as a compliment. Her smile cut her chubby cheeks like a knife through fresh dough.

The phone rang. Geoff answered it, despite it being on Hoggit's desk.

Duke continued.

'All she needs to know is that we're here to help. That woman has been practically on her own since the moment Elizabeth was snatched. Her husband just buggered off and left her. Which didn't help our bloody case one bit. So, what she needs from us is a strong support network. People she can trust. People who will be there for her. No matter what.'

'Got it.' Addison didn't mind. He'd only been in the office ten minutes and already he was feeling penned in. Looking around the room he felt a lot closer to his colleagues than he needed to be. He could almost smell the whiskey that had helped Hoggit get out of bed this morning. It was no coincidence that he'd started walking to work. Facing him, Maggie was busy making herself look presentable. She was approaching fifty, but the way she applied blusher you'd think she was a teenager let loose on her mum's posh make-up supply. Geoff, as always, just stared straight through him. If Addison didn't know better, he'd think that he'd really pissed Geoff off somehow. His eyes were fixed, but way past where Addison stood.

In fact, Geoff wasn't looking at him at all. Instead, his eyes were focused some hundred miles away, wherever that voice on the phone was taking him. His jaw had become square. He was clearly gritting his back teeth. Without saying a word, he lowered the phone to his side. His eyes focused back on the room.

'Duke,' Geoff raised the handset towards his Sergeant. 'You may want to get this.'

'If it's the press, tell them to fuck off. Politely.' Duke played to his small adoring crowd.

'No,' Geoff's tone was flat. 'It's serious. It seems another girl has been taken. Same MO as Farrow.'

'Oh, sweet Mary, mother of mine.' Maggie had kicked back into Irish quicker than she could complete the sign of the cross.

Hoggit's face was planted into his palms, already questioning where he'd hidden his last bottle of whiskey. It was usually behind the cistern in the lavatory.

Duke, on the other hand, had gone a lighter shade of pale, before blood quickly rushed to the surface.

'For God's sake...' He turned to Addison. 'Let's get over there. This bloody better not be linked to our boy Benjamin.'

Chapter 13

The drive to Queensford hadn't been a long one. Twenty minutes, maximum. But the scene was a little different to what Addison had grown used to in Claymore. As you turned onto the road from the motorway, rows of council houses sat on one side, as acres of fields faced them from the other. A small river ran the length of the road, straddling a small park which was now empty. Secreted, a lake sat at the summit of the street, tucking itself in behind a large, somewhat neglected nature reserve. It seemed a little out of place to Addison. Too tranquil. It was almost silent compared to the noise that greeted you at the other end of the road. Outside of the house, a small woodland blocked the view out onto the lake. Addison was glad he couldn't see the water. It always held a face that he would never not see.

I'm sorry Joe. I didn't know.

Shaking off the memory, Addison focused on the scene. A cordon had already been set, manned by a handful of uniformed officers. Strange for what was simply a missing-persons report. Back at his old station, these kind of reports weren't rare. Kids ran away from home all the time. But they always came back. Often it was just some disgruntled teenager acting out of angst towards their protective parents. Sometimes, the children weren't even missing, and the parents were just using the police as some form of posh taxi service. Addison had soon learned the difference between 'absent' and 'missing', and had no time for time-wasters.

Duke pulled up just before the cordon. He had insisted on driving, and had insisted further that Addison attend with him. The incident was a little outside their region, in a small estate just on the edge of Warwickshire. But the timing had made it relevant. It didn't take much to link the retrial of Benjamin Farrow with the disappearance of a young girl on the same night the news broke. Especially if they confirmed it to be an abduction.

'This better not be related,' Duke turned off the engine. 'Or at worst, some crazy cunt of a copycat.'

Addison noted the language. Duke was pissed. He usually punctuated his words with profanities, but this was the first time Addison had heard him drop the 'c-bomb'. He allowed Duke to take the lead as they got out of their car and approached the young officer stood nearest to the scene tape. Her uniform was sparkling clean without a mark on it, fresh out of the box. Just like her.

Green and keen to please, she smiled and nodded as Duke and Addison showed their badges. She noted the collar numbers and filled in her scene logbook as they passed. She was obviously too nervous to ask them who they were. They were both out of uniform, which often meant high ranking, or specialist department at the very least.

If only she knew.

Walking down the freshly tarmacked road, Addison could see small puddles that had formed in the mud that kissed the kerb which sat on the side of the nature reserve.

Had it been raining?

The skies were clear, and the sun was beating down on the back of the trees that offered huge screens of shade towards the houses. The whole estate had been well designed. Every garden neighboured the next, serving as a stage to the row of houses that circled the lawns like a modern-day, low-rent amphitheatre. The gardens enjoyed every spot of light from dawn until dusk. Only the forest that flanked the front of the houses offered anywhere to hide.

The guy came in from the front.

They didn't need to check the address. Another fresh-faced police officer stood under the front porch of the only house that seemed to hold any life in it. The doorway was a small hive of activity as SOCO buzzed in and out. One officer stood swabbing the front door. Directly opposite was a small white van perched on the kerb under the only streetlamp that sat on the small stretch of road. The back doors were open, and the busy work-ants – clad from head to toe in white paper body suits – marched from the van's boot and towards the house, each carrying some new piece of forensic equipment.

'A little excessive, don't you think?' Addison glanced at Duke.

'Depends on what they know.' His gut was starting to rumble. And not because of the small selection-box he'd already poured into it. The location. The timing. The victim. Duke already felt a connection.

Together, Addison and Duke stood and waited until they could see somebody in the know. The young lad manning the door clearly wasn't the one making the decisions, and Duke wasn't prepared to muddy the young man's name by trampling over someone else's crime scene. Duke knew all about reputation. He prided himself on his, and measured most by their own. Standing back from the house, Addison started to take in the scenery. The row of houses bent around at the road's base. There was no through traffic. No way to drive up without being seen. And nowhere to park. Each house had a small car-port that sat at the building's side. The house the girl had gone missing from was a twin facing, detached property. Access was only gained from the front or the back. There were no side doors. And only a single gate leading to the backyard was overlooked by five other houses. Plotting the scene, Addison could see through the lower windows. The bay window to the right led you to the living room. The one to the left held the large kitchen and dining area. Just above it was the only window that was open.

Her bedroom.

A woman in a smart grey suit stepped out of the front door. She was not unattractive, but her stern features offered a natural sense of authority that locked the knees of the young officer standing guard. A small polite smile flicked across his face as his eyes remained fixed straight ahead. He looked terrified.

She was clearly in charge.

'Ma'am.' The young officer nodded. His eyes daren't look directly at her. He stood like stone.

'Well, screw me sideways,' Duke laughed. 'If it isn't old Big Bangers Betty.'

'That's DCI Wilson, thank you.' The woman made her way directly towards Duke with a face that was torn between fury and friendship. 'A bit of respect please Derek.'

It was weird hearing somebody use Duke's real name. It didn't seem to fit him anymore.

'That's Sergeant Parker, please Ma'am.' Duke said with a wink.

'Jesus, they'll promote anyone these days.' DCI Wilson looked pleased to see him.

'Tell me about it. Three times over, by the looks of it.' Duke embraced his old friend. He was right about her nickname. She looked as though she was keeping him at arm's length as they quickly hugged it out. Her auburn hair smelt like it had been cleaned that morning with something expensive. Her coat was dry cleaned, and her leather gloves were non-standard issue.

'Enough of that.' DCI Wilson straightened out her suit jacket. 'We don't want anyone appearing unprofessional. And I'm certain the vultures will be descending soon.'

She removed her gloves and nodded towards the scene tape that divided them from the rest of the road. Already a few news vans were parked up. A handful of journalists shuffled for space near to the cordon.

'So, Ma'am,' Duke continued. 'What do we have here?'

'A kidnapping.' Addison didn't mean to interrupt. He was still looking at the open window.

'So it would seem,' said DCI Wilson with a curious glance towards Addison.

'I'm sorry.' Addison meant it. 'I'm DC Clarke. I work with DS Parker on the Tasking Team. I didn't mean to talk over you, Ma'am.'

'No apologies necessary.' She offered her hand. 'I'm DCI Wilson. It's a pleasure to meet you. Any friend of Derek's is a friend of mine.'

Addison noticed she wasn't wearing a wedding ring. Neither was Duke, for that matter. And he was sure this wasn't the only thing the pair had in common. There was a chemistry between them. A hidden story. A history.

'Why are they swabbing the door?'

Addison broke the short silence. DCI Wilson glanced to the doorway and then back at them both.

'I think you need to come inside.'

The interior was pretty, almost as if somebody had a spilled a complete homeware catalogue into the hallway and had it pour out into every room. Several framed ancient maps decorated one side of the hallway. Each destination seemed too sporadic to not be connected. Addison concluded that each of them signified their travels. He liked it. In front of him was a winding staircase that led to a small landing. Two bedrooms faced one another, separated by a large bathroom that also looked out onto the front of the building.

The landing was too cramped. He left the way he came in.

Duke allowed the DCI to lead. It was her scene after all. To their side, a woman could be heard crying in what must have been the living room. A man with stark red hair comforted her. But she wasn't listening. Instead she sobbed as she stared at the small drawing she was holding.

Inside the kitchen, SOCO had set up a small office space. The onetime dining table now served as a workstation. Various terminals partnered pieces of equipment that wouldn't look out of place in a low-budget Sci-Fi movie. USB sticks were passed from officer to officer, in a relay of recordings and reports. Somewhere amidst the chaos, a printer clunked into action, as two fresh photographs rolled out. Hot off the press.

DCI Wilson picked them up before showing them to her guests.

'This is why they were swabbing the door.'

Addison tried to take in what he was looking at. It was obviously linked to what had happened the night before. But how it was linked, or more precisely why, wasn't clear at all.

'Last night, between 8 p.m. and 7 a.m., Amber Costello disappeared from her room. When the house woke, they found Amber was no longer in her bedroom. Her window was open. And four birds had been nailed to the front door.'

That's what the picture showed. The A4 piece of paper was a colour printout of a photograph that had been taken that morning. It showed four birds with nails through their throats. All pinned to the front door.

'They're magpies', said Addison. 'Any connection?'

'Nothing obvious,' whispered DCI Wilson. She clearly didn't want the family to hear them struggling to make sense of the madness around them. 'Not at this stage anyway.'

'Why four?' Duke was looking at the printout. 'You said it was a girl who had gone missing. Her name's Amber... right?'

'Correct,' she replied.

'Well that doesn't match up. With the magpies, I mean.' Duke was riffing. 'When I was a kid, we used to say a poem. One for sorrow... two for joy. Three for a girl... four for a boy.'

They all knew the poem carried on for a few more verses, but Duke had reached his point.

'Why highlight a boy if it was a girl that had been taken?'

'As usual, at such an early stage we have little to no answers. Only further questions. You know how these things work.' DCI Wilson kept her voice low.

'What about the family? Do they check out?' Duke didn't care for the fact members of his audience were made up of Amber's parents.

'Yes...' DCI Wilson spoke more confidently now. 'No concerns that side. Both can account for the other. They usually keep to a strict routine with Amber. Dinner at 6 p.m., bed by 8 p.m. No compromises. Mr Collins apparently insisted on structure.'

'Collins?' Addison picked up on the discrepancy.

'Learning from the best I see, Derek.' DCI Wilson gave Addison a smile. It was almost flirtatious. 'Amber Costello was adopted by David Collins and his wife Lisa just over twelve months ago. They loved... I'm sorry... they *love* young Amber, beyond question. They've given her a lovely home here. From what the reports say, Amber was happy. They were becoming one big happy family.'

'Any threat of the parents coming back on the scene? I mean, the biological ones.' Duke was up to speed, and already trying to get ahead of the case.

'Not likely.' DCI Wilson picked up a small stack of papers. A small Post-it note had the word '*Background*' scribbled onto it. She flicked through them until she found the sheet she needed.

'It appears her dear old daddy is resident in HMP Fordbridge, looking at a six to eight stretch for armed robbery. And Amber's mother kindly handed her over to the authorities the day the local drug squad raided her bedsit. It was probably the most selfless thing she'd ever done for the girl, not that I'm sure how conscious a decision it was. The reports state that she still had a syringe hanging out of her arm when the raid took place. Amber got out just in time. Her mother was found coiled up and a whole heap of dead a week later. Coroner put it kindly when he recorded 'Accidental Overdose'. There was enough heroin in the whore's veins to keep an entire street out of their minds for a week.'

'So, how long was Amber in care?' Addison couldn't help but feel for the young girl. Finally, in a safe haven, away from the ghosts of her past, only to be dragged away from it all by something unimaginable.

'Doing the maths, Amber was in and out of care for around four, nearly five years. A few families flirted with the idea of fostering her, but nothing quite fitted. Not until the Collins family, that is.' DCI Wilson put her papers down. She'd already been generous with the information she'd shared. She knew that this incident wasn't in Claymore's jurisdiction. It shouldn't concern them. She knew this case was going to be led by her own taskforce, and her Superintendent would chew her up if he knew she was sharing information. But then, she also knew exactly why her old pal Derek Parker was stood in front of her asking questions. There were clear similarities – both on the surface and underneath.

'So,' Duke sounded almost serious, 'you know why I'm here; what I'm looking for. Is there...'

'I don't know.' She was being honest. 'Derek. Relax. You got your man. For all we know this could be some freak who just worships Farrow. Or, hopefully, something completely separate. But trust me. If I see a link... whether it binds your case, or breaks it... I'll let you know. I promise.'

'Thanks.' Duke was readying himself for leaving. He took a small copy of a photograph that had been printed out ready for some community leafleting. It showed David and Lisa Collins with their daughter, Amber. She looked nothing like them.

'And Ma'am,' Duke stopped and turned before leaving. 'Don't worry about me. Just find the creature that took this girl.'

Outside the house the press had been breeding. A swarm of photographers vibrated at the top of the road. At least a dozen now pressed up against each other, snapping away at anything they hoped had relevance. Passing through them Addison caught the gaze of a young reporter. Her hair was short, almost sharp, and was bleached peroxide blond. A sense of assured sexuality oozed out of her. He could almost feel it. She locked eyes with him as he continued to walk to the car. He felt her stare burning into the back of his head, as Duke started up the engine and pulled away.

She raised her hands up towards them. A small flash of light fired off the rear-view mirror.

Chapter 14

The news had reached him. It was pretty much what everyone was talking about. And now another had gone missing. But he wasn't convinced. He didn't believe in coincidences.

Benjamin has a lot to answer to.

His time in solitary confinement had given him time to think. Benjamin needed a friend. With his case being set for a possible retrial, it wouldn't surprise him if there was one last rush for blood. One last attempt at killing the child-killer amongst them.

Everybody on the inside insisted that they were innocent.

Except him.

He knew what he'd done. He'd confessed to it. All of it. And since that day he had vowed to confess to anything else he was guilty of. He knew he needed to be on the inside. He couldn't cope out there. Out there was a life of confusion, judgements and pain. However, inside offered him a chance for redemption. He'd reasoned that whatever scrap of his soul was left could be somehow salvaged if he faced his demons head on. Face to face.

He'd only been inside for a few months when his actions towards other inmates had grown increasingly violent. He often kept to himself, but when he saw people suffering at the hands of others, he had to act. These men had already been judged. It wasn't for others to punish them further. No matter how good it felt. No matter how much he wanted to. Each and every one of them had been called to account for their crimes, and each and every one of them had been found guilty. Their judgement had passed. That is, apart from Benjamin. The fact that he had been granted a review shifted the situation entirely. Benjamin was now on the inside trying to get out. Within the eyes of those that he moved amongst, Benjamin was now guilty until proven innocent. And this allowed just a short window for his haters to hurt him.

And they wanted to hurt him. Badly.

But not him. Not as things stood.

Since being moved to HMP Fordbridge, following the almost fatal mutilation of a fellow inmate, he had soon got to grips with the stance taken towards Benjamin Farrow. To all concerned, he was the top scalp to be taken. Granted, he sat amongst a sea of sex offenders, killers and maniacs, but there was something about Benjamin that made all the other inmates thirsty for his blood. And that 'something' went by the name of James Jenkins.

A murderer, part-time cannibal and full-time maniac, James Jenkins proclaimed to have a strict criminal code of ethics.

Do onto those what those could do onto you. And do it first.

He never hurt anybody that couldn't inflict the same amount of damage to him. And for that reason, he despised anybody who preyed on the weak. Especially children. To hurt a child was an act of irreversible guilt. No amount of time would ever atone for it. And so, Jenkins justified his barbaric brutality, and encouraged others to emulate him, to hurt those whose victims couldn't fight back. He saw himself as a saviour in Satan's clothing, and forced others to follow his cause. So much so that Jenkins had made it cutthroat-clear that if anybody failed to share his hatred for anyone he'd identified as worthy of punishment, then they themselves were condoning the man's actions, and would suffer a similar fate.

And so, according to the godless gospel of James Jenkins, every inmate of HMP Fordbridge hated Benjamin Farrow. And they ALL wanted to hurt him.

Without question.

All... except him.

He wasn't like the rest of them. He'd refused to bend to the bullying tactics of Jenkins, and was well aware that he'd soon face a visit from the psychopath. Especially after sending one of his finest followers to the hospital. But the threat didn't faze him at all. Fear wasn't his to feel. It didn't belong to him. Not now. All he had grown to know was death, so he wasn't scared of it. Instead, it was life that worried him. A life full of confusion, and questions.

Having been transferred to a Category A prison, he was now considered to be one of the country's most dangerous men. But he didn't feel like one. He traced his thumb across the long scar that cut through his eyelid and across his lips. It served as a reminder of who he had become. He was now blind in his left eye from where the blade had been dragged across his flesh. He can still hear the sound of his eye popping under the pressure of the knife. The few teeth that remained in his mouth were beginning to rot. And his scalp had never healed from where the hair had been pulled from his head. Recently, his battles had come to define him. To distinguish him. But this wasn't what haunted him the most. The darkness of his cell offered him no comfort. Sleep was the only way he could shift the stress that strained his every waking moment. Every so often he would wake up, surfacing briefly like the fin of a shark, cutting through the water's surface before plunging back into the depths below, stalking its prey. But even sleep plagued him. It brought with it another form of darkness. One that tricked and fooled you. One that shone a light on what could be, only to switch it off the second you woke. He hated the dark. Inside it, he couldn't see what he missed the most. His outline was blurred and unbroken, blended within the darkened walls of his cell. In the darkness, he cast no shadow.

The best of him was gone.

And now he was his very worst. Gnarled flesh stretched across broken, reformed bones that sagged in his face. The texture of his skin resembled cold wax that had quickly dried as it dripped over the busted lip of a mantelpiece. Covered in grease his entire face gleamed like melted marble. Nobody liked what they saw when they looked at him. At mealtimes he sat alone, and at night he heard them whisper about the terrible things he'd done.

They called him names.

They called him a monster.

He'd called himself Seth.

*

Seth's face had haunted Benjamin from the first moment he had seen it. The knotted features. The expression of fury framed by scarred skin. He had made Benjamin feel true fear. And yet, Benjamin knew that he owed the man they called 'the monster' his life. It seemed he was deeply indebted to this devil.

Having heard that Seth had been released from isolation, Benjamin felt compelled to seek him out with the sole intention to thank him at the very least. Maybe even get to understand him at most. After all, for whatever reason, the man had protected him. And although his solicitor had warned him of the company he kept, something told Benjamin that Seth was more than just an ally. He was key to his very survival.

Having allowed the morning to pass him by, the afternoon had eventually crawled up on him. The day so far had been a slow, uneventful one. But that wasn't a bad thing. He'd purposefully chosen to miss breakfast. Last night, there was something in the eyes of the inmates that made him think that they were plotting something; something that was likely to involve him, a blade, and an appointment with the reaper. It was clear he was the target. Before now, they would have no problem holding his gaze. But last night was different. Last night, they were looking everywhere else but directly at him. Like the shy boy caught staring at a crush, or the pervert in the bar with a tongue full of charm and a pocket full of date-rape. They didn't want to reveal their true agenda. So, Benjamin felt it wise to skip a meal. Even if it was breakfast. But then again, those that proclaimed that breakfast was the most important meal of the day didn't have to account for it potentially being their last. For now, the bellyful of breeding butterflies would do. Benjamin's main appetite was for survival, whether that came on an empty stomach or not.

If he was correct, Seth's cell wasn't far from his own, a minute's walk at most. The prison had recently been cleaned and the sharp scent of bleach bit into the air. Below him a few prisoner's played table tennis on the ground floor, whilst others sat in their gangs trying their best not to look too guarded. The scene looked strange, almost staged, as if everyone was trying too hard to look natural. Hardly anyone was talking, choosing instead to stare into the distance whilst their heads bopped in unison to an inaudible, imaginary beat. Some even thought pouting made them look tougher. It didn't.

Arriving at the cell door, Benjamin saw that it was already open, but the smell seeping out was far from inviting. Peering around the door, Benjamin could see Seth sleeping on his bed. He looked like a sack of soiled gym clothes. And smelt even worse.

If Benjamin had rehearsed an introduction, it was now redundant. As if the presence of a clean odour had cut through the solid cloud of ass-dust that had rendered him unconscious, Seth suddenly jumped out of his bed. He looked startled, like a teenager who had been caught by his mother whilst busy 'discovering' himself, and the Internet.

'What the hell...' he looked at Benjamin. 'Sorry... erm... shit... I just wasn't expecting to see you there.'

Seth looked around him as if to gather things that had scattered on the floor. He'd clearly been in a deep sleep.

'Do you often sleep with the door open?' Benjamin braved a step inside. 'You've got more balls than me.'

'There's a thin line between being fearless and being foolish.' Seth had gathered a little composure, although his posture always made him look slightly arched and on edge. His sunken shoulders sagged forward as he perched on the end of his bed. A cold bead of sweat stumbled across his once split skin.

'Either way, you wouldn't find me issuing an open invite to the world and its guard dog. The last thing anybody wants to see, inside and out, is me getting some rest. Although, they probably would want to see me inside-out.'

'And Rest In Peace, maybe?' Seth's face attempted what looked like a smile, but instead it resembled the expression of a baby with trapped wind.

'Oh, there'd be no peace in that... trust me.' Benjamin smiled back. 'Even dead, they wouldn't let me rest. Probably give them an opportunity to pin countless other crimes on me too.' He ran his hands through his blond hair. When had it grown so long? He obviously hadn't been taking care of himself.

'Good news though,' spittle spilt from Seth's split lip. 'I mean, about the court case... not the haters.'

'I guess. But not everybody seems to think so.' Benjamin leaned up against the wall. The bricks felt clammy against his back. The cotton of his T-shirt grew damp and clung to his cold skin. 'Strangely, that's why I'm here. I just wanted to say thank you... for what you did.'

'You're welcome.' Seth stood from his bed. His bent back suggested he was taller than he appeared. Sleep clogged up his left eye. 'They were going to kill you, you know? Those guys I met, they all wanted to be the one to do it.'

'Jesus, don't sugar the pill.' Benjamin took a breath. 'I know you're right of course. They might even still manage it. From what I've seen this morning, it's clear that they've got something on the boil out there. I can almost smell it, simmering away.' He didn't dare smell the air out of pure fear of throwing up and offending his host. He could already taste the bitter stench on the tip of his tongue as he talked.

'You're a child-killer,' Seth noticed the reaction on Benjamin's face. He looked surprised. 'To them, anyway.'

'But... not to you?' Benjamin had to choose his words carefully. He didn't want to scare off the only chance he had at surviving this place until his court date.

'I know what I know...' Seth held his hands out. 'And I also know what I don't.' He scuttled over to his windowsill and let the small sliver of sunlight kiss his face. His scattered skin looked like someone had shone a flashlight on a crime scene before reversing a ten-ton truck over it. Nothing seemed to be in the right place.

'I have to ask... why did you help me?' Benjamin stood and watched Seth. It was hard to picture this damaged man being able to tackle the thugs that had beaten him half to death.

'Because they have no right to judge you.' Seth turned to face his short-term cellmate. 'Let alone punish you.' He held his stare with his one good eye. 'Death's not something strangers should perform. It's as precious as giving life. And rarely is life given without careful thought or planning. It's often given because people truly care. Death should be the same.'

His voice was gruff, but not because he had just woken up. No amount of coughing or water could clear the gravel that rattled in his throat as he spoke.

'Benjamin, I saved you because they had no right to kill you.' Seth staggered his weight from one foot to the other. His hips kicked out as if his knees couldn't take the weight of him.

'Who does deserve to kill me?' said Benjamin. He was starting to feel uncomfortable. It had been stupid of him to forget how dangerous the man who stood before him was.

'None of that lot out there.' Seth nodded. 'They don't care about you. Not really. Their hatred is born out of a sense of fear that brings them closer to animals than the divine. They barely even know you. So, they don't deserve to even hate you.'

'Is that it? You saved my life because they weren't worthy to kill me. Is that all this is? One big power play to establish who gets the right to slit my throat? I'm not some prize goat picked for the slaughter. I'm a person, a real person who is hopefully getting the hell out of here the second those assholes at the court realise that my coffin isn't nailed shut just yet. Just like the case against me, it was more stitched up than sealed, and I'm hoping that the stacks of bull-crap they tried to bury me under shouldn't hold me for much longer. People are starting to smell it and, when they start digging through it, they are going to find an innocent man buried beneath it all.'

'And yet – here you are.' Seth watched the man's face. Every crease told a story. Every flinch or flicker of his flesh mapped out the truth behind his words. 'They must have had something.'

'Yeah, they did.' Benjamin's laugh was more of a sarcastic grunt. 'They had one whole shit-storm of a case they needed to sweep under the carpet, and who better to bin off than the lad who wasn't local. I was dispensable. Not even a ripple was caused by chucking me in at the deep end. Instead, they branded me a child-killer, strapped some weighted allegation to my ankles and left me to the sharks. With any luck I'd have sunk without a trace, never to surface again. No more reminder of the little girl lost to rock the boat.'

'But you must be causing a few waves now...' Seth stood closer. 'On the outside, I mean.'

'Good,' Benjamin looked almost spiteful. 'I just hope I survive to see it.'

'Is that what you want? To go back out there.' Seth looked towards his window. He squinted as if the light offended him.

'Who doesn't? I'd do absolutely anything to get back out there, away from here. There's too many corners in this place. Too many shadows.'

Seth flinched. He turned to study his guest. Benjamin looked thinner than the pictures the press had used, but he was still quite the poster-boy. Soft blond hair framed his youthful face. Only his eyes looked tired.

'I'd like to get to know you, Benjamin.' He staggered forwards. A sharp tongue dragged across his cut lip. 'If I'm going to help you then I'd like to see if you can help me.'

'Me... help you?' Benjamin observed the monster everyone else referred to. His cruel characteristics were almost cartoonish.

'Yes.' Seth practically hissed the word. 'I'd very much like to know your mind, so that I could then get to know mine.'

'What... the...'

'Fuck?' Seth tried his hand at a smile. 'I'm afraid you're not my type. No matter how pretty some of those out there find you. I hear some have plans for that toned frame of yours. Be sure to be careful in the showers now, won't you, things can get awfully messy in there. Not that all that interests me. I don't want to be inside you. No. I just want you to shed some light on the darkness that's inside me. I'm convinced that you can.'

'Me? What do I know about *your* mind?'

'Nothing, not in this moment anyway. But I was hoping that getting to know you might answer the questions that haunt me. Maybe offer a little clarity to the cravings I have. It might even help me become what I need to be.' He looked uneasy. 'To recover, that is.'

Benjamin was starting to get the sketch. The set up wasn't that uncommon. Given the fact he had been granted a review, inmates would often want to know what 'trick' was used to dupe the courts. It never occurred to them that the truth may be enough.

'Okay,' Benjamin said with a salesman's smile. 'What's it worth to me?'

Seth slid towards him. He looked towards the door and nodded. The heat of his halitosis could be felt on his ear as he whispered.

'Only your life.'

Chapter 15

The first three cups of coffee had done nothing. Like flicking a flea into a gorilla's face. He hadn't felt the impact one bit. He'd tried a few potions. Black coffee. Added sugar. Reduced sugar. Added alcohol. Even tried a few herbal teas. Nothing had an effect. Nothing helped him sleep. And none of them had woken him up either. Instead he had to mentally drag his mind out of the mud, and constantly force it to focus on whatever his eyes were pointed towards.

This time it was the rapid movement of Maggie's lips, punctuated by the occasional head tilt and stare that usually required a nod of the head from her audience to prompt her into the next monologue of trivial gossip and low-end local drama. Addison had perfected the technique of feigned interest. The police handbook had called it 'active-listening', which basically required you to add an enthusiastic 'uh-huh', 'okay' or 'hmm' at the end of someone's dull bombardment of boring news.

But never with victims. True victims were always interesting, and always had a story to tell.

However, Maggie McAndrew was not a true victim, though it was a part she often auditioned for. He began to zone in as her mouth slowed down.

'...four years it's been. Not even a bunch of flowers from my old station. You'd have thought they'd have checked up on me, right?'

'Uh-huh...'

The sound of the office door closing announced Duke's arrival.

'Jesus Christ, Addison.' Duke dunked a chunk of Dairy Milk into Maggie's tea. 'You look like death dug up. And shag me each day but Sunday, Maggie, your tea is stone bloody cold. It tastes like Jack Frost's piss! Which means you've either spent the best part of an hour talking this poor lad into the stupor he seems to be permanently stuck in, or you're starting out on some new fad diet that you've been conned into trying. Honestly, I'm really hoping that Addison is just exhausted and I haven't just wasted my chocolate in some sort of bumblebee sperm, or goat urine.'

Maggie's expression was one of such stone-cold outrage that it couldn't have been any worse had Duke actually thrown a mug of goat urine into it. Thankfully he hadn't because she'd have got a mouthful of it. Her lower jaw sank into the middle-aged waddle that was developing on her throat like some fleshy pockmarked neck-warmer.

Not that Addison was noticing. The flickering of the bulb from the windowless office made him feel uneasy, as if the whole room had a stammer. People's movement jittered around like a cheaply made time-lapse video. He needed to escape. Thankfully, Duke was his ticket out of there.

'We still need to go and see Beverly Silver,' said Duke as he wrote her name on the whiteboard, more out of courtesy than anything else. 'No doubt this latest episode will have dragged up a few buried emotions. If you'll pardon the pun.'

Addison recalled the house which Amber Costello had been taken from. Her family picture had now been stuck to the whiteboard, along with a few innocuous questions which really weren't theirs to answer. It was no surprise that the biggest letters, taking up at least twice as much room as the others, spelt out the name Benjamin Farrow. The question mark that followed seemed sharper than the rest, as if the pen had been scraped rather than stroked along the board.

'Do you think there's a connection to the Farrow case?' The question was asked through the gritted teeth of Geoff Talbot, who was still standing. A kettle bubbled behind him.

'Doubt it. At most we've got some weirdo whack-job trying to mock us. But I'm sure the press will invent a few links. It wouldn't be difficult. They'll only have to run it next to the story of Farrow's appeal and the public will start making their *own* minds up about it all.' The bunny ears Duke placed over the word 'own' seemed unnecessary. His tone was one of complete condemnation.

'Trust me,' Duke continued. 'If any of you ever get into bed with one of those parasitic pricks,' he pointed to the door as if the press were trying to smash it down like some horde of frenzied flesh hungry zombies, 'then you better not fall asleep, because those monsters will rip your heart out just so they have something hot and bloody to serve up to their beloved public for breakfast.'

Addison thought of the attention he'd received lately. The Elizabeth Silver story was big news. Never in all his time policing his old inner-city patch had he seen such press attention. But there wasn't anything novel about horror stories back there. Nobody cared about two rival gangs cutting each other up, or the aftermath of countless drunken domestics. Yet Claymore was different. Here, everybody seemed to care about this case.

'Come on then fuck-face,' Duke was looking at Addison. 'We've got a lost soul waiting for us. Let's get there before the press have pilfered whatever sense of privacy she has left.'

Duke had already left the room before Addison had chance to get up from his chair. The keys to the only pool car available were still hanging on the hook.

I guess I'm driving then.

The way his head was swirling, he didn't even feel close to capable. Out of more hope than expectation, he took one last drink from his double-strength coffee.

It did nothing.

*

The house looked like most of the others in the road. Unassuming. Plain. Dull. The fact that it had played home to the tragedy that now haunted the entire town seemed ill-fitting for a building that blended so well into its neighbours. The grass was cut, the flowers had been watered and the curtains were open. In all, appearances were being maintained, and whoever was inside wasn't planning on hiding away forever.

Stood near the window, Addison could see the outline of a woman stand up from her chair and walk towards the front door. The silhouette disappeared briefly as it passed from the living room to the hallway. The front door opened, revealing the fresh face of Beverly Silver. She was looking happier than Addison had seen on the news. In fact, it was a complete solar system away from the image of the sombre, anguished shell of a woman whose soul had been ripped out from the very root of her being.

'Good morning Sergeant,' she gave a knowing nod to Duke before offering a polite yet unfamiliar smile towards Addison.

'Beverly. How the hell are you?' Duke sounded his sincerest. 'May we come in?' He was already halfway inside the doorway before she could offer an answer. Not that she offered any resistance. She appeared almost glad of the company.

'Got to admit it, I thought it would be a lot louder around here.' Duke stood by the fireplace and fiddled with the small ornaments on top of them. His face was contorted into a small ball of concentration as if the answers to all he sought could be found on the porcelain figurine he was now twirling between his fingers. It was back in its place by the time Beverly reappeared. The sound of a kettle rumbled in the background.

'Oh, if you mean the press, they've been and gone I'm afraid. By the looks of it, I think they saw a link in the Queensford incident even quicker than you guys did.' Her voice lacked any trace of bitterness.

'That's because there's no bloody link to see. Don't listen to them Beverly. Vultures, the lot of them. Can't they just leave you alone? What is it with everybody? One sniff of another missing child and they're banging down your door.'

'I didn't think you knocked that loudly officer.' She was almost smiling as she spoke. Addison couldn't believe that this was the woman they'd intended to meet. She was too jovial. Too nice. Too normal. Nothing like the fallen angel twisted by pain and sorrow that he'd heard described by Maggie. But then Maggie wasn't shy with her exaggerations. Interesting only by association. That's how the rest of the office had described the meddlesome Ms McAndrew.

'Forgive me,' Duke remained serious for a moment. Addison wondered how long it would last before he said something inappropriate. He started to count.

'But those shit-spewing spasticated spin-artists don't care about you one little bit.'

Two seconds.

'Come now, of course I know that.' Beverly ushered the men into the kitchen where the kettle now raged. 'But they're only after their pound of flesh. Like everybody else.'

After three cups of tea were poured, stirred and suitably sweetened, they all took a seat around a small dining table that looked out onto the rear yard. Duke had dunked and devoured three bourbon biscuits in his before Addison had even had chance to reach for one.

'If you don't mind me asking,' Duke didn't wait for any indication of whether she did, 'what did the press have to say for themselves?'

Beverly took a long drink from her mug. Thin cracks where she had superglued the pieces back together cut across the picture printed upon it.

'Nothing much. I don't really give them anything. They asked if I'd heard about Mr Farrow's appeal, and whether I was aware another girl had gone missing. I admitted that I'd caught the news and seen that he was granted a review, but I'd only heard whispers of what had happened one town over. Such a shame. Have they found her?'

'I don't think so,' Duke's hand instinctively took hold of hers. 'That investigation is being run by another force, by a dear friend of mine. She'll let me know what she knows and I'll keep you updated as best I can.'

It was the first time Addison had seen a reaction even close to frustration. Until now Beverly had been the perfect hostess, seemingly more interested in her guests than the dramas that had engulfed her entire identity.

'Never mind me, Sergeant,' she took her hand away. 'As you said. That case has nothing to do with me. It's the poor girl I'm more concerned with. She must be terrified.'

'As well as her parents.' Addison's introduction to the conversation was a gamble. If he had sounded abrupt then it wasn't intentional. No sleep for four weeks can sometimes do that to you. Duke's eyes burned into the side of his face.

'I suppose so,' said Beverly in a tone that suggested she was growing suspicious of her guest.

'I'm sorry,' Addison held up his hands. 'All I meant was... well... if anybody knew what they were going through, it would be you. This whole episode must have freshened up a few buried emotions.'

'None of them are buried, Detective.' Beverly shot him a look. 'Nothing is.' She held the mug as if she was cradling the child printed upon it.

'Mrs Silver,' Addison tried to focus. His head felt like a force was pushing down on it, and based on the look Duke was giving him, it suggested he wanted to slam it straight through the table himself. 'Please. Maybe I should explain.'

'I think you sodding well should son.' Somehow Duke had come to sit closer to their hostess.

'I'm currently looking through the investigation into your daughter's disappearance. On an administrative level at most. What with the case being reviewed, we often review what we did ourselves, mainly to ensure that the case was airtight and the defendant doesn't slip through the system on any technicalities. After all, justice shouldn't be served through shoddy paperwork. And, if Benjamin Farrow were to get out of prison, then we don't want it to be down to poor police procedure.'

'Get out?' The shade of Duke's face alone could have re-boiled the kettle, and his tone could have silenced it. 'Mark my words. It'd be easier for him to chew through diamonds than put up any sort of decent argument for his release. As far as I'm concerned, that worthless scumbag is exactly where he belongs.'

'Unless he's innocent.'

Beverly had said the exact words that had rolled across Addison's mind like an unwanted screensaver. Her very openness to the concept of Benjamin Farrow's possible innocence shook Addison sharper than any amount of caffeine ever could have. He had to stand and move away from the table, as the heat coming from Duke's face threatened to set fire to the entire room.

'How in Christ's name can you say that?' Duke looked at his hostess like she had accused him of the murder herself.

'Sergeant,' Beverly maintained her composure. 'He was found guilty of taking my little girl. I trusted the system. I was told to trust it and so I did. But now it's having doubts, and I'm sorry if that causes me to have them too. The only truth I know is that something... someone... took my girl that night. Whether he's still out there, or we caught him and he now gets a shot at getting out. Either way concerns me. And with another young girl gone... what am I left to think?'

'We got our man.' Duke's words had no anger in them. His face held a conviction that reflected the certainty in his tone.

'I truly hope so,' she mirrored him. 'For everybody's sake.'

Addison left the two of them to talk it over. It was clear that the investigation had forged a deep connection between Beverly and Duke, almost a partnership that used the other's conviction as reassurance. It was a partnership that Addison had come into far too late to even have a chance of fully joining. It probably helped him with his task if he didn't. He knew only too well how duty could hurt those closest to you if you got it wrong. He flinched at the thought of his friend's face drowning in the waters. The image of Rosie with tears streaming down her face always followed.

Without really knowing why, he walked into the rear garden. The cold air brought him around from the self-harming slumber that threatened to swallow him up. Behind the glass patio doors, he could still hear Duke and Beverly talking. The tone was familiar. Pleasant. Soothing.

Knowing when it was his time to walk away, Addison took a small walk around the garden. The general state of it mirrored the one at the front. Well maintained. Manicured. It showed a mind seeking focus, or distraction. A shallow pond settled at the back, with a small rockery that held a simple water feature. Nothing fussy. It seemed to fit the style of the garden. Small, well-kept lawn. A few hanging baskets. Nothing that would make it stand out from any of the others that looked out towards the far fields behind them.

Then he saw them.

Two inanimate objects that sparked a memory. Stood towards the back of the garden was a shed, its roof in need of repair. Next to it was a set of swings. There was no mistaking what he was looking at. He'd seen them before, just not at this angle, and a little further away.

Maybe it wasn't relevant. Maybe it was unrelated.

Maybe wasn't good enough.

He had work to do.

Chapter 16

It was six o'clock – p.m. – and it was Thursday, which meant he was twenty minutes away from Marjorie's home-made pie and mash. Her supper menu was regimented, always had been, ever since he'd first married her some thirty years ago. What she would serve up was scheduled by the season and day of the week alone. No room for impulse – she had no time for that. Yesterday had been ham and eggs, sunny side up with a pinch of salt, not too much due to his weak heart, and tomorrow would be fish and chips. Always fish on a Friday. Always.

He'd become used to it. The regimented life, that is. Granted, the sex was a monthly occurrence if remembered, tucked in nicely between *Coronation Street* and whatever night-time reading he was into. Certainly, some would say it was dull having your days mapped out, but at least there weren't any surprises. He liked it like that. Which was why he was starting to get a little miffed at the young newbie asking far too many questions, far too close to his home time.

Marjorie will be pissed if the mash gets cold.

'I'm sorry DC Clarke, but I don't have those records to hand. You've seen how we police around here... more Stone Age than New Age I'm afraid. My guess is that they'll be buried under a pile of other reports that have gone untouched for the last twelve months. May I ask, why such urgency? Can it not wait until tomorrow?'

His questions were purposefully loaded and leading.

They were also purposefully ignored.

'I'm just after the reports from the Delta unit that covered the searches for the Elizabeth Silver case. I've got all the rest – the OSU statements, forensic reports, even the witness statements from all the volunteers that helped us out with the search. But I've got no report from your department. And reading the Operational Debrief, it mentions that you and your team assisted with the crime scene and surrounding land, but I can't seem to find your papers.'

He was right.

Sergeant Tucker and his dog-handling unit had been part of the search team. But they'd found nothing, which was half the reason why they didn't bother submitting their reports. Granted, they'd written them, but what was the point of saying that you'd found nothing. It hardly altered the case. And even the courts hadn't bothered to ask for them, so why the hell now were they so bloody important?

'Look here lad, I'm happy to help, but your timing's a little off. My tour of duty is up the second I'm off this phone and the chap who manages the filing isn't in until tomorrow. Can't it wait?'

'Sadly not.'

It could have. But ever since visiting the Silver residence, Addison had an itch that needed scratching, and six hours of rooting through rotting reports, coupled with a few re-reads and phone calls to submitting officers hadn't quite done it.

'Well there's only me here and I'm afraid I'm unable to assist you.' The Sergeant checked his watch. It was thirty seconds later than when he had last looked at it.

Marjorie would be plating up before I'm back at this rate.

'What if I come there? Just hand me the keys, I'll happily lock up. I'll even be there first thing in the morning to hand them back over.'

Routine had its own pressure, and Sergeant Tucker was yielding. On this occasion police protocol lost out to personal procedures. Home time had arrived.

'Look here son, don't worry about all that. You sound a decent lad. Just leave it as you find it. I'll prop open the door for you.'

The line went dead. Addison took this as an invite to head straight over.

Unbelievably, Sergeant Tucker wasn't lying. True to his word the front door to his small mobile station – which took the shape of an extended portacabin – had been left propped open by a stray brick that the Sergeant must have grabbed from the nearby construction site. The station itself was conveniently pitched at the entrance to the kennels where the majority of the Local Policing Unit's dogs were trained and initially housed before going to stay with their human handler. Seeing the young, maniacal spaniels search the small play area for their favourite toy brought a smile to Addison's face. It reminded him of when he and Rosie had first brought Marshall home as a puppy. He'd been a handful, and an absolute bugger to train. Quite unlike these spaniels who were well on track to sniffing out the next big drugs haul. He watched as one spun in delight when rewarded with his treasured tennis ball, completely oblivious that the ones served at Wimbledon didn't tend to smell of Class A narcotics. But it was all about association; the dog never saw the drugs. All it knew was whenever it got close to a certain smell, he was rewarded. It was a simple trick – presenting the bad as something good – but it was effective.

Making his way into the office, unannounced and completely unchallenged, Addison half-expected to find Sergeant Tucker still sat at his desk, manning the station until Addison had arrived there. But he wasn't. Instead, he was greeted by a stumpy, narrow office space that had a single window and two doors. One, Addison had just walked through, the other led to the extended section which was filled with filing cabinets. Pocketing the small Post-it note that read '*Help Yourself*', which had been slapped on the door, Addison made a record never to trust the Delta unit with the keys to his house.

The room itself was unsurprisingly sparse of any mod-cons. The light switch took the shape of a long piece of string that Addison had to almost pull from the ceiling before he heard it grace him with a click. The room was stone-cold, the bulb overhead shivered into life before casting out a pathetic patch of stale yellow that barley reached the walls.

Thank God for smartphones.

Addison flicked the home screen of his phone and pressed the torch icon. The bright white flashlight raised a firm middle finger to its energy saving piece-of-tat equivalent that quivered overhead. Thankfully the filing cabinets were titled by date and in some semblance of order. Whoever managed the files clearly took some pride in their work. Or, based on the piss-poor security, had made easy work for any would-be burglars. Not that that was likely. Somehow, Addison felt that Claymore wasn't quite the place for counterespionage cases, and if it was, he doubted that they'd find anything worth salvaging from the sinking ship that was Claymore's Dog Unit. The recession had bitten the public sector hard, especially the specialist departments which were now regarded as luxury items to any forces lucky enough to keep hold of them. The plan was to centralise everything, using a single hub station to cover wider areas. The smaller hubs like this one would become obsolete. Thinking about it, Sergeant Tucker's *'couldn't give a fuck, fill your boots'* attitude started to make sense. Most of this paperwork was either set for the scanner or the shredder, and you didn't need a Sergeant to do that job.

Silently thanking the anonymous filing clerk, Addison found the drawer he was after. Pulling it open it was almost overflowing with folders, all on the brink of bursting. Clearly it was a busy year, and it didn't take Addison more than one guess to establish what the subject of the searches was. No wonder Tucker was looking to bat the task onto someone else; there were at least three whole trees chopped up, flattened, pressed and blotted with pointless audit trails in this drawer alone. If he didn't get lucky and get the file he wanted soon, Addison guessed he was there for the night. Which was fine if it wasn't for his battery symbol indicating he had already lost twelve per cent of his phone battery. The flashlight was a ravenous little shit.

His battery was on ten per cent when Addison finally found what he was looking for. If the date box and twitching hands were anything to go by, the clock on the wall's battery had died at around ten past one some three weeks ago. Meanwhile, the clock on his phone said it was closer to three in the morning.

He prayed it had been worth it. An excitement washed over him like it always did when he felt close to unearthing something. Just like the moment when you've been bursting for the loo for the last half an hour of your drive home, and then you finally arrive at your door and your body kicks into overdrive because it feels just how close you are to that sweet relief, things could always go wrong. Sometimes, the bubble burst and there was nothing hidden away within it. And yet, that feeling – the one that stood between questions and answers, hope and knowledge, theory and fact – always felt the same.

It fuelled him.

Running his eyes over the document, a seemingly dull, unassuming report which detailed a dog-handler's search record, Addison knew this was the last roll of the dice. It had only been a hunch; a thump to the gut that refused to budge. But he couldn't ignore it. Somebody had targeted the Silver's address, just like someone had stalked the Collins'. Both held similarities. Both were as secluded as they were condensed within a small, nosey community. Neighbours would have seen something amiss, someone acting out of the ordinary. Where the Collins had a closed off setting, with no through road or adjacent properties, the Silvers had a boundary of high hedges and fencing. It was the perfect cover, but offered flawed, clumsy access. The dog units hadn't sniffed out any exit from the back, and whoever was doing this must have been a stone-hearted piece of work if they weren't drenched from head to toe in freshly squeezed adrenaline – the number one cologne for all tracking dogs. And yet so far, none of the reports showed a single pooch pounding the backyard. Therefore, whoever entered the houses, did so from the front.

Bold. Confident. Calculated.

Just like any form of access, familiarity was key. Both these houses had been scouted out, and watched. They hadn't been selected at random. A girl didn't just vanish into thin air because of opportunity alone, and your average opportunistic child-snatcher didn't happen to carry a hammer, four nails and a bunch of dead magpies on them just in case a young girl's window was left open. Both of these cases were planned. Someone had prepared. Someone had taken the time to look where they were going. And they'd left their mark.

The message behind the four birds didn't add up – not if they took it's meaning from the old folklore surrounding magpies.

Four for a boy.

But it was a message nonetheless. No matter how indecipherable, garbled, or even the ramblings of an unhinged mind, it was a message; a marking.

Just like the mount. Addison recalled what he had found when he was out jogging that first time. The town, the land, it was all new to him. The jog had helped him to map it all out, to get some sense of bearing.

Just like he had done.

Addison had seen Elizabeth Silver's house before. Not through any press or crime scene photography, but from a distance. A safe distance. A distance that allowed him to see almost all of Claymore in a single sight. A distance that would allow someone to draw out their approach. Thinking back, he remembered seeing the back garden, with its broken shed and set of swings. It was the one he had seen when he had stood on the mount and looked at the village below. It was the one that had been scratched out on the metal map that had stood by his side.

The crime scene reports hadn't given him the results he was looking for. There had been no record of any further birds, especially magpies, anywhere near the Silver residence. The search teams had recorded every cigarette butt, every trodden in piece of chewing gum, even almost every stone turned over within a mile radius of the house, and not a single one of them had found the remains of magpies. Not that anyone had been looking for them in particular, but when somebody makes a makeshift wreath out of them and pins them to your front door, you can't help but take notice.

And that's what had struck him about the Collins case. The message was placed in a way that it could not be overlooked. If, like Duke was declaring, this was some possible copycat, then why differentiate? Why do something that was so clearly different to the abduction of Elizabeth?

Unless it wasn't different at all. Maybe the only difference was that we didn't see it the first time.

Then he saw it. Two simple sentences that, without the knowledge of the feathered calling card at from the Amber Costello case, would have sat flat on the page just like the rest of the report.

PC 258 Lehane had been tasked with a scent trail within, and around, the neighbouring farmlands and fields. Unfortunately, his trusted canine companion wasn't able to write the report as Addison felt they may have shown a lot more interest in what was found compared to handler. Situated on top of the mount, next to the park bench and small stand – presumably holding the metal map – were the remains of three birds. Nothing obvious. Nothing exciting. Not even that noteworthy.

But it was noted. It was noted because it was odd. It was noted because it seemed to have a purpose. Granted, there was no clear link to the case, and PC Lehane was beyond any criticism. For Addison, he'd done enough, without even knowing it. He'd written it down, and referenced it. The reference number related to a photo record, one taken by a Scene of Crime Officer who had followed PC Lehane on his search. That way they were able to capture anything of note, whether it was latter discarded or introduced into the investigation. The photo itself, along with around a dozen others which showed images of bushes and trees which Addison assumed the dog had shown an interest in, was stapled to the report.

On paper, the finding was nothing. A dog had found the smell of rotting animals interesting. It was hardly press-worthy. But the picture told a different story. On paper, maybe a local cat had enjoyed a good night's hunt and forgotten to take them home as an unwanted gift to their master. Or maybe they'd just killed them for fun. On paper, it was anything. It was nothing. But in picture form it was something else. Just like the paper said, the photo showed three dead birds, lying side by side. What the paper didn't say was that these birds had the remains of white and black plumage. No big deal. It also didn't clarify that if this was the work of the local tabby, then that cat didn't just play with string, it was able to tie a knot with it.

There in beautiful high resolution was the image of three dead magpies, all bound together at their feet, by a piece of string.

Addison's gut took a punch.

Just like the birds, the cases were linked.

Chapter 17

For the first few days he'd kept her the same way her family would have remembered her. But now she was the way he'd intended. She'd cried a lot, at first. But she never really had the chance to learn that it wouldn't help her.

It never helped me.

The tears he had cried had only ever been greeted by the opportunity to cry some more. Those that had caused them always acted as if they could simply stamp the tears right out of him, like they were wringing out a wet towel. But he was just a boy. It took him some time to learn that each wail, each scream, each cry for help, only ever led to more pain, more punishment. They all wanted them to learn that it only ended when the noise did. If you were silent, then they'd stop. Only to start something even more destructive. Looking back, he could see how they needed him silenced before they could do what they did. He was never meant to talk about it. Not him, or any of the other children. You were told to keep your mouth shut. Even when they were kissing it.

He looked at her face, she was almost ready to be remembered the way he wanted her to be. The creases that the crying had brought defied her tender age. It wouldn't have been kind to her to leave her this way. The pictures in her home showed her to be a happy child. So, to be a child forever, her skin needed to be smooth. The clay was often so unforgiving.

Rolling his thumbs across her cheeks he could feel how cold she had become. She had such fire in her before, such fight. She had wanted to live. Most of them had been the same. He envied that about them. As a young boy, he had dreamt of escaping his childhood, of finding some form of release. Not for a moment would he have fought to remain exactly where he was, to remain a child utterly dependent on others. But these children did. They always did.

The young girl was lying face up on his workbench, her large afro hair had begun to flatten out around her like a sunken halo. She'd been dead for a little over two days now. He hadn't killed her straight away. That wouldn't have been fair to her memory. He needed to know what type of child she was. He needed to know her in detail. Every detail, it all mattered to him. He'd watched her before. With her family. She'd seemed happy.

He jotted down her measurements on a scrap of paper. The belly of an old wood-burner remained empty behind him, starved of any firewood. He preferred to work in the cold. The heat made him sweat, and he didn't want to have to alter the solution. The cold also kept the skin tight. He needed that.

She needed to look her best. After all, she was enjoying the most precious time of her life. And he was about to frame it for her. He was about to give her exactly what she wanted, what she had fought so hard for. He was about to capture her childhood, frozen and preserved so that nobody could ever take it away. She looked happy, he'd made sure of that. From what he knew of her, she often was.

The clay was ready but it wasn't needed just yet. First, he needed to focus on the negative. But this wouldn't take long. Pouring the solution over her face, he smoothed it in around every crease of her skin. She was so smooth. The plaster hadn't taken long to dry, and once it was set he peeled it off, careful not to cause any cracks. The feeling was almost therapeutic, like he was working in an expensive health spa. His client would have been delighted with the results. Not only had he captured their youth, he'd removed time itself. They would never age again.

The mould was ready.

Taking hold of the clay, he could feel the oil run down his forearms as it squelched between his fingers. Keeping the mould in place, he pressed the clay into all the crevices, massaging them into the area that had once held her face. This was one of his favourite parts, second only to watching the children take their last breath. His fingers hovered over the mould, precisely where her neck would have been. Allowing his hands to tremble at the recollection, he could almost feel her pulse slow beneath his thick thumbs. Her final breath had been her finest, like a flower in full bloom, presenting itself in all its beauty before embracing its inevitable demise. But it didn't need to be that way. She didn't need to rot. She didn't need to become her worst. This way – his way – she'd be frozen at her finest, preserved at perfection, and not allowed to wither and die. Her skin was like varnished oak. It would never chip, scratch or splinter. Not now.

Not like his. His had been cut, bitten, bruised, all from the very moment it began to fit him. As a child he'd been abandoned, like they all were. Whoever had brought him into this world had no space in their life for him. He had been discarded, thrown out, and left for the wolves to feed on. But this was no pack of wild beasts. They had no natural urge to fulfil. Their appetite was for something much more ceremonial. They liked to play with their food, toy with it. At night he could still hear them discussing whose turn it was next, what they were going to do to them, and all without ever any reason as to why. All he grew to know was that his life was worth nothing. His childhood belonged to them.

With the mask beginning to dry, he picked up the scalpel. The razor-sharp tip stole a flicker of moonlight from outside as he inspected it. Using his crooked teeth, he pulled down the sleeve of his winter jumper, revealing a thick forearm lined with thin horizontal scars. He counted them one by one. The next would be the twelfth. Feeling the blade split his skin apart, he bit down upon his fat tongue until he could taste blood filling his mouth. Feverishly, he placed his puckered lips across the wound and drank the warm, oily liquid fresh from his torn flesh. He turned towards the young girl. He knew she had felt pain. He could taste it on her. Slowly he flattened his wide tongue against the base of her chin. A mixture of blood and saliva smoothed his path as he dragged it across her ice-cold skin, past her sharp cheekbones, and around her closed eyes, until it came to rest upon the top of her sunken brow. He pulled away and admired her fresh face. A smile cut into his flesh, as his knife cut into hers.

Chapter 18

The atmosphere was thick, almost tangible. The narrow walls of the office somehow felt closer, as if they were standing over them, watching them. The press had died down a little, but Addison had a feeling that would change. For a couple of days the papers were saturated with stories about Farrow's appeal, but it was soon pushed from the front page by another story. There's always another story. But whatever was hogging the headlines today didn't seem to catch the eye of those in the office. Their eyes were focused firmly on the past; a period that seemed almost altered since the latest development.

'I don't fucking believe it. It can't be.' Duke was having trouble adapting to Addison's findings. 'Come on lad, one swallow doesn't make a summer, and a bunch of motherfucking magpies doesn't make a free man of Farrow. No chance.'

'I'm not saying he's innocent,' Addison knew his audience. He knew better than to suggest that all the hard work they had done had led to the wrong man being sent down. 'But we've got to have a look at the connection. Whoever left these birds, did so for a reason. It's been over a week since Amber has gone missing and we've not heard any positive noises. No possible phone calls home, no possible sightings. The girl's gone. We all know the statistics around missing persons: if they're not found within seventy-two hours, then the chances of them coming back alive are, well... crappy, to say the least. And they're the cases where some nutjob hasn't gone to the trouble of decorating the front door with four feathery little fuckers.'

Addison didn't often swear. Maybe it was the worry of having a man wrongly accused of murder that gave this matter a little more emphasis. Maybe it was the fact that he'd had as many nightmares as he had minutes' sleep over the last five weeks making every waking thought feel like a cannon ball rattling around in his skull. Or maybe it was because there was a missing girl still out there, terrified, and praying that she'd be saved. Either way, Addison was losing patience with niceties. Duke, on the other hand, had never had time for them.

'Bollocks to all that. We got *our* man.'

'Then who's got the girl?' Addison didn't care anymore. He didn't care that Hoggit looked like he was one bit of bad news away from seeing whether a noose would take his weight. And he refused to give a damn about the pointless mutterings of McAndrew who rolled her rosary beads through her chubby palms whilst aimlessly staring at the floor. Addison was pretty certain the young girl wasn't hidden under his colleague's desk, despite having not seen Maggie leave her seat once all day. And he cared even less for the five-mile stare that Geoff Talbot was pointing in his direction.

'Well, we'll need more than a bunch of bounded bird bones to convince DCI Wilson to hand over the case to us. I checked in with her last night, told her what you told me… she's keen to take a look at what you've got, but it's not altered anything. She's still going to run the case as a separate one to ours. Especially given the fact that the chap that did ours was locked up nice and tight when young Amber Costello went for her midnight stroll.'

'How the hell can you say that?' Addison was beginning to collect his car keys from his desk. His coat would be next. The walls were beginning to suffocate him.

'Quite easily. In fact, I'll happily reiterate… if I must. Amber Costello's abductor was not the same as the one who took Elizabeth Silver. I know this because we caught the man who took Elizabeth. Benjamin Farrow was hopefully having his head caved in when young Amber vanished. He didn't do it.'

My point entirely.

Addison dared not say the words out loud. He'd already seen Hoggit palm his less than secret bottle of whiskey and head off towards the toilets. But it wasn't hard to keep things hidden when all you have for company is a madman, a woman who looks for answers in an ancient book, and a supervisor too stubborn to bend towards anything other than what he wants the world to be.

He decided to take a walk. The autumn sun was trying in vain to hold off the incoming bitter winter winds. The day was bright, but the air held a bite. But Addison didn't care. His blood was on the brink of boiling over and his head felt like someone was rattling hot rocks inside it.

His phone started ringing. Looking at the screen he could see the soft face of Rosie vibrating in his hand. He loved that photo. He'd taken it when she wasn't expecting it. She always looked her most beautiful at her most natural.

'Hello.' Addison spoke with an inflection. There was no question, he knew who was calling, but wasn't entirely sure why.

'Hi.' Her voice was low, almost a whisper.

'Are you okay?'

'Fine.'

He hated that word. It never meant just that. It never meant *fine*. Instead it meant that the person was pissed off, they just wanted you to suffer before finding out why they hated you that day.

Rosie was anything but fine.

Six months ago, she had to bury her only brother because Addison made a mistake. Addison had acted foolishly, and Joe was the one who had paid for it. Maybe, he should have let the young girl drown that day. She wasn't their child, she wasn't their responsibility. Addison didn't have any real obligation to go into the lake. There was no crowd egging them on, no added pressure from an idle expectant audience compelling him to act more heroically than any of them would ever dare to. It had been just him, Rosie's brother Joe, and a drowning girl.

What if he had let the girl die?

Rosie would still love him. Joe would require no mourning. And his life would have been the same way that had made him happier than he had ever known.

He'd received no thanks from the girl's family, no personal gratitude. Granted, they were happy she'd been saved, but they didn't care that it was Addison who had done it. He was just another uniform simply doing his duty. Not unlike the one that had died trying to help.

Rosie had every right to be angry. But it didn't change a thing. Addison would still have saved the girl. They both knew that.

He swallowed the tennis ball that had been lodged in his throat.

'How have you been?' He knew the answer.

Sad. Alone. Angry.

'Fine.'

He waited. He could tell she wanted to say something. After all, she'd called him.

'Rosie...'

'I've met someone.'

The bullet hit him straight in the chest, bouncing around enough to hit almost all of the vital organs, before exiting through his gut.

'What? When?' The rocks in his head had joined forces to create a boulder that had bashed his brain in two. 'Who?'

'You don't know him,' Rosie sounded almost angry that he'd asked. 'He's not from your... world. I've known him for a while from work. Since you moved out, he was there for me, made me realise that we'd had feelings for each other for some time, but we'd just been ignoring the chemistry.'

'Jesus Christ!' Cold wind clogged his mouth as he filled his punctured lungs.

'Don't get angry with me. I don't deserve your anger Addison.'

A line that 'he'd' fed her no doubt.

'We've decided—'

Fucking 'We'!

'—it'd probably be best if I just bought you out of the house. From what I gather from your old station, your posting up there sounds pretty permanent, so there's no real need for you to have somewhere to live back here.'

'What the f—'

He couldn't get his breath.

'Stop it Addison. I don't want this to become any harder than it already is. Let's just accept, like adults, that you and I are through. We both knew it, so it was about time one of us accepted it. So, I made the choice. For both of us.'

'And when was that exactly?' Addison was pissed. 'Before or after that snake was inside you?'

'Addison!'

He knew he'd lost. He'd lost the argument the second he lost his cool with her. He always did. The fact was, he'd clearly lost her months before his phone had started ringing. She was right, there was no point getting angry. Anger didn't solve anything. It didn't bring her brother back to life. It didn't piece together the shattered life that he had once shared with Rosie. But sometimes anger, in times like this, just felt natural, almost necessary.

He said his goodbyes by smashing his phone against a nearby wall. There was no relief when the phone exploded into a collection of parts beyond repair. But he knew he needed to do it. He didn't need access to any means of contacting her, not at the moment. No strand of communication was going to be helpful. There was only hurt, and expected apologies waiting on the end of that line, and she didn't deserve his apology. She deserved silence. After all, he wasn't cutting her off from him, she'd said all she'd needed to say. She was gone. Now, he was cutting himself off from her.

She deserved that.

*

The pub was quite full for a Tuesday night. Strangers exchanged stories and smiles, whilst locals washed away their evenings with their favourite drink. The jukebox was playing a mixture of '90s love songs and '80s power-ballads. Queen introduced The Spice Girls, who paved the way for Bon Jovi to belt out his best. People seemed happy.

'Same again please.' Addison was on his fifth, maybe sixth, he wasn't sure anymore. He hadn't let the ice cubes from his first measure of Jack Daniels have the chance to dilute his drink. They still looked brand new when the barman filled up his glass.

'I'll have the same,' Duke's introduction was coupled with a gentle pat on Addison's shoulder. He left it there for a second too long, which made Addison look at him. His eyes had softened since the rage that had framed them from the last few days. 'You okay?'

'Fine,' Addison raised his glass and took a gulp. The whiskey was still warm.

'Sounds like it.' Duke gave a little sharp chuckle as he sat down on the stool next to Addison. 'I wanted to apologise to you. If you think I'm coming over a little stubborn about the case, I don't mean to. It just means a lot to me.'

'You don't have to explain yourself to me.' Addison ran his hand through his heavy black hair. How long had it been since he'd had it cut? His old force would have pulled him up on it by now. He remembered when he first joined having to have it cut three times before his trainer was satisfied with it. They couldn't have it touching the 'Queen's collar'. Like she gave a crap.

'Addison,' Duke continued. 'I know a bit about you, where you came from, what brought you here. It's all written down in your file, black and white. But that doesn't mean that I know you. What you find in files, folders and countless reports, doesn't define who you are, or what the true measure of the man is.'

'Okay.' Addison felt cold. The joy everyone was sharing around him felt like it was pressing in on him like a vacuum. There he was, in a strange town, amongst strangers, having been discarded by the one job he'd ever loved, and then dumped by the woman he had given his future to. Without her, he had nowhere to point himself, no plans that were made for just one person to enjoy. It didn't really make him feel his finest.

'Like I said,' Duke opened a packet of pork scratchings. The small backdraft from the packet made it seem like a tiny pig had farted on the bar. Duke tossed a large piece into his mouth. Addison was certain that he saw a hair still on it. Duke crunched as he continued. 'We'd be foolish to believe what we read.'

'Are you still talking about me, or are we back onto your fixation with the case?'

'Maybe a bit of both.' Duke smiled as he cracked a hard piece of fried pig skin between his teeth. 'You see these people around you? They're happy being oblivious. Tragedies, they just pass them by. Sure... they feel something when it's fresh. But after a while, they let it pass. It never belonged to them, so why own it? Us, on the other hand... you and me... we can't. We can't just let go. These things that are sent to test us, we have to own them. Invest in them. When everyone else is running away, or turning their backs on it all, we're the ones who have to face it, maybe even sprint towards it. It's the only way we can deal with it. After all, it's our duty. A duty we chose.'

'Deep,' Addison left half a smile unfold on his face as his finished off his drink. The barman began pouring another before he'd even begun to ask. It was clear he wasn't done for the night. 'But what exactly am I running into at the moment? It seems to me that I'm supposed to face up to it, look at it, but I'm not really expected to really run with it. No matter what I see. No matter what I find. I'm not running towards anything; I'm just in a hurry to find any mistakes before anyone else does, so that we can bury them before they bury us. That's a little messed up.'

Duke straightened up his shoulders.

'Addison, we all want you to do what you think is right. This case, it needs looking at. But maybe you ought to know something first. The Tasking Team, let's not kid ourselves, we all know what that is – just some hole in which to sweep all the troubled kids into. You're either crazy, incapable or too difficult to deal with. Maybe even a mixture of all three. You and me? We're the difficult ones: the "in the shite, so out of sight" officers that are kept hidden from everyone else, the runts of the litter. What happened back on your force, they had no idea what to do with you. Not that you had done anything wrong. Lord knows, if you had really messed up, then that would have been easier for them to deal with: a simple one-way ticket out the door, don't pass go, don't collect your pension – just one more anonymous entry into the disciplinary board for all the other officers to *learn* from. Or just read about and take the piss.'

'I know what happened to me.' Addison turned to face Duke. 'But what happened to you?'

'Elizabeth Silver.' Duke's smile faded. 'That's what happened to me. Back before I was heading up Claymore's career hospice, I was one of the Senior Investigating Officers heading up the case of Elizabeth's disappearance. Old God-bothering Maggie was a Family Liaison Officer back then, still is, which is how our paths crossed. Her orders were to be there for Beverly. Seems like they struck up quite a friendship. Anyway, it wasn't long until we knew who our man was. We had witnesses sticking him near to the scene, one even having a guy matching his description holding hands with Elizabeth down by the river on the night she was taken, and only two hours after her mum had tucked her up in bed.'

'But how can you be so sure that it was Farrow?'

'Who else would it have been?' Duke's pale skin twitched. 'He knew the girl, he'd been teaching her for a few terms. Maybe she'd caught his eye.'

'That's it? That's all you had? What about her dad? Where in hell is he right now?'

'God knows,' Duke finally finished his drink. He poured whatever dust and cut-offs had collected in the bottom of his crisp packet into his mouth. 'He was around at the start. We took our statements, looked into all possibilities: family accident, argument, abuse. None of it added up. They – Steven and Beverly – they were tight, solid. But they were aching. Not a pain brought by guilt, or feigned just to cover up what you'd done. No, they were broken in two. Families often are after a tragedy like this. Whether one blames the other, or whether it's just a simple matter of being unable to deal with your grief when you're living with a constant reminder of what you've lost – often couples in these circumstances break up, go their separate ways.'

It made him think of Rosie. Would they have made it if it wasn't for their tragedy? Was everything before that moment as perfect as he'd thought, or were they both jumping on an opportunity to make a clean break, to drop something that had been weighing them down, like an anchor attached through politeness alone.

'Anyway,' Duke wasn't finished. The smell of scampi and lemon soured the air as he opened another small bag of bar snacks. 'Once the news broke that we'd arrested Farrow, the press went crazy. We were front page news. You ever felt the eyes of the nation on you Addison? Do you know the pressure that can bring? And forget about your sportsmen, forget about some footballer begging for forgiveness having missed a penalty during an international match. Imagine how the world would turn if we didn't find who'd taken Elizabeth? Can you comprehend the scrutiny we'd have suffered if we'd let some child-snatcher slip through our fingers?'

'Is that all it is? Is that why you're so wound up?' Addison felt a fire in his belly that wasn't a blend of whiskey, but something deeper. 'You're worried that if I find a link between Elizabeth's disappearance and Amber Costello, that the press might call you a few names? What about the fact that there could still be – sorry, scrap that – there *is* a child-snatcher out there? Does that not concern you?'

'Of course it does.' Duke was trying to look relaxed but his skin had twitched itself tight. 'But as long as that case remains separate, then I'm fine. Kids go missing every day. Granted, not like this. But it happens. If the press catch wind of a connection – a real connection – then we're fucked. We lose our jobs, Farrow stands a chance of being released, and the case remains unclosed forever. Can you imagine what that must feel like for her parents? Could *you* live with never knowing?'

'No,' Addison drained his drink. 'And that's why I'll still be running this case. Like you said, we have to face up to it. Maybe there is a connection. Truth be told, my gut is yelling at me that there is one. And what's to say that if we help solve Amber Costello's case that we don't also solve our own? Maybe Farrow walks free, so what. If he didn't do it, and we catch who did, then that's the better result surely.'

'But he did it.' Duke's voice was an octave over Tony Hadley's, which made a few revellers stop for a second before dancing on to Spandau Ballet's 'Gold'.

'Really,' Addison lowered the tone. He hated an audience. 'Then tell me this. If you're so confident that you got your man, then why the hell are you where you are? Shouldn't you be held up as some local hero instead of being hidden away with cop-killers like me?'

'It's all just one big mother dry-humping cliché.' Duke smiled. But his eyes sank a little, as if saddened by the fact. 'You know as well as I do, when it comes to a crime – any crime – it's easy to know who did it, but a lot harder to prove it. In my experience, it goes one of two ways. Either the system works, or you work the system.'

The music played on. The whiskey continued to pour. At some point Duke had gone home, but Addison was left with what he had told him. He knew what he had to do. Either way somebody was going to be upset, that was just something he'd grown accustomed to. There was never a happy ending; only one a little less shitty than the others.

Once the drunken strangers had become acquainted, some coupling up to share a few regrets, others returning to what they found familiar, Addison watched as the life around him blurred into one big stage exit.

He knew his role.

He was set to play the bad guy.

Chapter 19

'He'll die in here. Trust me.' Jenkins seemed angrier than his usual mix of sadistic psychopath and messiah complex. In fact, today he had the devil in him. His inmates had seen it before. For some, it had been the last thing they'd ever seen; taking the wide unblinking stare of a mad man with you to the grave and beyond wasn't on many men's bucket list. But many had kicked the bucket that way.

They all nodded, cramped up into a single cell, smiling up at Jenkins like a pack of adoring delinquent disciples. Some were smiling out of fear, others mainly just happy that he wasn't talking about them.

'From what I hear,' the prophet continued, 'Farrow has gone and got himself a stinking case review. And word has it, he stands a bloody good chance of being listened to. Well, I for one ain't having it! That paedo,' he continued without evidence, 'has to pay. Now I don't care who does it, as long as it's done. The hands of time have already started ticking my brothers, so we need to strike. If he gets out of here, then that's it. Little Elizabeth would have died for nowt.'

The smiling continued, almost awkwardly. None of them wanted to be the one who started to cheer and clap too early. The last guy who interrupted Jenkins mid-flow had found it hard to clap again after having both of his wrists broken.

'So...' a silent sigh was shared by all, 'we've got to ask fast. A few of my guys tried their luck a while back, only for that stinky-assed sloth Seth to get in the way. Well, if you're worried about him, don't be. He'll be tended to. No homo hobo lays his shit-smeared hands on one of my boys without having to answer to me. And I only have one question for that slag...' he paused for effect. 'How's my fucking shank feel boy?'

He held out his arms. It was their cue to clap and laugh like they were watching some mainstream stand-up rather than a straight-up maniac. It didn't matter to them that they were talking about murder, it was just a good thing that it wasn't about theirs. In Fordbridge, that's all they'd grown to care about – survival. The guards had stopped caring about these meetings some time ago. They all knew that it would be some plot or other; some plan to hurt or even kill another inmate. But why should they care? As long as they killed each other, nobody got hurt who didn't deserve it. If they could, the guards would have armed them themselves. Death was just another inmate, housed for life.

Two floors and a couple of corridors away, Benjamin Farrow had no idea how close to death he stood.

'Have you seen today's papers?' Seth seemed to slur the words through a chewed lip as he leaned up against the doorway to Benjamin's cell. 'They mention something about a girl gone missing.' His breath was hot, almost as if it had never met with water before, let alone a mint.

'I heard.' Farrow didn't want to appear too excited, but this was massive news. From the moment Elizabeth had disappeared he, and he alone, had been firmly in the frame. There had never been the slightest hint of consideration that somebody else may be responsible. Instead, the police rounded up the local village outcast and ran him out of town with pitchforks and a twenty-year life sentence.

'Think it's got anything to do with you?' Seth's frame slithered against the wall as Benjamin passed him by. 'I mean, with what happened to that other girl... the one you're meant to have taken?' He scuttled his way back to Benjamin's side. The man appeared to be walking with purpose, with direction. And given the tired-looking towel that slumped over his shoulder, it wasn't any surprise that he took the turn that led to the communal shower rooms.

'I'm not really up for talking about it,' said Farrow as he slowed his pace a little. In truth, talking was the last thing he wanted to do. He wanted to scream at all the doubters. Shout down all those who had thrown him to lions, and out-roar all the beasts that heckled and spat out his name like it was acid on their tongue.

Seth was not far from him. His nose alone could have told him that. His stench was almost mythical, almost intentional. Surely he knew. Surely that blend of unwashed ass and sweat was something your senses could never get used to. He must know how bad it was. But then maybe it was on purpose. His vicious reputation had made people keep their distance, for now at least. So maybe the stench was some sort of force-field, some shit-smeared shield behind which he could hide.

Benjamin took the next left which led into the communal showers. The air was cold and sharp, twisted by a hint of bitter lemon and cheap bleach.

'You looking to take a shower? Brave move given the fact half the prison is waiting for a chance to slit your throat.' Seth's head leaned forward as his feet dragged behind him.

'No,' said Benjamin, almost smiling. 'You are.'

He tossed the towel towards the stench that masked his friend.

*

The shower was the first he'd had for as long as he could remember. He hadn't planned on having one, but Benjamin had clearly made his point, and he didn't want to lose any, not when he could feel them both getting closer to one another. Truth was, he almost liked him. Almost. There was still a side of him that he wanted to understand; a side he didn't even know if it existed, but if it did... it may help him come to terms with the urges that stirred beneath his skin.

The water trickled between the torn flesh of his face, forced into small streams as they staggered through his scars. He kept his eyes open as they became flooded. His one good eye became blurred beneath the shower, as steam rose from the floor like an explosion in slow motion. He hadn't any soap, but the water was enough. As the water dragged the dirt from his body, he finally felt its warm touch against his neck. Goosebumps rose to the surface of his skin, decorating his body like cheap leather. For a moment, he let the waters hold him. It had been so long since he had felt something touch his body. He flinched as it crawled between the cracks, kissing his inner thigh as it passed.

'No.'

As if the water threatened to wash him away, Seth jumped out from beneath the shower.

'Go away.'

Thoughts distracted him. Blurring his judgement. He longed for touch. Her touch.

'Not now. Leave me.'

Turning towards the door, he saw that he had an audience. Two of Jenkins' disciples stood in front of him, shadowed by a prison guard.

'I'm afraid we can't do that Seth. Orders are orders.' The man turned to the guard. 'I thought you said Benjamin had come this way?'

The one who spoke had a face that hadn't met with a salad for what looked like a lifetime. His fat frame leaned onto his left leg, his hip kicking out to the side. Clearly a weak point. The other had a pair of teeth that would disqualify him from any apple-bobbing competitions on the grounds of an unfair advantage. And if any other parts of his anatomy resembled that of a donkey, Seth was about to find out as Goofy dropped the towel that had been hooked around his waist. The blood rushed from his face as his wart-covered cock began to pulsate. Seth knew this wasn't your usual, everyday prison-rules beat down. As did the guard, who flicked off the light as he turned his back and left.

Darkness hit him, but not before he could feel an oversized tooth break between his knuckles. Lunging forward, his foot met with an explosion of squashed scrotum, at the exact time the wind was forced from his lungs and replaced by the shoulder of the salad-dodger.

Hit with such force, Seth's back smashed against the damp tiles of the washroom. Shadows screamed in front of him as he planted his knee into the weakened hip of his attacker. Steam smoked out the room as his eye struggled to adjust to the darkness. Scrambling around, fingers outstretched against the floor, he could feel it alter from damp tiles to dry sticky vinyl. The unmistakable scent of stale urine told him he was near the toilets.

Fat hands took hold of him and lifted him up off the ground, forcing him backwards. A thin wooden door broke upon his back, as his legs slammed into a metal latrine. Pain burst across his chest as a backhand slapped him to the floor. A hand grabbed his hair and spun him around before pushing his face beneath the water. Struggling for breath, water gargled and rushed around him, as his attacker pulled the flush with one hand, and used his entire weight behind the other to force Seth's head down.

But he'd done him a favour. The vacuum had pulled all the water from the toilet, allowing Seth to fill his lungs with air. Fuelled by the adrenaline that now invaded his bloodstream, Seth spun onto his knees, his back arched under the weight of his wannabe killer. If he wanted to, he could have killed the man. His thumbs were pleading to be plunged into the depths of the man's eyeballs. They screamed with desire to scramble the brain of the monster whose fingers had now begun to wrap around his throat.

But Seth had to be smart. He couldn't afford to be moved again. It wasn't just his life that concerned him. Not anymore. If he killed this man, then he could be moved away, and that would mean Benjamin would be defenceless.

That didn't serve Seth at all.

The first punch was only to distract his opponent, serving as a tracer for the one that mattered. The short jab had played its part perfectly. Caught on the side of the head, the man had reacted, letting out a small cry before making the unwise decision to shout out some witless obscenities, and unlocking his jaw in the process.

The next punch ensured his jaw remained that way. Feeling the bones break as he punched through his attacker's face, Seth pulled his arm back and fired it three more times in the same direction. As the fingers unravelled from around his windpipe, he knew he'd knocked the man clean out. All that was now left to do was to ensure that his ass-faced friend hadn't gathered his strength back. Feeling for his head, Seth took hold of his unconscious enemy's thick, greasy hair from the roots. His knuckles dug into the man's scalp as he dragged his limp body towards the muffled screams of his buck-toothed would-be rapist.

After a few steps the adrenaline was already beginning to fade, and his thighs burned beneath him. Soon, the floor became damp again; cold tiles licked at the soles of his feet. As the short, sharp, blood-clogged whimpers became louder, Seth knew the man was nearby. Letting his ears guide his hand, Seth forced his fist a foot further than he needed to. The dull thud that followed brought with it a blunt mixture of cracked skull and tile.

Careful not to touch the riddled rank groin of the now toothless wonder that was Goofy, Seth pulled the man's knees wide apart before he slammed the fat man's gawping face into his squalid lap. He counted to five to gauge any reaction. Happy he'd hurt but not killed, Seth walked out of the shower room, leaving the two men entwined, and broken, behind him.

Chapter 20

'We've got him.'

Hoggit's voice seemed nervous, almost apologetic. It was followed by the sound of the handset being wrestled from him, with little resistance.

'Sarge, we've got the fucker!'

The unmistakable anger in Geoff Talbot's voice now filled the phone.

'Uniform picked him up about an hour ago. They responded to some call on the 9s made by a freaked out young girl who'd been walking her dog in the woods. Apparently, this piece of dirt tried to grab her in broad daylight, but she shook him off. He was still there when the response team arrived, curled up in a bush like some weedy paedophilic plant.'

'Sounds more like pond-life to me mate, let's hope it was a thorn bush he was lying in. Or better yet, some poison ivy.' Duke was excited. Confused, but excited. If this was the same man that had taken Amber Costello, then if Addison was right, he may also be the man who could tell them where Elizabeth Silver was. 'Any sign of the girl?'

'Not that we know of. The call only just came in. Thought I'd let you know straight away.'

'No problem, you did the right thing. I'm guessing the scene is contained, the search team on their way? Do we have a name for this guy?'

'Not yet Sarge,' Geoff's voice bordered on a whisper, as if he was talking as an aside, away from the listening crowd. 'From what I gather, he's not giving much at all. Sounds like he was reared on the special farm and somehow missed the cull, if you catch my drift.'

'Well Geoff, prepare him for slaughter. I'm about to carve him up.'

The short five-mile commute had only been briefly extended by picking up Addison from his digs. He was still in the hazy midst of his hangover, but looked no different to his usual sleep-deprived, scruffy self. At most, his beard was a little fuller, but other than that, you wouldn't have known the difference.

'Late night?' Duke spoke out of one side of his mouth as half a pack of Hubba-Bubba filled the other.

'More early morning,' Addison braved a smile, but even the slight movement of his face caused his head to hurt.

'Really?' Duke tried to blow a bubble but failed, almost spitting the entire contents of his mouth onto the dashboard. 'I thought the time of day wasn't really an issue for insomniacs?'

Addison looked at his friend, puzzled.

'Don't think I haven't noticed. I can spot a night owl a mile off. Trust me, I've had a few sleepless nights myself of late, and there's no mistaking that Droopy D, hound-dog expression you've been lugging around. When was the last time you slept? I mean, a full nine hours.'

'God knows.' Addison reached for his sports drink. It amazed him how often the aching masses nursing a hangover from hell tended to opt for a drink supposedly designed for athletes. If pain was a true message, then his body wasn't quite up for a run today. 'I doubt I've amassed nine hours in total over the last month or so. You kind of get used to it.'

Rain had begun to blanket the windshield. Addison was praying Duke would make use of the wipers soon. Car washes, showers, anything that submerged him in water had a habit of encouraging hallucinations, and the last thing Addison's head needed right now was a flashback of a dead friend's face freaking him out.

'Well,' Duke flicked on the windscreen wipers and tossed another block of chewing gum into his packed mouth. 'I may have some news that will ease your worried mind and put to rest some of those theories of yours.'

'Eh?' Addison could only offer a grunt as he emptied the bottle of sugared water into his dry throat.

'Seems like this morning, whilst taking her designer mongrel for a walk, little Jessica Walker – you know, the one whose dad runs the ice cream parlour – well she only goes and escapes the dirty grasp of some stinky-assed creep. Thankfully, she had the presence of mind to call us before running home to soothe her woes with some rum and raisin... my favourite by the way. Response then swooped in and scooped up the fruit-nut before he has a chance to flee. And guess whose name falls out of his slack-jawed mouth as soon as the police lay hands on him...' Duke paused but saw Addison was in no state to guess. He took both hands off the wheel when he revealed the answer.

'Elizabeth.'

Addison swallowed his drink hard. It felt like it had washed over thick rows of razor blades that lined his throat. 'You think this is our guy?'

'No idea,' Duke indicated to turn right. They were around half a mile from the station. 'But how many kiddy-snatchers can one town possibly have?'

*

The custody suite was not unlike any other. Cold grey breezeblocks had been given a single lazy coat of paint, typically some variant of blue that looked almost as tired as the staff working within its walls. Void of any windows, the motion-sensor lights staggered into life, staining the ceiling with a stale tinge of yellow. The air felt heavy and drained, as if it clung to your clothes as you passed on through, hoping to hitch a lift out of the place.

As senior investigating officer, DCI Wilson was already in attendance. She'd been briefed that their suspect hadn't called for a solicitor, nor had he wished for anyone to be informed of his arrest. Addison could see her reading the front sheet of the detention log when Duke announced their arrival.

'Make room, make room,' Duke added a bit of swagger to his usual dangly gait. 'Claymore's finest are in the hiz-ouse.'

'Derek,' said Wilson, as she rolled her eyes. 'You know this is my case.'

'And you know this is my town, Chief Inspector.' He smiled as he offered an exaggerated wink. 'Sorry Ma'am, I've always wanted a jurisdiction stand-off like you see in the movies.' There was a genuine tension shared by both. Some of it professional, most of it sexual. Addison would have left them to it if it wasn't for the fact a young girl was missing, and the closest thing they had to a lead was stinking up a cell twenty feet away from them all.

'Well, I'm afraid this is real life Sergeant, not one of your make-believe adventures.' DCI Wilson spoke as if to dismiss them both but walked in a way that encouraged them to join her in the small doctor's office, just away from the front desk. Not too far to look suspicious, but far enough to avoid any angled ears.

'This guy's not saying anything. No details when being booked in; no name, date of birth. Damn it, the way he's acting, he doesn't even seem to be on the same planet as us. The custody officers have managed to Live-scan his fingerprints, so we'll get the results of any matches soon, and they've taken his DNA as well. If you ask me, the swab belongs in the biohazard section. Have you seen the state of this guy?'

DCI Wilson pointed to a small set of monitors that displayed live video footage of all the cells. Sure enough, amongst the small squares of men mostly pacing or sleeping, there was what appeared to be a walking mound of mud, with unblinking eyes. Eyes that knew exactly where the camera was. Eyes that were staring straight at them.

'Wow! Check Muddy Holly out! This guy is bizarre.' Duke gave an excited laugh. The high-pitched cackle echoed and bounced off every wall in the suite. A few of the sleeping inmates shuffled on their wafer-thin bed mats, but weren't completely stirred.

'When are you planning on speaking with him?' Addison looked at DCI Wilson. He could tell she was someone who had her day mapped out, no matter what happened, or whatever eventuality she encountered. From the very start of every incident, she had it all in order in an instant.

'After he's been run though a jet wash, I'd say.' Duke was still flirting, trying to appear less interested in the matter than he was, but it was clear to all that he was concerned about what could potentially unfold. Concerned, and nervous.

'Calm down Derek,' DCI Wilson lay a soft hand on his shoulder. 'You know how these things work. My unit are with the young girl now, taking a statement. Once done, we'll run through what we have. He's currently on the books for an attempt abduction; nothing to do with the Amber Costello enquiry just yet, and somewhere closer to another universe than the Elizabeth Silver case as far as we're concerned. So, you can relax for now.' She cast her eyes at Duke. The small needle holes where his eyes were meant to be flitted between hers and the screen. 'But all that's just process.' She looked down at her clipboard as if to check that she was to schedule. 'We don't do a thing until we know who we're dealing with.'

The woods where the incident happened weren't unlike any other that you'd see neighbouring a small council estate. Pockets appeared untouched, like nature's own little bolt-hole. Other parts played host to various fly tipping sprees. Seasonal plants suffocated under various fast-food buckets and bags, whilst empty cider cans choked the thin grass. Even the police presence wasn't a novelty, appearing as almost a natural element to the site. Local burglars and drug dealers often used the woods as a cut-through to avoid being pulled over by officers in their brightly lit, siren-loaded crime-detection preventers.

Between the custody block and the crime scene, Duke had somehow managed to locate a large bag of sweet chilli flavoured kettle chips. The front of the bag had the words 'Sharing Size' stretched across it, but Addison knew there'd be little of that going on.

'More space than spuds.' Duke spoke through the side of his mouth as the other half crunched and chewed. 'I'm sure you pay for the air these days.'

'Just like *Total Recall... Give these people air!'* Addison laughed to cover up his embarrassment of his terrible Schwarzenegger impression.

'Eh?' Duke looked puzzled as his hand plunged into the bag, rustled for a moment and then heaped a fresh fistful of crisps into his mouth.

'*Total Recall*... the film?'

'I don't remember it at all.' Duke let out a shriek of laughter that caused birds to leave their branches.

'Shit pun... really shit pun.'

'A man's gotta poo what a man's gotta poo. Now that's a shit pun!' Duke laughed again. It made the echo of his last one sound like it had gone full circle.

'Talking of bowel movements,' Addison nodded to Duke's snack, 'what the hell is going on with yours?'

Duke flashed Addison a look that resembled a greedy hamster stocking up for winter.

'All I see you do is shovel garbage into that gob of yours. What's the deal with that? You seem to have the metabolism of a twelve-year-old boy, and the sweet tooth to match.'

'Bull... crap.' Duke's hand appeared to be scraping the bottom of the bag as he spoke.

'No, it's not. All I've ever seen you eat is something from the sweet aisle. Your inevitable coronary will look like a confectionary cupboard.'

'Yeah... that's true. But the metabolism thing, that's all a load of bull. It's a myth that skinny people have raging metabolisms. Probably made up by some lard arse to excuse the fact that in-between sitting at his desk all day and then anchoring himself in front of his TV for six hours each evening, he hasn't been able to burn off the eight packets of biscuits he inhaled sometime between brunch and lunch.'

'Maybe,' Addison watched his supervisor tilt the bag in the air in an attempt to get every last crumb that had escaped his grasp, 'but that still doesn't answer as to why you have the diet plan of a suicidal diabetic.'

'A man's gotta chew what a man's gotta chew.' Duke look pleased with himself. With a slight skip in his step, he made his way over to the small group of officers that had gathered towards the bottom of a small quarry. A flimsy attempt at scene-tape had been wrapped from one tree to another, but half of the cordon was missing, allowing any man and his dog to walk on through. The failing was clear to see, but Duke still felt the need to make a point.

'Well boot me in the bollocks and try to charge me for the pleasure, what the hell's going on here then?' Duke walked through the invisible line with his arms outstretched. 'Hardly Fort Knox boys, and girls... sorry... I apologise. Criticism should know no gender.' Duke corrected himself as he noticed a small female officer holding an exhibits bag.

''What have you got there?' Addison tried to sound his most caring.

The girl wore an expression that hinted at a long shift of being a dogsbody to the bigger boys. Nobody wanted to be the exhibits officer, it amounted to two things: a long day of cataloguing every last piece of evidence taken, followed by an inevitable and even longer day in court facing a member of the defence team hell-bent on making you appear like you don't know how to seal a plastic bag.

'Sorry, who are you?' The girl seemed shy when asking. Even though she was right to.

'His name is Addison Clarke, he's a detective under my glorious guidance, Claymore's very own Tasking Team division.' Duke flashed his badge whilst never making eye contact with the girl. Partly because he was scanning the scene in front of him, but mostly because he'd seen television cops do it, and he thought it looked cool. 'What have we got here then...' Duke turned and scanned the nametag etched across the young officer's fleece, 'PC Alsopp.' His emphasis on her rank was a clear move to highlight the hierarchy.

'Well Sir...'

'Sarge...' Duke corrected her. 'But just call me Duke.'

'Oh, sorry Sarge.' She continued, struggling to work him out. 'This is the outer cordon, which is why we've done such a shoddy job with the scene-tape. It was only me and my partner sent down here originally. I wasn't really sure what kind of scene we were supposed to be protecting. Our only information was that the young girl was pounced on by a bush, but no idea which bush exactly. We decided to fence in as much of the place as we could, until SOCO arrived. Thing is, whist down here, my partner spotted something. They're all down there taking a look at it. Down there.'

The officer nodded towards the lower end of the quarry. Behind a hulking oak tree was a hive of police activity. It struck Addison how they hadn't spotted it earlier. Officers buzzed like worker-bees around the trunk of the tree.

'Who's down there?' Duke was back to not looking at her as he spoke.

'Scenes of Crime, a few response officers. Oh, and the press.'

'The press?' Addison was looking at her as he spoke. He wanted to gauge every reaction from her face. The way she mentioned that the press were here suggested as if their presence would have been obvious, almost expected. Her expression said the same thing. Her wide eyes, slightly slackened jaw and stuttering speech suggested a newbie who now feared they had done something wrong.

'I'm sorry, I thought it was all right for them to go in?'

'Relax... you did fine.' Duke didn't like seeing an officer take the blame for someone else's inadequacies. It was clear she'd been left with little guidance and even less instruction. If the press were down there, then the officers who allowed it to happen were still allowing it to happen. Not that it was difficult to bypass the five-foot-two officer with six metres of scene tape and a six-acre scene to protect. That wasn't her fault.

Down by the tree, the party was as described. It seemed the guest list had been quite generous on this occasion, with the dress code ranging from full forensic white suits to relaxed jeans, waterproofs and a wide-angled lens.

'Who's in charge of this circus?' Duke entered with a roar. It appeared the role of the lion tamer was to be played poorly by what Addison could only deduce to be the partner of the female officer left at the top of the hill. His tatty fleece suggested some mileage, but there was a slight gathering of dust around the small pen pockets that insinuated that this chap hadn't been practicing his literary skills for some time. His *I can't be dealing with this shit* body language also hinted at the common lazy, left-behind prick that Addison despised. No doubt this guy hadn't gone as far in his career as he had wished. But it never occurred to him that he'd have to put in some legwork to travel from side to side, as well as upwards. So, now he used his experience to make those with less time in the job feel worthless. It had never occurred to him that by leaving them with everything to do, they would soon become more skilled than him and actually go places, leaving him behind to wallow in his own rotting pile of procrastination.

Addison already hated him.

'Who are you?' The officer stood with his hands in his pockets. Addison's instinct was to push the man over, just to teach him a lesson in self-defence. But it wasn't his place to correct the man. Thankfully, Duke hadn't missed the opportunity to educate.

'Stop touching yourself when you look at me. I usually charge for that.' Duke flashed his badge again. 'DS Parker from Claymore, and this is DC Clarke.'

'Claymore... that's at least three miles away.' The officer clearly had no respect for rank. Instead, he was more focused on highlighting flaws in processes and procedures. It was the tactic of everybody out of their depth, finding it easier to criticise existing processes than create anything better. But given the carnival this sloth in a stab-vest had created with the scene, maybe it was wise to leave him on the sidelines when looking to re-paint the playing field.

'Well spotted.' Duke offered one slow, exaggerated clap. 'We're potentially dealing with a cross-border matter. My colleague and I are here to check whether there is a link between the two. So, if you could kindly let us take a look... we'd be most grateful. We won't intrude too much. You can even continue your long-distance tutelage of your young partner, if you wish. Just stand here... do diddly-squat all day... and go home happy. Or at least, not as unhappy as you should be.'

'Excuse me?'

'Gladly... you're excused' Duke expertly spun the officer as if to steer him away from the scene as he brushed past him. The officer was stood behind, seething as they surveyed what lay in front of them.

A handful of SOCO were scattered around, tweezers in hand, pulling some pieces of fabric from various bits of wood. In-between them was a sixty-foot oak tree, branches bare of any leaves, and a small alcove at its base. The remains of a fire sat at the front, the ash cold and damp. Duke went to take a closer look when Addison caught the flash of a camera bounce off the bark. None of the forensic team were taking photographs, so it was clear the press were interested in what they were all looking at. Turning, Addison saw one stood behind the nearest tree, examining the picture they had just taken.

'Mind if I take a look at that?' Addison was in front of the photographer before they had chance to take another picture.

'Oh... ignore me.' Her voice was kind, but assertive. It was clear she knew how to get her own way. Looking up from inspecting the image, a small smile flickered on her face at the sight of the officer now stood blocking her view. She was attractive, in a boyish way. Her short blond hair had been highlighted, but the roots were beginning to come back in. The lighter tones gave her hair a feathered effect. It suited her sharp features.

'I've seen you before.' Addison wasn't lying. The camera, the short blond hair, the interest in missing children. This was the same person that had taken a photograph of him and Duke leaving the Costello residence. He was certain of it. He was also certain that he wasn't going to tell her that – at that distance – he'd mistaken her for a man.

'Really?' She appeared uncomfortable. 'Where exactly?'

'Well, I can only say the one place. But I have the feeling that there have been others I may have missed. The fact that you didn't deny it means you know it's highly possible that I've seen you before. Partner that with the fact that you asked me where *exactly*, and I could be forgiven for thinking you've seen me more than I've seen you. Do I have a stalker on my hands?'

'Well, aren't we quite the detective.' She was relaxed again, almost flirtatious. 'You know I don't have to tell you anything, unless you're going to arrest me.' She flashed a smile his way. 'I'm not a suspect, am I?'

'Not yet,' he smiled back. It was nice to feel chemistry again. 'But you may have evidence on that camera of yours. I apologise in advance if I have to seize it sometime.'

'What's the matter? You worried your professionals may have missed something?' She shifted her weight onto one hip to add a little sass to her comment. It worked. The hint of a curve stirred Addison. There was something about this woman, something that lived somewhere between dangerous and sexy. And he liked it.

'Oh, don't worry ma'am. Us professionals... we don't miss a thing.'

'Yo! Addison...' Duke's voice hit the back of his head like a blunt fist. 'Get your ass over here. You're missing this!'

She giggled as she watched how uncomfortable his colleague made him. 'Go on then Detective. I wouldn't want you to miss something. Apart from me, maybe.'

'Thank you,' he said, still squirming from Duke's interruption.

'The pleasure's all mine... Addison.'

The namecheck stopped him. He paused for a moment before realising that Duke had just screamed it at the top of his lungs. Part of him was pleased that she'd picked it up. Walking away, he still had no idea who she was, but he was certain she'd surface again sometime. Hopefully, sometime soon.

'This mother-humper has a frigging shrine...' Duke stood back to allow Addison full access to the small alcove at the tree's base. The way he was standing was sure to block any prying, spying eyes. It was clear what was in there made him uncomfortable. His expression was a mixture of enthused disappointed rather than excitement, like somebody who had found the answers to an exam, but only after having taken the test and realising they'd answered all the questions wrong.

At the base of the tree was a collection of everything that was dear to whoever stayed there. A box of matches rested next to a few empty cans of extra-strength lager, a soiled sleeping bag scrunched between two branches in a vain effort to keep it dry, and a small carrier bag that had been flattened out to make a makeshift placemat, on top of which sat various newspaper cuttings, all from different publications, but all discussing the same thing. Or rather, the same girl.

Staring up at Addison, beneath various headlines and articles all using her name, was the image of the girl-ghost that haunted them all: the unmistakable image of Elizabeth Silver.

Duke knew Addison was up to speed with the scene in front of them. His hand was shaking as he rested it on Addison's shoulder and leaned in, speaking just above a breath.

'Who the fuck is this guy?'

Chapter 21

'Spike Harris... local urban camper with a Mental Health marker for paranoid schizophrenia. He once turned up at a police station smeared in his own excrement, saying it was the only way the King of Mercury couldn't see him. Numerous arrests for shoplifting, drunk and disorderly, and he was sectioned two years ago – but was released a day after. He hasn't surfaced since. Well, not until today that it is.'

The Livescan results had come back. Somewhere, beneath the muck and faecal matter, they'd found a fingerprint, and that print belonged to a man called Spike Harris. Addison handed Harris's PNC report to Duke as they headed back to the car. One of the operators back at the station had noticed that the log had been updated with the suspect's details and thought it apt to let Addison know. It had nothing to do with the fact that she had a huge crush on him, and just wanted an excuse to chat to him. Not that Addison was the chatty type, but she liked the mystery in him. Or at least that's how she described it. Others would have just taken him for rude.

Having checked the mound of muck against the man painted in his police-print, there was no point waiting for the DNA results. They knew they were one in the same. The rap sheet practically spelt out a paint by numbers kit for the guy who was last seen decorating his cell with his defecation.

'Still think this is our guy?' Addison waited until they were in the car before he asked.

'Not at all.' Duke seemed a little relaxed.

'Seriously... not a shred of doubt?'

Duke watched Addison as he spoke and offered nothing but a mock look of dismay. He tossed what appeared to be a toffee into his gaping mouth.

'Come on!' Addison knew Duke was bluffing. The class clown always played up when he felt uncomfortable. 'Not only does our guy scream the name Elizabeth when he's arrested—'

'The report didn't say he screamed it...'

'—we then go and find a makeshift shrine to the girl in the woods—'

'Hardly a monument...'

'What?' Addison was almost laughing. 'Are you in denial? Harrison has about three things to his name, and he uses two of them to create a shrine—'

'More like a memorial.'

'Are you kidding me? Duke, the Major Incidents team have been informed of what we found back there. SOCO are bagging up all of it. Before long, they'll have diggers ripping up that tree just in case there's a young girl's body feeding it from underneath. And you're telling me you're not in the slightest bit twitchy about this?'

'They'll find nothing.'

'Seriously?' Addison had to admire his Sergeant's defiance.

'Response went out with a sniffer dog this morning when they first went looking for Harris. The dog paid no interest to that site, even though the adrenaline pouring out of Harris's clogged pores led them right to that vicinity. The ground didn't look disturbed either, granted it's been over a year, but still... it didn't strike me as a grave. The man pissed, shat and slept there. If that was the girl's grave, do you really think he'd do that? Given the photographs and the images, it doesn't really strike me as someone who would show that level of disrespect.'

'Still could have killed her. People kill out of love... obsession?'

'True, but they don't then sleep on the grave when they do. Crimes of passion... they're heated moments of madness blurred and frenzied within a red mist. Once all that settles, the feelings that were hurt – the ones that made them react out of anger and anguish – they often return and cause a new form of pain. A slow-aching remorse that refuses to ever leave. Spike Harris, he's a madman, but he's no killer. There's no connection to him and the Silvers. There would be no reason for him to take her. Just look at his previous; it's not in his makeup. Elizabeth was taken from her bed at the dead of night, without a sound or a trace. That tells me two things: either she knew her abductor and went freely of her own will, or that the person who took her had the presence of mind to keep the place sterile. Harris can't even keep his pants clean. The last we heard of him was two years ago when he was sent on his merry little mad way because the doctors found he didn't quite fit into one of their pigeonholes. But we both know that he was crazy back then and, given today's performance, he still is. Yet, I'm meant to believe that he's capable of taking Elizabeth from under the noses of her mother and father without a trace? They'd have fucking smelt him!'

'He did fall off our radar around the same time as Elizabeth disappeared, only to surface a few days after Amber Costello was taken.

We have to take that into account.'

'Only if they're linked.' Duke tossed another toffee into his mouth. 'So far, it's only you making that connection, and what was that connection again... some bird bones? Well tell me Ace Ventura, pet-detective, did you see any dead birds back there? I sure as hell didn't. Trust me Addison, when talking about Spike Harris... I think we've got someone who is more cuckoo than magpie.'

'But there's still a link.'

'A link? Seriously? What, the bloody Missing Link they've just gone and arrested? Okay, fine. In fact, do me a favour and give David Attenborough a call and tell him we've found the legendary Sasquatch. Seriously, get dialling, tell him I told you to call. Because, I'd genuinely rather make that call than the one to Beverly Silver to tell her that we think her daughter was taken by the local village idiot.'

'You know what I think? I think you're just too scared to admit there could be another candidate for this case. You can't accept that you may have got it wrong!'

'Oh, well that's it then. You've solved it. Click, click, case closed. Where's Benjamin Farrow housed up? I'll go and let him out. Even run him a bath and let him have a pop at my wife...'

'You're not married.'

'Whatever Addison! We'll go along with what you suggest. We'll ignore the witness reports, and the fact that Farrow clearly did it. Let's release him right now, point him to the nearest playground and turn our backs on him, what harm could it do? Oh, and forgive me if my judgement is off, I must be getting tired from my twenty years of experience, but I don't seem to remember much of a mess back at the Costello residence. The night Amber was taken, there was a huge storm. Now, unless that storm washed the half-life we have in custody completely clean, and he then somehow managed to dry off before breaking into the house, I would have expected to see some kind of trail inside.'

Duke took a breath. Addison didn't take it personally. It was clear his Sergeant was carrying a much bigger weight than a mere personality clash.

The fact was, the Elizabeth Silver case meant almost everything to him: his team, his name, he'd laid it all on the line. He'd literally gone all-in on Benjamin Farrow, every chip he had left was placed on that one man, and it was a gamble that had so far seemed to have paid off. But that's exactly how it appeared to Addison... a gamble. It was like the whole town had rolled the dice and prayed that they'd got it right. For Addison though, there were too many question marks remaining. What exactly was it that Billy Jackson knew that time they'd caught him with the drugs? Where was the young girl's body? Why is nobody ready to connect the Amber case with Elizabeth's? Too many doors were left wide open for Addison to adopt the 'open and shut' case that the town proclaimed to own. It felt like people were trying to accept a lie. But Addison wasn't convinced, and now even the courts weren't too sure. The case was up for review, and it seemed that only Addison was prepared to twist, rather than stick with the hand that Claymore had dealt themselves.

They were back at the station and pulling into one of the parking bays. Duke hadn't spoken for the last five minutes of the drive. But neither had Addison. Both of them had the same thing on their mind, just with a different take, as if they were reviewing a film, which one of them had starred in. One take was heated and biased, the other cold and removed.

'Addison,' Duke spoke softer now. 'I'm from a different generation to you. The cloth that I'm cut from, it doesn't have much thread to it; it's made from two strands, right and wrong. One goes one way, and the other another. There's very little that overlaps and goes back on itself, and it makes for quite a stubborn material, trust me. It won't win any fashion shows, but it's the trend I'm sticking to. Today – this society we're in – it's all blinkered. There's no cut and dried, cold-pressed case, there's no simple right and wrong. These days, all things are considered, even when they don't deserve our consideration. People who act like animals are able to hide behind rights that belong to humans, regardless of the rights they took from their victims. I mean, what kind of world allows burglars to sue people if they break a bone falling through the roof of the house that they're about to break into? It's madness. A madness that's born through worry, a worry about offending others when there's no offence to be had. We're expected to be apologetic rather than just polite, to say sorry when somebody bumps into you, or offer your seat to a stranger and not be offended when they don't say thank you, but instead look at you like you've just pissed on their kids. It's a bullshit, false positive, silver-lined outlook. It's full of people who look beyond what's under their noses because they don't want to acknowledge the crap that's beneath their feet. It solves nothing. Ignorance doesn't remove the problem, it becomes it. We ignore the immediate and the obvious and pray... almost wish... that there's something more, something bigger. And this wish, it becomes a worry, a worry that controls and directs us. It makes us feel like there's something better; something we've missed. But it's just a wish... it's worthless. These people – these worry warriors - they'd rather toss a coin into a wishing-well than hand it to the homeless because maybe, if the wish came true, then they'd get away from the problem; they'd escape it all. And it would no longer be a problem for them to solve.

Addison, I solved my problem. I acknowledged the obvious. I accepted the immediate facts. The rest, the freedom of theory, it's all just madness to me.'

Duke looked more relieved than saddened, as if a huge weight had left his shoulders.

'Come on,' Duke threw his head towards the door that lead out to the custody suite. 'Let's go interview this lunatic. See if he knows who did this.'

Chapter 22

'Yeah, it was me.'

Benjamin seemed a little amused, somewhat playful, and part cocky. She noticed how relaxed he seemed in his chair, the same chairs he had spent so long complaining about.

'What makes you say that?'

At some point she had started twisting one of her thick curls around her finger. She knew it was as inappropriate as it was instinctive. She couldn't help it, there was something different about Benjamin Farrow... something genuine. Part of her hoped that the courts had got it right to review the case, that there was hope that this man would be cleared. If he was innocent, she could feel a little less guilty about the times she had allowed her hands to travel south when alone and thinking of him.

'I seem to be the highlight around here.' He'd noticed her blushing beneath her slapdash make-up. 'It appears I'm quite the headline act.' He nodded towards the folded tabloid on her once flat-packed coffee table. Beneath the redtop banner sat his name in bold capital letters. He couldn't see what came after the semicolon, but he could guess.

Child-killer Set for Review.

Second Chance for Elizabeth's Murderer.

Silver Lining on Claymore's Darkest Cloud.

'Have you been reading up on me Doc?' He set his tone to firm but partnered it with a smile. His eyes looked up through a brow of near golden hair.

'You know it wouldn't be in my professional interest to do so.'

'What about personal?'

She hesitated. She knew she had a leaky face. It wasn't always an issue, given that the majority of her clientele were used to being disliked. But when she started to show signs of affection, this posed a huge problem. Thankfully, Benjamin seemed decent enough not to take advantage of the situation. Instead, it appeared that he simply liked the thought of being liked.

And she did like him.

'I think we need to focus on the hidden parts of you... I mean, how you feel... inside... Oh Christ!' She composed herself. 'How are you feeling about recent events?'

Her face was on fire. He stayed cool.

'Well, as I was saying Monica...'

'Doctor Dawkins, Mr Farrow.'

'Well, you can call me Benjamin if you like Doc. I'm done with hiding behind countless masks and titles. It's about time people started seeing me for who I really am, and the sooner I'm out of this hellhole the better. The attack on Seth recently – that was because of me. If he wasn't close to me, if he wasn't my friend, people would have no reason to hurt him. Not that they managed to hurt him! It seems they didn't reckon him for a cold-blooded maniac. Seriously Doc, that man terrifies me.'

'And yet you call him a friend.'

'I suppose he is, to an extent. I'm not comfortable saying it though. He's a criminal, a crook. He also says weird stuff. Borderline *creepy* stuff.'

'How so?' She pretended to be taking notes. It stopped her from staring into his bright blue eyes.

'It's more around his interest in me. Not that that's anything new to me. I'm forever being asked questions about the reason I find myself in prison; questions about Elizabeth. Questions like... *Where is she? Why did you take her? What did you do to her?* Things I just can't answer. But with Seth... he doesn't ask questions like that. When he asks me things, it's more for his own benefit – like he's answering to some part of himself that he's struggling to control. I'm sorry...' He paused, waiting until she made eye contact with him. 'I'm not sure I should be sharing this with you. I just don't know who else I can trust in here.'

'It's okay. You know the situation. Nothing leaves this room.'

That wasn't strictly true. If she were to encounter information that pertained to a life or death situation, then she was obligated – both morally and professionally – to share what she knew. But she was certain that the ramblings of an unhinged hunchback like Seth hardly constituted any real risk. The man was a freak, and she shivered just thinking about him.

Looking at Benjamin, however, gave her an entirely different feeling. She applied her finest *don't worry, you can trust me* face, as Benjamin began to speak.

'It's probably nothing really, but he talks about a *side* of him – a shaded side. This side of him, it asks him to do dark things. Things he seems to be battling with. I've seen his handiwork and he's more than willing to hurt people. But the things he asks me, it's as if he's trying to understand some part of his mind. A part he can't come to terms with.'

'What exactly is he asking you?'

'How to kill somebody.'

'Anybody in particular?' She acted casual but knew she needed to write down the answer, just in case this was the first disclosure of a potential murder victim.

'I don't think so. It's more of a moral conflict. He says that the part of him that whispers to him at night – "*that scratches at his brain between the distractions of the day*" - it's constantly telling him to be ready to do what's necessary.'

'And you think he's version of "*what's necessary*" is to kill?'

'Without a doubt Doc. He's scrapping with some sort of inner conflict. It's as if he wants to know whether there's ever a reason to kill, whether there's ever an excuse to do it.'

'Does he ever give a reason?'

'Children.' The word seemed to burst from his mouth.

He took a breath. It sounded strange saying it out loud.

'Children?'

The more he heard it out loud, the more it began to make sense. Seth's interest in him was shaped solely on what he believed Benjamin had done. He had Benjamin down as a child-killer, just like everybody else did. The only difference was, Seth didn't seem to hold that against him. Instead, he saw it as a way to understand his own urges, to appease the shaded part of him that raged within.

'Doc, I think Seth wants answers from me so that he can understand the desire to kill a child.'

'Something you're not able to assist with?'

'Christ no!'

Benjamin couldn't filter his reaction. His guard was back up. What was this bitch trying to do? A little bit of cleavage and a whole heap of blusher and she thought she could get a confession from him? She must be mental. Just like the rest of them. And there he was beginning to trust her, beginning to relax and speak freely. Maybe it was the fact that she spoke to him like he was a human being, or the fact that he'd countlessly pictured pulling up her skirt and screwing her across her desk, that he'd foolishly let her in. And for what? A fantasy? Is this how the courts were going to test him... throw together a nice set of pins and a soothing voice, and I'll spill my guts for the world to pour over and parade through the streets. No chance.

'Benjamin,' she looked shocked, almost frightened, but more like a person worried to have offended a friend rather than somebody who was afraid. 'I didn't mean to cause you any offence, I promise. I was merely speaking from the perspective of your friend Seth.'

'Really,' he wasn't sure at what point it had happened but he was stood up and facing the door to leave. 'Well... it felt more like you were playing games with me, just like everybody else.'

'I can assure you that I wasn't.'

She'd joined him at the doorway, somehow finding the nerve to get in front of him and slam her hand against the door to stop him from leaving. She couldn't let the session end this way; they had been making progress, and she refused to risk losing any confidence he may have in her.

'It wouldn't surprise me though, somebody not believing me.'

He took hold of her shoulder and turned her to face him, her back pinned against the door. 'Have you any idea what it's like to have somebody look at you like you're a liar. Like everything you say is some calculated, considered statement, rather than just the truth? Imagine for a second seeing the look of hatred and dismissal in the eyes of people who hold your very future in their hands. Do you know how hard it is to keep it together when the world would rather you just accepted the title it had given you, and then just disappear? "*So long Benjamin... piss off now... don't bother us anymore.*" But the end for them is just the start for me. Now, I'm a killer, a man worthy of punishment. A man who deserves to be tortured and have his skin cut as his good name burns to the very ground he's beaten into.'

'Benjamin, I'm sorry. I meant no offence.' She held his gaze. Her hands touched his. 'Please let go of me.'

His hands remained where they were, gripping her shoulders.

'And then there was you... *wonderful* you. Finally, I thought I'd met someone who didn't see what everybody else did. You didn't see a monster. You looked beyond the label. And you saw me.'

He'd let go of her now. Beneath his furrowed brow, he could see her chest breathe in rhythm with his own. He mirrored her on purpose. Slowly he reached for the door, opening it from behind her. He paused for a moment to see whether she'd take the bait. He raised his eyes in line with hers. She was staring straight at him.

'Benjamin, do you need a friend?' Her lips were moistened.

'What do you mean?' He was close enough to share the same breath.

'Seth.' She turned her face to the side. 'Even the friends from your past that you mentioned in our last session; do you need friends to hide behind? Do they offer you comfort, some form of protection?'

'God knows,' he hung his head again. 'Who knows what Seth is up to. As for the guys from my childhood, I have no idea what they're up to these days. I wouldn't even know who they were anymore. Hell, I don't even know who I am anymore!'

'I think I do.'

He looked up intently. He felt her warm hand wrap around his fingers.

The door shut behind her pressed body, as her lips met with his.

Chapter 23

'Stop screwing around!'

Duke had taken on more of a talking role than DCI Wilson had originally hoped.

'You mean to tell me that you don't know why you tried to grab the girl earlier today? What was it, feeling frisky? After all, bacteria has a need to breed, right?'

Spike Harris said nothing. His tired eyes remained glazed over, as if whatever it was in front of him wasn't enough to hold his focus. Not even being arrested had shaken him from the crazed slumber his mind was floating in.

'Come on Spike, don't act all dumb now.' Duke had taken to his feet. He'd read somewhere that motion created emotion and he was now filling the small interview room with plenty of both. 'We've had you assessed – the nurse said you're okay. Aside from the need for a quick bath of bleach, you're ready to go to the ball. So, let's dance. You have no need for an appropriate adult. You chose not to have a brief in tow. You know exactly what's going on here. So... talk.'

He remained silent, whilst his clothes seemed to vibrate, as if they couldn't settle on his skin. Meanwhile, Harris maintained eye contact with something far away from the interview room.

'For Christ's sake... come on! *You* came to our attention Spike – you hardly made a quiet approach, did you? Screaming at the poor girl at the top of your voice – it was hardly the act of somebody who doesn't want to get noticed. You pretty much invited us to this party. So, stop being a terrible host and cut the cake. Forget the parlour games, they won't work. I was the master of charades, I won't be fooled. I also have no time for finger foods, and I'm not waiting around until the last dance. I want the main event, and I want it right now.'

Addison had already decided not to say a word. Officially, this case was none of their business. They'd only taken an interest because of the potential crossover between Amber Costello's disappearance and the Elizabeth Silver case review. Quite frankly, there was nothing to suggest that what Spike Harris had done was in anyway linked to DCI Wilson's case. That was, apart from the timing of it.

First, Benjamin Farrow gets granted a review, then Amber gets taken, followed shortly after by Jessica Walker having some guy try to take hold of her. It all seemed twitchy, a bit too frantic.

It just didn't fit. Addison's stomach was grumbling, and not because he'd been up for the last week and not eaten for at least a full day. Instead, Addison had a gut feeling that Amber's disappearance was connected to the Silver case completely; much more than just some copycat looking to grab a few headlines, or just raise a middle finger to the local police who were already coming under scrutiny. There was a definite connection. The timing of it was intentional, Addison had no doubt about that, and it was more than just a coincidence in the kidnapper's scheduling that it happened the day after the news of the case review broke. There was clear planning in the act, a message even. The manner in which Amber was taken mirrored Elizabeth's case meticulously. This wasn't somebody piecing together a plan from various scraps of newspaper and a collection of headlines. This was someone who knew the method intimately. Both times, there didn't appear to be any clear motive; the families had no known enemies, the young girls seemed sweet and far too young to be making any real relationships with anybody outside of their parent's radar. Both abductions were done too well. Couple that with the magpies – whatever message that may be – and you've got yourself a clear link.

Spike Harris on the other hand, he was just something else entirely.

'Jessica Walker – does that name mean anything to you?' DCI Wilson had taken over handling the questions, with Duke seemingly content to stand against the back wall, staring directly at Harris.

But he did nothing. There was no flinch, no reaction, no tell. If he was hiding the fact that the girl's name meant anything to him, then he was doing the finest poker face that Addison had ever encountered.

'And how about Amber Costello? Does that name mean anything to you?'

Still nothing.

'Okay, Mr Harris – what about Yorkswood? You were there this morning. We both know that because that's where my officers met you.' DCI Wilson used her firm but familiar tone. It was easier on the ears than Duke's audition for *The Sweeney*. 'Spike, please tell me what you were doing in the woods today.'

'Girls'.

It was the first thing that the guy had said for over an hour, and the word he used was even more surprising than the fact he'd decided to speak at all. Addison could feel a slight warmth radiating from Duke's face which was now one shade brighter than flowing lava, and just as hot.

DCI Wilson raised her hand. It was a clear signal for Duke to keep his distance. She didn't have to look at him to work out that a blend of adrenaline and anger was urging him to enter the ring.

'Mr Harris, please explain what you mean when you say *"Girls".*'

'Girls. Young girls. Not safe... boys... men... they take them away.'

Harris's voice seemed soft, somewhat younger than the years etched out across his forlorn face. Dry clay cloaked his face, hiding his true age. He was younger than the mask suggested. If Addison had to guess, he'd say that Harris was more than aware of what was going on right now. If anything, he was scared of it.

'What about Elizabeth Silver!' Duke couldn't hold onto his rage any longer. He knew there were several ways to skin a cat, with Duke preferring to cut straight through it and pray that it spilled its guts out.

And there it was.

A twitch. They all saw it. Tucked beneath the glaze, there was a definite flash of light in Harris's eyes. They bounced about the walls like a bluebottle looking for an open window. He began to hold his hands, in some weak attempt to offer himself comfort, but they seemed too awkward to fit within each other. His leg bounced at the knee, as if his toes had been nailed to the floor. It was clear he wanted to leave. It was unbelievable; almost every tell in the book, in an instant flash.

It made Addison even more confident that Harris had no idea who the young girl he spooked earlier was, as well as Amber Costello.

'Come on then!' Duke's voice clattered against the walls, ricocheting against every angle, ensuring that it hit everybody in the room. 'What do you know about Elizabeth Silver?'

The delivery was plosive, intentional. The room seemed to rest on pause, waiting for Harris's reply to bring everyone back into play.

'Wrong man.'

Harris's head sank into his chest. His hands formed a single fist perched between two trembling knees.

'What do you mean... wrong man? We're not asking whether you took her. We're asking you why – when you were arrested earlier today – did you say the name Elizabeth? It seems a little strange to be chasing a young girl through the woods whilst screaming the name of another, don't you think? Unless I've got this all wrong, and you do have something to do with it. So... this *wrong man* you mention – is it you? Come one then – spit it out! Why are you the wrong man?'

Harris's entire frame froze as Duke spoke. There was no doubting where his focus now sat. Every word that Duke uttered hung in front of

Spike Harris like the brightest stars at night, puncturing the darkness and demanding attention. A shimmer of life glimmered across his fallen face as he looked the detective directly in the eye.

'Not me detective... Benjamin Farrow. You have the wrong man.'

*

'And what!'

Duke wasn't holding back.

'So, whilst he's scrambling through the woods for some tabloid to jerk off to, he reads a headline, sees that the case is up for review and thinks he'll make a name for himself. Why not? He's now got a roof over his head and hot meal in waiting. Come on for Christ's sake, wake up, he's played us. I've already seen enough journalists dine out on that story, I won't have some hobo getting his fill as well.'

'Duke,' Addison had ushered him into a side room so they could speak in private. 'We both know that this guy has more than a healthy interest in this case. He's not stumbled over headlines, he's collected them.'

'Well, I won't let that schmuck turn me into one!'

'He won't. Trust me. But who knows what he knows? Wilson has one of her guys doing an intel debrief on him as we speak. After you stormed out, he mentioned that he went to the same children's home as Farrow. Did you know that?'

'Farrow was in care?' Duke looked confused, as if he'd just found out that he himself was adopted. 'There was no record of that on his profile.'

'There wouldn't be. Farrow changed his name at the age of sixteen, at the earliest opportunity. I checked with deed poll, seems like a certain Benjamin Randal was knocking down the door to the local offices on the morning of his sixteenth birthday. No idea why he picked the name Farrow, but he's been using it ever since. Never went back to the care home either.'

'Balls,' Duke rubbed his face with both hands. 'What care home?'

'They're digging that out of Harris right now. Seems like they knew each other as kids. Maybe that stirred up some loyalty within Harris, maybe he couldn't connect the kid he knew to the man that took Elizabeth. Either way, we'll have all he knows soon enough.'

'How did we miss that?'

'Maybe it wasn't relevant. Nobody else stepped forward to say that they recognised him. There weren't any character witnesses the first time around if I recall, so why wouldn't you accept the man for who he presented himself to be.'

'And this Benjamin Randal... much of a record?' Duke spoke as if they were two different people. Like he wasn't ready to connect the dots just yet.

'Clean. Granted, during his early years everything was recorded with good old-fashioned ink... but prints would have still been uploaded into the new systems once they went live. If there was a criminal past on record, you'd have had the connection the second you swabbed and scanned Farrow.'

'So, it doesn't change anything.'

'Not as it stands. Just strange that it didn't surface the first time around. His defence didn't bring it up because they didn't need to. He wasn't accounting for Elizabeth's murder, so there'd be no reason to paint a picture of the man as a boy. There was nothing to explain away, or excuse through some tragic event from his early years.'

'What makes you say there was anything there to talk about? Like you say, the defence didn't raise it.' Duke had started boiling the kettle. A small ball of stress was pounding inside his head and a bullet of caffeine was needed to blow it out of his skull.

'Well, that's it... they didn't. I've read the case files, all the transcripts and court notes, and the defence don't dig any deeper than his early adult years. The prosecution follows suit; they try to create a picture of a man, a loner, an unknown. But that's all they had. There were no friends on the radar to state otherwise, so the prosecution used that as a slight on his character – nobody was ever able to like him. And it worked. That way, if there was a past, one that showed him to have friends as a child, a past that could show him to be able to interact and hold normal relationships... why didn't the defence use it?'

'Maybe because his so-called friends are lunatics?' Duke nodded in the direction of the interview room that seemed to have begun to stem up now Spike Harris had started to talk.

'Maybe...' Addison felt excited. Like a dog who'd spotted a ball in his owner's hand. 'Or maybe there's something the defence didn't want to produce; maybe there's a story from Farrow's past that would have harmed him even more than the empty hole the prosecution were trying to bury him in.'

'You think they know something?'

'It's something for me to chase down... no?' Addison could see the look of hope colour Duke's grey face.

'Well go fetch boy!'

Duke laughed as he patted Addison on the shoulder. It was a relief to hear that the man wasn't just looking to pick holes in the case, but merely looking to gather the truth to what had happened. Who knows, maybe he'd find something that would offer them all some closure.

DCI Wilson entered the room and poured herself a coffee from the pot Duke had brewed. It was cooling down, but still warm enough to offer a kick.

'So, boss,' Duke spoke with a little more glee than when he first entered the room. The prospect of digging up some dirt on Farrow had excited him almost as much as the unearthing of an unknown past scared him. 'What do we know?'

'Well,' Wilson took a draw on her coffee. Addison could see it was too bitter for her liking, she squinted slightly as she swallowed. 'I'm not sure whether you heard, but Harris appears to have a past with Farrow. He says, back in the early eighties, they both attended a children's home by the name of Precious Moments, around twenty miles from here. It's no longer around, but I'm sure they'll have records somewhere, so we'll check his story out, see if it's not just our noses that he's filling full of crap. Meanwhile, he also denies trying to abduct the girl today.'

'Of course he does.' Duke looked at Addison in a way to say *told you so.*

'He also denies any link to the Elizabeth Silver case. States that his interest in her was brought about by his knowledge of Farrow. According to him, he'd never seen the girl before the night she was taken. Didn't even realise who she was until it matched the description in the press.'

'What?' Addison felt the air drop a degree.

'He's in there now offering a full witness statement for the night of Elizabeth Silver's disappearance. He says he saw a man with her. And it wasn't Farrow.'

Chapter 24

He'd got it wrong before.

First, he'd made the mistake of taking the mask with him, and then he'd taken another big risk with the door.

They wouldn't have been happy with him. Not that they were around to punish him, but he still didn't want to disappoint anyone. The birds were usually placed after the child was taken, that had always been the way. Always secure the child, then leave the birds. Always.

But there had been a storm that night and maybe the thunder could have muffled out the noise. Or so he thought.

You're not instructed to think. Just do as you are told.

He had been told to make this time more obvious. No little Easter eggs for the clever little bunnies to find. No more breadcrumbs to lead each missing child to the next one. This time it needed to be as bold as a brick in the face: blunt, bloody and brutal.

He had to admit that the location was a bit risky. He'd never left them so close before.

Close enough to be found, but not always seen.

The last time, there was no avoiding them. But he wanted that. *They* wanted that. There was no point enjoying the mystery anymore, no point toying with the authorities. He wanted them to see the connections. He wanted them to see his warning.

The new girl was in her place.

She looked happy enough, almost like she used to in the photographs her family had. Seeing what she had become, he was pleased with what he'd done. Since her death, her clay mask had kept him company for a few nights, but she had soon become a bit of a bore. There was no life within her frozen expression, no sign of personality or character. He just couldn't connect to it.

So, like the others, her mask was mounted and shelved. He now stood looking at it, hoping to see the face upon it change, to see a hint of expression. But it never did. Instead, her face remained still, cold and ungrateful. The rest of her, on the other hand, seemed quite at play. The pose he had her adopt captured the essence of the girl he had seen before. Before he'd taken her that is. She'd been a complete pain since.

But now she was a joy to behold.

He was pleased with this part of his work, the way he portrayed how the children were. For most people, life always had death, and death was the end. But for them, for his chosen, his way meant that death held within it a form of life. That way, the girl's capture had not been a complete waste of time. Instead, it captured time itself. And that's exactly what he did. He captured time. Or rather *a* time, to be more precise. A time when everything is meant to be happy, when worry and fear are not yet born but nestled only in those made to protect you. It was this moment that he fixed so that it could never be soiled or lost. What was stolen from him, he'd given back in abundance. This time had been broken for him, but now he fixed it. The pain of a youth removed with such force had caused him to want to make sure that all the children he took could never lost the innocence that their age afforded them.

They were all precious to him. Moments so precious they hurt.

He couldn't stare for too long. Images of happy children always caused a conflict within him, a swirling of joy and jealousy blended within his bloodstream and caused him to recall the horror of his own youth. But that was all done now. Now, he was a man. A man who had let time rush away from him. A man whose face wore an age far older than his years. Peering into the dusty mirror, he held the gaze of the dark holes that stared back at him. His skin had begun to sag around sharpened cheekbones. Some of his teeth warred with his gums for territory, as his mouth lay crooked and open. He rolled his thick tongue across the blunted edges of the teeth that had once been broken. There was little symmetry left to his appearance. But it wasn't a product of anything other than time. Something he had never fought against, because he was pleased with it passing.

He welcomed the end.

Picking up an old brush, he ran it through what remained of his once thick blond hair. Now, a wiry cloud of a dulled gold seemed to float above his flaky scalp. Sitting beneath the breached blanket of a once dense hairline, fierce freckles blotted the skin that had only seen the sunlight on the rarest of occasion. Since his childhood, he had always preferred the dark, despite the monsters that lived within it. In the dark, maybe they wouldn't see him, maybe the monsters wouldn't pick the face masked by time's cruel hand.

But his reflection had not always been so obscure. He had once been handsome, almost pretty. As a young boy, he had already begun to gather the attributes of a man. Although his mind seemed to have raced the other way. Hulking in stature, with a strength much greater than the other children, he struggled to restrain it when he grew frustrated at being unable to understand what the other children could.

When letters became words to them, and then those words became sentences, his eyes still only saw sharp shapes. Each letter was a splinter in his eye, each word was sharpened to a point, and each sentence a branch with which to prod and beat him with. Words were used to mock him. None of what he was told ever stuck, and he never knew the answer in class.

But his strength was beyond question. His hands could hold a child's face in each palm, and his colossal grip could have crushed it just as easily. And yet, despite the threat that his physique presented, others still dared to taunt him. Caged by his lack of intelligence, he become a shackled beast, an injured animal that the other children could throw names at that hit like bricks to his young face. But with time, and in the absence of any consequence, the children grew brave, and stupid.

Sticks and stones may break my bones. But names... they'll break yours.

It was almost inevitable. One day, one boy took it one name too far. The child, numbed and detached through privilege, had goaded the school's gargoyle for months, constantly beating him down until he was nothing.

Thinking back, he couldn't even remember what the boy had called him that had caused him to cross the line. But he could remember the red mist that closed in around him, the fire that forced his arms to reach out, and the acid that commanded his hands to squeeze until they were completely closed.

The men in matching suits all told him that the young boy had never woken up. His neck had been broken, and his windpipe crushed.

That had altered everything.

After he was taken away, the children were different in his new home. They seemed quieter, muted. But eventually, he made friends with two of them. Real, true friends, and he was never going to let go of them. They were all that he had. His parents never visited him after the incident, and the adults at the home were far from caring.

Not allowing himself to recall the nights that followed, he thought of the days to come. Allowing his hands to brush across the faces that stared down at him, his fingers danced across countless dimples and creases as he left the display room and entered the garden. Feeling sunlight against his skin for the first time that day, he smiled as his eyes squinted into two sharp slits. The sun was almost setting, but it was still a stark contrast to the cave from which he had just crawled. Every curtain on the building was drawn. Every door bolted, and every window barricaded.

He was not going to allow anything to see what he had created.

It wasn't ready yet.

Walking through the overgrown garden, he sulked beneath the shade of an overhanging tree. Within it he had hidden his favourite little toy. He could already hear the squawks from his new friends. He could feel their feathers ruffle against the steel bars as he pulled it from the branch it had been balanced on.

Standing to admire the cage, he looked at his home-made bird-trap. It had room for at least six birds, a large pit of seeds and two doors. But no exits. The stainless-steel bars were shiny enough to lure them in, and the food was far enough inside for them to have to fully commit to the trap. Once inside, the doors only opened one way. Yesterday some stupid sparrows had found their way inside, but they were easily disposed of. The useless little runts were silenced with just a click of his thick fingers.

Today, however, he had struck gold. Black and white feathered gold. Going berserk, with their beaks bouncing against the steel bars, were two trapped magpies.

He had already captured and prepared four. He smiled as he thought of the next child.

All he needed was one more.

Chapter 25

'I'll take another.'

Addison waved his empty pint glass towards the barman.

He'd poured him six already. Not that his commitment to the Carling was unusual for a Sunday evening. Many of the local men often leaned against the bar and drowned their days away. Other than explore the land, or add to the local gossip, there wasn't much else to do in Claymore.

The bar itself was as loud as expected for a Sunday night. Many had waddled off home to sleep off their belly-busting roast dinners, whilst those with nothing to go home to stayed and watched whatever sport filled the large flat-screen TV that occupied the wall above the large fireplace. Right now, a fire roared into life whilst some home crowd sat muted as they watched their team losing to another team from a much lower league in the English FA Cup. There were only six minutes to go until full-time and the team in red looked a little desperate.

No more Fergie time to save you now.

Addison watched on, more passively than he had intended. Others around him murmured, but there were no local loyalties to the two teams playing, so the atmosphere was simply an appreciation of the sport rather than the game itself. They all chugged and chanted like a disengaged pack of tribal worshippers. The words were nonsense, but they all said enough to gain acceptance to the pack.

The oath of allegiance was simple.

We are men. We love football. We love beer. And we love women.

Sadly, there were none of the latter, so instead they all had to pretend that their priorities were to the drink and the dross that was playing out in front of them. Politely, Addison had engaged with the other lonely publicans who had generously offered up generic comments about the match: how the manager will be getting sacked in the morning, that the recent transfer was an overpriced prima donna who spent more time on his backside than with the ball at his feet. But it all meant nothing, just fleeting, inconsequential comments that served only as a dress rehearsal for when the next match started. It didn't form bonds, or friendships. At most, it merely warded off exclusion. Not that Addison wasn't grateful for the light conversation. His mind was too full to take on anything more demanding. There were too many questions rattling inside his tired brain for him to give any time to any real weighted debate. The Elizabeth Silver case was consuming him. And not because he had taken too much on, but because he hadn't been given enough. All around him there were officers who appeared so sure about the conviction of Benjamin Farrow that they were either too blind to see the parallels to the abduction of Amber Costello, or they were in sight of something that he wasn't.

Either way, it pissed him off.

His sole role since moving to Claymore was to form part of the 'Oversight Programme'. He would take cases under review and make sure that the police hadn't cut any corners. But when looking at the case against Benjamin Farrow, there weren't any corners to cut. The whole case was a straight-line prosecution of one man. The case was loaded, rifled and aimed at one man only. There were no documented enquiries that looked at other angles. There were no attempts to see whether Farrow's own account of that evening held up. It was all streamlined, sharpened and fired towards a single target.

Farrow was guilty.

Nothing else would explain it.

Maybe they'd got it right. Maybe they'd bought one ticket and hit the jackpot. Maybe. But maybe wasn't enough to convict somebody. Following his charge, there was no further evidence that came to light that pinned the disappearance of Elizabeth Silver to Benjamin Farrow. Nothing. No body. No blood. No DNA. No confession. Nothing.

And yet he was found guilty. It baffled Addison that a jury of his peers could all see beyond what he couldn't. He prayed, for the sake of the entire judicial system, that they had somehow struck gold. Justice shouldn't be a gamble; just some game we all passively watch unfold, where sides are taken based on suggestion alone, and where a person's fate is decided upon by little more than chance. Everybody involved deserved more than that. The young girl, her family, her friends. Even the convicted.

He considered Spike Harris's recent revelation. Both he and Duke had read over his statement at least a dozen times, and both of them had disagreed with each other on every reading. Harris wasn't credible. They both knew that. His statement ruled Farrow in as much as it ruled him out. Nevertheless, his account of seeing Elizabeth being taken had to be sent to the case reviewers. Not that it caused much of a reaction. To them, Harris was just an inebriate who confirmed that somebody matching Farrow's description took Elizabeth. Both sides, prosecution and defence, would use the information to strengthen their case equally. It was a stalemate. A bore draw.

He was finishing his drink as the whistle for full-time caused men to break from the bar like birds at dawn. Glasses chinked before being plopped onto dampened paper coasters, and the ice-cold air from outside battled with the log fire every time the door was opened. The strangers didn't hold the door open for one another, so it swung like a saloon bar door until every last one of the single-filed singletons had left. A couple of minutes after the door finally came to a stop, the bar was beginning to warm up again when Addison felt the cold kiss of the night upon his neck.

'Same again… Addison?'

It was her. The girl from the Yorkswood scene. Minus her camera this time, which was a welcome subtraction given that Addison hadn't slept for three weeks and was feeling less than picture perfect.

'Please, let me…' Addison gestured for her to take up the stool next to his. The addition of a female in the pub hadn't gone unnoticed and the barman was already walking over to where they were both perched. 'Can I get one more lager, and…' He looked to her.

'Oh… gin and tonic please. Slimline.'

'Check you.' Addison smiled under tired eyes. 'Didn't have you down as someone on a health kick.'

She flashed him a look of confusion and mock offence.

'I mean,' Addison put the gearstick into reverse, 'they say a healthy body leads to a healthy mind. That doesn't quite fit with someone who shows an interest in weird crime scenes and missing children.'

'Well, what did you expect me to order? I'm not sure they do a cocktail called *Caught in the Woods*, or *Flashing from a Distance*.'

They shared a smile. It warmed him more than the fire did.

'So, what do I call you?' Addison rummaged for his bank card. He always stored it in the sleeve of his warrant card. He hated carrying a wallet.

'Whatever you want to.' Her flirting was a reflex. The cliché didn't give anything away. It was too obvious, too much of a conversation template to be read as anything other than what she would have said to anybody else in that moment.

'Okay…' He handed the barman his card in exchange for two drinks, gesturing for him to keep it behind the bar in case he needed to open up a tab. 'What if I was arresting you? What would I say then?'

'Oh, I don't know. Maybe "get on your knees, you filthy scumbag".'

'Or spread 'em, smartarse.' He pretended to look tired of her. It was an act.

'Very well, officer. I'll come clean. My name is Piper.' She held out her hand. 'It's a pleasure to meet you DC Clarke.'

'How did you...'

'Well first of all, you didn't need to flash your badge just now to impress me. And secondly, given that you were at two crime scenes – both of which involved child abduction – and you didn't leave there in cuffs... makes me think that you must be the one carrying them. Couple that with a quick and dirty name check of local police officers, and only one has the first name Addison.'

Thank God for transparent policing.

'Well it appears I'm not hard to find. Luckily for me, I don't have any enemies.'

'Yes, you do.' She let her comment hang in the air as she took a sip from her drink. 'After all... isn't that why you're here?'

His mood changed as quickly as switching a channel. From recreational sports to breaking news in an instance.

Now, it wasn't just the booze getting him pissed.

'Has this become a business drink Piper? Because I'm off the clock and all out of time for snooping journalists looking to scoop up the dead. Trust me, my story puts the old in told. It's done to death... buried.'

'Like your friend?'

'Fuck you.' He slammed his drink down. 'How's that suit for a headline?'

He rubbed his hands over his face. What was this girl's deal? It was clear he was trying to distance himself from his past. Here he was enjoying the little downtime his overactive mind would allow, and she rocks up with a shovel primed for digging up dirt and a silver spoon for stirring the shit. Is this all the work she had on? There was the biggest case in the town's history ripe and ready for review, and her focus was solely on him? It couldn't be. Granted, he had some small part to play in the months ahead, but it was nothing more than an administrative one. If only she knew what he did, then she'd have a few other officers under her microscope. So what if the man checking over the books travelled with a cloud above him, it changed nothing. He wasn't part of the investigation. He hadn't been around when Farrow had been arrested. His past had nothing to do with where this case had come from.

But it did have a little to do with where it went.

Maybe that was it. What if she was already aware that Farrow was fingered from the start? He knew nothing about her. Maybe she'd followed the case from the beginning and knew more than he did. He couldn't recall seeing her name in any of the tabloids that picked Farrow as their monster-boy pin-up for that summer. But then again, he hadn't read them all. One was enough to get a flavour for the rest, and you only needed to catch a whiff to know that the rest of it didn't taste great.

He was confused, she didn't give off the scent of the usual desperation-dipped, caffeine-fuelled media vulture that often circled these kinds of stories. But she had done her homework on him. Maybe it was time for him to start paying attention in class; he had the feeling Piper could teach him a thing or two.

That's when he noticed her voice. For someone seemingly on the lookout for a story, she sounded almost friendly. There was no anger in it. No accusation. No challenge. Just somebody talking. However bluntly.

'Come now Addison,' she placed her hand on his knee. 'The battle-worn detective is an overplayed role. Surely, it doesn't get you laid, does it?'

He looked out from between his hands, not quite sure of what was happening.

'Excuse me?' He reached for his drink.

'Don't worry, I come in peace.' She took another drink of her G&T. Her eyes were alive as she peered over her glass.

'Why are you here?' Addison drained at least a quarter of his glass in one gulp.

'To see you.' She put her glass down and looked almost serious as she spoke. 'Addison, I think I love you.'

He spat his drink out before looking up at her. She was on the brink of laughing.

'There's the smile you've been burying. I saw it in the woods the other day and needed to see whether it was a one-off. I could have gone with "I'm having your child", or the classic "Addison I am your father", but none of them really made sense... so I went for the old tried and tested. Nothing rocks a guy more than the L-bomb.'

'Lunatic?'

'Proper.' She tilted her head to the side and offered a maniacal stare. It suited her somehow. It gave her face an almost comical, Harley Quinn appearance.

That mixture of dangerous and sexy again.

'You have problems. I mean, why stalk a guy just to take the piss out of him?'

'Don't act like you didn't want to see me again'. She pretended to twirl a non-existent curl. Her hair was still short and feathered. Under the weak lights of the pub it looked almost grey, like a soft steel. He liked it.

'What can I say, I'll admit it's not half-bad seeing you at the scene of a kidnapping.'

She looked confused.

'Don't you mean attempted? The girl got away didn't she?'

'That one did.'

Her look of confusion drifted towards concern. She slowly pointed at her chest as she mouthed the word 'Me?'.

'Don't worry,' Addison adopted his reassuring tone, 'I'm not going to abduct you.'

'Shame,' she smiled again. There was a hint of menace in it. 'Nobody knows I'm here. You could have done what you liked with me, and no one would have ever known.' She looked to measure his reaction, but he wasn't giving anything away. He was sat somewhere between handsome and battle-bruised. No doubt he'd have had female attention before, and her lines were far from original. It disappointed her that she hadn't allowed herself to show him how truly different she was. Ditching the seduction for a second, she attempted to steer the conversation back to the real reason she was there.

'Going back to what you said…' she stroked the straw in her drink as she spoke. 'You only spoke to me at the scene in Yorkswood, where that poor tramp almost got the rap for something that he clearly didn't do. I have to say detective… it seems like this town is starting to make a habit of that.'

'I meant what I said…' he kept eye contact with her. 'You were also at the Amber Costello scene, camera and all. I don't tend to miss much.'

'But you missed me…'

'Is that what this is? A simple flirt and fish exercise?'

'Eww! I'm not sure where all your conversations with women go, Addison, but that kind of sounded like it ends up somewhere pretty horrid.'

He blushed.

'I meant…'

'I know what you meant. And no, that isn't what this is. I'm not flirting with you just to get some inside scoop. I'm not one of those tin-pot, two-bit journalists that deceive in an attempt to seek the truth. Not always, anyway.' She smiled.

'But you *are* a journalist?' He raised his guard. He knew she must have been some form of media to get so close to the scene before, but it was so easy to forget whose company you were in when chemistry clogged up the vision. Partner that with several months of insomnia and half a dozen pints of booze and you had yourself a well-fed, cold-case bred, cash cow ready for the milking.

'Yes… I'm a journalist… of sorts. But I'm pretty much freelance.

You won't find me contracted to any of the tabloids or mainstream magazines, I prefer to go down the more investigatory role. I find that much more interesting than your usual celeb gossip, or scaremongering, not to mention a hell of a lot more ethical. Honestly, I think there's a lot of excitement out there, and we don't need to invent it. The truth can be just as surprising as it is obvious. And I believe people deserve to know the truth. Don't you agree?'

'Totally.'

The next hour was a bit of a blur. He remembered it involved at least two more orders at the bar, and maybe a few shots from her. But other than that, the time seemed to blend into a blissful escape from all the shit that he'd become buried in. Piper had been a blessing; a timely reminder that there was an exciting world taking place outside of the village walls. Smart, honest, attractive. It was exactly the type of distraction that he needed. Granted, she'd asked a few probing questions, sandwiched between the listing of favourite movies from the '80s and a series of poor old action-hero impressions, but they were lost in there, amongst the casual chat. Addison knew he couldn't let his guard down just yet. He wasn't foolish enough to believe that the brief moment in the woods was enough for her to seek him out. She had no apparent ties to Claymore, and he found it hard to believe that he was the sole reason that she was sticking around.

Looking at the devilish twinkle in her eye, and the way the small curve upon her shoulders suggested she possessed a strength that betrayed her petite frame, he decided he was going to enjoy her company.

Danger and all.

Chapter 26

'Jesus Christ ladies, will you two stop flirting and get a room.'

The guard was more talkative than his usual '*don't look at me or I'll break your neck*' demeanour.

Then again, they were currently the most talked about inmates in HMP Fordbridge. Everybody knew their story. Benjamin's case review had already caused quite a stir, way before his newfound 'BFF' Seth decided to redecorate the shower rooms with two of their less welcoming neighbours.

Since that incident, Seth and Addison were all the prison talked about, and given their raised profile, Jenkins had bitten his tongue. For now. There could only be so long that a man like Jenkins would allow another to own his spotlight. No doubt, the stage would soon be set for another tragedy to be played out for all to see.

Benjamin knew his part.

'Come on you pair of tits...' the guard had a tone that would have suited a much older, fuller man than the ratty frame that barely filled their doorway. 'The bill for your grub has kindly been covered by the lovely law-abiding taxpayer. Now, you've already pissed them off royally by stealing one of their loved ones and killing one of their kids... so don't insult them any further by missing the meal they paid for.'

'I'll just be a minute...' Benjamin was feeling on edge. 'Prick.'

He whispered the last part. There was no point giving the guards an excuse to break his face. He'd grown accustomed to chewing his food again and had no plans to go back to having dinner served through a straw.

And anyway, between the empty insults and starved allegations, they were simply being called for dinner. For many of the inmates, dinner was the highlight of the day. Having seemingly become institutionalized the very moment that they'd reached criminal responsibility, many of them saw no difference between the food they were being served up in prison and the school dinners that they'd scoffed when they were kids. Both were better than the sausage-roll pacifier they'd been raised on, and infinitely more filling than the empty fridge and bare cupboards that they'd often returned home to.

But on the *inside* they were provided with three honest meals a day. Nothing like this waited for them outside. There was no structure for them to lean on or rely upon outside of the prison walls. In its place were responsibilities, expectations, duties, things they had no time for whatsoever. On the outside, it was the wrong people making all the rules. The law, the shades, the feds: a bunch of uniformed bullies hell-bent on making their life more difficult than it already was. But on the *inside*, the law couldn't touch them. They were beyond its grasp. It made them feel out of reach, untouchable. So, for the agoraphobic outlaws, dinner was a social occasion: a break from the mundane and a chance to talk with friends; a chance to break bread away from the legal fingers that wanted to choke and silence them; a chance to speak freely, to plot and to scheme. Dinner was the best time of the day. For some.

But for others, others like Benjamin Farrow, dinner was just another chance to find a knife dragged across your throat.

'Sorry if my little episode caused your case any bother.' Seth looked to the ground as if he were addressing the ants that scurried along the sticky floor tiles of the cell. 'I know it wouldn't look good, me doing that and all. Especially now that we spend so much time together. What is it they say… guilt by association?'

'Tell me about it.' Benjamin ran his hand through his dulled blond hair. He could still smell her on his fingers.

The sex with his therapist had been as wild and as frantic as it was foolish. Any good character that she would be able to offer in court would be dismissed the moment the prosecution caught whiff of anything more than a professional relationship between them. In his opinion, if she had any sense, Monica Dawkins would remove herself from the case review entirely. It was the best move for them both. And, who knows, maybe he could speak more freely to her now. After all, she wouldn't dare testify against him. Not now.

Hooking up once could be seen as a mistake on both of their parts. To repeat it would be professional suicide on her part. But for Benjamin, it wouldn't look any worse than the one-off. Nothing more than an attractive shoulder to lean on at a time when he was exposed and vulnerable. And the presence of an adult lover would go some way to dismiss all the poisonous paedophile rumours. No, Monica Dawkins wasn't something he was looking to quit just yet.

'How's your therapy going?' Seth could see that Benjamin's mind had wandered off. It often did after his sessions with the painted lady.

'It's not therapy Seth... hardly even counselling. More like an...' he let his mind wander, '...exercise.'

'Well, as long as it's helping. I could do with some honest exercise myself. It must be quite the relief, not having to rely on just the fear of death to get your heart racing. That's all this place provides, death. No life. There's no light at the end of the tunnel, just monsters hiding in the dark.'

'Are you still struggling with what you told me before, the voices? I could ask Monica if she'd talk with you?'

'No.' His voice dropped an octave until a look of embarrassment crossed his face. 'Her perfume makes me sneeze.' He rubbed his nose with the back of his hand. 'Anyway, I doubt she'd be any help to what I've got going on. I know she claims to read into people's thoughts, but only through what we decide to tell her. She could be fooled, no problem. A mention of an abusive father here, a hint of sexual insecurity, and all of a sudden you've got yourself an excuse for being broken. It wouldn't be hard to play the victim with someone like her. Trust me. But to sit and talk, to open up, when really you're forever holding back the side of you that would rather explode out of your mouth than remain hidden away, that's something I couldn't risk, and something that she'd never understand. The dark desires that fog my thoughts are better left unspoken.'

'Are you sure?' Benjamin looked at Seth. He was all hunched over and curled up, rocking back and forth upon the balls of his feet. It was a wonder to Benjamin that this man could do so much damage to another human being. He looked too fragile, too delicate to be capable of anything so bloodthirsty.

'I don't need her help.' Seth continued to rock. 'I need yours. I think you can help me more than anybody in here. Something calls to me when I look at you, something that tells me that you will help me understand what plagues me, much more than that nymph nurse that you see.'

'And how's that?' Benjamin was beginning to question his doubts. In just a few seconds Seth had transformed from a folded man into a coiled sinister spring that looked ready to strike at any given moment. His soft tone had since become acidic, as if venom tipped his tongue.

'Because you've been where I'm going. You've seen more than I've seen, experienced what I need to know. Every night, I welcome the darkness, it's a friend of mine. I can rely on it to hide my face, to mask what I am... who I am. At night, the shadows consume me, leaving no room for reflection. Under the cloaked air you can think freely. You can be released. But the daylight lies in wait to trap you. It skulks behind the shade of night, waiting to show the world what you truly are. And that's what I need from you. I need to know how you disguise what you are.'

'You what! Hide what I am?!' Benjamin couldn't believe what he was hearing. He felt such a fool that once again he had allowed himself to feel betrayed by thinking that somebody had considered him to be innocent.

'You're not the person I know.' Seth's head seemed to have locked into place like a predator who had spotted his unsuspecting prey.

'Too right I'm not. Clearly, you're no different from everybody else... just another member of the mob who see me as responsible for something that scares them. But you're wrong. You're *all* wrong. And what's the deal with you anyway? Do you see me as some form of mentor, as someone to teach you? I mean, what the hell do you think I can teach? What do you think I know? And as for the darkness being your friend... are you crazy? You're hardly hiding, Seth. You've got one of the highest profiles in this place. The whole prison saw what you did to those guys, and they'd barely had time to forget what happened to the bunch before them either.'

'They deserved it. They all did.' He stopped rocking and rested on the heels of his feet. His eyes had a pained focus as he looked up from his arched frame. 'I don't need your help with the likes of them. None of them could ever cause me the sort of bother that others do. You see, people in here deserve it. They deserve the pain they get, every last bit of it. But what about the ones that could never deserve it? What about the ones who haven't had time to do deeds so foul that they warrant the actions of a man like me?'

Benjamin had a feeling he knew where this was going.

Seth sensed his friend tense a little.

'Like who exactly? Kids? Are you talking about a child?' Benjamin watched as a frenzied look of acknowledgement flashed through Seth's eyes.

'Precisely...' his speech was strained through a violent smile. 'What about a child? What about when they get hurt... can we really ever justify it? Can we? What if I wanted to cause pain because of the pain a child had caused me? Is there justification there for killing?' He panted as he spoke, both breathless and motionless at the same time. 'You see, this is what daylight brings me. Nothing but questions. Questions in the form of people circling me, surrounding my life, causing and calling me to act. Because the light brings shadows with it. Shadows that follow you and haunt your every move. But not the night. When everybody else welcomes the delicious security that sleep gives them, the seeming escape from all the monsters that hide in waiting, I welcome them, each and every one of them. I greet those lurking beasts that bug your brain, the crippled creatures that claw at your mind. Benjamin, I want them to destroy me. Because it's right to let them do it, to allow them to release me. And I pray for the day when I am ripped from the world that I know, and find myself hurtled towards an endless oblivion of judgement. I'll fully embrace that life. The life that death brings.'

The air seemed to chill as Seth brought his speech to a close. It was clear that he didn't need Benjamin to answer the questions he had let erupt from within him. Instead, Benjamin had just sat there in silence as a wash of torment and anguish ruptured the once awkward form that his friend had adopted.

'Seth, I can't help you. I'm sorry.'

'Don't be sorry unless you truly need to be.'

'Well, right now, I think I need to be. I'm not sure what you think I can help with... these monsters that you speak of... the urges that you have. I can't relate to them. I don't act on impulse. I'm sorry.'

'Don't be. If you can't help me, then you needn't be sorry. Maybe I just need to rest. Feel free to eat without me. I'd rather starve than eat that tripe they serve. I doubt I'll ever get used to it. Not like those vultures out there. How those fleas flock to the cafeteria as if some form of nectar is being dished up goes to show that their deviant ways may be down to nurture as much as they are nature. Unlike you and me. With us, there's more than just the stench of circumstance as to explain the paths that we have taken. We had a choice. We had options and we chose to be different. But those bastards, that's how they cope inside. Remain no different from the rest. For them the inside is no worse than the outside is. For some, it's probably even better.'

'But not all of them?'

'Not for the likes of you, no. But for some... this is their hunting ground, and their favourite prey is all caged up, with no way out.'

*

Out in the canteen, James Jenkins had taken his seat. Three of his freshest followers had already wisely offered him their pudding, and now sat watching him eat them without even a muttering of thanks. His mouth was still half-full of chocolate mousse when he began talking.

'So, one paedo and his little bitch are beginning to think that they're untouchable in my joint?'

He didn't wait for an answer.

'Wrong! I'll give the little weird one his dues. It seems my boys have been underestimating him. Problem is, you'd be forgiven for thinking he was a full-blown retard, given that he spends most nights talking to little girls in the dark. Our boy Tony sleeps in the cell next to him and he swears that the wasted spot of spunk that calls himself Seth can be heard whispering to himself all through the night... about dead kids! Tony reckons he can hear him beating it as if it owes him money. No wonder he's partnered himself up with Farrow, the local kiddy-fiddler. I bet they tug each other off as they share tales of their little playground adventures, the disgusting bastards. Well, I for one am sick of it. And to think that the law are considering letting one of those predators out on the loose! Well, paint my nails, call me Shirley, and leave it in my ass until it falls out! Because I'm fucked if I can wrap my head around that one. None of those animals should be let out of their cage. Not a single one of them. So what if they never found the little girl, you only have to take a look into the pretty boy's eyes to know that he did it. The smug cunt. Was it too easy for the blue-eyed bitch to get some pussy that he fancied more of a challenge? Did he get so bored of the chase that he became a creep instead? Why run after long-legged ladies when little kids were only a short step away? Well, I say fuck him... and his limp-dicked lapdog! They need to go, and I'm happy to serve the time for anyone that manages to put an end to either of theirs. I'll take the blame for every last drop of blood that gets spilt. I'll even skip on down to the courts and sing them a merry tune on exactly how I did it. I don't give a shit! Hand me the weapon. Put their blood on my hands. I don't care. I don't care... as long as it gets done. As long as I'm here, Farrow, and his little puppy for that matter, don't get to leave this prison alive.'

Chapter 27

The birds. The timing. The method.

They all linked up. Somehow. But what was causing Addison more grief than anything else was the one thing that didn't seem to fit in to any of it: Benjamin Farrow.

From the little that was known of this man, the town seemed certain that they'd caught their killer. But what they had on him just wasn't adequate for Addison to accept. Looking at Farrow's subject profile, there was barely enough detail to hang a positive ID on him, let alone a murder conviction.

Thirty-two years of age, approximately 6ft tall, medium build, with blond hair and blue eyes. That was it. No previous convictions. No known next of kin. No previous known addresses, although he had offered a few previous schools as references when applying for his placement as a substitute teacher in Claymore's primary school. And yet, despite the generic description – no marks, no scars, no tattoos – the police were convinced that they'd identified Elizabeth's killer.

And because of what?

A single witness statement.

Billy Jackson was the one witness that placed Elizabeth, hand in hand, with a person matching Farrow's description. The reports of seeing him out on his bike were judged to be inconclusive, Farrow was already known to ride a bike, and to make the case as clear as mud, Farrow stated in interview that his bicycle had been stolen a few days before Elizabeth's disappearance. He went on to explain that he didn't want to bother the police with the report because it was only an old bike and the chances of finding it were slim to none. Couple that with how busy the police were with the young girl's disappearance, and you simply had someone not wishing to burden a division stretched thinner than fresh pasta.

Not a bad defence.

But the prosecution took a whole different stance, suggesting it to be a clear sign of deceit. The report after his arrest, and the fact Farrow didn't want to waste the police's time, didn't add up. If the bike had been stolen before the girl was taken, then the police would have been free to deal with it – a conundrum Farrow failed to answer with any reasonable explanation in court. According to the prosecution, Farrow was either lying about the theft entirely or had let it slip that he knew that Elizabeth Silver was going to be taken. The question was damning enough to show Farrow as dishonest, as someone with something to hide. His report of a theft was represented in court as a plot to remove himself from any physical evidence that could link him to the crime scene.

'Still finding it hard to put him in the frame?'

Addison wasn't sure how long Duke had been watching him work. It was still a few hours before both of their shifts started and whilst Addison could explain why he was there, he couldn't find a reason as to why his supervisor was stood watching over him.

'Tough night?' Addison noticed that Duke looked like crap. His skin was ashen, and the bags under his eyes looked like the sandman had fly-tipped a beach into them.

'You could say that.' Duke was leaning against the doorframe as he dunked a chocolate bar into an overly milky coffee. 'Got a few things on my mind lately.'

'Anything I can help with?'

Addison noted the irony. There he was tackling his insomnia by throwing himself into a high-profile investigation, when the very papers he was diving into were causing his manager to lose sleep at night. And the worry lines that had formed like thick trenches across Duke's forehead went some way to confirming what Addison feared the most. Somewhere, buried deep within the pages of these reports, was a mistake, and whether honest, misguided or just plain poisonous, Addison's gut was telling him the person responsible for it was stood only a few yards away.

'Don't worry about me Addison,' Duke tried to appear relaxed as he chewed on his half-melted Mars bar. 'Do what you've got to do.'

He took a mouthful of his drink in the same way some smug comedian might do when they say something smart, rather than funny, on a panel show. It was a statement more than anything. An act to suppress a glee that was borderline gloating. However, it was a failed gesture, it only highlighted the point they were trying to disguise, a point punctuated by a sudden urge to cover the smile that was stretched across their face.

But the eyes didn't lie. They always showed what hid beneath them. And right now, Duke's eyes were smiling widely above one of the most blatant victory-sips Addison had ever seen.

'Oh... I forgot.' Duke shifted his stance as he pulled out a rolled-up file from his back pocket. 'Before you go looking for any blind leaps of faith that me and the team may have taken, you might want to start by seeing exactly what we saw.'

Duke placed the file on the desk. The corners were kinked, and the pages looked tired and weathered. Small indents sat where the signatures had been made. Whatever these papers were, they were the originals.

'What's all this?' Addison didn't mean to sound pissed-off, but everybody at the force knew he had a crappy job to do, and if Duke was hell-bent on proving that he didn't cut any corners, then withholding information wasn't the wisest move to make.

'It's the forensic report from the Silver scene. Complete with photographs, floor maps, officer statements. Oh...' Duke tried to act casual, 'and the DNA they found.'

'DNA!'

Addison felt like somebody had hit him in the chest with an epi-pen. He'd read every report, every dull, drawn-out court manuscript, every single case paper, even the minutes to all of the above, and there wasn't a single reference to any DNA being found. Not a drop of it.

'That's right, poor-man's Poirot. Seems to me as if this little mystery of yours was solved long before it ever became one.' Duke had turned to a page that was titled *DNA Sample Results*. Beneath his long, surprisingly hairy, finger was a name that Addison – along with the prosecution – had been completely unable to place inside the crime scene. But there it was, as plain as the sunlight that had just begun to clamber over the high hilltops of Claymore.

DNA Sample Result: Positive Match.

Benjamin Farrow.

*

So, there was DNA.

Benjamin Farrow's to be precise.

Amazingly, this had failed to reach the press as the evidence bag appeared to have been dismissed before the case was ever presented to the Crown Prosecution Service. In fact, there was never any mention of the finding in any interview either; or at least not within any of the records of taped interviews submitted within the case file. Further to that, having scoured through all the case reports and countless court manuscripts, Addison couldn't find a single reference to any foreign

DNA being found at the scene of Elizabeth's abduction. Not once was it presented in court, or anywhere else for that matter.

Why did they have to remove it as evidence? Clearly this was the most damning piece that the prosecution had at their disposal, and yet here it was, tucked away like some miscellaneous file that got swept up and discounted like countless others.

But this report was vital.

According to the file, when SOCO first attended the scene they recorded finding a few strands of medium-length blond hair. This was located near to the bedside cabinet belonging to Elizabeth. Four single strands, all belonging to Benjamin Farrow.

Understandably, the police had fast-tracked the enquiry and had the results back within a day – triggering the dawn raid on Farrow's rented flat. Their swift swoop now made sense. On the face of all the published facts, the move to bring Farrow in appeared to be based solely upon a distant description.

But this would have been a huge stretch to say the least. Duke would have known that this was the one of the biggest moves his department were ever going to make, and by far the most public. Luckily, the papers seized upon how quickly the police had moved, interpreting this to be a strong sign of confidence on their behalf. It was enough for them to get the ball rolling. And with the radio silence that came from the police's media department, the press were provided with a license to be creative.

What followed was a frenzy.

If only they knew the truth.

It was clear Duke had given his protégé a couple of minutes to digest what he'd served up. He'd now returned with two hot cups of coffee and a fresh pack of chocolate bourbons. He placed one cup in front of Addison and tore off the seal to the biscuits before dunking two at once, stuffing them into his mouth, and taking a seat.

'It's an interesting read, isn't it?'

'You're telling me! Why wasn't any of this disclosed first time around? Surely they wouldn't be any need for a case review if the courts had hold of this?'

'Nobody will touch it.' Duke dunked another biscuit. 'It's utterly worthless now. After the balls-up, that is.'

'The balls-up?'

'Two, to be precise. Two of which conceived one hell of a bastard for us to manage. Both were by the same goddamn officer... PC dip-shit Pyke.' Duke openly sighed. 'This complete *Jonny-No-Stars* of an officer failed to seal the original evidence bag correctly. This in itself left the door wide open for any defence brief to suggest cross-contamination.

That's the first page of policing right there. Couple that with the fact that this *same* officer had also encountered Farrow on the morning of the search, and you've not just gone and burned the best evidence that you could imagine... you've just covered it in oil, tossed on a match, and then tried to put out the inferno with your own stinking piss.'

Aside from admiring just how one man could house so much anger, Addison was still trying to grasp the existence of the evidence.

'But why not let the courts toss it out? Surely it would have been better to make the jury aware of it. That way, even if the judge asks them to discount it, the damage is done – they already know.'

'Great minds, DC Clarke, great minds.' Duke reached for another bourbon. He was still chewing the last one when he spoke. 'That's exactly what I suggested. Turns out... because we were already aware of the flaws in the case, it was *unethical* to submit it. Now, we've all taken the hit and taken home a regret in a red dress when pickings were dry. But everyone gets what they're after, and then you just have to live with the compromises that you made. You simply shake it off, right? Well, not if the Chief Constable is offering the diagnosis you don't. This thing was a cancer to the case... lurking like some messed-up malignant melanoma, just lying in wait to lay claim to my low-hanging balls. In the end, we had to ditch all of the officer's records and reports. *All* of them. The CPS was already a bit twitchy about how quickly we'd moved in on Farrow, and the chief stated that we couldn't submit anything that had the slightest whiff of a stitch up about it. We couldn't even put it to the son-of-a-bitch in interview. He just sat there, acting all innocent, not knowing what we knew. The moral of the story, always double bag.'

'So, you just buried it?'

'Yep. Had to.' Duke spoke out the side of his mouth. 'The damn thing deserved its own ceremony: headstone, hymns, the lot. It left me in mourning for some time, trust me. That's why I kept this copy, it helps me keep my sanity. Whenever I find myself questioning whether we got the right guy, I just take a look at the report. It helps me sleep at night. I mean, come on, it puts him there. It puts the guy *right* there.'

Duke downed the rest of his coffee. It did little to douse the fire in his belly, but he took a moment to collect himself.

'Anyhow,' Duke stood up, holding onto his belt like an underpaid extra from an old western. 'I've got myself a town here to run. Keep up the good work Deputy.' And with a gentle nod and a slow turn on his heels, Duke moseyed on out of the office, the report securely holstered in his trouser pocket.

For Addison the revelation was enough. He could now see that the Claymore Police Department had every reason to arrest Benjamin Farrow. It was just a tragedy that they couldn't use the evidence in interview.

With little else left to occupy his day, he spent the next couple of hours listening to the first taped interviews that were held with Farrow. He'd heard it all before, and he knew them almost word for word. But now they sounded different to him. Not the way Farrow spoke; he still sounded like the confused passer-by who was happy to assist enquiries whilst at the same time utterly bewildered as to why he'd been swept up in all the chaos. But above all, he was calm, as if he was sat within the very eye of the storm that raged around him. A complete and utter shit-storm forecasted for a possible twenty years to life.

But the difference wasn't found within Farrow's tone. It was in Duke's. What initially passed as blind rage was now clearly an exercise of ragged restraint. The gravel that rattled in his voice was like somebody had put their foot down on an Aston Martin whilst being forced to leave the handbrake on. Frustration screamed out behind the gritted teeth that ground through the gears of what were, in truth, generic questions. It was clear to the ear, Duke had been forced to drive with the brakes on, and it almost broke him.

'What is your relationship with Elizabeth Silver?'

She was a student at the school where I worked.

'Where were you on the night of her disappearance?'

Alone.

'What did you do today, leading up until your arrest?'

Nothing.

That's when it hit him.

Nothing.

Not a thing.

All of a sudden, Addison had an itch that needed scratching. Tossing a biscuit into his mouth, he took a note of the date Farrow was arrested and logged into the local intelligence system that covered Claymore. Like the village walls, the program was ancient, it was nothing more than an electronic filing system that was fast becoming a relic. But that's all he needed. Having keyed in the relevant details, Addison found the report he was hoping for. Like some forgotten fossil, buried beneath countless intelligence logs was the often ignored encounter form. Introduced by the police mainly as a tool to defend themselves against any claims of profiling, the form was used to record any significant encounter an officer may have had whilst on duty. Often, they were used as a numbers-game by lazy officers who wanted to appear more proactive than they actually were. Some were even written out retrospectively. If the officer had seen someone on the street that day but the importance of it wasn't relevant until later on, it wasn't unheard of that they'd document it in light of the new information. Nothing wrong about that. Just an officer recording what was relevant.

And that's exactly what Addison was banking on.

Understandably, a quick chat on the street with a local teacher wouldn't be worthy of recording. Not at first. Especially in a town like Claymore where the local bobby was an integrated part of the community. But what if that chat was more significant than you could have possibly known?

What if you were talking to a killer?

Duke had stated that all of PC Pyke's reports were to be ignored. All of them. The fact that Pyke had messed up with the evidence bag wouldn't have been documented by him at the time, but rather surfaced through one of SOCO's records. So that wasn't the report Duke was pissed about. Instead, the fatal blow was dealt when it was discovered that Pyke had interacted with Farrow in the morning, a day *before* his arrest. A move that Addison had felt a little extreme, especially given the fact that the defence may never have had reason to link PC Pyke and Benjamin Farrow prior to the arrest – not unless Farrow happened to disclose it in interview. But he didn't. The decision to dismiss the evidence was because the link must have already been recorded, by PC Pyke himself.

And here it was. Timed and dated, PC Pyke had thought it best to submit a retrospective encounter for his chance meeting with Benjamin Farrow, ironically because he probably felt that it may come in handy evidentially. But here it was, on police record, the chink in the armour, the feckless fly in the ointment, detailing every last piece of detail of their exchange. The Encounter Pedestrian form detailed Farrow's appearance, his clothing, even his account for being in the area. By all accounts he was out cycling to the greengrocers to gather something for his breakfast.

Cycling.

Benjamin Farrow was on his bike when he spoke with PC Pyke. A day after he had claimed it was stolen.

The lying son-of-bitch.

Chapter 28

'Joseph, come on. You'll be late for school.'

She was running late herself. Brian, the department head, had decided he was going to visit the office this morning, bringing her presentation for the new HR business proposal forward by two days. The same two days that she'd set aside specifically to work on it.

Balls to it!

She'd just have to wing it, she knew what she was talking about. Mix a little bit of conviction with charm and she'd convince Brian that her proposals were his idea, ones that he'd no doubt take credit for once the benefits were celebrated. But time for celebration was a few months away, and right now she just had to blind him with technical jargon until his confused little mind caved in.

Bullshit with confidence Karen, that's all you have to do.

'Joseph! Come on.'

He wasn't the quickest at the best of times, but this morning the boy was almost stationary. She should never have let him have that extra hour on his computer before bedtime.

She climbed the stairs, taking care to avoid the toy soldiers and jagged wrestling figures that were scattered from top to bottom.

'Jo-Jo...' She slowed as she reached his door, rapping lightly before entering. She'd invaded his privacy before and it had not gone well. For three nights straight he'd wet the bed, terrified that someone was at his door, waiting to take him away, to take him back. She'd only wanted to watch him sleep for a while, but she'd learned that a little distance often made them grow closer to one another. It established a mutual trust.

The settling period was tough. He's come on so well since.

Joseph was a blessing.

Since his promotion, Nick was away from home more often, and the brief time that they did get to share was upon increasingly uncommon ground. Being separated was beginning to pull at all the things that had once bound them. The love was still there. But the mutual understanding, the natural chemistry, it was all waning.

Until Joseph.

He gave them something to invest in, a shared outlet for all their unspent affection and attention. Through the love they shared with him, they reflected their love for one another. It had saved them. And just in time.

Her lonely nights had invited paranoia to move in. After a while, she was convinced Nick was having an affair. The late nights, the business trips, the complete lack of libido: it was all beginning to tell her that she wasn't good enough anymore. At her lowest, she'd taken to checking his pockets for receipts – never deterred by the fact that every one of them married up with his account of where he'd been that evening. But she was convinced he was lying. He had a charm, a certain way that made everybody like him. Even that new young secretary with the blond hair and high heels, no doubt.

Fixated by an unproven guilt, she was no longer looking for good news, only bad. She'd insisted that it would be '*fun*' if they set up location-sharing software on their smartphones. But this was inconclusive. It only told her that his phone was more often than not sat in his office for twelve hours a day. His cheating ass could always be elsewhere.

But then Joseph came along.

Now, when Nick was home, he no longer talked about Janice, his demanding, yet very attractive, boss. Karen had seen her at a Christmas ball the one time and had immediately felt a sense of intimidation. It was strange how power often turned the bland into beautiful. The woman wouldn't have turned anywhere near as many heads if the men at the office didn't need to kiss her ass as she walked past. But now, even Janice was a lost topic of conversation. Home was finally a healthy distraction for Nick. He no longer talked about the countless business lunches that she shared no interest in, professional or personal. Instead, he poured all his heart into the young boy that truly needed a father figure, a man of firm, clear morals.

She made sure she was delicate when she entered the room. She didn't want to surprise him again. Peering past the door, the bedroom looked untouched from when she had last tucked him in the night before. The bedside lamp was still off, and the clothes she had folded for him to wear today were still piled neatly on his small wooden stool. All that was missing was the boy.

Behind her, the toilet flushed, followed by the slow staggering sound of flat feet slapping along the wooden floorboards. Turning, she saw the young yawning boy using his entire fist to try and rub a small crumb of sleep from his squashed eye.

'Jesus Christ, Joseph!' She hurried him into the room and began to dress him as she spoke. His arms pointed to the heavens as she pulled his Superman pyjama top over his head.

'I'm sorry Mummy,' he said through half a yawn. Her frosty demeanour melted instantly. The boy was nothing if not heart-warming.

The drive to school had been less stressful than the usual rage-filled procession of sparkling clean four-by-fours and roughly abandoned vehicles that resembled some low-rent post-apocalyptic movie. In fact, the slight delay had given time for sanity to resume upon the road, and Karen was starting to think that being late could have some benefits. Choosing to relax rather than stress out, she turned up the radio and flicked on the windscreen wipers. Heavy rain had begun to fall, thudding against the rooftop like a thousand feet all dancing to some forgotten song. She had always enjoyed the sound. It acted like white noise, blocking out all the racket that poured from the radio. As usual, the presenter filled the ever-increasing gaps between the music with endless empty insights into their personal lives, using the show as a platform for self-promotion rather than an opportunity to just play some decent music.

She knocked the indicator up to show she was taking the next left.

Joseph was sat quietly in the back seat, seemingly content with his latest action figure. She wasn't sure whether this one could fly, shoot fire from his eyes or act like a spider. That area of knowledge was left to Nick, he'd been a bit of a geek when he was younger, loving his comics and toys. The recent surge in super-hero movies had allowed him to rekindle the magic of his lost youth.

Pulling up alongside the small primary school, she was spoilt for choice when it came to parking. The school run squadron had completed its morning mission, and all that was left on the road was a small green van and a couple of pushbikes. Karen felt sorry for the poor sods who had taken the healthy option only to have been hit by this shower. The raindrops continued to rap upon the roof as she turned to see her little boy still fixated by his figurine.

'Jo-Jo.' She shook his leg a little to ensure he was listening. 'Can you do Mummy a big favour? There's a brolly tucked in behind my seat. Why don't you be a good boy and pass it to me.'

A few seconds passed before he replied. He hadn't budged an inch, but his eyes had at least looked for what she had asked.

'There's nothing here Mummy.'

'What?' Leaning awkwardly, she was able to pat the back of her chair. Sure enough, the small sleeve was empty.

Balls.

The rain continued to fall, tapping at the window like a nuisance you just couldn't ignore. It wasn't going anywhere. Looking at the front of the school, she guessed it was a hundred yards max from door to door. More than enough to soak a woman right through and make her look like a drowned rat for her presentation. She knew Brian would be tougher to sway if she was both late and looking like she'd swam to work.

But for a young boy with a hooded jacket and a wild imagination? The rain was an adventure.

'Jo-Jo,' she turned her whole upper body around to face the little man. 'Are you ready to be Mummy's little hero?' He nodded slowly. 'Now, I'm about to turn your coat into a magic costume. All you need to do is pull your hood up and you'll be invisible. Not even a drop of rain will be able to find you. But we can't use it against our teachers because they won't be able to help you learn cool stuff if they don't know you're there... so just use this power from the car until you reach the school. Okay?'

Joseph seemed excited. He was almost nine years old and wasn't ready to start finding grown-ups uncool just yet. So, he decided to play along.

Looking at her watch – which was telling her she was already twenty minutes late – she began a countdown from ten. By the time she'd reach *five*, Joseph's jacket was zipped up to the top, his hood was up, and he was reaching for the door.

Four.

Three.

Two.

One.

And he was gone.

Blanketed by rain she watched as the young boy faded into the falling water. Realising the time, she didn't wait to see him enter the school gates. Like a panicked reflex, her mind had switched back to the focus group she was meant to be chairing right now. Shifting her car into gear, she pulled away, forgetting to look back to see whether Joseph had completed his mission. She trusted her little hero was up to the task.

But maybe she should have waited. Maybe, if she wasn't in such a rush, she would have walked him in herself. Maybe she would have seen him in safely. And maybe she would have seen the blond-haired man who was watching them. He'd been stood in the rain for some time.

She was late.

Chapter 29

He wasn't sure what to do.

Should he order her a drink? Get himself one whilst he waited for her to arrive? It had been such a long time since he'd done this sort of thing. But then, was it even a date? It wasn't strictly pleasure. Despite having a fun time in the pub the other night, Addison still wanted to pick Piper's brains about a few things. She'd shown an interest in the case after all. Maybe she'd seen a few links he hadn't; known of other similar cases that he was yet to dig up or identify. He'd arranged to meet with her for a coffee to see whether there was something he'd overlooked. That, and the fact he liked the way she made him feel. He hadn't felt like fun company for over a year. Causing a friend's death had a strange way of doing that to you.

He'd picked this café on purpose. Unofficially, he would say it was because they served free refills on fresh filter coffee – which was a lifeline to somebody who had long accepted to try to cope with his insomnia rather than cure it. However, the real reason he'd picked it was because it was probably the coolest looking place Claymore had to offer. The eclectic décor was more considered than just a jumbled-up pile of junk. The staggered stag heads that stared back at him from the walls provided a more beatnik than bookshop vibe. He'd already picked up over a few drinks that Piper was a little more alternative than most, but not enough to be scary or bogus. She knew who she was, and that comfort bred a confidence that he was cool with.

'Morning tiger.' Her voice was slightly stressed, but her touch was quite tender as she rested her hand upon his shoulder. 'Sorry I'm late. The weather is shocking.'

He'd already noticed the rain. It was the reason he'd chosen to sit with his back facing the large windows that walled the front of the café. The sight of water cloaking the glass would only have dragged him back to his darkest hour, and Piper had already made it clear by the fourth pint that playing the fallen angel scored you no brownie points with her.

'My round?' She smiled as she sat down, shaking off the large cotton coat that looked like it had just come straight out of the wash. Pebbles of rain clung to the fabric like paused tears.

'Don't think they serve that type of drink in here.' He smiled and checked his watch like he didn't already know the time. 'Well, not before midday, anyhow.'

'Ha!' Her smile was infectious. 'Trust me, I meant a coffee. I let my guard down around you last time; letting you get me drunk the way you did. Nope. Not for me. Not again. Something tells me that I need to keep my wits about me when I'm around you... officer.'

'Please,' he was determined not to make this meeting completely business. 'You don't have to call me that.'

'Okay,' she gestured for the hipster waiter to come over. 'I'll call you whatever you prefer. I'm just glad you called.'

They both ordered the filter coffee and, whilst he had his eye on the large slice of chocolate fudge cake that sat on the bar, he didn't really feel it was a one cake, two spoons situation. Not yet anyway.

Like the last time, the chemistry was obvious.

'I like this place,' she held her mug close to her chest with both hands. 'Nice choice.'

'Thanks.' He couldn't deny that there was some design in his choice. 'I thought you'd like it. It's very...' he looked around the place trying to make sense of the mixture of styles, '... you.'

'Oh really?' She playfully feigned a mixture of excitement and intrigue. 'And what exactly might I be?'

'Right now? A mystery.' He smiled as he took a small drink from his cup. 'But I'll crack it. Don't worry about that. I'll work you out soon enough.'

'I bet you will.'

They shared a laugh and let a few minutes pass, talking only of little things that illustrated the bigger picture – their likes, dislikes; nothing more than detail, a true measure of who they were, or at least wanted to present themselves to be. There was little change from the first hour before Addison brought the conversation around to what was soon becoming the screensaver to his subconscious, a constant thorn in his paw, refusing to ever allow him a single idle thought.

'I wanted to pick your brains, if I may.' He'd lost count of how many coffees he'd had so far, but it was enough for the waiter to come accustomed to pouring him a refill every time he passed by. Addison waited for the man with the coffee pot and well-oiled beard to leave before he spoke in almost a whisper. 'What's your take on the Elizabeth Silver case?'

There was little reaction from her. Not a reflexive one anyway. Instead she appeared to slow down a little, as if every movement she made had now become more intentional.

'Hmm...' she was looking at him, but with an expression that suggested her mind was somewhere outside of the room. 'It's a tricky one really. I reckon they've got their guy. I mean, they moved pretty quickly on it.'

'True. But is there anything you remember from the case? Something that I may not be seeing? It always appears easier looking back and seeming to know everything once all the little secrets have presented themselves to you. But this one's different. I feel almost as if I'm walking backwards through the case – tracing the steps made by the police – but I have my back turned to everything. I don't see the clear path that they chose. Instead, I see all the enquiries that were brushed to the side, and questions buried in shallow graves. It's as if I'm expected to step back and just hope that there'll be firm ground to stand on. Like the whole thing is just a huge messed-up trust exercise.'

'So, what, you don't believe that they've got their man?' She spoke in a broken rhythm, as if every word brought with it another question.

'I didn't.' He thought about the DNA that they'd found. 'Not until recently anyway.'

'I don't envy your job Addison. Not one bit.' Her hand rested on his knee. It sent a charge up his leg.

'Don't worry about me. I'm fine.' He didn't sound it. 'I just don't want anybody to get hurt because of me. I have a tendency to enter people's lives like a bullet: smooth entrance, messy exit.'

'Sounds painful.'

He smiled.

'Maybe I was just hoping to see whether you saw something at the time that might assist me?'

'Aren't you supposed to just check over what the police department did, to ensure they didn't drop the ball at all? This isn't a mystery that you need to solve. I'm sorry to break it to you sweetie, but your job is a lot less sexy than that. It's basic admin.'

'It's called the Oversight Programme, actually.' He picked up her slam-down with the sense of humour with which it was intended. 'But seriously, what if there are things I can't overlook?'

'Like what?' The café had begun to fill up with the lunchtime trade. According to the last three loud-enough-so-everybody-could-hear orders, it seemed the café did an adequate organic chicken and avocado on rye.

It sounded dreadful.

'No idea. I just get a feeling that there was a lot happening that people just ignored.' Addison decreased the detail the more the crowd increased. For all he knew, there could have been someone connected to the entire thing stood next to him.

'Well, I can't help I'm afraid.' Piper offered a small shrug. 'I was nowhere near this mess when it all went down.' She spotted the confused look on his face. 'I'm freelance, Addison. I'd have to count myself pretty lucky to be around a sleepy-hollow like this one at the very same time the biggest case in its history burst open.'

'Oh,' he mulled it over. 'Didn't you piggyback onto the case like the rest of the country's media?'

'Nope,' she took a small drink. 'I was miles away, working some spurious child abuse story if I remember rightly. You know the sort, the usual children's-home-commits-abuse scandal. Turns out the place had been shut down for years, and the previous suspects had become impossible to track down, so there were no real legs in it. By the time I'd taken a look at the Elizabeth Silver case, I was playing catch-up with the big guns. Couldn't get anywhere near a sniff at a press conference. It seemed like all the seats were reserved for the nationals. Who's interested in the little local voice when you've got the lungs of all the red-top tabloids ready to sing whatever song you fed them? That was my take on it all anyway. The press, the police, it was all just one big hymn sheet. Problem was, Benjamin Farrow refused to sing.'

'Just like a bird in a cage, right?'

'Too right.' She nodded at him. 'But now that the case is up for review – well that changes it all. Granted, the nationals are going to run a little with it, but you can bet they won't pass any form of opinion until a decision has been made in court. There's too much on the line this time for them to be completely outspoken. The way they ran the story last time, it was a one-way road. The turn's too sharp to manoeuvre at speed right now, so they'll act casual. Until the decision, at least. If Farrow's conviction stands, then they'll carry on as if they always knew that they were right. And if he's released, well by then they'll have distanced themselves enough to not cause too much alarm when they offer their spin on the whole damn thing.'

'Wow. Thanks for the lesson.' He offered a wry smile to show that he was only half ripping the piss. 'How do you fit into all this?'

'Well, isn't it obvious?' She opened up her arms. 'I was a ghost back then. I was as muted as a monk.' She could see by his puzzled look that he wasn't quite getting it. 'There's a whole heap of freedom in being non-committal. I can report on the whole matter however I want now. I'm free to bend whichever way it takes me.' She let the last sentence hang in the air until she could see his mind register the innuendo.

'And, that's why you can be found at various crime scenes?'

'Yep.' She sounded her most serious. 'Addison, I also want to know what people know. I see the connection too.'

His chest thumped loud enough to mute the dull drone of the chatter around him. Something about Piper drew him in. Something that scared him as much as it excited him. He went to speak before he was interrupted by his leg beginning to vibrate.

'Either your phone's ringing in your pocket, or you are very excited to see me.' Piper mirrored his smile. It suited him. She just hoped he thought the same about her.

'Hello, Addison speaking.'

The number was unknown. More often than not Addison wouldn't have bothered to take the call. Unknown numbers were never good news. This one was no different. He stayed still as he listened, as if it in some way made the caller on the line any louder. The lunchtime crowd had really picked up. Small pockets of rich opinion dressed in cheap suits began to compete over who could air their grievances louder about either their dumbass co-workers or the jumped-up supervisor who was overlooking their true potential. Addison had heard it all before. The self-centred dross of days stuck on repeat.

Sadly, the content of the phone call was also becoming all too familiar.

Another one. Gone.

As he hung up the noise around him seemed to amplify. Droves of people continued to complain for complaining's sake. Addison couldn't help but feel contempt for them. Part of him wanted to go and tell them that if *all* they had to worry about in their vapid little lives was what Terry from Accounts thought of them, or that Steve had got the girl from HR pregnant at the Christmas party, then they should rush to church and thank every god imaginable for being so damn lucky.

Because, right now, Addison was certain that there were a couple of people whose worlds were caving in around them. Worlds built around something that was now in immediate danger.

He noticed Piper looking at him as he tried to regain his focus. He didn't know what to say, but his face said it all.

'There's been another one, hasn't there?' she said.

'Yes...' his voice was a whispered blend of rage and exasperation. 'A young boy's been taken.'

Chapter 30

The result could only be bad.

Even positive news was simply going to be the lesser of many evils. But given the way he was feeling today, he'd gladly welcome something a little crappy compared to catastrophic. Times had been hard for everybody lately, and they were all depending on him to protect them. No matter how many hits were coming his way.

The lighting inside the waiting room looked tired and overworked, not too dissimilar to the staff that scurried around him; both had been working through the night and it was beginning to show. The once bright light in their eyes now blended into the same stale glow that coloured the walls around them. They weren't there to stop, to simply cease working. They were there to assist, care and maybe even cure. But they couldn't always do all three. Not always.

Refusing to feel sorry for himself, he unwrapped a small spearmint and popped it into his mouth. He could still smell a trace of the cheap liquid sanitizer on his fingers. The pumps were everywhere, located on every wall and next to every doorway, and you didn't have to wait long to hear the slow churn of the pump as it coughed out another glob of the alcoholic handwash. The smell was so strong it surprised him how it never dragged any of the local bums inside like the alluring scent of a hot cartoon pie left on a windowsill. Then again, even he'd drank worse before. He flinched at the memories of his misspent youth, with the countless moments lost to mindless drinking, hopeful memories obliterated by booze. Thinking back, he felt foolish for wasting so much time.

But time could keep those memories that he'd squandered. Those memories would only serve to embarrass him if he was ever able to recall what he'd been up to when he'd pressed the button to oblivion so hard that he'd not surfaced for days.

However, all the other memories... the good ones... they were all that he had left.

That's what happens when a future is taken from you – all you have is what's left of the past. The parts you can remember, anyway.

If there was one side effect to his condition that the countless paper-thin pamphlets seemed to consistently miss out, it was crippling nostalgia. That was the real killer. The clock ticked for everybody. But when it felt like you could almost hear your time drawing to a close then there was only one way you could focus.

Forward.

What sat in front was rapidly becoming shorter by the day, arriving and passing in an instant, and constantly filling up the space behind you; the space where everything you can ever be turns into all the things you were. A space where your victories sat with defeats, where love lies with loss, and where happiness is bound by hurt.

There was no cure for what he had. There was no escaping what was to come. He'd known it for some time now. Initially he'd fought it, even looked like he was winning for a short time, but in truth, it was already out of reach. There was no prevention or cure, just postponement at best.

Quite the brutal little bastard, is cancer. Not content with just attacking one area, it feigns retreat only to surface somewhere else, somewhere less detectable at first. And that's when the bugger becomes brave. Like the hidden coward that lays the boot into an already fallen foe, cancer can become its most aggressive once the fight is already lost. It constantly plays you, forever bluffing, and changing its cards whenever it wants. You could win a few hands, maybe even fool a few people that you're okay, but the house always won in the end.

Waiting his turn to see what card he'd been dealt, he discovered that he wasn't actually filled with much regret. He'd owned his mistakes as much as he'd savoured his successes. But there was one shortcoming that he would never have the time to address, nor ever regret. Sat around him were a few families, scattered across the waiting room, each fulfilling some role or another. Some acted like gatherers, collecting food and drink for the rest of the group in an attempt to distract themselves and appear useful, whilst others sat sedentary, like rocks of full support for their loved ones to lean upon.

And that's all people really needed on this side, a bit of strength and support. In truth, if you were sat on this side of the doors then there was often somebody much worse off on the other side. Scanning the room, nobody around him looked injured, wounded... maybe, but there were no obvious emergencies. Experience taught him that this meant there'd be somebody else who was causing all this anguish and pain; an agony that can only be born out of a love. And that was something he'd never regret. When it was his time to go through those doors, there wouldn't be anybody sat where he was now, crying or hurting over him. His pain wouldn't cause others to feel it. And he took that as a blessing in some part.

'Mr Parker.' The doctor holding the door open looked around for his next patient.

He stood up, wondering exactly what sort of timeframe was written on the other side of the report the doctor was holding.

'That's me Doc. I'm Derek Parker.'

He tossed another mint into his mouth as he left the waiting room.

Chapter 31

He got the call because the operator couldn't get hold of his line manager.

Addison had tried to call Duke a few times, but no luck. Having already left one voicemail, he decided not to leave another; that and six missed calls within the space of five minutes should be enough to strike a little urgency into the matter.

Where the hell is he?

Addison felt it odd that his supervisor hadn't pounced like a tramp on hot chips. After all, the Elizabeth Silver case only went some way to defining Duke's entire career. If there was another creep out there, copycat or otherwise, then Duke clearly had cause to get involved, or at the very least appear the slight bit interested. Instead, the deeper Addison found himself – the thicker the connections were between Elizabeth's disappearance and the recent spate of kidnappings – the more distant Duke became. Granted, he showed a little interest to begin with, but the more Addison began to dig, the more buried Duke appeared. Maybe he wanted to keep things neutral, make sure that Farrow's appeal wasn't affected by his involvement. But if this was the case, then Addison didn't know his friend at all. Duke could take the hit. If Farrow was innocent, then whatever criticism came his way, both he and Addison knew – what with the DNA at least – that Farrow needed to come in. Duke had made the right call. The rest of it – the decision to charge, the press frenzy, and the sentencing – none of that could be levelled at Duke. And even more so, if Farrow was innocent, then that left the real killer out there. The mystery was still waiting to be solved, and there's no way Duke would rest until the truth was known.

Unless he was certain he already knew it. Either way, another child – a boy this time – had been taken, and there was no way of pinning this one of Farrow. He was safely stuck inside secure accommodation, courtesy of the taxpayer.

However, this monster, whoever they were, was still out there.

Failing to get through to his Sergeant, Addison saw no harm in taking Piper along with him. No doubt she'd had just turned up there anyway, and he was still enjoying her company too much to let some small matter of a child abduction get in the way. Who knows, maybe she could see a connection that he'd overlooked.

'So, what have we got?' Piper leaned back into the passenger seat, almost too relaxed for her wannabe partner's liking.

'Don't start playing cop with me,' Addison flashed a smile. 'We ain't partners. Not yet, anyway. The deal for today is simple. Because I figured that you'd only turn up at the scene anyway, I thought I'd do my bit for the environment and offer you a lift. But once we're there, you'll be on one side of the tape, and I'll be on the other. This isn't my crime scene, and it isn't yours. I have to respect whoever owns the job. So please, keep your distance. Trust me, the way this is all developing, you don't want to get yourself caught up in it.'

'Yes, officer.' She feigned a sulk, but her playful salute showed she was cool with it.

It took them almost an hour to push through the diverted traffic. The local school run had been brought forward on account of the missing boy, and the neighbourhood officers managing all the road closures were doing a good job at keeping the scene as sterile as possible. But people still had to be places. And if you ever broke the norm, then the ripple effect fractured the routine, forcing change, which always seemed to bring the stupid out in people. Especially drivers. Ignoring several traffic violations, and at least four road rage incidents, Addison manoeuvred his way through the mindless motorists. He could see the disgruntled faces of the other drivers in his rear-view mirror after the officer on the cordon allowed him to pass. Pissed was an understatement. It always baffled Addison how it never occurred to people that the presence of the police meant that something bad had already happened. They weren't there to simply piss people off, or disrupt their day. Not the law-abiding ones anyway.

If it wasn't for the scatterings of various press vans, police forensic vehicles and half a dozen scene officers, the school would have appeared like any other public state school. Housing both infants and juniors, St Anthony's Roman Catholic primary school had two main entrances. The one leading to the infants' side of the building was directly attached to the school car park, on account of the fact the school also ran a nursery and playschool. The entrance for the junior school, on the other hand, sat on the opposite side of the building. Access was gained from the street, with no off-the-street parking causing those on the school run to share the space with a couple of busy bus stops and people popping to the small row of stores that sat on the opposite side of the road. It was at this entrance that eight-year-old Joseph Farnham was last seen.

Unsurprisingly, DCI Wilson was already on site, and if she was unhappy to see Addison, then she didn't show it.

'DC Clarke,' she extended her hand as she smiled. 'I have to be honest, I half expected to already find you and your sidekick Derek here when I arrived.' She looked over his shoulder as she spoke. 'Don't tell him I called him that. He hates playing second fiddle does our Derek. Where is he, by the way?'

It took Addison a second to realise that the Chief Inspector was referring to Duke. It always threw him to hear people using his real name.

'I'm sorry Ma'am. I've been unable to get hold of him. Seems to have completely dropped off the radar. Not like him at all. Like yourself, half of me was hoping that he'd already be here.'

'Sadly not,' she sighed. For a moment she looked more attractive than she had before. Addison had to admit that behind all of DCI Wilson's smiles and courtesies, he knew there was a force of nature that you simply didn't mess around with. He'd sensed it from the moment they'd first met. But she could be disarmed. Whenever Duke was mentioned, she always softened. It was only slight, like a single ray of sunshine breaking through a crack in the wall.

'Ma'am, I'm sorry to just turn up like this. If you need me to clear off, I can.' He waited for her to respond but her expression showed she was aware he had more to say. 'As you know, I'm still in the middle of the Elizabeth Silver case review and... well... it keeps on growing.'

She took his arm and led him away from the small crowd of officers that had gathered to hand out a few hot drinks for those on the cordons. She didn't look at him as she spoke, as if they were sharing a secret.

'You think they're all linked as well?'

Addison flinched. It was obvious that DCI Wilson would have spotted what he had. It was clear she still had an ear to the ground and her eyes fixed on her department. After all, it's easy to lose your footing at the top if you didn't know what stood beneath you.

'I do, Ma'am. Whether directly or indirectly, there's something tangible at all these scenes that links them to one another. I'm not entirely sure what it is, but it feels close. I believe if I can just do a bit more digging, gain a few more perspectives, it will eventually present itself to me like some messed-up magic eye puzzle.'

'I agree.' DCI Wilson straightened up a little. 'That's why I'm going to give you full access to all the case files we have. There's no point looking at this from individual stances anymore. Somebody needs to be sighted on everything. The spectator gets to see more of the game than the players involved, and it's clear you've picked up on the pattern at play here. So, we're happy to have you onboard. It's the best way to ensure that no clues, big or small, get overlooked.'

'Thank you, Ma'am.'

'Our pleasure.' Her smile was soft, until her hard face tightened it up. 'Naturally, we'll run you like a consultant; someone with oversight on operations, but with no strategic authority. I don't want to go pissing off my detectives. They're pretty shit-hot at what they do, but they can be slightly crippled by their sense of pride and ability. Let's just say that some of them can get a little bit selfish with their toys, so don't expect an invitation from them to come out to play. You'll still answer to DS Parker, who can answer to me... for once.'

The smile returned.

With regards to the detective's ego, Addison knew exactly what she meant. He hadn't forgotten the countless times he'd walked into the old CID office back home only to appear invisible to everybody in there, like an ant walking through Olympus. The uniform didn't matter, in fact, it was a burden, a cloak. It seemed that if you weren't wearing some cheap Next clearance suit and a two-for-one George from ASDA tie, then apparently you weren't worth looking at.

'Come over here,' she took his arm again. 'Tell me what you think of this.' She led him across the small footpath that ran between two overgrown hedgerows. The wind had become trapped within the tops of the thick branches, causing it to howl above them. Beneath it, a group of SOCOs were dusting every shiny or smooth surface that they could find, whilst officers in poorly fitted suits spoke with a few bookish-looking bystanders. Their exhausted expressions, coupled by the strong mixed scent of coffee and cigarettes led Addison to deduce that these people were the teachers from the school. Overworked, underpaid – well, for at least two thirds of the year, that was, Addison couldn't imagine what he'd do with six weeks holiday every summer, and a couple more for Christmas and any other holiday for that matter. All that time would lead him into madness. Too much time gave him too much to think about. The unwelcome ghosts of his past only came to visit him when his mind afforded them room to sneak in. So, instead of playing host to these uninvited guests, he filled his brain with whatever case he was working on. It became his default setting – trying to understand the criminal mind. Before the death of his partner, before the crippling insomnia, his work often kept him up at night. But what once was an unhealthy obsession had now become his opium.

Keeping the demons at bay for one more day, he focused on the scene in front of him. Taking the lead, DCI Wilson led him to a small bag that was still being photographed from every imaginable angle. The large zipper that ran across the top was already open.

'I'm guessing this is Joseph's bag?'

'Yep,' she nodded for the photographer to stop. They obliged. 'Any guesses what's inside?'

'I think I can hazard a guess. Small, beaky little bastards, with black and white feathers, recently used by jumped-up psychopaths to make some form of ominous messed-up message?'

She nodded.

'Thought so. But what I can't call is the number of them...' Addison knew there was a pattern he wasn't seeing. DCI Wilson opened the bag a little wider to reveal several dead faces looking back up at them.

'Magpies... seven of them.' She almost sighed as she spoke, like the number brought with it a heavy weight that pressed upon her heart.

'Seven?' Addison was stumped. All the others suggested a gender: three for a girl, four for a boy. 'I don't get it boss.'

'Sadly... I do.' DCI Wilson smiled as if being held by a warm memory. 'My mother used to recite the poem all the time. She was a superstitious old soul. Black cats, ladders, cracks in the pavement, even the smashed mirror; every single one of them held a power over her... as if anything bad that proceeded was a direct result of her breaking a rule. And, according to my dear old mother... magpies were the worst of all. I remember how she'd always salute them on sight, like some monochrome mini-Hitler. Those things bloody terrified her.'

'But they don't seem to make sense,' Addison looked to correct himself quickly before causing any offence to Wilson's presumably deceased, somewhat deluded mother. 'In this case I mean. I remember the poem from when I was a kid. But with our guy, none of it adds up.'

'How come?' DCI Wilson was still caught between their conversation and a distant memory.

'Well, when I did some digging, I found that there were three dead bird carcasses found overlooking Elizabeth Silver's residence... which tallies up... *three for a girl.* Fast-forward to Amber Costello's disappearance and we have four birds nailed to the front door. This is where the pattern breaks a little. Four is meant to represent a boy. *Four for a boy.* Right? But a girl was taken. And now that we actually have a missing boy, we're stood here being stared at by *seven* of the silver-stealing little sods. It doesn't add up. Unless that's it... the three at Elizabeth's plus the four at Amber's equals seven? I don't know.'

'No,' she was back with him. 'Well, yes it does add up to that, but that's not the link. Like all things...' she contemplated the best way of putting it, '...*superstitious...* the magpies are omens. They serve to *foretell* something bad to come. In this case, when Elizabeth was taken, the killer wasn't telling us what they'd done, they were telling us what they were going to do next. The three magpies you found didn't represent Elizabeth Silver, they represented Amber Costello.'

It all started to make sense.

'So, the three that we found at the Costello property... they stood for the next victim... the boy.'

'Joseph Farnham.' Wilson nodded towards the small rucksack. Just below the set of seven dead eyes was a small nametag stitched into the seam of the bag. The name JoJo was written in neat handwriting.

'Well, that certainly does add up.' Addison still felt like the sum was only half solved. 'But what the hell does seven mean?'

DCI Wilson started counting them out on her fingers. She already knew the answer, but she was interested to see what Addison made of it.

'Five for silver... six for gold.' She looked at Addison. 'Seven for a secret never to be told.' She watched the message register.

'This guy's showing out. He wants us to know that there's a reason to all of this madness... some twisted justification, some contorted conscience behind all of his actions. A *secret.* Never to be told. But he's telling us there is one. Is he teasing us? Or does he want us to discover it?' Addison's mind was on fire. The killer was clearly sharing a message. One that demanded acknowledgment. Addison knew the killer was showing that there was a link to all the abductions. That somehow Elizabeth Silver, Amber Costello and Joseph Farnham all held a connection to one another.

Maybe it was simple.

Maybe, they were all taken by the same person.

The winds began to whirl overhead, softly breathing life into the feathered forecast that filled the young boy's bag. Addison stared into their black eyes and felt nothing but rage.

'It gets worse.' Wilson could see the story unravel in Addison's mind.

'How?' Addison's blood carried a heat to it. He could feel it pulsing through his brain, as if it no longer needed the heart to pump it around, the fire that fuelled his head was enough alone. 'How can it possibly get any worse than this? We already have at least three missing children, and to top that off we also appear to have an innocent man locked up for an act that somebody else is clearly quite keen to continue.'

'Well, that's exactly it.' DCI Wilson ran a hand through her silver hair. It occurred to Addison that she was wearing it down, possibly in vain, on Duke's behalf. 'Whenever my dear mental matriarch would meet a magpie – as well as saluting like a maniac – she'd also say *Hello Mr Magpie, how's your wife today?*' Wilson could see in Addison's expression that he was beginning to wonder whether her mother's condition was hereditary. 'Now, stick with me on this one... Magpies mate for life. Apparently, one on its own was bad fortune as a loved one was apparently lost.'

'Okay...' Addison wondered where this was going. He hoped the wind didn't change and freeze his confused expression for good. His own mother warned him about that one.

'Well, as you know, seven is the end of the poem. There is no eight, do you understand? And it's fair to say that whomever is doing all this knows that. It's their message after all.'

'You think that's it? The seventh bird is the final secret – like there's some sort of lost tragedy to all of this?'

A small sense of relief washed over Addison. He already held little to no hope for the lives of the missing children, but he'd much rather track the breadcrumbs of a retired psychopath than the warm blood splatter of one with something left to say. 'Do you think our guy has said all that he has to? Leaving it like this for us to solve, confident that we never will.'

'No.' Her voice was firm. 'Not this time.'

Addison's heart sank. He watched Wilson as she stretched her arm out towards the school. Her finger pointed out something that Addison wished he hadn't seen. Above the fresh trail of blood that crept towards the pavement was the body of another bird. The black and white wings had been nailed to the front door like a mock crucifixion. Its body had been gutted. The small head slumped upon the sunken chest, staring at the internal organs that now hung out from its split skin.

'One more? You said it yourself, it ends at seven. There is no eight.'

'One for sorrow.' Wilson sighed. 'The seven were to signify the existence of a secret. It marked the end of them hiding something, or at least admitting that there was a reason to all this. Every ending marks a new beginning. There's every chance that now this guy has our full attention, he can start telling us what the reason is.'

'Sorrow?' Dread weighted the word as it fell from Addison's mouth.

'More than that. A single magpie is an omen of impending death. If attached to a building, it meant that anybody inside it was doomed.'

'The children?' Addison looked around. The scene lacked the urgency that he hoped he'd see if the lives of an entire school had been threatened.

'Exactly.' Wilson surveyed the scene. She could feel Addison's frustration. The sense of calm alarmed him. 'Addison, understand. Elizabeth, Amber, Joseph. None of them went to the same school. That's not the connection. If you ask me, our guy is being quite clear. He means to tell us that *all* children are doomed.'

'All of them?'

'None of them are safe. Not anymore.'

32

DCI Wilson had been true to her word.

Although he wasn't allowed to get within reach of any of the witnesses, she had forwarded Addison all the statements gathered by her squad. The majority were from school teachers, mainly offering nothing more than character references, all of them dishing up the usual generic assessment of any child Joseph's age: he was a good kid, sweet, polite, quiet, popular. To Addison, most of them read like alibis, as if their opinions could somehow distance themselves from suspicion, and any form of criticism of character was cruel and therefore deviant; *he caused me no problems, I liked him, he liked me, I wouldn't kill him, please leave me alone.* And he would. None of the teachers in this case caused Addison any concern – all of them were in class with around a dozen schoolchildren all answering morning register at the time somebody snatched Joseph.

Joseph hadn't made it into school that day.

But he'd got close.

Perched on the edge of his sofa, too tired to open up the curtains to his flat, Addison was reading the statement of the last person to see Joseph that day. There was little to glean from it. It was clear that the person providing their account could barely get past their own sense of blame and responsibility. There were no enquiries to follow up on, no opportunities to explore. Just utter grief.

Karen Farnham's initial witness statement was one shackled by a sense of shame and guilt. She held herself responsible, maybe in the same way victims try to rationalise the unnatural actions of others by wondering whether they could have done something different to stop it. A black-eye could be avoided if less questions were asked. In Karen's case, her bad timekeeping was the reason Joseph had been abducted. According to her account, she'd been running late for an important meeting. It seemed she'd been somewhat delayed by Joseph – frequently referred to as JoJo – when he'd dawdled around his bedroom instead of getting dressed. She hadn't been angry at him by all accounts, and instead had taken her time to make sure he had everything he needed. Even when stressed, she seemed to have an eye for detail – something Addison noted in case she needed to be revisited. It was remarkable what people saw once the dust had settled. Karen went on to explain how the weather had been awful that morning, and so she was going to blame any accusations of tardiness from her bosses on that. JoJo was not to blame. It would be the weather.

However, according to the grief she was now wrestling with, it was actually the weather that had caused her to make her biggest mistake. Because of the rain, she feared she'd get soaked and look a state for her meeting, which she didn't really explain. Addison noticed that under job description, the officer had scrawled the term *Media Executive*. No doubt the meeting would have been for that. In all honesty, Addison was just happy not to see the job role of 'Full-time Mum' recorded like it was some form of qualification. Granted, it took nine months to complete, when some college courses only took three, but Addison disliked how it suggested that those mothers that did work were in some way only part-time parents. Being a mum wasn't a job, it was a duty, and one Karen Farnham clearly took seriously.

And now she would be haunted by a single bad decision. According to her statement, rather than risk ruining her appearance by braving the rain, she instead let her boy walk inside on his own. She insisted that she'd waited until Joseph was out of sight before leaving, more in an attempt to distil her crushing recognition of irresponsibility rather than to offer any evidential value.

Having read the statement four times, Addison was only able to scrape a little meat to flesh out the scene. Karen Farnham's tardiness had offered a distinct timeframe for when this offence could have taken place. Granted, being on time would have possibly offered far more witnesses, maybe even prevented the event, but it would have also increased the window of opportunity for when little JoJo was abducted. It was clear that this act was not impromptu or opportunistic. It had been planned meticulously. The kidnapper was prepared and ready. Which also meant that he would have been expecting his prey to have been on time. Addison had scribbled down that Karen Farnham mentioned that a few pushbikes and a green van were the only things on the road when she parked up. Well, unless some wannabe Elliot was looking for some child to play the role of ET, Addison discarded the possibility that the kidnapper was using the bike to make children disappear. Which only left the green van. Making a quick call into the CID office, he requested the results from the CCTV trawl. He remembered the small row of shops that faced the school. Hopefully, one of their cameras would have picked up the vehicle at some point. He also asked for a copy of the witness list and whether any of the parents dropping the children off in the morning had been spoken to. It appeared they had, and initial accounts had been taken from them. None had mentioned seeing a van. But then, none of them were looking. Or at least, none of them were seeing anything different. The normal things tend to blend and fade out. Our eyes are trained to spot the obscure. Maybe the van belonged to one of the local stores and was parked there quite often. That, or maybe some scumbag got his kicks by scouting out the place before he saw his opportunity. Either way, it was a four-wheeled rock yet to be turned over. Hopefully it was a rock that Addison could pick up, run with, and ultimately use to cave some child-snatcher's face in.

His phone lit up.

Seeing the name that flashed back, he couldn't help but smile.

Piper.

That girl was something else.

'Hey,' his voice was coarser than he'd expected. He coughed to clear his throat. His coffee mug was empty, the remains of his last drink having dried out some two hours ago. The blackout blinds were pulled closed on his apartment, but he could see the sun trying to burn through. The edges glowed like framed fire.

'Hi you.' She sounded more awake than he did. 'I just wanted to see what you were up to? You disappeared from the scene yesterday. I didn't get a chance to say goodbye.'

Balls.

He'd left her there. Piper had gone to that scene with him. Having stepped across the lines of the scene-tape, Addison had completely forgotten everything that stood outside of it. It had often been a blessing, allowing him to focus on the task at hand when the rest of his life just swirled like fog around him. But it was also a curse, shifting his sight to all work and no play. It had cost him before. Loved ones, friends, family. All of them had said that they understood the role that he did, how busy he was. But none of them really understood, not truly. Eventually, having seen the worst in people, the time Addison spent alone was always taken personally by those closest to him. To those who were close enough to feel his absence, they never saw a man who was simply trying to cope, but rather a man who held no interest in them anymore. It didn't matter that he held the times they'd shared close to him like a comfort blanket, woven by memories of moments that reassured him that not all people were bad. It didn't matter that, having seen true tragedy, he often struggled to listen to people with charmed lives moan about the colossally trivial dramas that plagued their otherwise carefree existences. Their worlds appeared closed off to him, bubbled by ignorance. And he wanted it to stay that way. What he knew would blow their lives wide open, introducing them to a fear so real and resident, that they'd never feel the bliss of ignorance again. So, he removed himself, blunting his impact on those that were once his closest friends.

So, it was no surprise that he'd forgotten Piper the evening before. Although, she did seem to have a foot in both of his worlds.

'Sorry for that.' He ran his hands through his hair. It had grown heavy and dense. A few strands stuck to his sweated palms.

'It's okay.' Her tone remained breezy, light, almost chirpy. 'Fancy meeting up? Would be kind of cool to see what you saw down there. Maybe I can offer some assistance?'

'Fine,' Addison wasn't exactly sure how Piper could help, but with his Sergeant going AWOL, he could do with running the case by someone, if only to hear it all out loud.

'Cool. I can come over to yours if you like? It's not far from where I'm staying. I can pick us up a couple of coffees. It's my round, and it sounds like you could do with a java-based jumpstart.'

Almost an hour passed until she arrived. Not that he was clock-watching. He didn't need any reminders to the lack of sleep he'd had. Days had become blended into weeks now, and he'd taken enough Pro-plus to set a dead man's pulse racing.

'Knock knock,' she was halfway through the door as he turned to greet her. 'Not very safe of you to keep the door open like that... any old maniac could just walk right in.'

He laughed.

'By all means, send them my way. I could do with finding one twisted son-of-a-bitch in particular; he has a penchant for young children, nails dead birds to buildings. Do you know him?'

Her smirk was playful. Intentionally cute.

'Sounds like a catch.' She handed Addison the coffee. It was red-hot. She'd balanced some fancy pastry on top of it. Small flecks of dusted sugar coated her fingers. She licked it off as she spoke. 'Any further forward with this guy? I mean, what did the scene back at the school tell you?'

He waited until she'd finished with her finger food. If she wasn't aware of what she was doing, then she was a natural flirt. Probably even got her into trouble a few times. There was a thin angry line between a guy misreading a signal and his ego. No doubt some morons flattered themselves into thinking she was keen, only to feel crushed when she rejected them.

'Well,' he took a small sip of coffee, trying his hardest to style out the fact it had just scorched his tongue. 'What I do know is that this is far from over. Joseph Farnham, eight years old, who was last seen by his mother when she dropped him off to school, was soon replaced by a bagful of murdered magpies, with one ceremoniously crucified against the main entrance to the school.'

'Shit,' her eyebrows climbed the small space that was her forehead, tucking themselves under a short sharp fringe. 'Any leads? Links, patterns? Surely, this guy is picking his targets for a reason.'

'Yeah he is. But there doesn't seem to be a type... girls, boys, all different in terms of appearance. If there's a sexual element to this, then either this guy is an animal who just likes them young, or there's something much larger that I'm missing.'

'Well, if you ask me...'

'I didn't.' He smiled, before braving another drink from the overpriced molten lava she'd served him.

'Well...' she raised a finger in front of his mouth. 'If you were kind enough to seek my counsel, I'd say that this thing wasn't sexual in the slightest.'

Part of him questioned whether she was still talking about the case. Maybe that was a half-message to him.

Keep it professional.

'Go on...' He leaned back in his chair. Maybe the distance would show her he wasn't in this for anything more than a soundboard. Whether that soundboard happened to be the most attractive, intriguing person he'd met for some time, was neither here nor there.

'Correct me if I'm wrong, but if this was sexual, wouldn't the guy be more... rash? More prone to impulse? Couple that with the recent frequency, and timing of it all, and I don't think that this is some frenzied fetish. Whoever this is, they're doing it for a reason. Whatever kind of twisted logic they may be applying, it's with purpose. The magpies, the fact it coincides with the Benjamin Farrow review... there's a message in there somewhere. You see, the sexual deviants, they don't tend to sign off their work quite like this guy does.'

She was right. Everything she said had already been noted by Addison. As gruesome as the fact would have been, part of him wanted this guy to be perverted. The motive would have been clear, traceable. But this guy was different. There was no ignoring that.

'So, what's the pattern?'

He watched her mull it over. He'd already let her read what DCI Wilson had shared with him.

'I'm not sure. I've tracked quite a few missing children cases in my time, and none of them share the characteristics of this one. Each of the cases are linked... that's clear. But the rest isn't. Ironically, they're so distinct in how dissimilar they are to the usual abduction cases that I've seen before. Most of those tended to be somebody who knew the child, or the family at least. There tends to be a clear connection between the victim and their abductor; a clear line of access. But there's nothing to connect these kids or their families to each other. Looking over the statement you gave me, it seems the Farnhams were a young, professional couple, looking to raise a family. They were obviously keen to have a child because they seem quite young to adopt. Maybe there's a medical reason for them not being able to have one of their own, it's not clear. But you don't take on a commitment like that unless you really give a damn about the child's welfare.'

'Excuse me?' Something popped in his mind. 'What did you just say?'

'Oh...' she looked a little flustered. 'I wasn't taking the piss. That wasn't a jab at the mother making Joseph walk alone. I was serious when I said I admired Karen Farnham's commitment to being a mother.'

'No, not that...' he rubbed his brow. 'Well, actually... yeah... exactly that. Mainly the part about the adoption. Are you telling me Joseph Farnham was adopted?'

'Don't shoot the messenger,' she leaned back from the statement with her hands raised, as if she had been caught red-handed. 'I'm just repeating what it says in the statement. Or at least hints at. The part where Karen Farnham is referring to JoJo's settling-in period, and how he's adjusting to their home. The electoral records put the Farnhams living at their current address for the last six years. That's more than enough time for their son to *settle in*.' She did the bunny ears with her fingers. 'So, I gathered she was talking about the family unit as a whole.'

'Balls,' he looked impressed. 'That had slipped me by. We may have something here. Amber Costello was passed around households like some seasonal toy; fun at first, but with a short shelf-life. Poor girl had had her dreams crushed half a dozen times before the Costellos came along. Are you saying JoJo had the same thing?'

'No idea,' she looked a little distant as she spoke. 'Each case is different, I guess.'

'Well it's the clearest link we've had so far.' He stood with a sense of urgency that betrayed the fatigue that framed his face. 'Come on, get your coat.'

'Ooh,' she winked. 'Have I pulled already?'

'Sadly not.' He smiled. 'I've got a date with another woman.'

'Really?'

'Yeah,' Addison was heading for the door before he stopped, and turned to usher Piper out. 'I need to speak with Beverly Silver. I think she forgot to tell us something.'

Chapter 33

The Silver address was as he remembered it. Quaint, discrete, seemingly tucked away from the media frenzy that surrounded it once more. With the case review of Benjamin Farrow and the recent disappearances, the Elizabeth Silver case had once again become a topic of daily media musing; around the clock news channels reported 'breaking news' on almost any minor development or leak, whilst loose-lipped basement-level celebrities from various unrelated and uninformed backgrounds offered their *specialist* opinion, sandwiched between tea, biscuits and the stapled dose of generic hate-mob motivated gossip. There was poison everywhere. Towards the police, towards the killer; even the victims' families were under scrutiny. To the neutral observer, everybody was culpable, everybody had an angle, the lack of evidence was too damning for those close to the case to not be involved. And so, nobody was who they presented themselves to be. Simple facts were boring, predictable. Instead, the public had begun to present conspiracies, tales of police corruption and family cover-ups. They couldn't just accept the facts as they were laid out. Benjamin Farrow couldn't just be guilty. The Silvers had something to do with all this. Maybe Elizabeth wasn't even dead. To some, her death had become tedious, a dull tale with no twist or scandal. Opinions became theories, and these theories only held any value if they were twisted, often suggesting a conclusion that nobody had considered before.

But the facts remained the same. All things had been considered. And the police had caught their man. Now, they just had to do it all over again.

Addison still hadn't heard from Duke. Almost two whole days had passed since he'd had the pleasure of listening to his Sergeant's controversial rantings. He almost missed the mad bastard. Almost. Addison had to admire the force behind the man's conviction, it always countered any doubts that ever rose towards the original investigation. But now that he was absent all that remained were unanswered questions. One of which, Addison was just about to ask for himself.

He hadn't been able to shake Piper off, so he'd allowed her to come along for the show.

He knocked on the door as Piper stood next to him, straightening herself up a little. If he didn't know her, he'd say she was coming across a little nervous.

True to form, Beverly casually opened the door, looking like she had been caught in the middle of filming a bakery show. A small apron, dusted by flour and sugar, clung to the bottom of her colourful summer dress. Her blond hair was pinned back with a small clip decorated with a painted metal daisy. She smiled and wiped her hands on her apron before welcoming her guests inside.

'DC Clarke,' she almost breathed the words as she was half-panting as she spoke. 'I apologise for the state you find me in. The church is running its annual springtime bake sale and – of course – I've promised to help out.' She feigned the appearance of a fool, as if she'd let herself in for something way over her head.

The welcoming smell of fresh cakes suggested otherwise.

'Please, come in. How can I help you today?' Her tone was a thin attempt at casual. It was clear that she was accepting any interruption to her day that came her way. No doubt the recent events would have invited old ghosts to visit, and maybe a few fresh faces would scare them away. Problem was, Addison had brought a shovel, and was hell-bent on doing a little digging of his own.

'Just thought we'd call in. See how you were doing. We were just passing by.' Addison gestured towards a coy-looking Piper before realising that he'd failed to offer an introduction. 'Mrs Silver, this is a friend of mine. Piper...'

'Piper Thomas. Pleasure to meet you, Ma'am.' Piper flashed out a hand and held Beverly's with the other as they shook hands briefly. 'I hope you don't mind me being here. I'm simply accompanying Addison... forgive me... DC Clarke, with his enquiries.'

Piper offered an awkward smile as she felt Beverly's inquisitive gaze upon her. It was clear the woman seemed puzzled, almost put off by Piper's presence. She continued to scan her face curiously as she spoke to Addison.

'Not a problem at all.' Her focus remained still locked on Piper. 'Like I said before, please come in. Anyone for tea?'

What was that?

Addison couldn't help but notice the awkward exchange. Did they know each other? Had Piper already been here before, simply adding to the countless reporters that had preyed on Beverly when she was at her weakest? He didn't think so. Although, Piper didn't exactly volunteer her information, and there was no mention of her profession when she introduced herself. Why did she pretend she was his associate? Why hide who you are? Maybe it was just so that Addison could gain access to the place. No doubt Beverly Silver's guard would have been raised if she knew another reporter had entered the house; another scavenger sniffing around for scraps. Or, the awkwardness could simply be that Beverly didn't like the look of Piper. There was always that possibility. Beverly – traditional and the picture-book version of a middle-class mother – simply didn't like the *alternative* appearance of Piper. It hadn't escaped Addison that Piper, with her feathered hair and boyish attire, was one of those girls who would state that she always found it easier to get on with boys rather than her female peers. Guys, though misguided and wholly inaccurate, tended to call them ladettes, whilst girls just called them bitches. Either way, Addison made a note to google his new friend Ms Thomas when he returned to the office.

The cup of tea had been accompanied by a slice of lemon drizzle cake and a short anecdote from Beverly about how her estranged husband, Steven, would have seen their sweet treat as a plated cardio session and a thousand push-ups. Addison remembered the reference from when he first visited with Duke. After a few polite smiles, it took Piper to ask the natural follow-on message.

'So, where is Steven these days? Do you still hear from him?' She took a small nibble at her cake in an attempt to act casual, like the question wasn't a complete intrusion into a clearly sensitive subject. Beverly appeared unfazed. Rehearsed almost. No doubt she'd been asked the same thing a thousand times over, so she'd had her story straight for some time.

'Truth be known, I have no idea what place that man is in right now. He had his form of coping, and I had mine. What with Elizabeth not being from our blood and all... maybe we didn't really need one another to get past it. Is grief genetically linked? It sure doesn't feel that way. I'm guessing that's why you're really here today.' She looked at Addison. 'I've seen the recent spate of abductions in the news. I saw the same pattern as I imagine you have. Both of the children have been taken from adopted families, and you wanted to know whether it was the same with Elizabeth and us. Well, DC Clarke... it is. But that doesn't mean the man who took my girl wasn't caught.'

The air felt cold, almost sharp. Outside, the sun was shining, blazing through the high hedgerows, but the light that broke past now felt like shards of ice upon Addison's skin.

'Steven and I found out that we couldn't have children of our own. We'd tried for years, but it never took. For whatever reason, Steven felt responsible. Like he'd failed me somehow. But in truth, we didn't really know why we couldn't. And we refused to find out, medically I mean. It didn't feel right to know... to see where the issue sat. We were a couple and that was that. For a while Steven wondered whether it was God punishing us, on account of him being Jewish and me Catholic. But I don't believe any god would do such a thing. The cause was medical, not spiritual. We couldn't have children the natural way, that's all. I still loved him, he loved me, and we wanted a family... together. So, after months of classes and countless checks on the type of people we are, we got the nod. Elizabeth was the first girl we'd seen. Instantly, we knew. Her mother, a young girl in care herself, had died during childbirth, and there was no other known family around. There was no record whatsoever of her real father; nobody had stepped forward, even after Elizabeth's birth-mother had died. Nobody wanted the responsibility. That pulled on Steven. And from that moment on, he couldn't let the thought of the young girl go. She was the one. She needed him. And now he needs her.'

'I have to say Mrs Silver...' Addison spoke in a soothing tone.

'Beverly... please. I always feel like I'm in trouble when you call me Mrs Silver. Sounds too official.' Her smile was genuine.

'Well, Beverly, I have to admit, there is a striking physical resemblance between you and Elizabeth. You really could be her family.'

'We *are* her family.' She allowed her temper to simmer before carrying on. 'But you are right. We did look alike. But that was just pure luck. Steven and I adopted Elizabeth when she was a few months old and still just a bald bundle of joy. We had no idea what she would look like. Yet it did help somewhat when she turned out looking like she was a mixture of both of us. Not that it would have mattered to us, but at least it stopped the questions from others. Thankfully, Elizabeth never had to feel any *different* from us. If that's the best way of putting it.'

'She never knew any different.' Piper spoke solemnly, as if the story resonated with her. 'That's a blessing for a girl her age. I have no doubt she felt loved... cared for... valued.'

'She did,' Beverly practically cut Piper off. 'She also felt protected. But that didn't stop some creep breaking into our home and taking her away from us. Did it?'

A heavy hush hung over them all. There was no worth in refuting what she had said. No matter what theory you accepted, the fact remained: somebody took the young girl. And that somebody had never given her back.

'And before you raise the question of whether Mr Farrow was responsible, don't bother. In my eyes... he did it. We both know the courts didn't get to hear the half of it.' Somewhere in the background, a small beeper rang out. The homely scent of bread began to fill the air. 'I don't need another group of people to look over the evidence. There's nothing fresh to consider. And, no disrespect to yourself Addison, there's no point looking over what the police did. I know all about their good work as I do their mistakes. The DNA, for example. A catastrophe yes, but it's conclusive enough for me. I've learned to live with it.'

Piper looked confused. Like she was being told something new. Addison noted it.

'You know about that?' He turned his attention back to Beverly.

'Of course.' She paused, as if considering what she should say next. 'The police messed up. But it was an honest mistake.'

'Excuse me,' Piper sounded meek in her approach. 'But what do you mean, DNA?'

'It would appear she's not a cop after all.' Beverly nodded in the direction of Piper. 'Young lady, everybody in the department knows about the error. After all, it almost destroyed the entire case. But I can't blame the officer for simply trying to do their job. It wasn't them that climbed through my window and stole my daughter. I don't care that they forgot to bag up the evidence correctly... that they spoke with Benjamin Farrow at some point along the way. All that matters is what they found. A sample of hair, belonging to the abductor, inside my daughter's bedroom. Hair belonging to Benjamin Farrow. That man was in my house that night. No failed procedure can remove that fact.'

'Crap.' Piper spoke under her breath, looking down to the floor. Her entire body language seemed to melt away, as if she was leaving the conversation to be elsewhere in her head.

'I understand,' Addison meant it. 'Sergeant Parker only told me the facts recently. I guess it's quite frustrating holding something like that back from everybody else. I still have a job to do. And trust me, I'm not looking to get someone off on a technicality. In our line of work, it's always easier to know something than being able to prove it. All that I'm doing is making sure that if we have our man, then we haven't left any doors open for him to walk out of.'

Beverly smiled softly.

'I know.' Her voice was warm. 'And I know it must be confusing now that these two other children have gone missing. The connections must seem so clear, what with the similar backgrounds and all? I can't deny that there has to be something in the care home link. There simply has to be.'

'Hang on...' Addison was confused. 'I thought you were certain that they were separate, that Benjamin Farrow was guilty.'

'I am, and he is. But there's no ignoring the fact that all of those involved have come from care homes. Elizabeth, the two children taken recently, even Mr Farrow himself. That swine would often talk to Elizabeth about their shared backgrounds, not that she could relate in any way whatsoever, given how young she was when we adopted her. But he somehow knew about Elizabeth's upbringing, even that of her biological mother. He said that they'd experienced the same things – asked themselves the same questions – and if Elizabeth ever wanted to know more, he was there for her to talk to.'

'Hold on... Farrow knew Elizabeth was from the care system? Why didn't I know this?' Addison looked from Beverly to Piper, shocked that neither of them saw the significance that was slapping him across the face like some enormous, overlooked motive. He felt the hairs on his arms reach for the skies. He wasn't sure when he'd made the move, but he was now standing up and walking towards the door.

'Mrs Silver... forgive me... I mean, Beverly...' A sense of urgency was pulling his mind away from where he was. He was already keying in DCI Wilson's number as he opened the front door. 'It appears I have some work to do. Piper, are you coming?'

It was more of an order than a question. It was clear to all that Piper had overstayed her welcome after about two footsteps inside the property.

'Thanks again for the tea and cakes. I'll need the energy boost for what I've got planned. It looks as though I've got a whole lot of digging to do.'

Luckily, he'd already brought his shovel with him.

Chapter 34

He hadn't kept the boy locked up for too long. He'd always hated it when they'd done that to him. No, he was kinder than his former keepers, he ended the boy's misery early.

He cried too much.

Part of him was glad that the screaming had stopped. The sound always dragged him back to a place when all the pain belonged to him. A time when he wasn't strong enough to fight back. He had found friends back then and he didn't want them to get hurt because of the things he did. It became their code. They all had their own paths, their own goals, their own demons to destroy.

Or embrace.

It was really a matter of perspective. His was clear – he captured what had been taken from him, a youth stolen in its prime, when all that existed was innocence. That was his ambition, to give children eternal innocence. He didn't know what exactly his friends' ambitions were, but he'd heard that they'd had achieved some success at least. Back when they were children, his friends protected him from their abusers. He missed them dearly. His friends that is. Not the adults that had hurt them all. No, they were still out there acting as though they were decent folk. Acting like they didn't beat, kick, kiss or rape the children they were employed to take care of. They'd made the monster he'd become. If that's what he was – a monster. He didn't see it that way. If anything, he was an angel, freeing the children before they were stolen, liberating them from a life of make-believe. Their new families didn't truly care for them, how could they? All they offered them was a lie, an act of acceptance that only painted over the utter abandonment from which they had all come.

He missed his friends. The first, they had done together. The rest, he'd done alone, with some guidance. Each of them had their reasons; their justification for what they were doing. But in the end, it all boiled down to the same thing – freedom. All of them wanted to be free from what had happened to them. And whatever road they had chosen to take, be it bloody, sheltered or masked, he was certain they would all find their way.

He was close to his end. He hoped they were too.

At some point, the small boy's back had been broken. It had been a mistake, but not one he couldn't work with. When he emptied the boy's rucksack, he'd found a few action figurines inside. The boy clearly had his heroes.

I wonder if he'd call me his hero?

Looking at the toys, the largest of them wore a long cape, presumably to help him fly. He liked that. He liked how life was captured in motion. This had given him an idea for where to place the boy. The playful scene that he had been slaving over was now all set. Countless hours had been poured into every nail, every piece of wood and every lick of paint that had been used to build his playground. Artificial turf had been laid down to replace real grass, as no sunlight had been allowed to find its way inside. He didn't want the world outside ruining his creation. The large replica house that he had built was solely from a stolen memory, and only a fraction of the size of the one in which his nightmares had begun. Now it served as a mere background to the joy that was played out before it. The joy of youth.

Seeing how happy the others had been made to look, he considered where he would frame the small boy. His skin had already been removed and treated the same way as the others. The parts of him that would have rotten away had all been discarded. His flesh had been filled, and his bones had been polished. The brightness of the boy's once blue eyes could not be matched by any of the glass marbles that he often used to replace them, but that was a small compromise for the way in which the boy would now forever appear.

The scene demanded movement. Or a sense of it at least. Within it, joy lived forever. It was movement that freed us all, the sense that no shackles could keep us where we did not belong. He remembered running when he was a child. Running deep into the woods with his friends, wherein they all played and laughed, ignoring their inevitable return to where they slept, to where they meant to rest, but were taken, shackled and broken. He remembers the last time that he ran. The way the darkness held him, the way the cold night air melted against the fire that burned from his chest, and the way the moonlight coloured the blood that covered his body.

He walked to the side of the room, near to where an old crank and winch connected a thin wire to a set of makeshift children's swings that sat on the opposite side of the scene. He had already placed the boy upon the wooden seat of the swing, driving a thick nail through each thigh to make sure he stayed in his place. His hands had been tightly fastened to the ropes, having stitched the skin of each finger into the fabric. But the look wasn't complete. Right now, the boy's body sagged, slumped upon the seat, lifeless, with no sign of motion. Wrapping his long fingers around the crank, he felt the cold brush of rust within his palms. Slowly, he wound the crank until the wire began to tighten. With each turn of the winch the wire pulled, lifting the seat of the swing towards the sky. Feeling the line become taught, and the gears begin to grind to a halt, he locked it in place.

The boy looked magnificent. His darkened eyes stared towards the heavens above, his arms locked, stretched out high in front of him, as his feet dangled below. The smile he had woven into the boy's cheeks was one of sheer joy. Upon his shoulders clung a dark red cape, which he had made for the boy as a gift. It didn't match the memory, but even memories rippled in the mind, distorting reality. The boy could have his deviation. The fabric fell downwards, in the opposite direction to the boy's flight, completing the look. At the very top of his ascent, the boy looked truly alive.

Motion breeds emotion.

Admiring his collection, he smiled at the scene that he had created. The playground had become full of life, full of joy and freedom from the terrors that sat behind it. But there was always room for more.

Outside, the shutting of a steel trap brought with it a short, sharp squawk. A smile slithered across his face.

'One for sorrow.'

Freedom has its price.

Chapter 35

He felt the hand on his shoulder at exactly the same time as the knife going into his side. Pain exploded, forcing his legs forward and arching his back.

Focus.

His attacker was left-handed. The thin trembling fingers of their right hand dug into his shoulder as the blade began to drag towards the lower part of his spine. Stood before him were a group of prisoners, all smiling, almost laughing at his agony. Their smug faces were all he could see. That, and the five frail fingers he was about to break.

Taking hold of his attacker's hand, he was surprised how easily the wrist snapped when he twisted it towards him. The bone left the joint with a satisfying *pop*. The scream that followed echoed along the corridor, bouncing off the cold concrete walls and dumbing down the stupid grins that sat upon the faces of his audience. The knife was still inside him, tucked nicely behind his lower rib. He needed to leave it there, he'd bleed out otherwise.

His attacker must have struck him across the head at some point, or scratched him at least. Blood now streamed from his scalp, masking his face. It was nothing more than a mere graze, but the head always liked to exaggerate an injury. The fresh blood flowed down the creases of his scarred skin, pooling in the jagged ridge that split his upper lip in two. Droplets tapped on his thick lower lip that hung loose above a slack jaw.

Pain gripped his body.

Don't let them see what hurts you.

The crowd had begun to disperse. A few guards had arrived, pumped-up and flustered by the adrenaline that action demanded. Somebody must have pressed the alarm as the pulse of the claxon beat at his head. One of the guards clubbed his attacker until his body lay still.

Another brought his baton crashing down across Seth's bloodied face.

Then the lights went out.

*

When his eyes finally adjusted to the bright white lights, he recognised where he was. It was the same room that he had dragged Benjamin's lifeless body to some several months before.

The pillows that hugged his back were little relief to the wound that perched somewhere between healing and hurting. Sometimes, they were the same thing. At least they were both there. Only hurt ever came alone; there was no guarantee that healing would follow. The nurse who had no doubt saved his life had made sure she had done a rough job of it. There was no point being pretty about procedures in this prison. The sad-sacks of human waste that resided here only needed sewing up whenever they had been torn open. There was nothing correctional about the process at all. Soon enough they'd each fill their battered bodies up with the countless sins that suited them. There was no point keeping procedures clean, no need to waste stiches when a blunt staple would do, no need to offer clean dressings, when the bloodied rags that had been ripped from his body would do the job.

He could smell the scent of the clotted blood on the strips that were now wrapped around his head. The flow of blood had been stemmed, and the broken flesh of his back had been bolted together like Frankenstein's monster. Whatever painkillers he had been given had worn off, and the pain that followed was probably the reason he had woken up. That, and the fact that there was a man talking quite casually next to him.

'Morning champ.' Benjamin's voice was one of friendly familiarity. 'How's the head doing? Sounds like that guard caught you a cracker across that messed-up melon of yours.'

'There goes my modelling contract...' Seth stopped himself from laughing as the muscles in his back tensed, causing a bolt of agony to run down both of his legs. At least he could feel them, he thought. The blade had come pretty close to his spinal column; one more inch or so and he could have been seeing his time out in a wheelchair. And he wasn't exactly sure this place was handicap-friendly.

'What the hell happened?' Benjamin moved out of sight, somewhere towards the only window in the ward. 'Why would someone want to attack you?'

'Believe me... it's not the first time someone has hurt me. I've been cut way deeper than that. But I always hurt them back. Twice as hard, and ten times slower.'

'Exactly!' Benjamin had picked something up. Seth could hear the clunk of something heavy lift from the windowsill. His friend continued to talk.

'Every time someone has attacked you – or had the balls to even try – they've come off worse. So why do they bother trying?'

'Really?' Seth looked around the ward. 'I don't see anyone keeping me company.'

'Trust me… that guy who attacked you… he's hurting. From what I heard, they had to rush him off to the local A&E. Word is, they may not even be able to repair that wrist you shattered.'

'Well, forgive me for not being sorry. The son-of-a-bitch can still shank with his strong hand. He was a leftie. I broke his right wrist. Who knows, maybe he can still find use for the bust one… it'll just feel like someone else's when he's having a cheeky shank.'

'Ha! Maybe he should thank you.'

'I doubt he's feeling grateful.'

The sound of liquid being poured entered his left ear. Benjamin came into sight with a plastic cup and a large jug of water. He poured a little into Seth's mouth, but the majority got swallowed up by the dry cuts that decorated his split lips. Standing back a little, it surprised Benjamin just how quickly he had become used to the grotesque appearance of his friend. He was like the unmasked Phantom. Half of his skin was scorched and marbled. His hair nothing but loose remains of wisps and dry scalp. And the scar that cut his face in two, blinding his one eye, and cutting his lip so that the few remnants of teeth were on permanent display, seemed to suit him somehow. Benjamin had almost grown accustomed to his fiendish features, no matter how monstrous they were. And Benjamin knew more than most, that when you were in hell, monsters made great friends.

'Who the hell are you staring at?' Seth tried to sit up. He felt vulnerable with Benjamin stood over him. 'Stop flirting with me and pass me that water.'

Benjamin did as he was told. Which was a first. Often he was the one giving the orders, pulling the strings. Pausing, he allowed the image of Monica's naked body to wash over him. He didn't miss her. But he loved the way she looked at him, eyes wide open; as innocent as she was naïve. She'd made a big mistake with him. A mistake he planned to help her repeat whenever he could get his hands on her.

Seth felt like he'd swallowed nettles. The cold water cut through the jagged edges of his throat. Had one of the guards squeezed his neck as he hit him? He allowed the agony to pass before speaking again.

'Thanks for the drink. I don't suppose you have anything a little stronger?'

'Are you kidding me?' Benjamin offered a smile. It appeared genuine. 'What's stronger than you around here? You're invincible! People are starting to talk about you as if you're some demon or…'

'Monster?'

'I was thinking more Angel of Retribution.' Benjamin laughed as he refilled his own cup with water. 'I mean, how many times have Jenkins' boys had a pop at you, and yet you still live to tell the tale? Not only that, they end up worse off. That's unheard of.'

'Doesn't really feel like surviving from where I'm sat. And I wouldn't credit any of those creeps in my story. They're simply extras, making up the numbers in the background. I've got enough history to haunt a thousand lifetimes. I don't require any cameos from those cavemen. And as for me being the undead… well, you better hope I keep resurfacing because the second those boys bury me, Jenkins will be coming for you alone. Now I don't for a moment flatter myself with thinking that I'm the single object of his affection. It's all about you.' He tried another swig of the water, it tasted like sharpened glass. 'As for me? I'm just an ugly obstacle that your admirers keep tripping over.'

'Don't I know it!'

For a moment he looked frightened, but then he put his face back on. The face he wore to everybody in here. He had many, for all environments, all built for survival. The one he wore on the inside belonged to a defiant fool, a man with no idea how deep he was under.

Seth's throat scratched as he spoke.

'They're getting brave – almost bold. To attack me in broad daylight, with a weapon. That took some balls and planning. Jenkins has mobilised his mob, and they come tooled up. How did he manage to get hold of that?'

Benjamin smiled and nodded to a small steel counter that stood by the side of Seth's hospital bed. On it sat a small, stale uneaten sandwich and a napkin. Benjamin saw the confusion that crawled across his friend's face.

'Ignore the sandwich. Probably do more harm than good anyway. That was just some poor excuse for a lunch. Forget that. I think you'll have more of an appetite for what's under the napkin.' He looked to the doorway to check that the place was clear before performing the big reveal like some low-rent magician.

'Tadaa!' He whisked the napkin away from the counter.

There, sat upon the steel plate was a bloodied piece of steel, roughly sharpened and strapped amateurishly to what looked like a small part of a wooden chair leg. It was around six inches long, four of which had recently been dragged through Seth's own flesh.

'How did you get that?' Seth couldn't take his eyes away from the cell-made shank.

'Well, earlier, when they were operating on you – being the concerned friend that I am – I couldn't help but burst into the ward. So overcome with emotion was I that I proved quite the distraction to the nurses working on you. So much so, they didn't even see me pull the weapon from out of your back! Luckily, the pool of blood that then burst from the wound kept them occupied enough for me to palm that little beauty and slide right on out of there.'

'I could have died!'

'Calm down. Technically, you already *were* dying. That's what the nurses were there to deal with. That blade over there was coming out either way, and the blood with it. It didn't matter who had a hand on it, really. What matters more, is that we now have a hold of it.'

Benjamin seemed really pleased with himself, completely ignorant of the risks he had flirted with. And whilst Seth was far from the forgiving type, he already had one use in mind for his new toy.

'Oh, I forgot to mention...' Benjamin went out of view briefly before returning with a small vase of flowers. He placed the bunch of closed-cup lilies onto the small table that ran along the end of Seth's bed. 'The nurses got you these. Personally, I'm not sure lilies were the wisest choice, given their affiliation with death and all, but maybe they didn't know you like I do. They probably thought you weren't going to make it.'

'How sweet. Not a bad choice really.'

'Really?' Benjamin looked displeased, as if the flowers pushed out a scent that left a bitter taste in his mouth. 'Flowers annoy me. They're for the dead alone. Especially lilies like these ones. Look at them, closed, dull, lifeless, selfishly demanding our attention until they allow us to briefly see them in their full beauty. Like I said, they annoy me... up to a point, that is. A friend once explained to me that it's not until they're dying that we see any true life in them at all. The moment they open up, they're already taking their last breath. And, for me, that's the only time when they hold any value – any purpose. Stupidly, we cherish what we see, hoping that it will last forever. But it's already too late. We stand in idle adulation as we watch the life slowly leak out of them. So, that's why flowers are for the dead. It's because we only recall what was beautiful once it begins to leave us; the pain of mourning always outweighs the joy of having it in the first place. Watching those flowers accept their fate – when they show their true colours – is probably the finest moment we can share with them.'

Seth watched Benjamin grow more fascinated with the flowers in front of him. His eyes were glazed over by some distant image, some far-off memory of a loss not quite forgotten. Seth watched him the entire time. Making note of everything he was doing. His eyes didn't shift.

He watched Benjamin the entire time.

Especially whilst Seth slipped the shank into own pocket.

Chapter 36

'And you don't think that's important?'

'It certainly wasn't overlooked.'

'So, what was it then... discounted? Discredited? Forgotten?'

Addison was almost out of line.

'DC Clarke,' her voice was stern, almost blunt. 'Your role is one of a consultancy basis – based solely on your current case review alone, and any potential crossovers therein. If you happen to have found anything pertinent, then please feel free to refer this information to our team. Otherwise, I order you to leave your opinions regarding our conduct at the door, as you not only show yourself out of my office, but of this entire investigation.'

DCI Wilson had every right to kick him out of the enquiry. After all, all he was doing was looking over the Benjamin Farrow case and making sure there hadn't been any local cock-ups. He'd already entered this town under a cloud, and with the media looking to shake up a storm with the missing children story, Addison Clarke's little rain dance was nothing more than an unwelcome gust of hot air blowing in from where he was standing. It shook nobody, and guided no one. It barely even kicked up old leaves.

But he couldn't care less.

The incident room was a small office, set away from those shared by other units. The clichéd corkboard had recently been replaced by a stained whiteboard, cluttered by several photos, all connected by thick lines of removable marker pen. It was easier to hide your mistakes that way. Or just plain erase them.

'Ma'am, with all due respect, I'm just making sure I've got this all clear in my head. Beverly Silver said her daughter, Elizabeth, often spoke with Benjamin Farrow about their similar upbringings. Turns out, they were both from care homes. Then suddenly, whilst Farrow hits the headlines due to his possible release, even more kids go missing – all from care homes. There has to be a link. There just has to be.'

'And how might you think that could be?' Her voice remained sterile; no heat, no frosty bite, just the sting that comes from cleaning an open wound. 'I seriously doubt your friend Farrow is orchestrating all this from the inside.'

'He's no friend of mine.' Addison thought about the last real friend he'd had. The way they'd laughed, shared stories, made plans. The way they could always just pick up from where they left off, no matter how long it had been since they'd last seen each other. The way he'd looked that day, their last day. The way he'd been banned from attending the funeral. The way he missed him more than anything else.

'What is he then? A criminal mastermind, a child-killer, or just some poor misunderstood fool who found himself at the wrong place at the wrong time, stealing the wrong girl.'

'The girl was the right one...' Addison could feel the blood starting to surface. 'All the facts from the latest kidnappings show clear links. Similar age ranges, backgrounds, not long adopted. All these kids had managed to beat the system – they had got out. And now, for whatever reason, somebody is dragging them back in. So, yes Ma'am, they got the right girl. I just don't know if we got the right guy.'

'Oh... we fucking got him all right.'

The man's voice was more refreshing than the stale statement.

Duke.

'You're alive then?' Addison tried to act casual, but inside he was a mess of mixed emotions. Worry, anger, suspicion, all swirled around beneath the overriding feelings of joy and relief. The man always made an impact, and Addison loved that about him.

'For now.' His voice waivered for a fraction. Nobody noticed. 'I had a few things I needed to address... which I did... and now I'm done. So, DC Clarke, consider me firmly back in the frame. And whilst I'm in said frame, the picture I plan to paint is one that captures the pure essence of me knocking some sense back into your stupid overworked brain.'

Duke twirled a lollipop stick around as he entered the middle of the room. Motion always seemed to bring with it emotion, and Duke loved to walk and talk. The man always performed perfectly. But this time, it was no act.

'Just doing my job... nothing more.'

'Really? Is that right? Your *job*.' He paused and glanced at Addison through a slanted head. 'Because from what my spies seem to be telling me, you've also been doing a little bit of freelance romance on the side. Apparently, you've been flashing with a flasher.' His face blended rage with concern. 'What did I tell you about journalists? Danger, my friend.

Danger. But balls to all that. Forget what the old owl tells you. I'm only out of the way for a few minutes and already you're both flashing away at each other. You flash your badge, she flashes a smile – amongst other things no doubt – and just like that... you think you've unearthed some major scoop. Ever pause to think how this new friend of yours might be making all this work for her?'

'Piper?' Her name fell out of his mouth like it had been clinging to the tip of his tongue.

'First-name terms I see... strictly professional, I'm sure. Of course. Don't get me wrong, she's attractive in that broken, edgy, more issues than the *Beano* kind of vibe. Just not my type. In all honesty, I prefer the more straight forward, drama-free, less stab-you-in-the-back-the-second-I've-got-my-scoop kind of girls.'

'Really? I'll be sure that she's seated when I break the news to her.' Addison knew he'd fallen for Duke's test. The man had probed him, gone under his skin and prodded around, looking for any raw nerve endings, and like a fool, he'd shown out. It was true, he was intrigued by Piper. But maybe it was just loneliness talking.

'Have you finished your reunion yet boys?' DCI Wilson took ownership of the room in an instant. 'Honestly, I enjoyed your thrilling game of cock-conkers, I really did, but if you hadn't noticed, we have several missing children, and I plan on finding them.'

'Of course Ma'am... just establishing the hierarchy. Chain of command and all.' Duke put on his most humble smile. 'Just tell me what shit you're dealing with and I'll make sure that when it rolls on down the hill, my boy Addison here doesn't step in it and leave a stink wherever he treads.'

It took her only a couple of minutes to bring Duke up to speed. That was something that all the good tree-toppers had: the ability to summarise. Brief, but informative, with a shit-filter set to the tightest degree.

Once briefed, and DCI Wilson had begun to task out her team of investigators, Duke and Addison took their cue to leave. Outside the sun had begun to set, washing the sky in a burnt orange shade. It was the first time Duke's skin seemed to hold any colour.

'Are you all right, Sarge?' Addison spoke as a friend.

'God knows.' Duke tossed his lollipop stick into the bin. 'I've been called all kinds of wrong in the past, but rarely right. Trust me.' His eyes defied his smile as he spoke. 'I know I'm right on this case. I know it. I knew it from the start. And so did everybody else. Well, they did at first. Yet now, every bastard with a spare brain cell seems to be wasting it on conjuring up theories and countless cock-sure conspiracies. But it's all bollocks. One day, over all this twisted mess, I'll lose my mind.

And despite the relief that that may bring, it would still be nice to know that when I do go – full throttle into oblivious oblivion – then at least one of my last sober thoughts would be that I got it right. That I hadn't let little Elizabeth down.'

'Who's saying you have?'

'Nobody that matters. But the doubts aren't just creeping in anymore. Instead, they've now booted down the door, urinated all over my name, and beat me to the ground with a rolled-up case review with Farrow's name written in bold just so it hurts more.' He chucked a piece of chewing gum into his mouth. It was a few exaggerated chews before he offered Addison one.

'No thanks.' Addison shifted from one foot to the other, and back again. Looking at his friend, he could see a realisation etched into his face. An expression perched right on the very edge of defeat. But he wasn't about to let Duke accept his loss just yet. Like any good friend seeing another drifting out to sea, he pulled him back in.

'You can see a connection... can't you? Between the Silver case and the missing children?'

Duke nodded as his jaw clenched.

'Me too.' Addison stopped rocking from one foot to the other. 'However, that doesn't rule out Farrow at all. Who knows, maybe exploring him can go some way to solving these cases. Maybe he knows something... or someone. Did we ever look into whether he had others working with him? Maybe we never caught them all... maybe they're out here finishing off his work. It would be the perfect fit for someone having their case reviewed if the "real" killer continued to commit the crime you were sentenced for.'

Duke let out a small laugh.

'Maybe in the movies mate. But not this time. Farrow was your off-the-shelf, vacuum-packed, tabloid-ready deviant. It was as if the clichés were invented for him. He'd collected them all like some morbid set of retro Panini football stickers. Loner – got. Out-of-towner – got. Quiet, therefore mysterious, demeanour – got. Alibi – need. When it came to suspects that were guilty before proven innocent, Farrow was the tabloid template. At first, they would have panicked as he looked relatively normal – almost inoffensive really. He had all his teeth, his hairline was solid, some would say he was borderline handsome if you could look past the fact that he'd just abducted and more than likely murdered a young girl. But you get my point – he looked like everybody else. And that was the scariest part. He could have been anyone. But they used this to their advantage, like a blank canvas on which the press painted him as this creep, this scary, foreign weirdo with psychopathic tendencies. His relative silence was a blessing, as it ended up being spun quite nicely into him being remorseless. These journalists, they know what they're doing. Once you're on their page, they can distract and deflect you. Especially the ones with tits.' Duke looked at Addison and smiled. 'But in all seriousness, it wasn't the press that spun it for me. It was the evidence. It always has to be the evidence. For me at least. Truth be known, Benjamin Farrow was normal. During the interviews, he didn't show any signs of mental injury or illness. In fact, the bastard was friendly – insisting he was there to help in any way he could. He wasn't a demon, he wasn't this deformed monster that the press produced just so that all the people could huddle up against each other, hiding their own faults and failings, as they waved pitchforks in the air and called for blood. But there was no ogre waiting in the traps for them. He was just like us. Apart from one crucial thing. He was guilty. No doubt about it.'

'Did he have any friends, family even?'

Duke blew a perfect bubblegum bubble before he spoke.

'Funny you should say that.' He flicked his head back towards where their office building sat. 'Come with me.'

Apart from the smell of stale coffee and the occasional half-filled mug, the office was empty. Duke flicked on the light that eventually, after a few flirtatious flutters, came to life. The sound of computers on standby hummed, and the heating was chuntering away in the corridor outside. It struck Addison just how loud quiet could be. The room seemed at rest but in no way relaxed. Duke's energy was no different.

Disappearing into a small storeroom, he quickly reappeared with a small paper file which had been bound with a piece of string.

'Bloody hell,' Addison looked at the file, and then towards the storeroom. 'What have you got back there... the 1960s?'

'What?' Duke looked confused. 'Oh, because of the string. That one's on me. Just call me Theseus.' He offered a proud wink. 'Back there is my labyrinth. Countless documents, all labelled up, all from previous cases which have either been mislaid, duplicated or deemed of no real value. However, having had the fear of death from the claws of the IPCC pumped into our blue blood since our very first day in uniform, the police have inadvertently bred a bunch of cowardly hoarders. Go into any station and no doubt you'll find countless interview tapes from closed cases simply scattered within people's pigeonholes – all stored in the *Just in Case* file, right next to the ones labelled *What If* and *Too Difficult to Deal With.*'

'Your point being?' Addison had taken it upon himself to pour them both a cup of tea. Duke was already dunking a chocolate bar into his before Addison had sat down.

'My point... thanks for the tea by the way... is,' said Duke, muffled by a melted Mars bar, 'why hide something when you can leave it in clear sight? This file contains papers I put together when first looking into Farrow's past. Nobody seemed to give a damn about it when I first made it, but I didn't want to destroy it and I felt it would've been seen as a bit creepy if I took it home with me. Granted, I know I'm a little job-pissed, but even that's beyond my obsession.'

Job-pissed was a phrase used to describe those that took the job with them wherever they went. More often than not, it was those officers that had little else going for them and used incidents to appear interesting by association. Duke, on the other hand, didn't need the job to make him more interesting. Instead, he made the job more interesting by simply being part of it.

'And the string?'

'My label.' Duke took a gulp of his tea. 'I gathered there was no point labelling it up, for two reasons. One, it's not hidden if you're showing out. And two, I couldn't risk it being caught up in some other investigation by mistake. So, I put string around it so that I could navigate through that maze of lost files back there. You know, *just in case*.'

'What did you find out? More stuff on Farrow?' Addison held his cup of tea with both hands. The heater outside was clearly knackered.

'Very little.' Despite Duke's anticlimax he still opened the file with a flourish. 'Well, not first time around anyway. But after what Spike Harris has told us in interview, about Farrow's childhood, I did a little extra digging.'

Inside the file were three pieces of paper all relating to Farrow's time in care. Two were nothing more than registration papers, showing how Farrow had been bounced from care home to care home up until the age of twelve, by which time he had come to settle at Precious Moments, the children's home DCI Wilson was told about by Spike Harris. It was a renovated bed and breakfast just outside Stratford Upon Avon. Back then Farrow went under the name Benjamin Randal, presumably his family name. But there was no record after that.

'The care home is now closed down, has been for some time. For the last few years it's just been a pile of wood and rubble, like some broken shrine to what the place used to be.'

'Used to be?' Addison looked up from the papers he was reading.

'Yup.' Duke paused. 'Place burned down over fifteen years ago. That's why they closed the business. Not sure why they didn't start it back up again.'

'Do you think...'

'It's connected? Doubtful. It was empty at the time. Seems like the managers were downing tools as they had no kids on their books at the time. For all we know, it could have just been some junkie squatter being a little overzealous when sparking up their crack-pipe. The urban campers probably moved in the same day they all moved out.'

'What did the fire report say?'

'That wood is flammable. There was no investigation as there was nobody filing any complaint. No insurance was claimed either.'

'What about the previous managers?'

'Either dead or too old to care. I haven't had chance to track them down yet. I did get to meet the old landlord though. He'd been on site when Farrow – then Randal – was there. He said that the boy had been "complicated", somewhat troubled by the fact nobody was "picking" him for adoption. The older he got, the more troubled he became. Seemed to make friends easily though. The chap gave me that last bit of the file there. Said he'd found it in the wreckage. Apparently, it's part of some larger photo they'd taken of the place.'

Duke pointed to a fragment of an old photograph showing three young boys stood outside. They looked similar to one another but then altogether different. All three had bright blond hair, cut short above their ears, and they all had the same hollow stare. But one was petite, mostly emphasised by the hulking frame of the larger boy next to them. The other, propped up by a sibling on each side, was unmistakably Benjamin Farrow.

Chapter 37

'There has to be a connection.'

His body was almost as restless as his mind. Addison paced around his apartment. He'd found it hard to relax after his long night paper-sifting with Duke. The file on Benjamin Farrow was brief but pointed one way.

His past.

The care home.

The photograph.

A fire?

He'd taken the opportunity to call Piper. Partly because he thought she could help, but mainly because he wanted to hear her voice.

'Do you have any contacts within social services?'

'Sorry, not anymore.'

Her voice sounded hoarse on the phone. He liked it. A small flame sparked into life in his chest as her tones continued. 'Sadly, I lost touch with the guys I did used to know. Promised myself I'd reconnect someday, but you know how it is with people from your past. Always seems like a good idea at the time, but tomorrow always drags you one day further away. Why do you ask, anyway?'

'Just a hunch.' He wanted to tell her everything, but he could hear Duke's voice scratching away at the back of his mind.

'Check you out, detective. You sound like the classic troubled cop. Working the case into the long hours. I have to admit... I'm loving the commitment.'

'You know I don't sleep too well. The chronic insomnia that's been kicking my ass for months has to take some of the credit. Saying that, there is something about this case that doesn't fit. Something's missing. Or we just missed something.'

He didn't want her to see him as one-dimensional, defined by his work alone. But that's all that connected them: this case. Deep down, he wanted her to like him. For some reason, she was beginning to matter.

'Need some company? I don't have anything on right now...' She knew what she was doing. She paused to allow the idea of her naked body to play out in the silence. 'I'm sure there's a couple of bottles of wine here that are just itching for an excuse to be opened.'

'Fine.' He smiled as he spoke. She could hear it. 'Sounds like a plan.'

Thirty minutes later, Piper was sat on Addison's two-seater sofa with a half-empty wine glass in her hand. He'd already stoked up the fire and dimmed the lighting. The pub beneath them had closed for the night, and all that could be heard were the cold night winds, hugging the windows tightly.

'So... you missed me?' She tilted her head to the side. Exposing her neckline.

'Maybe. But I'm not sure whether you can miss what you don't really know.'

'Come now...' She chinked her glass with his. 'We're hardly strangers.'

'Why are you here?' He watched her reaction. His words felt like they had come from Duke's mouth more than his own.

'You invited me.'

'Technically, I didn't.' His smile sat under his tired eyes. 'But that's not what I mean. Right now. This town, this case. Why are you here?'

She looked confused.

'I've told you all this before... that time in the café with the hipsters and their health kicks. This case interests me. And given my freelance role, I can move between the lines a little, unlike the nationals who, if you ask me, committed far too early to Team Guilty. It makes me laugh how muted they all are now. Now that some things are brought into question – be it the evidence they had, or the way the case was managed – they're all just staying distanced and quiet. Until a result is found, that is, and then they'll announce it like they discovered it first. But right now is where I have my fun. I love seeing them all hiding under the rock that they first threw at Farrow, and it'll end either of two ways. They'll either stay hidden under the rock if he's innocent, or they'll bash his brains in with it if his case review finds nothing new. They're laughable, the lot of them. Just a bunch of overpaid headline-hunting hookers if you ask me. Leave your morals at the door, opinions in your locker, and pick a topic so as to scare or generate hate only. Mass categories to control the masses, that's all the news is now. I'm sorry Addison, that's just not my bag.'

'I know all that.' Addison leaned back from her. 'It's just, in the café you said that you'd been working on a case at a care home before.'

'That's right.' She finished off her glass of wine and poured herself another. 'I'd been tipped off about a historic abuse case, but the story was dead on arrival. The home was closed, and so were my leads. Quite frustrating really.'

'See, that's why I believe you're here for a reason. Be it fate, fortune or design.' Addison filled his own glass. He felt an excitement crawl across his skin. 'Duke had a few additional files on Farrow's past that I hadn't seen before. All of it points to a nomadic upbringing. Bounced from care home to foster home, and back again, like some broken misdirected piece of junk mail, permanently stamped *Return to Sender.* He never made it out of that place. Not until it closed down anyway. But Elizabeth, Amber and JoJo: they all made it out. They escaped. They were wanted. Was that it? *Is* that all it is... envy? There must be a link in there somewhere.' He took a drink from his glass as if mulling over his point. Instead, he was waiting to measure a reaction.

He held her gaze he spoke.

'That's why I wondered whether you already knew all of this. Had you always known the connection?'

He placed the polaroid Duke had given him on the coffee table. Three young boys stared back at them.

She reacted.

'Holy shit! Are you kidding me?' Her face went from relaxed to perplexed. 'I wasn't even looking at Farrow at the start of all this. It was just a missing child case when I arrived. As for the link, I only know what you've shared with me. JoJo... I got that from the statement you showed me. As for Elizabeth, you were right there when I found that out. Trust me.'

She was right. He'd been with her every time the details surfaced. He'd seen her reaction, a swirled twist of confusion and anger. The innocent often acted this way when they were accused. And so did liars, the very best of them at least. But she was right. He'd been there all along, she had as much right to accuse him of already knowing. The idea was absurd. He'd made a mistake. His measurements were off. He was no longer removed from the enquiries, he'd caught the itch, and he'd scratched it so hard that the details poured into him like a clouded poison, twisting his thoughts, and forcing him to bend a twisted mystery into the straight shape of reason and fact. He had a better chance ironing steam. The allure of the unknown was as infectious as it was contagious. He'd allowed himself to be influenced by another. Duke had made him so suspicious up to the point where he was becoming paranoid.

'Addison, if you want me to leave, I will. I'll back right off, you won't have to hear from me again. But if you really want to know why I'm here... right now... it's because of you. I'm here because of you.'

She put her hand against the side of his face. Her nails fired electricity through his skin.

The pounding in his chest muted his dull head long enough for him to make his move.

The kiss was tender at first, and then as wild as he'd imagined it would be. Her hands were running through his hair as he scooped her up and carried her to the bedroom.

What happened next had been inevitable.

Afterwards, for the first time in months, with his body spent and his limbs as loose as rubber, he finally fell asleep, her head nestled against his chest.

*

She was still there in the morning. He didn't know what he had expected. It had been so long since he'd been with a woman, especially for the first time, that he'd forgotten how the next day felt. The world had moved on since his early dating days, with online hook-ups happening as easy as a swipe of the finger. The world just seemed more highly sexed. Access was everywhere. First the Internet was exploited as one big porn storage centre, before social networks were stripped down to a simple 'would you, wouldn't you' filtering system. No longer did anybody have to quietly accept that their fantasies were unobtainable, instead a few clicks and you had every preference tagged and filed like one gigantic fetish farm, with smartphones acting like miniature porn ATMs. And like all things, with access comes excess, followed swiftly by either regret or unhealthy expectation. The millennials were the first generation of porn-fed guinea pigs, fatted by fetish and access. Every man's body now needed to be carved from marble, with veins pumping protein to each inflated extremity, whilst the young girls idealised the fabricated lifestyles of the frivolous reality stars, who coupled narcissism with a complete disregard for true self-worth. Sex was just a casual exchange. So, he truly didn't know what to expect when he woke up. But the fact that she remained there could only be a good thing.

He left her sleeping as he walked into his kitchen and poured himself a filtered coffee, more out of habit than necessity. For the first time in a long time, he didn't feel the draining ache that came with insomnia. Instead he felt rested, relaxed. Almost happy even.

His mood picked up a level further when he saw Piper enter the room wearing nothing but the shirt he had worn the night before.

'Morning tiger. Got any more of that hot stuff for me?' She nodded towards the cup of coffee he was holding.

He poured her a cup and followed her to the sofa. He perched on the edge as she gently ran her nails down his back. It felt like lightning had struck his skin.

'I really enjoyed myself last night.' Her voice passed over his shoulder like an ocean breeze.

'Me too.' He turned to face her. 'I'm sorry about the grilling beforehand.'

'Oh, don't worry about that. Let's put that down to experimental foreplay. Tried, tested, and put to one side. Unless we fancy some roleplay that is... you be the frustrated detective and I'll be the sexy suspect who's not only looking to get herself off.'

'I am genuinely sorry. I shouldn't have come down on you so hard like that.'

'Innuendo overload.' Her eyes opened widely as she took a drink of her coffee. 'But *seriously*, relax. I had a good time. And I'm used to boys going hard on me. No sex-pun intended.' Her soft shoulders shrugged beneath the oversized shirt. 'I had brothers growing up.'

'Had?' He put his arm around her, as she nestled into his chest again.

'Oh, you know how things are. Life pulls you apart sometimes. Like most people, we just all took different directions in life. It doesn't matter where you all came from, how inseparable you all seemed, family may share the same start-point but not always share the same end. As kids we were typical. They gave me a hard time, toughening me up, whilst I played a mini-mother to them whenever they felt low. I suppose we always knew we'd end up apart. That's why we shared a little bit of ourselves with each other, so that we'd always be together, in all that we do.'

'Do you ever hear from them?' Addison stroked the back of her neck.

'Not really. I hear things about them now and then. The world's not as big as when we were kids. Seems you're only ever a few clicks apart from anybody these days. But we don't talk anymore, for no other reason than we don't feel the need. We're all happy doing our own thing. It's what we're used to doing: finding our own way in life.' She looked up from his chest, all doe-eyed beneath her brow. 'How about you? Do you have any brothers or sisters that I could tap up for information?' She pinched his arm playfully as they cuddled.

'No... I'm afraid I'm all alone in this scary world of ours.'

'Not anymore you're not.'

She pulled him in closer as she kissed him. Her legs wrapped around his waist as he pulled the shirt from her body.

He wasn't expecting it. But he was glad she'd stayed.

Chapter 38

The sex served more than one purpose. It was fun, but it was also necessary, especially if an element of control was still required. Everything else about his life hung in the balance: the evidence, the case review, his imprisonment. But his character, that was something he could control.

He watched as Monica buttoned up her blouse and made a loose attempt at making herself look decent. She always looked ashamed of herself. He liked that about her, it showed a sense of pride. One that would get lost from time to time, but at least it was there. He knew what he was doing was wrong. But he did enjoy her. The way she looked at him like they could have been anywhere. To her, the walls didn't seem to define him. He wasn't just a prisoner, he was a man. One that she appeared to actually like. Monica Dawkins wasn't some infatuated teenager who enjoyed the buzz of being misguided and deviant. She didn't kiss him because she wasn't supposed to. She did it because she wanted to. Because she believed in him.

Their sin was complete. It didn't matter how many times it was repeated. Not for either of them. Once was enough to ruin her career forever. For him, it would paint him as a man of urges, seemingly uncontrollable. He needed to show restraint, and anything sexual would serve only to alter how people saw him. Sex soiled a person in the eyes of the law, regardless of how consensual and conventional it was. It remained taboo, a matter that should remain private. Once public, it showed weakness, demanded shame. If it became public, the sex they shared served neither of them well. But if it were to remain private, it served them both. Him even more than her.

The threat of exposure caused enough fear to control Monica Dawkins' opinion of Benjamin Farrow. Whatever report she submitted would have to compliment the man, not too much to raise suspicion or bias, but enough to present him as a human, and enough to keep him quiet about their misdemeanours. The shame would silence anything negative she had to say about him.

However, unknown to him, it wasn't just fear that guided her mind. Her heart also played some part. Despite all her professional judgement begging her not to, she knew she was beginning to love him. She looked at him as he sat in her chair, running his hands through his golden hair and his blue eyes across her body. He made her feel something she had never felt since she began her career.

Trust.

For the first time, she not only listened to what a patient was saying, but she truly heard them. She heard the way he spoke about his life before prison. She could see the man he once was, and who he deserved to be again. In all her time with him, he had never demonstrated any of the character traits synonymous with his crime. Undoubtedly his past was a broken one, pieced together by fragments of broken hope and shattered dreams. As a boy, all he had wanted was to belong to somebody, to something, to be part of a unit. Instead, he had nothing but rejection for company. After somehow dragging himself out of the dark depths of a broken care system he had begun to make a life for himself, even gather an education and a job. He was a success. He had no reason to ruin what he had made. There was no true motive. He was free. But once again, the world he'd entered chose to reject him. But she wouldn't. No matter what.

She did up her last button and walked over to where he sat. His boyish features and golden hair brought his face to life. On the outside, with his grey jogging bottoms and matching sweater, he could be easily mistaken for an athlete, fresh from the track and with a life of promise ahead of him. But then the outside had never been kind to him. All they saw was a prisoner, stripped of all potential and personality, and placed exactly where he belonged.

'I really should get out of here.' He looked at the clock behind her desk. 'Our session was meant to have finished five minutes ago. People will start to think I'm getting some kind of preferential treatment.' He touched her arm as he spoke. It forced blood to flush her cheeks.

'Don't be daft.' She tried her best not to sound all giggly. 'Nobody really pays attention to these visits. The next guy will just think you're doing him a favour by eating into his appointment. I know none of *them* want to be here. It makes them feel vulnerable, like I have some form of X-ray vision into who they really are.'

'Do you see through me? I have to admit, you've seen more of me than most of my usual doctors.' He picked up her glasses from her desk and put them on. 'Wow, these really are X-ray specs. If I'm not mistaken, it appears you have the cutest little birthmark on the inside of your right thigh.'

Her face went a deeper shade of red.

'Benjamin!' Her feigned outrage was cut short by the kiss that he planted on her. She felt her knees buckle slightly as he stole her breath.

She was his. Completely.

*

'It's all going to plan.'

He shuffled the papers and bounced them on his desk, the way people do to simply say 'we're done here'. It was a false act of tidying up, suggesting everything was wrapped up in a tidy little package, as if to imply that Benjamin's freedom was just a simple matter of procedure. In truth, his freedom was simply a matter of time. All prison sentences were. The papers his solicitor was shuffling went some way to determining whether that 'time' amounted to two months, or somewhere closer to twenty years. He'd already served nearly three years of his sentence, but it wasn't unheard of for Serious Case Reviews to go the other way and result in people's sentences being extended. Life could really become life. He only had to look around at some of his fellow inmates to see the ones that were never going to see the outside world again. Some by design, others through doing nothing more than satisfying their darkest of urges. He thought about Seth, how quickly the man's offending escalated whilst on the inside. First, he found himself charged with a few minor run-of-the-mill crimes, nothing too violent, but once inside something inside of him cracked wide open. So much so that his bloodied footprints led to here, HMP Fordbridge, the number one Category A prison in the country, home to the most dangerous men this little island ever produced.

How did that happen? How does a man spiral out of control so much that he's beyond recognition? Benjamin had heard him mumbling at night, he'd heard Seth's inner voice leak out. There was a ghost inside of him, something that haunted him to the core. It scratched at his soul, chipping away at whatever man existed before.

'Now, it's natural that you should be getting a little anxious, maybe even a little suspicious of those around you. It's pretty much textbook.'

'Excuse me?' Benjamin focused on his brief. The man's waxy hair had been slicked back so tight it served as a budget facelift, the comb marks matching the thick pinstripes on his cheap-looking suit. Not that it was cheap. It probably cost a small fortune, but the build of this man caused everything that touched him to cheapen. A decorated disaster of a man.

'Mr Farrow, you're currently at the mercy of various legal and law enforcement agencies. You're surrounded by prison officers, wardens, psychiatrists, even the goddamn cook is probably part of the same system that somehow allowed you to be here. No doubt, they've been heavy-handed, turned a blind eye to your enemies, made you appear psychotic, and even spat in your food. And that's best-case scenario. In short, none of them like you. None of them value you. Do you think that smile you get from them is genuine? It's not. It's a plea for you to behave. For you to make their already unpleasant day no more unpleasant.'

'Aren't you from the same system?'

Benjamin wasn't in the mood for pep talks. Firstly, he wanted out from this asshole. The only reason he chose him was through an ex-con's recommendation, who'd told him that if you ever wanted to slip through the bars you needed grease and a whole lot of wriggle room, and this guy – Russell Alderman of Alderman's & Co – was the oiliest space-maker of them all. His reputation was fierce. According to the legends, Russell Alderman could pour his clients through cracks so small, it was almost impossible to see the daylight behind them.

'Mr Farrow,' he cracked his fingers before planting both hands on this head. 'You must understand that the system has several sides to it. Some are sharp... some are smooth. Some sides are a lot rougher than others, so just be glad that I'm on yours.'

'I am,' he lied.

There was something about the guy that bugged him. Something sleazy, and not even in a subtle way. It seemed that oil just poured from his pores, and his tongue appeared too big for his mouth and made a squalid squelch when he spoke. It concerned Benjamin that he was entrusting his entire life to a man he would have no reason to be friends with in the outside world. However, if prison had taught him anything, it was that sometimes there was great value in making friends with monsters.

'Glad to hear it.' Alderman fired off a smile that was cheesier than a wheel of brie. His entire fat frame looked as if it had been blasted from a cannon against the dull grey walls of the office. Flesh fell wherever it could, hanging off the back of his neck and bulging out from his wrists. His wedding band strangled his ring-finger, causing the tip to turn a shade just two shy from dead, and his fatted forehead forced his brow into a permanent frown.

'Well...' the diabetic demon continued. 'You'll be happy to know that the police are yet to find anything new during their case review of the papers.'

'But that's bad, isn't it? If everything stays the same, then there's no reason for reviewing the case at all.'

'Not exactly.' The smile returned. 'Everybody knows that the police had very little to go on the first time around. The fact that you were a suspect seemed enough for them. Nobody else presented themselves as a possible, so it had to be you. It just *had* to be. But both you and I know that there were enough holes in this case for the courts to play a couple rounds of golf on. The fact that the police have been unable to fill these gaps only helps us out. Forget all the press hype that hit the first time around. The witch-hunt is over. There's no pitchfork-wielding angry mob outside looking for an ogre to run out of town. The balance has shifted. Time does that. You no longer have to prove your innocence like you did before. All you need to create is doubt. Doubt that you didn't take Elizabeth. Doubt that you were even capable of such an act. Jesus Christ, let's make them doubt that she's even dead!'

'But she is.' Benjamin looked at the ball of grease sat in front of him. 'She must be.'

'I agree. But people love a good conspiracy. And stranger things have happened. Like you having the grim reaper as a guardian angel, for example.'

'What?' Benjamin felt a chill on the back of his neck.

'Come now... don't tell me you weren't happy to hear about all those kids going missing? It's a freaking godsend. Talk about timing!'

'Those kids are probably dead too. I doubt it will look good if that's seen to make me happy.'

'True.' Alderman nodded to him as he forced home a point he'd made several times before. 'Remember to keep that mask on at all times. It's the smart move. Appear sorry that they're gone... for sure... but sure as hell capitalise on it. Make the public realise that the real guy is still out there. Make them scared. Make them fear that they got it wrong.'

'But they have.'

'Maybe so.' Alderman leaned back in his chair. Given his frame, you wouldn't have been able to tell, apart from the fact that now his gut kissed the edge of the table. 'None of us know that the psychopath out there is the same one that took Elizabeth. Yet he *could* be. And... if he could be, then there's also a chance that you might not be. Understand? Doubt. The science of law and order can often just boil down to a state of mind, and doubt alone is the greatest enemy of the state. Trust me on that one.'

Later that night Benjamin thought about Alderman's sign-off, how it made him realise that there was little left in this world that he could truly trust. A life of rejection and occasional abandonment had threatened to remove the very word from his vocabulary altogether.

And yet, buried deep within him somewhere, somewhere where the darkness was at its thickest, lived a small lantern that shone for those who knew him the most. They'd all gone away now, but what they once shared together would always bind them to one another.

'What haunts you?'

Benjamin hadn't seen Seth enter his cell. Despite looking so rigid that all his bones could crack and snap at any given moment, the man had a strange knack for creeping up on you. His body was almost bent double as he walked, his one shoulder tilted higher than the next, making him look like something plucked from an old black-and-white horror movie. Almost as if by design. Who knew, maybe somewhere in an old hilltop castle a mad doctor was missing his creepiest creation.

The shadow Seth now stood within shaded his blind eye, masking the parts of him that looked the most monstrous.

'How long have you been there?' Benjamin sat up from his bed.

'I've not been here long. Just long enough to know that the shadows may be a friend of mine. Maybe even yours.'

'Jesus, Seth, you say some weird shit. Why do you have to be so strange?'

'I'm no stranger than you are. After all, we're both here for a reason, the same reason in fact. That's what binds us.' His breathing slowed down as it got louder. There was a sinister volume to his stillness. The shadow seemed to vibrate around him.

'What's all this about? Are you off your meds again?' Benjamin's body felt tense. Whatever relief was found from Monica's soft body, or Alderman's prickly positivity, was instantly washed away by looking at the creep in the corner. Granted, Seth was an ally on the inside, but there was no denying that he would be a distant stranger on the outside. All that united them were the walls that housed them, and as soon as he was out of there, whatever linked him and Seth together would be dead and gone.

'You're in demand.'

Seth brought his head out into the light that shone through the open cell door. He quickly glanced out into the corridor before sulking back into the shade. 'I overheard some of Jenkins' boys plotting again. Sounds like the closer you get to that exit door, the further they're willing to go to keep you here. You and I know that they won't make it easy for you to leave. I heard one say that he'd be disappointed to even see you wheeled out of this place, especially if you were sitting upright. If you were to leave, they want it to be lying down and ready for the ground. I think their terms are, "he can leave when he doesn't breathe". Kind of catchy, really.' His laugh was similar to a young girl's. A timid giggle muffled by the curled hand that cupped his grinning mouth.

'Why are they obsessed with me?'

'Because you killed a child.' Seth stopped giggling.

'Are you serious right now?'

Benjamin's instinct warned him away from Seth. But it was clear the man was simply standing guard, and though it often bordered on creepy, there was some comfort in the blanket of protection the madman offered him.

'But you were found to be guilty. It's this guilt that they are obsessed with.' Seth watched from the corner. He saw the words land – watched them register – and timed the pause before the reaction.

The flash to bang was instant.

'You fucking what? What was that you just said... my guilt?' The anger ran to his legs, causing him to stand up. He was now pacing the room as he spoke. 'Don't you dare toy with me Seth. Everybody thinks that they can do that with me. They think they can prod and poke, push and...'

'Provoke.'

'Exactly.' He continued to pace. 'Just because they know their sins, doesn't mean that they know mine. We're not all in this together. What we've all done does not connect us. The rape victim doesn't feel connected to the little old lady who was robbed in the street, so why the hell do the ones doing the crime think that they're bound together in all of this? Those pretentious pricks... those fucking beasts out there have nothing to do with me and my life. Yeah, maybe our pasts are all a bit shitty, but that doesn't go half as far as to explain their actions, let alone excuse them. So, if they think they're all obliged to punish me, they're wrong. I'll be walking out of those gates one day, and not a single creature in here is going to stop me.'

He sat back on his bed. The adrenaline had begun to wane and he needed rest. The fear, however, remained in the room. And the thing that was to be most afraid of stood by his side. At least he had that, the shield that fear brings, the distance that people keep from that which disgusts them the most.

The scariest thing inside this prison was by his side. Wrapped within his own shadow, Seth watched as Benjamin rested. The man had briefly nodded to him before turning over and lying on his side, almost like a child.

Seth shook the thought from his mind, pushing away the urge to cradle the child before him. It took a few seconds for him to see Benjamin as a man again, and not a boy ripe for the taking.

The cold cell door remained open and the small trail of light began to retreat as one by one the lights from outside were turned off. Seth waited until the prison guard came to lock Benjamin's cell, before making his way down to his own. But for the dull buzz and humming of the security lamps, the entire block was soon silent. All that sounded out were the chilling voices that filled his head.

You'll know soon.

You know you're damned.

His shadow followed him into the cell and lay with him inside the darkness. Like a tidal wave the voices continued to flood his ruptured mind, pounding at the bones of his skull, dulling his senses. Inside his pocket he pressed his thumb on the blade that he'd kept concealed from his friend. He pressed until he could feel warm blood blanketing his fingers, and the sharp voices began to slowly soften.

Life meant life.

Chapter 39

The instructions had been clear.

He needed to find the small book that the first girl was carrying when she was taken. The masks were his mementos, little frozen faces etched into clay for him to keep forever. But an accessory to his art was always welcome. He remembered how she had been clutching the book when he first saw her, clinging onto her past whilst strangers decided her fate. He frowned when he considered her complete ingratitude towards what they were willing to do for her, the way she cried impetuously whilst they made her immortal. She had looked at him like he was a beast to be feared. But he had a heart. He saw how much the book meant to her, how she clutched it close to her chest. That's why he stitched it into her cold dead hands.

That's how he found her now, propped up against a park bench he'd fashioned out of old timber, still holding her beloved book. Her eyes were no longer able to read the words she had once excitedly scribbled alone in her room, sharing secrets with herself, and documenting the dreams her days had dared to conjure. Instead, her dull eyes now stared at him coldly. Rough marbles sat where her soft eyes once did. She was his first creation within his scene of recreation, and possibly his worst attempt at capturing what he had imagined. She truly brought death into his dedication to the freedom of youth. But he had improved since. Her friends all brought an energy that allowed her to hide in the background, lost within her daydreams, her hands forever wrapped around her precious diary.

His knife needed sharpening. The last carving must had blunted his blade a little. Not that you could tell. He recalled how the boy's skin had slid from his flesh like butter rolling down a warm joint of lamb. Maybe it was the bones that had dulled his knife. Some were always more awkward to remove.

Each stitching offered a faint twang as the knife drew through them.

Her cold hands offered little fight as he plucked the book away from the girl with the saddest face of them all. He was certain her mask held a hint of a smile, but what remained of her now was grey and depressing. Her skin looked damp and darkened in patches, scolded by the cold air that he pumped through the room. She had been pretty once. But now he was glad she was only part of the background. The girl she was taking the role of was not too dissimilar. He had liked her. She wasn't as cruel as the other children. Granted, she could never love him like he had begun to love her, but at least she didn't call him the names that all the other children had called him. Apart from two. Apart from those he had called his family. In the photograph he was standing next to them, and he had stood by them ever since.

*

She wasn't there anymore.

Last time he had checked she was by his side, sleeping with a face framed by satisfaction. He was glad she'd stayed, and partly happy she had left before he woke up.

Piper had been a healthy distraction for Addison, helping him forget the troubles that had pushed him away from his hometown, but she was also becoming an inconvenient priority of his, the same way any person does when you start to develop real feelings for them, and that was no good for the job he was sent to do.

The fact that she was gone, that her soft milky skin wasn't only a bedsheet away from him, gave him back his morning. And if he couldn't spend it with her, he wasn't going to let it go to waste.

He poured himself a black coffee from a small percolator perched upon his breakfast bar. It was still hot, so Piper hadn't long left. A small part of him had hoped that she had popped out to bring some breakfast back in for the two of them to eat whilst watching the morning disappear within various cooking shows and property programmes, but the crumb-dusted butter knife and a small note leaning against a slice of toast which read '*Some warm toast from your hot crumpet*' made it clear that she was gone for the day.

Which was fine. Addison had a job to do and the last thing he needed was a clouded head when trying to unthread all that had happened recently.

The Benjamin Farrow case review had become a daily news article. Various legal teams had been meeting, solicitors from both sides took it in turns to offer positive but non-committal soundbites that the media miraculously made a meal from. Farrow's representative had basked in the limelight, which seemed to suit his slithery demeanour. His job was arguably easier the second time around, now that the general public had forgotten the victim, and so Farrow could be freshly served to them as a result of a flawed system, a product of a corrupt police investigation who were under pressure to close the biggest case in their history. Every piece of the procedure was now under question, each statement scrutinised, each signature tested for authenticity. All he needed was doubt, wherever it was lurking.

The problem for the prosecution was that Addison had found plenty. Interrogation of each part of the case had raised another question without an answer.

Why was the manhunt stopped once Farrow was arrested?

Why was nobody linking the new cases?

Where is Elizabeth?

All Addison knew was that this case was more complicated than any he had ever worked on. All evidence was doubted, and all doubts were dismissed. And yet, there was guilt.

Addison's gut was rumbling too loud to ignore. Benjamin Farrow had left DNA at the scene. He'd also lied in interview, suggesting that his bike had been stolen before Elizabeth's disappearance, but PC Pyke encountered him the next day cycling through the town. Couple that with the links between his past and the recent victims, and everything put Farrow in the frame.

But was that what it was?

A frame.

Had Farrow fitted someone else's plan? Was he the easy target? Maybe the true killer had used Farrow to hide behind, and now that the case was up for review maybe they fancied a little fun at the expense of everybody involved.

No matter what it was, children were still being taken, and until Addison could be convinced otherwise, he was treating them as connected. And, although it wasn't his case to solve, he couldn't help but feel that the disappearance of Elizabeth Silver was at the heart of it all.

He stuck the piece of toast Piper had left him into his mouth and threw on his navy peacoat. The weather outside held a grey gloom, mounting a day with little promise. The town looked no different to the day before. The quaint feel of a connected community hummed through the narrow streets, filling the air with an energy often absent in larger towns. It gave most people the feeling of protection, a blanket of comfort from the community you were part of.

But Addison wasn't part of it, and all he could feel were eyes on him, all the time.

Passing through the high street, he was greeted by soft smiles, all of them followed by a look to the floor. Nobody was prepared to connect with him completely. Politeness above all else was present, but there were no friendships to be made. Not for him anyway. He was once from the outside, just like Farrow had been, and now that he was inside, they all feared he'd break the monster out once more. Their firewall had been breached by a foreigner bearing gifts of closure, but he served only to open up the belly of the beast, and bring the stench of spewed blood back onto the streets of this once hidden town.

Wilted smiles continued to line his route, until a set of eyes lingered a second too long. They soon followed suit to the rest, finding feigned interest in the floor, but they had been looking at him for a moment more than the others.

Addison walked past the boy who now pretended to tie his shoelaces. The scent of cannabis kicked up from where he crouched. Addison walked on, glancing in the store window across the road. He saw what he suspected. The young boy was now getting to his feet. He pulled the hood of his jacket over his face and followed Addison through the small crowd that were waiting for the butchers to open.

Addison hooked a right, and quickly entered the first store along the road. His entrance into the small charity shop was announced by the jingling of an old-fashioned bell. Not ideal when you're trying to shake a tail, but the boy didn't hear it. Instead, he walked a few more yards up the road before stopping and looking around him. Having not seen his mark pass him, the boy followed his instinct and pressed on up the road, away from the charity shop.

A small hand landed on Addison's shoulder. It belonged to one of the weekend volunteers at the store. Her skin was almost purple, and sunk between the bones of her hand. Her words were partnered by the smell of coffee and Murray mints.

'Can I help you at all?' She peered up through lenses as thick as milk bottles.

'No, thank you.' Addison began to leave. He raised his voice as he stepped onto the street. 'You've been a great help. Have a lovely weekend.'

He'd said the last part towards the boy walking away from him. He wanted him to hear it. It was spoken with baited breath, and the young boy took it hook, line and sinker.

The boy's step shuffled a little before coming to a complete stop. After a small piece of theatrics, checking his watch and pretending like he needed to be somewhere else, the boy turned around. But Addison was already walking away.

The boy saw which way this time. His mark had turned right at the end of the road.

Bad move, he thought.

There was no through road that way, only a footpath that lead directly into Oakland Woods.

The pathway was shaded and penned by rows of old oak trees. Many were overgrown and their branches reached across the path, forcing you to duck beneath them. Having left the high street behind him, the boy was a hundred yards inside the woods before he saw something strange enough to stop him in his tracks.

Up in front of him, placed neatly over the stump of a fallen tree, was the mark's navy peacoat. It hadn't been tossed, but rather wrapped around the stump, and buttoned up.

It was enough to confuse the boy. He raised a roll-up to his lips and took a long draw. The smell was undeniable.

Billy Jackson was still smoking cannabis. Maybe if he hadn't been, he would have seen Addison sneaking up on him.

The coat was a clear distraction and gave Addison enough time to wrap Billy's arm into a gooseneck. He pushed on the pressure points of the wrist and steered the boy away from the path until they were out of sight. Spinning him around, Addison grabbed the drawstrings of Billy's hooded top and crossed them over, twirling the young man to his knees in one motion. He pulled the strings tighter until they choked at the boy's neck and forced Billy's head to the sky.

'Why are you following me?'

Addison released his grip to allow Billy to speak. His face turned a lighter shade of blue as he caught his breath.

'I needed to make sure you were alone.' Billy's voice was higher than usual.

'What?' Addison was confused. 'Why? So, you could pick me off? Thought you had a better chance if I was alone?'

'No... honestly.' Billy tried to get to his feet but Addison pushed his foot into the boy's thigh, forcing him back to his knees. 'For fuck's sake. I just wanted to talk to you. Alone!'

'Well, here we are. All alone. So, talk.'

'It's about the case.' Billy held his hands up as if the mere mention of the case would cause Addison to strike him. His flinch soon relaxed after a second passed by without an assault.

'What about the case? From what I remember, you were seen as a local hero. Your statement alone was enough to put a man away, for life. It's pretty much what the whole case leaned on.'

Addison had picked up the scent quick enough. He'd caught a whiff of it the first time he'd seen Duke and Billy together. There was something unspoken between them both that was too loud to ignore.

'That's why I needed to speak with you.'

The sound of footsteps drew closer. Taking stock of the scene he'd created, Addison dragged Billy further into the woods and pinned him up against a large oak tree. His hand was planted firmly across the boy's chapped lips as he waited for the footsteps to come and go.

It was a dog-walker. Just an old man and his beagle out for a morning stroll. The dog had picked up the scent of something interesting, most likely the adrenaline that the two men hidden behind the tree were sharing. Or the stale stench of the spliff that Billy had dropped once his knees had first hit the ground.

It was the latter scent that caused the old man to increase his pace a yard or two. That smell often meant youths, and this pensioner had read enough tabloid horror stories to know that he needed to leave.

It felt like a whole minute had passed by the time the dog-walker was gone. Addison's palm had been dampened by the panicked breath of young Billy Jackson.

He removed his palm and wiped it on the back of his jeans.

'Talk.'

'I need your word first.' Billy looked around him as if they may not have been alone in the bushes. 'I need you to promise not to share what I'm about to tell you. Not Sergeant Parker, not that reporter who stayed at your flat last night, nobody.'

'How the hell...'

'I see things, remember.' Billy flashed a smile. 'Things when the rest of the world are asleep. I see what people get up to when they themselves should be tucked up in bed.'

'So, what *did* you see?' Addison watched the boy intently. He saw him processing what he was about to say, calculating his options, assessing which one worked out better for him.

'Well... I saw your reporter friend leave about half an hour before you left this morning. Quite early for an interview, no? Or was it more of a debrief... or exposé?'

He laughed at his own poor joke, exposing the teeth that had been stained by wasted hours of drug abuse. At one point his poor mother would have adored that smile, but now all it reminded her of was how weak she had been in giving this waster everything he could bully out of her. Addison could have quite happily broken his jaw if he didn't need the creep to keep talking.

'Now listen here, you complete biscuit. I seriously doubt you stalked me into the woods just to tell me about things I already know. Unless you're trying to threaten me, is that it? Am I getting too close to something? Because – trust me – nothing would motivate me more than somebody warning me away from something. That's how cops work. We run towards the things others run from. So, which one is it? Are you here to educate me, or piss me off?'

'Maybe a little bit of both.' His face was one of genuine concern. 'I lied. All right. I... fucking... lied.'

'About what?' Addison already knew.

'That Farrow guy... the night Elizabeth was taken. What can I say? I saw an opportunity, and I took it. I didn't realise it would become such a big deal.'

'A big deal?' Addison gripped the boy by the throat before dropping him. 'Are you kidding... a big deal! A guy is inside because you were able to put him at the scene of the crime. Are you telling me that all that was pure bullshit?'

'Yeah...' he squirmed. 'No... well... kind of. Jesus, I don't know, all right. I was told that there was plenty more evidence to prove that the cops knew their guy. Something about DNA at the scene, some shit like that. All my account was going to do was firm up the fact that he was there that night. For some reason, the shades needed him near the place that night. Apparently, it closed doors for the defence. That's what your boy Parker said anyhow.'

'Parker? Are you saying Duke was in on this?'

'He's balls-deep in this bitch, believe me. He fathered this bastard. And yet it's me that gets grief all the time.'

'Is that so?' Addison could feel the blood rushing to his head. 'You?'

'Fuck yeah. All I wanted was a bit part... just enough to earn me a bit of leverage with the local feds if they caught me with my medicine, if you know what I mean. Clearly, I absolutely smashed my audition because, before I know it, I'm the star of the whole goddamn show. In a blink, the press are at my door, the locals are buying me drinks, people bothered to keep their eyes on me rather than have them shift to the floor when I walked by. Jesus Christ, even my own mum looked proud of me. I was a hero, a local star. So, tell me this, what was I supposed to do?'

'How about stick to the truth?'

'I did! Trust me, I did. But your boys in blue didn't make it easy for me. They practically made out that if I didn't place Farrow's hand in Elizabeth's, then I was helping him get away with it. They even suggested that I'd become a suspect, because I'd already admitted to being near to the house that night. So, if I couldn't say it was Farrow, then the cops could easily say it was me. Thankfully, a couple of other people had seen a guy near the Silvers' house as well, and he didn't match my description. Your boys took statements from them, even began a sketch of the offender, until they quickly realised that both of the witnesses were blind drunk. By the time they were fit to be dealt with, these witnesses had had a few sober thoughts of their own, eventually working out the true cost of their honesty. They were having an affair. Statements can lead to court dates... witness testimony, cross-examination. Neither of them wanted their secret to come out, so they kept it secret, the best they knew how: by keeping their mouths shut.'

'Okay.' Addison was beginning to get the picture. He could almost feel the frustration the officers dealing with the case would have felt at the time. It was a thick line between knowing something and proving it, especially when witnesses bailed out.

'Thing is, they still had their sketch, didn't they?' Billy shrugged his shoulders. 'Now, I don't know whether they'd finished this with the two secret shaggers, or sometime after they'd dropped out, but that picture looked just like Farrow. I mean... it was almost intentional. Desperate for a witness, they pulled me in and lay out photos of various guys all loosely looking the same. Then they stuck the sketch in front of me and asked me who I had seen that night. We all knew what they were really asking. So... I pointed to Farrow. Who wouldn't? They then got me to sign a statement, and before I know it I'm in a brand-new suit – courtesy of your boys in blue – and standing in court, playing public hero number one.'

'Why are you only talking now?' Addison felt a wave of fatigue wash over him.

'Because of you: because of the whole case review. It all suggests that this wasn't as cut and dry as we all first thought. It started to raise questions. What if I potted an innocent man? Would I be blamed for what we did? Would you come forward knowing that you'd not only be cast out of your hometown, but you'd probably do time as well? The whole thing is a huge hot steaming stink of a mess. Why the hell do you think everybody is on edge around here? We're all feeling it. We all know the risks we took. But you have to believe me, we only did it because we thought we had the right guy. Or at least, I was told we did.'

'Don't give me that shit!' Addison held his clenched fist next to Billy's clenched jaw. 'You only did it for a free ride. You're a parasite Billy, nothing more. I see the way you feed off others, exploiting your mum, working countless angles with the police just so that you can waste your life without having to face up to the fact that you've offered nothing of worth to anybody ever. You said it yourself, this case made you somebody. Suddenly, you mattered. Your mum didn't regret you, the town didn't resent you. You were no longer the one staining the town's good name with your pathetic calls for attention. And now, all of a sudden, you expect me to believe that you've grown a conscience? Bullshit. What is it that you're really after? Do you think that if you blow the whistle early enough that you get to bury everybody else under you? Maybe you think you can play some form of victim and gather sympathy, or even be seen as a saint, or martyr for the cause. I'm sorry, the world doesn't work like that. If what you're saying is true, then you're as guilty as everybody else.'

'Don't you think I know that?' Billy's voice was one squeaky note above crying. 'I'm scared all right. That's why I've been acting out. The drugs help me cope, but they also make me lash out. More stupid than brave I guess, but that's why I started painting those images. Of the crying eye?'

Addison had seen them around and had always gathered that it would have been Billy doing them, but not up until now did he understand why.

'I regret what I saw. And also... what I didn't see. If I wasn't so high that night, maybe I wouldn't have had to lie. Maybe I'd have been able to say for definite whether it was Farrow or not. Do you know what that feels like, to have the answer but have no idea of knowing it? Instead, all I can honestly say is that I saw what looked like a young girl walking with somebody with light-coloured hair. Would that really be enough to put an innocent man behind bars? And is it enough to set a killer free?'

'That's not for you to decide.'

'No, maybe not.' Billy looked up from the floor and into Addison's eyes. 'Maybe that decision belongs to you.'

Chapter 40

Addison needed to speak with Duke.

Alone.

After dressing down Billy Jackson, and disrobing a tree stump of a perfectly good navy peacoat, Addison walked the long road that led to the small Tasking Team's base. Whilst the shutters were down in the front office, he could see that the lights at the back of the building were on. Pausing, he entered the small shared kitchen area where a tuck shop had been set up along with a trust box that had more Post-it-note IOUs inside than coins. The kettle had long since been replaced by a small boiler with a tap connected to it, offering scalding hot water on demand. Addison remembered an old tip his father had taught him of pouring the milk in first, so as not to burn the cheap coffee granules. Having poured himself a drink he hoped the caffeine would help him process the morning's revelations.

It was the first time he'd thought of Piper since leaving his apartment. The deep sleep had left him feeling groggy and, if that wasn't enough to cloud his head, Billy Jackson's newsflash had left him almost punch drunk. The whole case for the prosecution was now on the ropes.

He checked his phone. Three missed calls from Piper. None of them were followed up by a text or voicemail. He'd call her back later.

He was pocketing his phone as he walked into the briefing room. What greeted him was a room that looked more serious than he'd ever seen it before. Everybody was in attendance. Forming a small horseshoe, Maggie McAndrew, Darren Hoggit and Geoff Talbot all faced their leading man.

Pacing the room, working the stage, Sergeant Derek Parker played out to his mini-amphitheatre. His opening monologue was to the point.

'We're fucked.'

It wasn't quite *Hamlet*, but it said it all. There was no madness. No method. Just facts. Addison remained in the cheap seats, watching the meeting play out.

Finding Elizabeth Silver's diary had been a crushing blow to the case against Benjamin Farrow.

It wasn't a mystery how the search teams had missed it. It was never there. If it was, it would have been the first thing they found.

Whenever a person was reported missing, one of the very first enquiries was to check whether that person had a diary. Modern times had almost made such things obsolete, with people documenting their every move through a variety of online stalker-porn mobile-phone apps, and countless social media platforms. The days of self-reflection had been replaced by self-projection. Sharing had distorted into styling. It was now a time to present the reinvention of one's own reality, to filter and tailor true events for the sake of external acceptance. Introspection was a dying art. As long as others accepted your pretence, then you could fool yourself into believing it also. Waistlines were altered by the flick of a finger, and landscapes tailored by the thump of a thumb. Nobody presented themselves in their true form anymore, instead they opted to play lead role in their very own fiction.

But not everybody stuck to the script. For Elizabeth Silver, her diary was her world, her place to share, and even dare to dream. It was a safe place, free from judgements and rejection. She didn't need to convince the world she was a better version of herself. Just two people. Beverly and Steven. Her new parents.

Nothing had made her happier than their acceptance of her.

Having now read the young girl's diary, it was clear Elizabeth was happy. Finally, she had a family: two people committed to giving her a life, a future. She also appeared to have someone she trusted, and considered to be quite a dear friend. A dear friend that could cost the prosecution everything.

'Her and Benjamin Farrow were very close. Friends even.' Duke cast his arms out wide. 'Do you know what this means?'

He was right to be concerned. The diary laid out a clear relationship between Elizabeth and her teacher. How they'd discussed their backgrounds, how he'd protected her from those that called her names, even how he'd held her when she cried. There were countless pages dedicated to the man.

'It's not the end of the world.' Maggie's voice slipped into the Irish twang she adopted whenever she was nervous. 'Maybe Farrow knew we'd find the diary. Maybe he knew we'd see the connection they had. That's why he took it the same night he took Elizabeth.'

'Then why the hell is the book here and she isn't?' Geoff Talbot's tone never wavered from rage restrained.

'Nor is Farrow for that matter.' Darren Hoggit nervously looked around to see whether he was permitted to speak. 'How has he managed to return something whilst locked up?'

'He hasn't.' Duke looked defeated. 'That's why the shit is about to hit the fan. And, unfortunately people, we're the goddamn fan.'

The audience whirred for a minute before grinding to a dull hum. Addison waited until the small crowd had dispersed before approaching Duke.

'Can we talk?' Addison nodded towards the fire door. 'Outside.'

The early evening air held a bitter bite. Fallen leaves crackled beneath each footstep.

'You okay?' Addison watched his friend shrug his shoulders and toss a piece of chewing gum into his mouth. The man looked defeated, completely beat.

'Duke, I spoke with Billy Johnson earlier today. I know you put a little weight on him to put Farrow in the frame.'

'Shit.' Duke's voice was a muted whisper.

'Why take such a risk?'

'Because Farrow did it. The DNA put him there, as did two cowardly cheats who would rather not hurt their partners with the truth than give a little girl the justice she deserved. We had two witnesses who saw the man, clear as day. I was there when they were describing him.'

'Him, or someone who looked like him?'

'It was enough. Trust me.' Duke cracked open a can of fizzy orange pop. He chugged it back, tossed the empty can in the bin and rested his crinkled forehead in his hands. His knuckles were a lighter shade of pale.

'Are you okay?'

'I was.' Duke flashed a small smile. It was fleeting. 'I was certain we'd caught our man. Certain. The facts all pointed to him. When we found the DNA, it was a done deal. But you know what they say about pointing the finger at somebody... at least three are always pointing back at you. Billy Jackson, the diary, the missing kids: three nails in my coffin. I *need* to find out the truth. I need to know I was right before it's too late.'

It was clear Duke's fight was closer to despair than someone simply being stubborn and standing by their beliefs. Everything Addison had uncovered only challenged the conviction, it didn't prove innocence.

'Duke, it's not too late.'

'It is for me.' He looked at his friend. 'I'm checking out, Addison. I have a brain tumour. It's inoperable. I don't know how long I have left, but soon every day will be a downward spiral. It's irreversible, so I simply have to wait it out. Could be a year before it kicks in, could be any time before then.' Duke clicked his fingers as his head fell lower.

Addison felt cold. It broke his heart to see his friend this way.

'At the start, my memory began to go. Only the short-term, forgetting where I'd put things: what day it was, trivial things. Gradually my mind became fogged over and, with each day, the mist took a little longer to fade away. Luckily, I've always been overworked, so it was easy to hide initially. People would put it down to exhaustion or too little sleep. Some even thought my diet was causing sugar crashes. Ha! The truth is: I only started eating everything that was sweet when I got the sour news. Life's too short to spend it sucking on salad leaves. I suppose in some way, it's feels good to know that none of my bad habits will be the death of me.'

His smile was tired. With each indulgence, Duke was raising a middle finger to the reaper.

'Who else knows?' Addison placed his hand on Duke's shoulder.

'Nobody. Apart from the guy whose medical degree and nine years of education can do nothing for me. I've got no family to tell... upwards, downwards, sideways. I was the lonely child of a lonely child. Both my parents are dead now, so at least the only funeral I'll have to go to is my own.' His smile was genuine, defiant. 'That's why I wanted to get this last case right, before my memory goes for good, before it's lights out. I need to know the truth.'

'Maybe you already do.'

'Right now, we know nothing. I can't lose my marbles before I've locked the truth in. I'm forgetting new things, it's just not sticking. But if Farrow did it, I'll remember that because I already believe it.'

'And if he didn't?'

'Then other people deserve the truth more than me.'

'Few do. I'll make sure you know it. How about you and I go smash this case out of the park? Apologies, but screw DCI Wilson.'

'Again?' A flash of life returned to Duke's face.

'Knew it.' Addison smiled. 'I've seen where both of your eyes travel when you're together. Saying that, it seems like nobody is looking where they should be. Especially with this case. The beginning starts here. Elizabeth Silver may be lost, but the truth isn't. We'll find it.'

'And where do you suppose we start?'

'Where – for some – it ends.' Addison was already turning towards the car as he handed Duke a piece of paper with an address scribbled on it. Duke knew the place well. The doctors had recommended that he consider living there if his condition got too much for him to cope on his own. He'd torn up the pamphlet they'd given him, and insisted that he'd never step foot in that place. And now he was heading straight for it.

He smiled to himself. Whenever he felt like he was walking his own path, life had a funny way of kicking him in the balls.

Chapter 41

Addison appeared to have struck gold with his latest line of enquiry.

The two former managers of Precious Moments, the children's home that Benjamin Farrow attended, were now based at the same care home. And it was only a few miles away from Claymore. Before setting off, he'd briefly returned Piper's call, telling her his plans. She only seemed semi-interested, and said she'd catch him afterwards.

The place they were looking for was called Ferndown, a care home that looked after nearly fifty elderly residents. One such resident was Norris Draper. Now seventy years old, and suffering the late stages of dementia, Draper was once the co-owner of Precious Moments, along with his business partner Mitchell Mason. However, whilst Draper was a resident, Mason was not. A few years junior to his one-time business partner, Mason was still working. A career in care had eventually led him to Ferndown, and now he worked part-time as an acquaintance. The role simply asked him to keep the residents company and provide them with a little attention. It didn't pay much, but it gave him something to do and removed a little strain from the nurses' heavy workload.

The man who greeted Addison and Duke on their arrival had a bulk which betrayed his frail age, though his hands were long and withered. Small patches of purple blotched his skin and what was left of his silver hair had been tied back into a ponytail. His handshake lacked the blunt strength his physique suggested, and the skin on his arm resembled the surface of a tired balloon.

'Good morning.' Addison's palm felt clammy after being released from the man's limp grip. 'My name is DC Clarke, and this is my supervisor DS Parker. We were hoping to speak to Mitchell Mason and Norris Draper.'

'Can I enquire as to what this is about?' The man shifted his weight. His smile was as stale as the once white tunic he was wearing. It gave him the look of a demented dentist.

'We simply need a chat about their former employment.'

'Bollocks to all the charades, it's to do with the missing children.' Duke's tone startled a few residents for a second before they sloped back into permanent distraction. 'Are they here or not?'

'There's no need to take that tone, officer. I'm simply doing my job.'

'Which is what exactly? Playing an extra in *Little Shop of Horrors*? None of these people here look like they require a root canal, so why don't you stop standing there like the tooth fairy's fossil and go fetch me the men we need to talk to.'

'Because, one... I don't have to, and two... I cannot.' The skin between the man's purple blotches had changed to a flushed red.

'Oh, trust me Captain Colgate, you do.' Duke took one step forward. 'And... you will.'

'No,' the man replied. 'I don't have to because I am Mitchell Mason and, if you follow me this way, I'll show you why I can't "summon" Mr Draper.'

The only blessing about their awkward walk was that it was a short one. Mason had led them through the overheated communal cauldron which was the television and games room, and into a private room just off from the main corridor. The room was not too unlike a hospital ward, although there were a couple of comfy sofas facing out across the landscaped gardens.

The state they found Draper in suggested he hadn't enjoyed the view for some time. Bed-stricken and wired up to various monitors, the man was completely dependent on others. A distant gaze sat within a sunken face. He looked much older than Mason, his shrunken body struggled to fill its skin.

'Norris,' Mason spoke in a friendly reassuring tone. 'These are two gentlemen who wanted to say hello.'

'Tell them to fuck their mothers with their dead dads' dicks.'

Draper's face was a knot of temporary rage, before it relaxed and sagged around his skull once more.

'Now, now Norris,' Mason persevered. 'That's not the way to greet people, is it? Especially ones from the police.'

Draper's head flashed in their direction.

'The filth? Are you mad?' He looked around in disbelief. 'You'll get us all locked up. What are you doing inviting them into our house? Snitches wear stitches, you rat-faced bitch!'

Draper took a weak swing at Mason, who caught his friend's frail arm in one hand. He leaned in close, as if to whisper something, but paused halfway.

Addison noticed Mason swallow whatever he wanted to say. He was clearly denying his instincts. His reflex hit his throat like acid reflux, burning on the way down, and left to simmer in his stomach. The man seemed more considered when he next spoke.

'Norris, you're not at home. You know that. This is Ferndown, where the nurses look after you. Remember?'

'Remember? How could I forget.' Draper sprung to life again. 'The bleeding horror of it all. Care they call it. Monsters the lot of us.'

'Us?' Duke spoke directly to Draper.

'He's confused. He still thinks he works here. Seeing me in my role probably doesn't help him.'

'Why would he consider you monsters?' Addison spoke just above a whisper. He wanted to appear secretive to Mason, but would have been happy to get Draper's angle.

'What would you consider your captors?' Mason offered a defeated grin. 'Norris, like everybody else in Ferndown, doesn't want to be here, being fed spoon to mouth, having your arse wiped for you, these are things we do for children. Imagine being an adult and requiring that sort of assistance, it reduces you, weakens your position in life. It can breed bitterness towards the ones caring for you. It's not unnatural to resent the very people that remind you that you're no longer independent.'

'Mitchell did it.' Draper sat up as he spoke. 'The reason you're here. It was Mitchell, not me. I didn't do anything, I promise. Lock him up officers. Lock him up. I didn't hurt anyone.'

The man was almost crying as he spoke. Tears glazed his cold shark eyes.

'What is he talking about?' Addison watched every wrinkle on Mason's face as he spoke.

'Christ knows, he suffers with dementia. Two police officers turn up and he starts to feel paranoid. He's like this when the nurses come to treat him, he's certain they're either poisoning him or giving him pills to make him lose his mind. It's tragic to witness, the decline. When we were younger, Norris was the driving force behind our partnership. He loved his job, and in all my time working with him I can't recall him losing his temper once. But to see him like this, each and every day he grows stranger to me. It's like Norris began to leave us when the illness moved in. He was still Norris for the first few months, same bright smile, same gusto for life. But it's just the disease that greets us now. It's hard not to take it personally, his temper and outbursts, but it's not Norris, it's the Alzheimer's.'

Addison could feel Duke's posture collapse next to him. A wave of nausea washed over his entire body, staining him with guilt. Why the hell had he brought his friend here, especially so soon after finding out his fate.

You're a stupid shit Addison.

But the look Duke offered him was one of nothing but reassurance. A look that simply said, *'Don't worry... it's cool'*.

Mason had offered them both a coffee, and having said goodbye to Draper, which involved two grins and a round of untargeted obscenities, they all found themselves in a small kitchen. The brushed stainless-steel fittings made Addison's spine shiver. There was something too cold and clinical about the space. Couple that with the countless knives that decorated the walls on magnetic strips like a butcher's bunting, and you had yourself a set primed for a slasher movie.

'We're sorry to find your friend in such a way,' Duke spoke as Addison adjusted to his surroundings. 'It must be hard for you.'

'It is, sometimes.' Mason held his novelty-sized coffee cup with both hands, the size of which made it look like he was palming a small shit-pit.

The coffee didn't taste much better.

'You scalded them,' said Addison.

'Excuse me?' Mason's reply was a mixture of anger and insult. A clear defensive reflex.

'The coffee.' Addison nodded to his mug. 'You scalded them. A simple trick is to put the milk in before the water, if you're using cheap granules.'

'Thanks for the tip.' Mason's sarcasm was a lot thicker than his patience. 'May I ask, is this going to take much longer?'

'Not at all.' Addison spoke before Duke had the chance to offer both barrels. It was a power play he often deployed, used to ensure people knew their place, and that they would take as long as they needed. They were in control; the tail didn't wag this dog. However, Addison felt that he needed something softer, more surgical than Duke's sledgehammer to crack this nut. 'We just need to ask you a few questions about Precious Moments.'

'Wow, I haven't heard that name for some time. I'm guessing you already know that Norris and I used to manage the place. So, why else would you be asking after that place?'

'Because one of the guys you looked after grew up to kill a young girl.' Duke was now speaking. 'What I want to know is why, now that Benjamin Farrow has been granted another crack at fooling us all, have more kids disappeared? Any clues?'

Mason looked confused.

'Excuse me? Farrow, you say? I don't recall having a child by that name.'

'How about Randal?' Addison saw a flash of recognition. 'Benjamin Farrow went by that name as a child.'

'Randal?' Mason's pondering was a bluff. He was stalling. 'Yeah, I remember a kid by that name. Is he the same guy that is in the press now? I had no idea. Honest.'

'Most liars use that word. *Honest.* The truthful don't tend to see the need to say it.' Duke clearly didn't like this guy.

'With all due respect officers, go to hell.' Mason's patience was checking out. 'I've not seen Randal, or whatever... Farrow, for nearly twenty years. And it clearly wasn't me that failed to see the dots the first time around, let alone link them. How was I meant to know they were the same people, and so what anyway? No cops came ruining my day when the first girl was taken, so I'm guessing they didn't make the link either, or even care about it.'

'Well, we're here now.' Addison was starting to agree with Duke.

'I'd say better late than never, but I can't see how I could have helped you back then anyway. Randal was a boy when we looked after him. Not a bad kid to be honest. Kept himself to himself. Ended up being one of the oldest there if I remember right. Quite a bright boy, quiet, polite. No trouble. Now you say more children have gone missing? Well, I can't see how your man could do that from behind bars.'

'Did he have any friends?' Addison took the old polaroid from his pocket. 'Do you know any of the children in this picture?'

Mason took a second to look over the picture.

'That's definitely Randal. Or Farrow as you know him. Not sure of the other two, names-wise anyway. The big lad, I remember him a little. As strong as an ox he was. Came to us after he had throttled a lad into a coma. Now... he *was* troubled.'

'No shit,' said Duke. 'Do you remember his name?'

'No idea, sorry.'

'Is there anything about Precious Moments, some event, something that could have triggered something inside of these kids? We have reason to believe that recent events are connected to Farrow's past.'

Mason knew something.

'Nope. Nothing.' He shrugged. 'These kids come with every issue in the book. Places like ours, they are there to support these children, not nurture their bad nature.'

'And yet it got burned down?' Duke delivered his jab casually. It landed.

'Only because the place was abandoned and flammable. The site had been closed down for a while before someone decided to raze it to the ground. Norris and I had closed the doors, we didn't have the resources to carry on. Overheads were increasing, whilst local financial support was removed. We simply couldn't keep it afloat.'

'What happened to the children that were there when you had to close?' Addison finished his coffee.

'Just farmed out somewhere else I suppose. Social services would have just relocated them. Happens all the time.'

'And that was that?'

'That was that.' Mason offered an insincere smile, like the smug cousin you can't hit because you were visiting their house.

No words were exchanged as they left.

Outside, Addison walked with Duke to their car. The afternoon had passed them by, visitors to the centre were leaving, forming a small queue of cars by the barriers.

'He's lying,' Addison said what they were both thinking. 'That guy knows something and has no intention of sharing it.'

'Why would he?' Duke offered Addison a stick of gum. He declined. 'We haven't got anything to press him with, no leverage, nothing.'

'Still keeps the care home link on the table, I suppose.'

'Firmly.' Duke filled one side of his mouth with gum. 'I want to know who the big goon in the picture is.'

*

He watched as the two nosey pigs got into their car and drove away. He hadn't expected them. It had been some time since the first girl went missing and, because no questions were asked back then, they'd caught him off-guard today. That annoyed him. It could have cost him everything. He'd thought they would have seen the link sooner. From now on, he had to be careful once more. For a time, he had thought he was in the clear: that he'd got away with what he'd done. But now, they threatened to bring his sins into the light. Their questions had forced his hand.

Loose ends needed to be cut off.

The next few hours passed slower than usual, and now only a few staff members remained. His window had opened, but it would quickly close if he didn't act. He couldn't afford to be the last person to leave; he needed someone to see him go. But only after it was done.

Walking through the communal room, the central heating showered him with the bitter stench of hot piss which emanated from a shrivelled, abandoned figure curled up in an old recliner chair. Her eyes were fixed to the floor, as her fingers fidgeted in her damp lap.

Passing by where she was sat, he spat into her hair. He didn't even break his stride. He would have laughed if it wasn't for the risk of drawing breath in her proximity. Her stench alone was enough to choke him.

He continued to walk casually as he continued his rounds. Ducking into the first room along the corridor, he smiled as he saw his old friend. He was lying on his bed, wide awake but frozen within fractured thought.

Moving slowly but smoothly, he closed the door behind him. The lock clunked into place.

He approached the bed.

'Evening Norris.'

His voice brought his friend back into the room. His smile was one of familiarity, like a napping child woken softly by their mother.

Mason lifted his friend and straightened his bed.

'Do you remember the men who came to see us today?' He spoke calmly.

'Men?' Draper was oblivious. 'No, not at all. Were they nice?'

'More nosey than nice.' Mason smiled as he plumped up his friend's pillow. 'They were asking questions, too many questions if you ask me. Do you remember the questions we never wanted people to ask?'

A flash of fright filled Draper's eyes.

He remembered everything.

'*You* did it. *You* hurt them.'

Mason sighed.

'I was afraid you'd say that.' He pressed the pillow into Draper's face. 'I'm sorry my old friend, but I can't let them know what we did to the children.'

His friend tried to fight it, but he had no chance. Mason pressed harder.

He pressed until the force beneath his hands collapsed.

Draper's body relaxed.

He was gone. Forever silenced.

Chapter 42

His body rolled over to the cold side of the bed.

They'd spent the last few minutes frantically sharing the side closest to the door, before both of them, loosened by their spent lust, fell apart. The sex had sedated them. Feeling Piper's hands creep onto his heaving chest he shivered under the sparks her touch created. It was still early evening, but having missed four calls from Piper, Addison felt that he had some making up to do.

'Well, whatever kind of day you've had, make sure you see me next time you have another one just like it.' She hopped out of bed and threw one of his loose T-shirts on. He loved the way it smothered her. He tried to focus on the day he'd had, but Piper had a fantastic talent for distraction.

'Anyhow, whether it was great or shitty, it better had been a big one for you to keep missing my calls.'

'I missed more than just your calls.' He pulled her back onto the bed. They kissed briefly, before she lay by him and buried her head in his chest.

'So, which one was it. Good or bad?'

'Are you after a review?' He laughed.

'Oh, trust me, the faces you pulled... I know I did all right.'

'Was this one of them?' Addison pulled a face, crossing his eyes and curling his lip to one side.

'It was! Those were the eyes you undressed me with.'

'Well that will explain why one half of your clothes are on one side of the room, and the other half on the other side.'

They shared a small laugh. He was happy with her. She had a way to make him forget everything else.

'Have you ever heard of a man called Mitchell Mason, or Norris Draper?'

He could sense a pause in her.

'Nope. Why? Are they linked to your case somehow?'

'I think so. Just not sure how. You said you'd run a few missing children's stories before. Bit of a long shot, but I just wondered if you'd dealt with these guys in the past. They used to run the children's home that Farrow went to back when he was just a small troubled child. You know, before he became a child-killing bastard.'

'Now, now. It seems you're spending too much time with Duke, you're even starting to sound like him.'

'Is that how it works? I thought the phrase suggests that you are what you eat, not what you hear?'

'Well then, in that case Mr Generous, you are one fine pus...'

'Don't say it.'

'See. Point proven. You're not a fan of the naughty words, so you should leave them to Duke. I prefer a dirty tongue to a dirty mouth anyhow.' She flashed a wicked smile and skipped out of the room. Addison could hear the kettle click into life from the kitchen as he looked for his jeans.

Half-dressed, he joined Piper at his breakfast bar. Between them, they could almost make a whole outfit. She handed him a coffee.

'What was it about these guys that grabbed your attention?' She watched him over her mug.

'Just a feeling. Mainly from Mason, Draper wasn't really with us today.'

'What do you mean? You actually met these guys? How did you manage to track them down?'

'Yup,' Addison feigned smugness. 'Wasn't too difficult for a top detective like myself. Pulled a few favours in from some undercover contacts of mine. You know how it is?'

'Really?'

'Nah,' he gave her his killer smile. 'I wish it was that sexy. Mason works at a place called Ferndown, a few miles north from here. Luckily, he'd called the police a few times, on the rare occasion that some of the residents were playing up too much. Not sure how a guy his size couldn't handle a few old boys.'

'Well, he's used to dealing with kids, isn't he?'

'Excuse me?'

'The children's home,' Piper offered a shrug which simply said *you know*. 'Didn't you say he worked where Farrow had been housed as a kid? Maybe he was more adjusted to tackling children than adults.'

'Funny you should say that.' Addison took a drink of his coffee. 'There was something about the guy that bugged me. He was holding back.'

'Are you going to talk to him again?'

'Doubt it. Not for now anyway. We don't have much cause, and I hate to empower the suspicious with a case of police harassment. That way both our hands and feet get tied. It sometimes better to let things run. People don't always act naturally when they think we're watching.'

A mini-drumroll rang out from the breakfast bar. Addison's phone had been set to vibrate.

'Hello.'

It was DCI Wilson. Her team were working late and she wanted to check in. Her voice was strained but still strong enough to give Addison little room to refuse when she told him she'd prefer to speak to him in person.

The call ended on a rhetorical question, rather than an order.

Addison offered Piper a shackled smile. He told Piper that she was free to stay the night, or let herself out if she didn't want to crash. He wanted to appear cool, happy either way. Secretly he wanted her there for when he got back. Whenever that might be.

She was still half naked when he left.

Duke had taken the same call. Addison agreed to swing by and pick him up. The man was eating a small bag of popcorn as they entered the crisis room. A mocked-up sign with bold lettering declaring '*Major Cases Unit*' clung to the door like a forgotten Christmas decoration. A tired-looking DCI greeted them. A handful of red-eyed detectives typed out reports in silence, scornfully overlooked by large photographs of Amber Costello and Joseph Farnham.

Duke and Addison had been ushered into a small corner office which contained a small table cluttered with equipment used for video conferencing. The way Wilson closed the door suggested that this meeting was discreet, no need to fire up the projector.

'Gentleman, thank you for coming so quickly.'

Duke stifled a snigger. The opportunity was too easy to comment on. He was better than that.

'I hope your approach to this investigation has been a little more mature than that, Sergeant.' Wilson was too exhausted to entertain Duke's flippancy. 'I called you here to update you as to where we are with our case. As you may recall, our guy last signed off his work with seven magpies. Given that the scent has almost completely dropped off, I believe our assessment that their motivation was to remain a secret was accurate. My team have begun to hit brick walls at every turn. They've exhausted every obvious avenue, explored each angle, and still nothing. The Costello and Farnham families remain hopeful, which is our official stance also. But we all know that finding those children alive is unlikely.'

'Anybody raise any suspicions? Family, friends?' Addison already knew the answer.

'Nobody. We've spoken to everybody, searched every house, knocked every door within a three-mile radius of the home addresses. We cast the net out wide on this one, and not once have we had a reason to draw it in a little. Spike Harris was a dead end, initially anyway.'

'How do you mean?' Addison hadn't heard that name in a while. It seemed like forever since he'd surfaced from the swamp, and yet they were no further forward.

'Well, as you both know, Harris's statement proved to be a raindrop in the ocean. Didn't even cause a ripple with the case-review board on account of the witness's poor credibility. Not sure if you know this, but we showed Harris a few images of men matching the description he gave us, even slipped in Farrow's custody image from when you guys first scooped him up. Turns out Harris's memory wasn't so sharp after all. Didn't even recognise him at first, admitting that it was an old picture the press had used that caused him to work out who it was at the time, which meant that he had no clue what Farrow looked like at the time of the offence. And to top it off, he eventually said that it could have been any of the guys we showed him.'

'So why did swampy say that he knew Farrow didn't do it?' Duke was furious.

'Because he was working from the memory of the young boy he once knew. Which is interesting. For all his faults, Harris did give us Randal. Until Harris came along, we had no idea Farrow was ever Randal. And whilst Harris appears to know nothing about the man Farrow, he knew quite a bit about the boy Randal.'

'Meaning?' Addison felt a buzz in the air. Maybe it was the humming from all the electric equipment set on standby, but there was certainly something hanging around.

'What made Harris so sure that Farrow wouldn't hurt a child was the fact that Farrow himself suffered when he was young. I pulled a few strings with a friend from social services and they were able to find some old reports about Precious Moments. During the period Farrow was a resident, there were nearly twelve reports from children claiming that they were being abused.'

'Jesus Christ,' said Duke. 'What happened with the reports?'

'Something sat snuggly between very little and not a single thing,' replied Wilson. 'The kids were regarded as broken, troublesome, looking to exploit and escape the system any way they could. Hate to say it, but times were different back then. There was bliss in ignorance, people didn't want to believe that such horror existed, so they swept it under the carpet, turned a blind eye to it. Out of sight, out of mind.'

'Did Farrow ever make a call?' Addison knew a piece to the puzzle was forming. He just didn't know where to place it.

'No,' replied Wilson. 'But he does get a mention in one of the reports. A young boy, named Quinton Harvey, complained to his social worker that the staff members were *hurting* the children. He said that the men had a type, and he and Randal fitted into it. Now, Harvey appears to have been a bit slow, but if you read the report it is clear what he was trying to say.'

Wilson handed both the men a photocopy of an old letter. The note was handwritten, most likely by a social worker given the mesh of lines and squiggles that sat above the section which required Quinton Harvey's signature. His childish markings made what he was reporting even more disturbing. According to Harvey, he – as well as other boys that looked like him – were singled out and disciplined for no obvious reason. What started as a slap across the legs soon developed into a belt around the face. A push in the back became a push down the stairs leading into the cellar. It was in here that the children were raped.

'And this was overlooked?' Addison held up the note in disbelief.

'Seems so,' Wilson continued. 'We've been trying to locate members of staff, as well as previous residents. Given these reports, and the links our missing children have to being in care, I have to draw a line between the two, even if it's only in pencil until we can either rule it out or firm it up. We've narrowed down who the managers were at the time of this report, two guys by the names of Mitchell Mason and Norris Draper.'

Both men nodded.

'You know these men?' Wilson was surprised.

'We spoke with them earlier today.' Addison was glad he'd followed his gut.

Wilson's face went from surprised to completely confused.

'Today? You spoke with them today?'

'Yes Ma'am,' said Addison with a small smile. 'We had an itch we needed to scratch.'

'So then, you'll already be aware that Norris Draper died earlier today.'

Alarm bells.

'What?' Addison's gut took a hit. 'How exactly? Ma'am, Draper was alive when we saw him, not in a good way, but a lot better than dead.'

'He simply passed away, by all accounts. When we called the home the receptionist informed us. She was helpful, if not a little shocked by our timing. Seems that Norris had only just been found in his bed by one of the nurses doing her final evening checks. You say you spoke to him?'

'Barely, he has – sorry, had – dementia. We saw him briefly, spoke mainly to Mitchell Mason. Feel free to talk to that one, there's something not quite right with him. We asked about Farrow's background, whether there were any concerns about his time in care. If what you're telling me about Quinton Harvey is true, then we need to get hold of Mason as soon as possible.' Addison could feel his heartbeat racing.

'You don't think this is all a series of coincidences?' Wilson knew the answer.

'Ma'am, we're cops.' Duke took the stage. 'We don't believe in coincidence.'

Chapter 43

The net was drawing in. The line had tightened.

Time was becoming precious. If everything stayed in place, it wouldn't be long until the truth was revealed.

I'm not ready for that. I have more work to do.

Instead of staying put, they had decided to act. And fast. They always knew that more blood would be spilled, but they usually preferred to plan their movements, rather than react because of others outside of the plan.

The night was drawing in. Parked up outside Ferndown, they waited for everybody to leave. They needed to make sure they weren't being followed. The drive out of there was smooth enough, no obvious compromises. After seeing where they needed to go, they found a small place to park on a street two roads from where they were heading. They walked the rest of the way, cutting through a small playing field. It was poorly lit, which was perfect.

No eyes on me.

The tower block where Mitchell Mason lived was a rundown slab of litter-filled balconies and broken windows. The kind of place where the stairwells doubled up as a public toilet, and the secure door had been propped open by a loose house-brick.

The place was used by local drug addicts and their dealers, so whatever CCTV footage had been in place, it had long been removed. The concierge desk in the communal hallway hadn't been manned for months, and both lifts were out of use.

There was no point being overly discreet. The people that passed through the block were a faceless flock, overlooked and ignored by their neighbours. Everybody knew what type of person ended up in a place like this, and nobody cared what happened to them, as long as they stayed where they were.

Passing through the doorway, they kicked the loose house-brick, causing the door to shut behind them. The small clunk of the lock felt satisfying, it gave them time. As they'd hoped, a series of small post boxes had been bolted to the wall. Amongst the countless flyers for cheap take-outs was a mountain of junk mail. Any legitimate post had been crammed into the individual boxes assigned to each flat. It only took a couple of minutes to find the one they were after.

Number 34.

The keypad to the broken lift informed them that this flat was on the third floor.

Nobody had seen them use the stairs. The third-floor corridor was filled with the scent of cheap deep-fat fryers and the noise from stolen surround-sound systems. Standing outside the door to number 34, they could hear the sounds of a battlefield from inside. The thin wooden door vibrated with every blast, shots were being fired and shouts could be heard ringing out above the chaos.

But only one voice.

A voice that poured ice-cold water down their spine.

Picking the lock was easy. They'd learned that trick when they were a child.

The cellar door was always the hardest.

One quick glance to make sure nobody was watching, and then they were in. Shutting the door slowly, they could have slammed it for all the noise that was being made from the back room.

Explosions, gunshots, boys screaming in anger.

The voice issued a laugh that washed away twenty years of freedom in an instant. It was the same laugh they had heard when they were a child. The same laugh that was as blunt as his hands, and as deep as his fingers.

Walking through the small hallway, it was clear he was alone. All of the lights inside were off, apart from the flashes of colour that bounced out from the far room. The door was wide open.

Moving slowly, they entered the room.

He was sat there, back to the doorway, slouched in a crinkled leather recliner. A head set with a small microphone was perched across his fat sweating head.

They heard his voice again.

'Ha ha! I'll get you, just you wait.'

Images of a warzone filled the flat-screen in front of him. Various usernames and tags ran down the right-hand side. In his bulky palms rested a small games controller, but his thumbs were still, the character on the screen motionless.

'You're so good at this.' He whispered down the microphone.

The softness of his tone crawled up their skin, forcing every hair on their arm to tremble. They held their breath.

'You need to teach me how to be as good as you.' His right hand reached into his pants.

Fire filled their veins.

Mason continued to whisper into his headset.

They took a step closer to him.

'Tell me. How old are you?'

'Old enough to fight back.'

The expression on his face was what they had been waiting to see for as long as they could remember. Since the hurt had started and all the innocence before was removed. It was the same face they had all pulled whenever Mason visited them in the dead of night. It was the face that came just before he started to do cruel things to them. The face that told him they were at his mercy.

Pure fear.

Chapter 44

He wanted blood.

He wanted the hurt to transfer the screams from his head into another's. To silence the shadow that haunted him.

A child's voice rattled inside his skull, tearing his mind into fragments that no longer fit together. Their face was like he had never seen it before, a twisted imagining of something that was once so beautiful to him. It made him want to do bad things.

The worst things.

Cold sweat cloaked him, clothing his broken body. The floor to his cell felt cold beneath his knuckles. He could feel them begin to bleed with every thrust and push. His arms ached as he pressed on, pushing himself to the brink. His muscles were exhausted, but his mind raged. With every press-up his breath became more visible, more forced, more desperate.

He deserved to be where he was; hidden from the world outside. The world he had shamed and let down. But he didn't deserve his torment. To him, his feelings were natural, nothing more than reflex. But not everybody agreed with his motives. He'd been able to hide his urges from the countless doctors and psychiatrists, all probing and prodding him into some casebook pigeonhole. But he didn't fit into any of them. He belonged where he was, he knew that. Only those that truly knew him understood why he needed to be inside.

Collapsing under his spent arms, Seth felt the cold floor kiss his face. All he wanted was to close his eyes and feel nothing at all. But the voice always came calling.

Never let me go.

He closed his eyes.

Hold me.

Tears traced the scars on his face.

Love me.

'I do.'

*

They'd chosen to act now.

Something was telling him they were closer to their guy. Addison called Piper. After several rings he was preparing to leave a message, until her soft voice answered. He explained that he wasn't going to be back for a while. She had sensed the excitement in his voice and after some loose probing he revealed the source of his enthusiasm.

'So, you're heading over to his address now?' asked Piper.

'We are,' his reply was hurried. 'Mitchell Mason was holding back today, and now I think I know why.'

'Funny you should say that.' Piper was calmer than her caller. 'After you asked me earlier whether I'd heard of the two guys, Mason and Draper, I made a few calls to my freelance mafia and one of them came back to me with a few things you might want to hear.'

'That's great,' Addison's voice was muffled by the sound of the engine. 'But it may have to wait for when I get back.' Parking sensors punctuated his words. 'We're here now.'

'What?' Piper sounded panicked. 'You're there already? Addison, trust me... if you're about to go and meet this guy, then you'd do better knowing exactly what type of person you'll be dealing with. He's dangerous. Seriously, why don't you hold on for a bit, wait for me to meet you there. I won't slow you down. I promise.'

He gave her the address.

'Come along, but we can't wait around. Just let us do our thing,' Addison insisted. 'Hang back from the location. I'll speak to you after.'

They parked in the small car park next to the tower block. There were no other cars around, none drivable at least. Addison stared at the burnt-out carcass of an old transit van as he got out of his car.

Had that been green?

'What are you doing?' Duke was bouncing on the balls of his feet. 'We need to get up there.' He flicked his bald head in the direction of the block of flats. 'Jesus Christ... come on!'

Addison knew he couldn't hold them up. Whatever Piper had to tell him, it would have to wait, he already had enough experience to get a true measure of the man. Mason was a low-life, a mainstream hitchhiker, thumbing around until he could get his next fix. Guys like him hid in plain sight, in places that gave them authority, that gave them *access*. Addison had a measure of exactly what he was dealing with. He didn't need to mull that one over. Instead, his brain was firing out possible connections to his case. Links, appetites, motives. Maybe Mason was taking the children? Maybe after his access was removed when the children's home was closed down, he was forced to branch out, take risks, go public? Maybe he'd gathered a taste for something that he just couldn't quit?

The front door to the block was closed. DCI Wilson pressed the trade button but got no reply. She then chose one at random.

After three loud droning tones on the intercom, a gruff voice answered.

'Yuh?'

'Police.' DCI Wilson flashed a badge towards a camera lens that was likely to be broken. 'We need access to the building.'

The intercom gave out a crackle as the connection ended.

The door clunked.

They were in.

The block was no different to countless others they had all attended throughout their careers. Stale lighting stained the tired walls of the stairwell, cheap bulbs buzzed and flickered above them, whilst the smell of bleach did little to mask the piss.

'Some stairway to heaven this,' Duke laughed as he took two steps at a time. 'More like hell's own colon.'

DCI Wilson chuckled. 'We've been to worse places than this in our time Derek.'

'Well, you've never let me take you to anywhere nicer.' He winked before spinning on his heels and bounding ahead.

'He's one of a kind, that guy,' Addison smiled.

'He sure is,' replied Wilson. 'Addison...' she paused for a moment, 'I know.' She watched the words land. 'And I know you do also. I can tell he's already told you. It shows in your face when you talk to him.'

'Ma'am?' Addison tried his best 'confused' face. It bombed.

'Cut the act. One of his doctors called me. He shouldn't have, but I could see why he did. They thought I ought to know in case it jeopardised him on the job; put him and others at risk, clouded his judgements.'

'And?'

'And I'll tell you what I told them. I'd keep hold of him until the end. There's nobody I respect more in this job than that fool in front of us.'

A door opened one floor above them.

'Hurry up you couple of reprobates,' Duke spoke in a raised whisper. 'The knob lives on this floor.'

Stood outside the door to number 34, a sense of dread greeted them. It was palpable, a tangible tension that they had all greeted many times before. It was never the noisy jobs, the loud fights or street squabbles that unnerved them, it was the still ones. The ones where a sense of spent violence vibrated in the air around them.

The door was closed.

They knocked. Five times, then twice. Classic cop knock.

No movement.

No answer.

No sign of life.

And then they saw it. They didn't know who saw it first, but without saying a word, all three of them were now staring at a small trail of red droplets on the floor.

There were only two drops in the hallway. None beyond what they could see. If there were to be any more, then they all knew where it would be.

On the inside.

The next knock came from Duke's boot. The cheap lock broke on impact, the broken door stood shocked against the hallway wall, its handle impaled through thin plasterboard.

All the lights were off. All, apart from the rear room.

Instinct drew them in, through the dark, narrow hallway, past the still walls and closed doors, towards where the air felt thickest.

The bloodstained breadcrumbs outside had led them into a feast of pure carnage.

'Oh my...' DCI Wilson put a hand to her mouth.

Addison flinched. Part of him wanted to help, to try and save the man in front of them. But it was clearly too late.

Slumped in a soiled leather recliner was the body of Mitchell Mason. A polythene bag had been placed over his head and sealed by reams of industrial-strength tape, choking at his throat. In his lap was a smashed photo frame. Pieces of the glass had been dug into his thighs.

Addison assumed the killer had used a large knife for the rest of the attack. The cuts were deep and wide. The thick warm blood that pooled in every crease of his folded frame made it impossible to see how many wounds decorated his body. The attack on his chest had been frenzied, ferocious, visceral. The attack on his neck, however, appeared more final. A single long, dense, drawn-out entry wound had forced Mason's head backwards, splitting the skin of his throat into a deathly dark smile.

'Jesus Christ!'

Addison turned to see Piper stood in the doorway.

'What the hell is she doing here!' Duke stepped between Piper and Mason's body, but she had already got close enough to see the bloodbath.

'I'm so sorry,' said Piper. 'I couldn't help it. I thought you needed to know what I knew about Mr Mason before you spoke with him. I messed up. I shouldn't have come here.'

'You gave her the address?' DCI Wilson's voice was as authoritative as Duke's was angry. 'DC Clarke, escort this woman from this scene immediately.'

Outside, Piper was her most apologetic.

'Addison, honestly... I didn't know.'

'Listen, how could you have known? None of us did. Don't worry about it, seriously. I'm sorry you had to see that.'

'It's okay. Maybe if I'd have called earlier... who knows, maybe you could have saved him. From what I found out, it's clear a guy like Mason would have his enemies.'

'I know about his past,' said Addison. 'About the allegations.'

Piper seemed relieved, as if the news that she wouldn't have to repeat what she knew somehow saved her from reliving it all. The allegations had been gruesome and graphic, words that now belonged to how Mason had met his end. She slumped into Addison's arms, relaxing as she felt them tighten around her.

Already officers were beginning to arrive, securing the scene. Blue lights bounced from every surface.

After a minute, Piper hugged her man, and spoke with a controlled sadness.

'Do you want to know what Mason did exactly? The details?' She didn't wait for a reply. 'From what I've learned, Mitchell Mason was a monster. A bully, a thug and a predator. He liked them young, illegal. They were children. For days on end he'd keep a child tied up in the basement of the care home, until it was time to rotate his stock. Believe me, what he did to those children down there fully justifies what happened to him up there.' Piper looked at the tower block. 'That man had earned his ending.'

*

Upstairs, Wilson and Duke were waiting for SOCO to arrive. They'd done the best they could to preserve the crime scene, although that fool Piper had gone some way to contaminating it completely. Forensics would be a minefield. Technically, anyone she'd been in touch with recently had just been dragged into play. All it took was a single transferred fibre, or fragment of skin or hair, and you could be in places you'd never even set foot.

However, this crime had a sense of the familiar about it. There was a pause in the act, something about it that suggested it wasn't done by a stranger. The detail, the anger, the wrath, all of them pointed to someone with a motive more than material. Although difficult to say, it didn't look as if anything had been disturbed. No drawers pulled out, no sign of a search. Mason himself had been the target. He was the prize. Whoever killed him enjoyed what they'd done. It wasn't panic that punctured his jugular, tearing his windpipe in two, it was clarity, pure lethal intent.

'Do you think this is linked to our case?' Wilson knew there was a piece missing. She could see the dots, just didn't know how they connected.

'Too coincidental not to be. Too far removed to join up.' Duke bit at his thumbnail as he spoke.

SOCO hadn't taken long to arrive. Flashbulbs had punched fits of bright white light into the small room, strobing the butchered body, freezing Mitchell Mason's final moments frame by frame.

One of the forensics team removed the polythene bag, careful not to cause Mason's head to detach completely, before continuing with their photography. It was only when Mason was modelling for his close-up that the officer finally spoke.

'Ma'am,' his voice was muted by the paper mask. 'You may want to see this.' He signalled for a colleague to join him. After a quick inspection, the colleague went to his small toolbox before returning with a pair of tweezers and an evidence bag.

Slowly, he began to remove a thick square of folded paper. It was mottled by blood and phlegm.

'Hold on a second.' Duke stopped the officer from sealing the square in an evidence bag. 'What is that? Let me take a look.'

Thick spit glossed over his gloves as he carefully opened up the folded paper.

Holding it by its edges, Duke felt the shot of adrenaline coursing towards his fingertips. He showed it to Wilson.

It meant nothing to her.

Embossed on a yellowed piece of paper was the image of several children at play. One sat reading their book, as another enjoyed a nearby makeshift swing. Behind them stood a large white-bricked house. Two adults stood watching from the entrance, their faces crowned by deep, scathing frowns. At the very front were three small children, all similar in appearance. Fair hair framed their solemn stares.

Chapter 45

The photograph had been an original. It was a much larger version than the one Duke had stored in Benjamin Farrow's case file. All he had was the image of the three children, he had no idea what story sat behind them. It was the first time Duke had seen the other children, all enjoying the moment, each and every one of them serving to accentuate the misery on the familiar faces at the front.

Farrow's was one of complete contempt.

'Is that Mason?' Addison was stood behind Duke, who was examining a copy of the exhibit at his desk. Mason's body had been swabbed, snapped and was now en route to be bagged and toe-tagged. SOCO would still be combing the scene along with the OSU.

'The guy looked a creep even back then,' said Duke. 'The other guy must be Draper, hard to tell seeing him stood upright and not gurning.'

'Duke, I spoke with Piper.' Addison could see the flash of anger cross his supervisor's face. 'I know... I know... she messed up royally back there, but she was only trying to help. She'd done some digging, turns out that Mason and Draper dished out their own form of care at this place. Towards the end of their tenure, there were some serious allegations of abuse.'

'I know,' Duke was still transfixed by the photo. 'DCI Wilson told me that the place had been peppered with complaints of paedophilia. None were taken seriously, and none were from this miserable shit here.' He pointed to the young Benjamin Farrow. 'He got a name-drop in a report from a kid called Quentin Harvey though. By all accounts, Farrow was often flavour of the month with the staff, due to his ill-temper, arrogance and complete disobedience. It seemed the staff chose "alternative methods" of discipline on him. The sick bastards. Do monstrosities make monsters?'

'You mean, the classic "abused becomes the abuser" theory? It can happen. Most of the time it doesn't, but then most of the time we don't get to hear about somebody's pain. You have to wonder what gets rebuilt when a person is destroyed like that. Surely, rage, anger, hatred bleed into the gaps, and cement parts of their mind together again.' Addison watched Duke's head slowly bob in approval. He landed his finger on the photo like a mini-missile. 'We need to check this place out. There has to be a link.'

'To our case?' Duke shrugged. 'Maybe. Could just be that Farrow's case review has kicked up some dirt that one kid had buried a long time ago. Maybe that's why Mason got what he was due. I'm a firm believer that there's no smoke without fire.'

'Like the fire at Precious Moments?'

'Exactly. Whilst you rummage around the rubble of what remains of that place, I'm going to check in with scenes-of-crime, see if they've found anything to finally put some distance between this and our investigation. Everything's getting a bit too close, it's starting to fog up the brain. I need some space to breathe, and think clearly.'

*

Addison didn't fancy the trip on his own. Eventually, with the promise of some good wine and a home-cooked meal, he'd been able to persuade Piper to join him. She'd sounded reluctant at first, most likely because she'd had her head blown clean from her shoulders the last time she'd visited a crime scene.

But this was different. There was no preserved scene, no police cordon, no official interest whatsoever. Yet Addison knew he had to see the place in person: to be amongst it, to feel the atmosphere that hung in the air. No matter how much time had passed, sites that had suffered pure trauma always carried a weight with them, as if gravity clung to it for fear of letting it spreading any further.

He had no idea what he expected to find there, maybe nothing. But he was getting itchy.

Pulling up, he parked at the side of the road. The driveway was blocked by an old rotten gate. Behind it sat a neglected pebble-stone path that ran all the way up to where the house once sat.

'Looks like we can get in through here.' Piper had found a small wooden stile in the fencing. She was making her way through scattered trees and hedgerows when Addison caught up with her.

'Have you been here before?' He laughed as he watched her navigate her way through the overgrown bushes.

'Come now Detective,' she fired a smile his way. 'It's not hard to see where *we're* heading.'

Her emphasis was intentional. She always flirted when she was uncomfortable. It could be used to deflect, disarm or misdirect, all with the purpose of gaining some form of control. In this instance it was most likely to distract herself from the thought of what lay ahead. Either way, her emphasis still made his heart thump in his chest to an unfamiliar beat. She knew exactly how to play him.

It took a couple of minutes to reach the rubble. Charred rocks and broken bricks were strewn amongst rotten wood, as fragments of wall hinted at the layout.

'Did anything survive?' Addison sighed.

'From what the reports said, it seems the fire had taken hold for some time before the emergency services arrived. There was a suspicion of foul play on account of the possible use of an accelerant, but this was found to be inconclusive. A fire this big takes everything with it.' Piper stood with her hands planted on her slim hips.

'Hold on,' Addison spoke excitedly. 'Didn't you say that some of the reports of abuse suggested the use of a basement? Maybe if we can find that, then there could be something that the flames couldn't reach.'

Piper flinched.

'Are you okay?' Addison rested his hand on her shoulder.

'I'm fine... honest.' She smiled solemnly. 'It's just the idea of basements. Not a girl's idea of a great date.'

'Is that what you think this is?' Addison laughed. 'Don't go telling your family you've found a guy that has a habit of taking you to crime scenes for kicks.'

He could see she was serious.

'Okay, no problem. If we find it, I'll go and check it out. You can keep watch and shout for me if the ghosts of Mason and Draper come calling.'

The basement was easy to find. A cellar door sat to the side of where the building would have stood. Two busted doors clung to old hinges, pinned to the ground by a combination of time and decay. Nature had moved in a long time ago. Vines entwined the handrail that lead down the moss-covered stairwell. At the bottom an open doorway invited both the brave and the stupid inside.

'Are you sure you don't want to come?' Addison shouted back to Piper, who hadn't moved a muscle since he last spoke with her. After a few seconds of silence, he made his way inside.

It was a portal to hell.

The darkness threatened to pull the hairs from his skin. A chill whistled through the walls, dancing in the shadows. The burned bleach and petrol stuck to the back of his throat, as if he had to chew the air before he could breathe it in. Moisture licked his fingers as he fondled his way through the dark.

Fumbling for his phone, he flicked on the touch-light function.

The face of a child greeted him.

His heart hit his stomach, his last meal hit the roof of his mouth.

Nailed to the wall was the head of a life-sized doll. Maggots crawled from within the sunken eye sockets and gaping mouth. It's once blond hair was now raven black with dirt and grime. Beneath the head, chains clung to the walls, their shackles slumped upon the ground.

There was little else left in the room. A steel bucket sat in one corner, just within reach of the chain-linked bonds, and a hollowed-out fireplace broke the far wall in two.

On the end of the wall where the cellar doorway sat was another doorway, presumably leading back into the house. Half a dozen steep wooden steps welcomed you at the foot of the door. There were no windows. No radiators. Just the odd copper pipe which crawled up the walls and into the flooring above. A mattress with the remains of the doll took centre-stage. The springs were broken as the material sagged beneath the countless suspicious stains.

Beneath the doll's head, well within reach of the chains, several names had been scratched into the wall.

Francis.

William.

Quentin.

Jacob.

Benjamin.

Two of them – William and Jacob – had been scratched out. Their names a lot fainter than the other three. The letters to those remaining were much deeper, more pronounced, as if they had been given more time, more attention.

Addison had seen enough.

The air that greeted him outside tasted like cold purified water. He let it wash down his throat as he tried to stop his mind from picturing what the children had endured inside that room.

The warmth of the mid-afternoon did little to thaw the chill that had gripped his skin.

Piper was stood next to an old makeshift swing. Her arms were wrapped around her chest. She made no attempt to approach Addison. The look she gave him was more of fear and concern than anything else.

'This place gives me the chills. Did you find anything?' Her voice was soft.

'Trust me,' Addison walked towards her. 'You do not want to be going down there. Something terrible was housed within those hidden walls. Something that had been able to skulk in the shadows for decades, until we went digging, until something we did allowed it to escape and rip Mitchel Mason's throat in two. The ghost of what was left to die down there is what's haunting us all. Whatever happened down there Piper... I just don't know how you'd live with that.'

His pocket vibrated.

It was Duke.

'Hello,' Addison did that thing when people answer the phone and turn away, as if it offered any more privacy. His voice was still loud enough to be heard. Duke's was even louder.

'How was the field trip? Get yourself a souvenir?'

'Not quite the place for keepsakes, but I have a feeling whatever we're dealing with was conceived here. The missing kids in care, Mason and Draper, Farrow... they're all strokes in the same painting.'

'Can you tell what it is yet?'

'Poor joke.'

'Well, my boy... whilst you were playing *Rolf's Cartoon Club* amongst the ashes of a paedophile's playground, I was doing some proper police work.'

'Go on.' Addison hoped for some good news.

'Remember the burnt-out van outside Mason's tower block? It got me thinking. Joseph Farnham's mum stated that she'd seen a green transit van acting suspiciously near to where she dropped her boy off at school. Mums on their school runs tend to spot these things... things out of the ordinary. Apart from child-snatchers, that is. Anyway, I got the guys at the scene to run some checks on the burnout, and...'

'It was a green van?' Addison had the scent of a trail picking up.

'Nope.' Duke laughed. 'However, it made me wonder about the original. Turns out Wilson had tasked some squeaky-clean, green and keen detective to trawl through the CCTV. The newbies are always given the soul-destroying tasks. Why do you think you're out in the cold and I'm inside with a hot cup of coffee? Well, thank whatever god you follow for creating sycophants, because this butt-kisser really went the extra mile to impress his new gaffer.'

'What did they find?'

'Two vans.' Duke paused. 'Two distinctive green transit vans in the same area at the same time. Never in the same shot, mind you. Just like me and Bruce Willis... you never see us in the same space, do you? Gets you thinking... are they the same? What are the odds on two distinctively green vans, with similar markings, being in the same area at the same time? These kidnapper wagons are like buses. You pray for a lifetime that one doesn't show up and then two come along at once, ready to steal your kids right from under your nose. Unless, that is... we are only dealing with just the one. A quick switch of the registration plates is enough to cause that confusion. So, we tested the theory. ANPR cameras picked up the van leaving the area of the school. We ran the plates and there were no records on that one. The plate was a fake. Swing and a miss. No camera picked it up entering the local area at all either. However, the plates on the van coming into the area before the snatch happened...'

'Yeah?'

'We got a hit.'

Chapter 46

He'd heard the news.

Most of him was glad. He hoped they had suffered.

The same way that they had made him suffer.

The torture that Mitchell Mason and his friends had subjected him to still visited him at night, creeping into his sleep, scratching at his sanity when he was at his most vulnerable. The cold chains, the countless faces, the depraved appetites of strangers – all catered for by Mason – had left him without a past, without a childhood, his youth utterly lost and broken beyond repair. His only option was reinvention. It was what they all had to do if they wanted to survive. Nobody could ever know who they were, or what had happened to them.

Recovery required anonymity.

Otherwise, the abused could easily become the accused.

That was the problem with being a victim, life treated you differently. It saw you as somehow different to normal folk. The damage defined you. Failure to recover was expected, anticipated, and any tiny degree of appearing 'normal' was greeted with patronising applause, and diluted by empty compliments and feigned interest. The only thing that *truly* interested people about the victim was the crime they had been a victim of. The consequence was irrelevant, a discarded by-product to morbid fascination, serving only to illustrate the depravity of the act itself. If anything, the damage glorified the deed.

That's why some of them had acted out, why those in pain felt driven to inflict it on others. When pain is in every single weighted breath, the pressure in comfort could drown you, make you feel unworthy of real care and attention.

Unworthy of honest affection.

Utterly unlovable.

So... of course he was happy that they were dead.

But the fear they created remained. Even beyond the grave, Draper and Mason threatened his freedom. Their untimely deaths, though welcome, made him relevant once more.

Having already stolen his youth, their murders had the potential to rob him of his future. He was not going to let that happen. Even if it meant siding with beasts.

'Trust me... we'll ensure that our case is distanced from recent developments.'

Russell Alderman was sweatier than usual. The oiled hair on his head sat atop a forehead filmed by grease. He looked uneasy, almost uncomfortable. He suppressed a belch into a tissue before he continued.

'Just because there is a link between the two dead guys and your childhood, the matter is irrelevant. A complete side story to our case at best.'

'But what if there *is* a link?' Benjamin couldn't look at his legal representative for longer than a few seconds. 'What if all of this is linked to those guys? Both of those bastards are from my past, and now that my case is up for review, not only does someone start copying the original crime, two people who abused me are dead. One murdered, the other, who knows? It's all a little convenient. And I don't care how you try to spin it, it still puts me squarely in the middle.'

'I don't see how.' Alderman gave a look that appeared more constipated than considered.

'Really?' Benjamin was losing his patience. 'You can't see how this makes me relevant? The public hate me. Once they'd completed their witch-hunt the first time around, they were done with me. I was gone. Neatly packaged off and out of sight, nobody needed to fear the bogeyman anymore. They'd caught him! "Sleep well kids, there's nobody under your bed." Until I get my case review that is, and like the uninvited guest that causes a stinking scene, I'm back in everybody's lives, destroying their sanctuary. Buried enquiries get dug up. Original answers questioned. And this just pisses the people off even more. I'm the boil on their balls that they thought they'd got rid of, the wart on the face that makes people look at them differently. They want me gone. Even quicker this time. But then – when the children started to disappear – the public had to reconsider everything. They even dared to take the idea of my innocence seriously. Soon, too many questions and not enough answers filled their heads. Fear snuck in. These questions cloud my guilt. How could I be responsible when I'm under lock and key of Her Majesty? How could the monster who killed Elizabeth Silver be committing these crimes from behind bars? Maybe he's innocent after all. Maybe... just maybe... we got the wrong guy. Jackpot! The focus shifts, it starts to look into new facts, the ones that track a different animal altogether. Suddenly, I'm in the background, a blur in the blurb. Gradually, I become invisible, inconsequential… irrelevant. Irrelevant, until the blood of the men that molested me stains every new article available. Now I'm part of the narrative again. My past is again interesting. My entire life, seemingly one long motive for murder. None of this shit can help my case. Time has already put two decades of distance between those men and me. Twenty years of sleepless nights, countless nightmares, with only the soft hum of terror to get me back to sleep. But all of that was bliss compared to what happened before. Not once has my sleep been broken by their hands. The memories may haunt me, but the men can no longer hurt me. Not physically. Time has put me out of their reach. Until now. Now everybody will know my past, and the man I built will be once again reduced to a broken boy. I can't see what somebody like you can do to help.'

'I can turn heads.' Alderman raised his fat hands. They rested on his inflated wrists like two slabs of old steak that were on the turn. 'Mr Farrow, your head is facing behind you. Whether you're watching over your shoulder for your next attacker in the showers, or whether you're fixating on the past, your perspective is backwards. It'll only slow you down. Sprinters don't check behind them, they focus in front, and that's what I'm here to do, to get you focused on what's ahead of you. I want you walking with blinkers on. Walking in a single straight line, with pure tunnel vision, no detours, directly towards your pardon and freedom.'

'And how exactly do you plan to achieve that?' Benjamin watched the man regain his shallow breath.

'The same way everybody takes control: through fear. Present, real, tangible fear. My campaign will stir up the public, make them realise that a killer walks amongst them. I'll make them look over their shoulders, leave them distracted by a current threat. I'll let the red mist blind them, cloud their peripherals to the point that nothing but the man responsible for the recent abductions matters. They won't care about you. And that's a good thing. They'll be no outcry for forgiveness, no plea for you to accept their apology. That will never come. With my help, you will become an aside to it all. An ugly obstacle between them and the truth: a scrawny obstruction simply bulldozed by the sheer force of their fear. You'll be nothing to them. Your freedom will be signed for by a distracted, preoccupied public, more concerned about capturing what threatens them than considering the risks of setting a "guilty" man free.' His bunny ears looked more like trotters. He grunted on. 'I'll turn you into a man who no longer endangers the public. A man whose conviction only serves to slow down their collective incessant stampede towards safety. They won't want to look over their shoulders at you anymore. All we need now is to play on that fear. Show them that the two dead men were monsters. Monsters that have more enemies than just you alone. *Everybody* would want them dead. They deserved it. That way, your link means nothing, because *they* hate monsters too. Finally, a miracle... you and them have something in common. You're not on the outside anymore. Wow, they may even sympathise with you. You are a victim, after all. Soon, they'll see that too.'

*

Deep down he knew Alderman was right.

If his past was to become relevant, then they should flavour it with the same fear that the public were feeling. By tossing it into the mix, it became part of the blend, just another ingredient to the concoction that confused the masses. His crime was no longer the main course. People had dined out on his guilt for far too long, and now they had to plate up something else for the people to feast upon. Granted, serving them up a serial killer was going off-menu. Nobody would have ordered that. And yet, they were all hooked; addicts to the end, clawing at the scraps served up to them in the tabloids, digesting it piece by piece before regurgitating their own version in gossip sessions over the neighbour's fence, or within online theories fired out by bored thumbs, longing for general acceptance.

Identifying what was different helps to define us. For a while Benjamin Farrow had been the difference. But not anymore.

'There's the dirty stinking deviant now.'

The sound of James Jenkins' voice dragged down his back like a blunt knife. He didn't bother to turn around. The scattering of several feet told him all he needed to know.

His time was up.

Jenkins and his pack of caged dogs had decided today was the day that Benjamin Farrow met his end. It was now or never. The more innocent he looked, the more he slipped away from them.

They couldn't allow that.

The first punch was thick but a little too high. It grazed the side of Benjamin's head but caught enough to leave him dazed. Things went a little fuzzy, like he'd stood up too fast. The second came in low, straight into the kidneys. Warm bile filled his mouth, then the wind left his lungs as the third fist hit.

Benjamin's knees met the ground a moment before somebody's boot almost cracked his neck in two. In vain, he covered his eyes. There was no fight in his fists. No fire in his belly. Just kick after kick. Boot after boot.

Jenkins was at the front this time, no longer hiding behind his orders. This time he wanted to watch his work in action. He wanted to see the man hurt, maybe even see him die. A tethered excitement was captured in his voice, a mixture of joy and fear, the same way a child giggles with tempered glee when they know they shouldn't be doing whatever they're doing.

Jenkins knew the consequence of killing Benjamin. But his life sat beyond consequence. That was the perk of being damned.

He ran his fingers through Benjamin's hair, gripped a lump of it near to the roots, and lifted Benjamin's head until his neck was at his mercy.

'Confess, and I'll make it quick.' Jenkins' voice hissed through gritted teeth. Phlegm frothed on his lips. 'Tell me where the girl is.'

'I don't know.'

He wasn't lying.

'Admit it!' Jenkins used his fist for punctuation. Benjamin could feel a tooth loosen in his jaw.

'I can't.' Benjamin's breath was bloodied. Thick liquid pooled inside his gaping mouth.

'Then I'm afraid this is going to be really painful for you.' Jenkins let out an excited giggle which he cut short. He leaned in so that the heat of his words could be felt on Benjamin's face. 'I don't know what part of you I want to eat first. I'd bite the tongue straight out of your mouth, but that would rob me of the chance to hear you beg for your life. Maybe...' He ran his tongue across Benjamin's cheek. 'I'll start with an ear.'

Benjamin could feel the pinch of teeth against his ear. Thick saliva caked the skin, before blood began to pour down the side of his face.

But there was no pain. No pull of flesh from his skin.

Only sound.

The sound of Jenkins screaming.

His grip had loosened from his hair. His hands became too busy trying to hold his own jaw together. The screams continued, but they became choked by blood. The cries turned to gargled splutters, and coughs gurgled beneath pure panic.

Benjamin looked up. The entire mob stood like statues, before slowly retreating, one tiny step at a time, never once taking their eyes from the scene in front of them.

Only one man remained standing, his fist clenched, violence vibrating within.

Seth.

His saviour once more.

Unfolding his fingers, Seth offered Benjamin his hand. He could see that it had already begun to swell. For a moment Benjamin almost felt sorry for what had been on the end of it until he quickly realised *who* that had been.

Coiled up in a ball of defeat and despair, James Jenkins lay at their feet. His jaw was shattered. His teeth smashed with such force that he had bitten off his own tongue.

The flap of flesh lay still, growing cold as its former owner shivered with agony beside it.

Chapter 47

The van was registered to a florist ten miles out of town.

Addison had a warrant sworn out to search both the premises and vehicle, but that was a last resort. They were planning to rely on good old-fashioned goodwill. People were often more than helpful with police enquiries, and there was no intelligence to suggest that anybody at 'Bouquets By Bonnie' was any different.

It took them nearly an hour to reach the store. It was coming up to the end of the financial year and councils were looking to blow their budgets on countless roadworks in a bid to justify their funding for the next twelve months.

'Come on... for fuck's sake!' Duke bibbed his horn for the sixth time in twenty minutes. Not that the car in front had anywhere to go. The busy high street had been reduced to one lane. A stream of burnt orange traffic cones dripped towards a group of workers gathered around a collection of machinery and tools. None of them being used.

'Good to see you're busy, pricks.' Duke didn't seem to mind that his parting shot was met with gridlocked traffic. Addison could feel the scowl of the half-dozen workers burning into the side of his face. The one in charge tapped on the passenger window. Duke pressed the button to lower it.

'You got a problem mate? Us lads are on our lunch.' He leant his thick forearms on the door frame. A mixture of sweat and mud clogged up the dark hair on his arms.

'Lunch? It's half past three in the afternoon.' If Duke felt uncomfortable by the invasion into his personal space, he wasn't showing it.

'We started late. Out of courtesy for the morning commuters.'

Addison could hear the approving murmurs from the man's minions in high-vis and hardhats.

The temporary traffic lights were taking their usual laissez-faire approach to traffic control. Despite no cars looking to come from the opposite way, they remained on red.

'So, you thought you'd just mess up people's school run instead?' Duke had a point. Whoever was organising this relaxed rabble could have arranged for them to start in the early hours of the morning, blocking the road completely for just the morning run, and then freeing it up entirely before midday. Everyone could have been re-routed once, rather than sit and stew in this stress-pit. Not that the council cared, as long as they had their invoice to add to their next funding bid, public inconvenience was an afterthought.

'Look here pal,' the guy put a deeper voice on to stress that he was the alpha. It didn't work. 'We've had the signs up for a few weeks now, warning everybody about the disruption. I'm sorry if you didn't bother planning ahead.' The guy noticed the lights turn to green. 'Now please, go forth and multiply, you scrawny runt.'

Duke laughed.

'My brain beats your brawn any day of the week, you thick ape. Be careful not to hurt your knuckles as you drag them back to your single-brain-cell-sharing bunch of reprobates, you'll need them to help scratch your head as you figure out how to use those tools of yours. Clearly you haven't got a clue so far.'

Duke felt triumphant as Addison pulled away.

'What the hell was all that about?' Addison was surprised by Duke's attitude. 'Granted, they could have planned a little better, but they're still decent hard-working folk. They didn't deserve you going in so hard on them.'

'I know.' Duke sighed. 'I was just a little pissed off by the delay. My condition, it's left me a little quick to anger. I didn't mean to be such a shit back there. I just go a bit cloudy sometimes, and it makes me go defensive. Remind me to send a letter of apology later.'

'Will do. No doubt you'll forget.' Addison winced. Duke had been dealing with his condition so well, he often forgot it was even there. 'What's your head saying about this place?' Addison nodded to the front of the flower shop as he pulled the car over.

'Who the hell knows anymore? The little sod that's skull-shagging me is slowly leaving me with nothing to go by but instinct and improvisation.'

'Nothing new there.' Addison smiled. 'Seems you've made a whole career out of that.'

'Ha! Bullshit with confidence my good man. It can get you a long way.'

Duke got out of the car first. It was only him and Addison on this job. Duke had insisted that Addison arrange an alternative little play-date with Piper. This was police business after all, and whilst the press could play their part, whilst Duke was conducting the enquiries, it would only be under his strict direction.

Apart from a middle-aged woman tending to some tiger-lilies, the store was empty. Bunches of daffodils ready to bloom were stockpiled towards the entrance, whilst the grander, more impressive bouquets sat towards the window. Like most florists these days, the business relied on both walk-ins and delivery orders. Duke was already palming one of the business cards that sat at the till-desk when the lady approached them.

'Good afternoon gentlemen. May I help you at all?' Her voice was soft, but came with perfect crystal-cut pronunciation. She stood at around five-foot-two, and was as threatening as fresh cotton wool. It was clear she found a serene quality in her work. If Addison had to put money on it, he'd say this lady was the owner. The way she had put herself together reflected the neat perfection of the store.

'Hello,' Duke flashed a smile. 'Do you do deliveries?'

He already knew the answer, but Duke had decided to pick the lock rather than polish off the battering ram.

'Why, yes we do.' The lady smiled. 'But given the fact that you're holding one of my cards, I assume you already know that. Is the order for anything in particular?'

'I'm afraid we're here on a different kind of business today, Mrs...?'

'Coxon, Bonnie Coxon. And you are?'

'Sergeant Derek Parker, and this here is Constable Addison Clarke.'

'Pleasure to meet you Mrs Coxon.' Addison popped his head around from Duke. 'This is a lovely store you have here.'

'Why, thank you.' Bonnie didn't look flustered by their presence. In fact, she looked pleased to see them. No doubt she was a key part of her community, keen to bother all at the community church groups and monthly village hall meetings with the town's current affairs. 'Is there anything in particular that I can help you with?'

'Well, it's to do with your delivery service. Is that something you run locally, or do you use a separate company?' Duke spoke as if he was an interested investor rather than a seasoned detective on the lookout for a cold-blooded child-snatcher.

'Oh no,' Bonnie gave a modest grin. 'We're too small to outsource my dear. Most of our business is local, regular customers with the odd word-of-mouth recommendation. We only have one delivery vehicle, for the very rare occasions that we get booked to do an event or for any online orders. Though, it's not many. Most of the folk that use us tend to know us personally, so they tend to fit us in as part of their weekly shop. I must say, I prefer it that way. The Internet is far too big for a small little florist like this one. We have a site of course, but Google have nothing to fear just yet.'

Her laugh was sweet, an endearing mix of humility and pride.

'Is the van here?' Duke was making his target known. He already had the measure of Bonnie. She was exactly how she presented herself. He didn't need to hide his interest from her. She was clean.

'I'm afraid not. Has it been involved in an accident, or been caught speeding? I did mention to Harv to be mindful of the new cameras that they have put in on the road out of town. Not that we've ever had trouble like that before. But then again, I wouldn't know. Like I said, we have little need for deliveries so we let Harv keep the van with him. As long as he tops up the petrol, he can have it.'

'This vehicle, are we talking about a green transit van, with an 07 plate?' Addison was a stickler for firming up details.

'That's right.' Bonnie's smile remained intact, despite the officer's refusal to clarify why they were interested. She reeled off the registration plate from memory. It was a match for the one seen in the area at the time of Joseph Farnham's abduction.

'Is everything okay?'

'Quite all right, Mrs Coxon, I assure you.' Duke placed his hand on her arm. 'We're just looking into a few witnesses for a matter back in Claymore. It seems your car was nearby, that's all.'

'Claymore?' A look of confusion contorted her face. 'I'm not aware of any business we've done over that way recently. But then again, as I said, Harv is allowed to use the vehicle as he wishes in his own time.'

Not if that involves sweeping young children up off the street he isn't.

Addison and Duke both had the same thought at the same time.

'Is Harv due in today? What exactly is his role here?' Duke looked behind Bonnie as if to indicate that he thought the man may have been hiding out the back somewhere.

'Oh, he's been with us for years. He helps out in the store three times a week, and is happy to do all our deliveries when called upon. Sadly, he's not due back in for a few days. Maybe I can give you his number and you could give him a call? Or, if you'd prefer, his address is in that old Rolodex file on the counter.' She pointed to a dusty, but well-thumbed rotary file.

'That would be great. Thank you.' Addison took out his phone as Duke went over to the counter. He began to spin the cards that had been arranged alphabetically. The majority of them were faded business cards and notes under names where numbers had been crossed out and corrected over time. Mostly when people stopped using landlines.

'Sorry,' Duke paused. 'I'm a fool, I should have asked. What's Harv's surname?'

Bonnie smiled as if sharing a naughty secret.

'No need to apologise officer. Force of habit on my part. We call him Harv because he insists on it, on account of him not being too fond of his first name. Harv is actually short for his surname. So, look under H for Harvey. First name Quentin.'

Duke's heart stopped. Addison froze.

Quentin Harvey.

Chapter 48

Quentin wasn't due back at work for a few days, so he had time.

Time for one more at least.

Now that his abusers were dead, no doubt the net would be tightening around him. Not that he was alone. Mason had abused dozens of them. Of course, he had his favourites, the ones he used to call upon maybe once, twice a week. The others, they were just part of Mason's taster menu, sampled so that he knew what to offer up to his guests.

And there were many guests. Familiar faces, wrapped in guilt, fear and lust. Quentin had seen them at countless charity events and awards evenings where he had delivered the table settings, some were even celebrated by their peers for their contribution to the community. If only they knew the truth.

He couldn't read until he was a young adult, but as a child he remembered seeing the same faces in newspaper articles and local leaflets. Some wore uniforms, others had nice expensive-looking suits on.

He mostly remembered them naked.

The first time he was sampled had been as a punishment. At five years old, Quentin had the body of a boy twice his age, though the brain of someone nearly half it. He never knew his parents. From what he was told they were either dead or happier without him. That's what his caregivers had told him anyway. Not that they tended to give much in the way of care.

He'd been in the system for two years before the abuse started happening. Before then, he remembered how children would be woken from their beds and taken away, not to be seen for days. He remembered never wanting to find out why.

But he did find out.

One day, the smaller man called Norris had accused Quentin of stealing from him. Some other children had dared Quentin to sneak into the main office and steal back the toys that had been confiscated from them. As a boy, he simply wanted to fit in, to find friends. He'd do anything for friends. People he could trust. People who understood him. People who he could relate to.

Ironically, Norris didn't see it that way. He had friends of his own. Friends he acted only to please. Friends who could take care of disobedient little boys like Quentin.

People used to think that Norris was the 'nonce'. He had that weak, rat-like frame that people often made cruel assumptions about. But Norris was nothing more than a middle man, a source for fresh meat. He knew what he was doing was wrong, farming children off to whomever had the right ratio between wealth and depravity. But he was too weak to stop it. Mitchel Mason was in control. Norris was just the paedophile's Pinocchio, a spineless puppet on a poisoned string.

After Norris caught Quentin, it wasn't long before he was the one being woken up at night. When everyone else in the home was asleep, Norris had covered his mouth with one hand and gripped his wrist with the other, gently leading him down the stairs and quietly into the basement.

That's where Mason was waiting.

'So, what do we have here then? A dirty rotten magpie, stealing from those that provide and look after him?'

He remembered the cold metal of the shackles on his wrists. Mason's whispers whistled in the cold air.

'Was it something shiny you were after?'

He was unable to answer. A damp sock was forced into his mouth before thick tape was wrapped around his head, covering his lips completely. Mason removed his belt. The steel buckle was covered in small dents.

'I guess we're going to have to teach this little bird a life lesson.'

His breath smelt of stale whiskey and cigarettes. The heat of it hovered upon the small boy's neck.

'Well, Magpie... maybe you'll remember this little poem. Maybe, we'll get a measure of what we're dealing with.'

That's when the beating began. Each sentence was met by a hit much harder than the last.

'One for sorrow...'

The buckle struck the bare skin of his back.

'Two for joy...'

Mason grabbed at his crotch and licked his lips.

'Three for a girl...'

The strike drew blood.

'Four for a boy...'

The chains didn't let him cover his face.

'Five for silver...'

His legs gave.

'Six for gold…'

Darkness closed in.

'Seven for a secret… NEVER to be told.'

He passed out.

But there was no escape for the boy. Mason kindly woke him up before he raped him.

It was that wicked way for the next twelve nights. During the day, Mason and Draper would refer to him as Quentin, but he was known to all those that ordered his services as the Magpie. It was their codeword for him. All the chosen children had them. Names such as Buttermilk, Moonlight and Biscuit. Even his close friend Francis was known as Sunshine. It helped the men cover up who they were going to order. Each disgusting act was also given the name of a cocktail. That way the police couldn't decipher exactly what was being sought when, for instance, a highly-respected businessman – with a wife and two children waiting for him at home – ordered a '*Manhattan for Magpie*'.

But Quentin could work it out.

He knew what was coming. Four years of abuse offers a twisted education in the sheer depths of man's depravity. It was only the first and last time that really surprised him. The first time felt like he had slipped into an abyss, constantly falling, twisting out of shape until he was numb to it all. His descent continued for four long years. Each time he was visited, a fragment of himself was lost forever. Until the last time.

That's when he woke up.

And like the day that follows any stupor – any period when the brain is forced to switch off to protect itself – all that came was the pain of it all. His mind felt like bare hands trying to piece together sharpened, shattered glass. His recovery would never be complete. Every attempt to piece his life together would only cut him deeper, and distort how he saw himself.

But before picking up the pieces, he had to escape the fire.

Following the last time, he and two other children had been locked inside the basement by Mason and Draper. He could still smell the petrol that had decorated the walls, and he could still feel the heat from when Draper lit the match, and locked the door.

They were meant to die. To take all that had happened with them. All the abuse, all the faces, all the masks that had slipped to reveal the monsters behind them. All to be lost to the flames.

But somehow, they had survived. And now, others would not.

Admiring his craftwork, Quentin examined the scene. The set had been easy to construct, it was mainly wood and paint, although the swing had been quite a technical challenge. Instead, what had been the biggest task were the actors. It had taken him years to collect his cast. All of them perfect for their role, some would go as far as to say that they were made for it.

It was a role of a lifetime. A performance set to define them forever.

It was a shame that he couldn't access the bodies of the men who had ruined his life, they would have made perfect backdrops to the scene that played out in front of where they had once stood. Scores of children enjoying being just that – children. He had copied the photograph perfectly. All the children were at play, all oblivious to the danger that watched over them. All of them ignorant to the horror. All of them, apart from the three that looked directly into the camera's lens.

Back then, the photograph had been used as a form of monstrous menu, developed and dished out to all who had an appetite for horror. Quentin was one of the children at the front. So were his friends Francis and Randal. It was only these that the men could choose from. There had been many pictures taken like this before them, crowded scenes used to hide the real reason, but this was the last one. All of the children behind them had escaped the torture. None of them were there at the end. One by one they had been selected for salvation. Various couples had picked them like ripe cherries, set to sweeten and crown their home-baked domestic bliss. But unlike the chosen, Quentin and his friends had been left to sour and rot. Tainted by what had happened to them, they were too bitter to blend into anybody else's lives. They carried with them a poison that threatened to destroy the lives of all that touched them.

There was no escape for them. Others like them had often disappeared, with no families ready to collect them. He'd seen the bags in the basement. The boy-shaped bundles that were thrown onto the fire. They wanted him to watch, to see the truth. Only the untouched were allowed to leave.

That's why Quentin had taken them back. The untouched. These children had all escaped. They'd found their freedom, but they were now back where they belonged, as members of the crowd used to cloud who Quentin and his friends really were. Amongst them, Quentin could hide his past. He could melt into the scene, and be regarded like any other child. The stage was set to bring him peace. The picture that had once trapped him, now could set him free.

He knew the children he had taken would be grateful. Yes, they cried at first, many until the very end. But he had saved them. Now, they would remain untouched forever. No doubt the world, with all its pain and poison, had eventually reached the children that had escaped his past. No doubt their dreams had been snatched away by adult life and all its pressures, all its expectations and demands that suffocate a child's imagination and ambition, all delivered by the cruel unrelenting hands of time.

Time strangled all, squeezing every inch of life from every single body.

That's why he loved flowers. Their time was fleeting, but they always fully revealed themselves, in all their wonder and glory, immediately before they began to die.

People were the same. Their eyes revealed who they were. Angry, upset, scared... delicate. All of it seen in its entirety as they drew their last breath. This is what his work preserved. When childhood is lost and abandoned, so are we. Instead of growing into who that child imagined, we mould masks for ourselves so that we can greet the many other masks that await us outside.

His children would never meet such a horror. They would never wear a mask other than that which showed their true, purest, untouched self.

These were the things that he mounted. Things that he elevated and preserved for an eternity. He smiled as he looked at the masks that sat proudly upon his shelves. Eventually, their bodies would decompose. Elizabeth Silver's was already showing signs of decay. But their faces, their faces would remain forever.

Turning towards his worktop, he examined the young girl he had bound to the table. Norris Draper had told him about this one. Before he began to lose his mind, Quentin had exploited Draper for his resources. Having met at a charity event by pure chance, Quentin had threatened him with exposure – unless, that is, he assisted him fully. Not one to disappoint the depraved, Draper stayed true to his weak nature, had done everything he was told. Well, almost everything. Sadly, he would never give up the names of the men who had once ordered Magpie. But the man still had his spies inside the care system, and it had proved remarkably easy to gather the details of children who had been adopted.

The young girl bound to the table was such a child. Looking at his watch, Quentin estimated that the young girl's adoptive parents would only just be finding out that their child had been taken. Recent roadworks had played an oblivious yet wonderful part in delaying the school run. Unless, that is, you had planned ahead.

And Quentin Harvey was a man with a definite plan.

Chapter 49

The traffic was no longer an issue.

Not when Duke was driving. One-way roads were being ignored, traffic lights and speed cameras were nothing more than merely suggestive.

Two minutes after leaving the store, Addison had taken a call from the Tasking Team.

'Another girl has been taken.'

Geoff Talbot's tone was his usual blend of rage and contempt, this time with a twist of urgency.

Eight-year-old Christine Pritchard was snatched outside her school gates whilst waiting for her mother to pick her up. There were no witnesses. Christine always left early at the end of the week as she had to attend a 'contact meeting' between her new parents and their social worker. Her parents dropped her off this morning, but the plan was for the social worker to pick her up after school.

'There was no way that the social worker would have known about the traffic works.' Addison was trying to make sense of the opportunity.

'Jesus wept!' Duke had half his mind on the road and the other half trying to thread the facts together. Addison was right, Christine was only reported missing by the school once her lift had arrived some ten minutes late. It was a small window of opportunity, but an opportunity somebody exploited.

What were initially soft apologies from the social worker to Christine's teacher for poor planning and timekeeping, had now escalated to hard pleas for forgiveness to a family utterly lost in agony and panic.

But this wasn't their fault. People just needed someone to blame. Someone to target their confusion towards.

Addison and Duke were no different.

'Whoever took her must have been local... they must have known about the roadworks.' Addison was thinking out loud.

'And it's another child from the goddamn care system.' Duke spat the words onto the windscreen as he headed into oncoming traffic, taking one corner before sweeping back into the correct lane. The sound of a car horn flew past the open window.

'Whoever did this, they knew they had an opportunity. There's too much chance to suggest this was someone working only on instinct and impulse.' Addison was acting as a second foot on the gas pedal. He wanted Duke to realise they were already heading towards where Addison's gut was pointing him.

Duke was already up to speed.

'Quentin Harvey's about to order a new front door.'

They knew they were on their own, rushing towards the complete unknown. Addison had called for backup but the controllers had refused to resource their request. Technically, they were out of their force area and also off-duty. Their earlier warrant only covered the florist and the van, and until the van was found, there were no extra troops heading in their direction. Instead, a local 'All-Out' shout had been issued, and now every local officer locked down an area that the offender had probably left some twenty minutes ago.

All of them would stand still, whilst their prey ran away. An animal which had already snared its catch.

Above them the police helicopter circled the school grounds that Christine had been taken from. Rubberneckers slowed traffic as they pointed their bored eyes to the skies.

Honest acts by the police, but all fruitless.

The man they wanted was housed elsewhere.

According to their GPS, it would take Duke another nine minutes to reach the home of Quentin Harvey. Addison watched as every manoeuvre and road taken at twice the speed limit shaved another minute off the ETA.

Left turn.

Right turn.

Overtake.

Undertake.

Foot to the floor.

Emergency stop.

You have reached your destination.

The building was huge, guarded by a tall red-brick wall that was cut in half by a giant iron swing-gate. The gardens were overgrown, the driveway sprinkled with weeds and litter. The green van was parked at the side of the house, with the front facing towards the gate. Lights off. Doors shut.

'It's been reversed in,' Duke nodded to the van. 'Looks like someone's trying to hide what was in the back.'

Despite being equipped with enough adrenaline to rip the gates clean off their hinges, Addison held his breath and slowly lifted the latch, causing the gate to swing open without dragging along the floor. They didn't want to give their guy a heads-up. If there was a girl inside, then any alert of their presence could cause Quentin to panic, and nobody ever benefitted from a maniac panicking.

'What is this place?' Addison whispered as they crept up the driveway, gravel crunching beneath their feet. 'Looks more like an old village hall.'

'That's exactly what it is.' Duke lifted the branches of a bush that had grown over a small sign. 'Tiny Tippy-Tappers – it's an old performing arts hall used by local kids. Looks like it's been closed down for a decade or two.'

'The guy lives here?' Addison spoke one octave above a breath.

Duke nodded.

'No doubt a place like this has some sort of living quarters for a groundskeeper or caretaker. I bet the freak is holed up inside there somewhere.'

Duke was right, behind the old red-brick village hall sat a small white cottage. Crouched within the undergrowth, it hid its broken original features from the main road. All the lights were off, but the curtains were wide open. They crept up to the small bay window. Addison peered inside and could see nothing but the remains of a meal growing cold on a tiny table. It looked like a scene preserved from recent history, dated furniture and forgotten furnishings strived to add some hint of décor to the dead room. The table setting had been for one. One chair, one plate, one cup. Duke was trying the door, but it was locked.

'Can you smell gas?'

Duke had a wry smile.

It was an old trick used to justify forcing entry into a house. Gas equalled danger, and it was their duty to 'serve and protect', and nothing unlocked a door quicker than the sense of somebody in danger on the other side. Addison knew that Duke was half-joking. There was no smell of gas. No signs of life or distress. No justification for breaking in.

Then the girl screamed.

They both heard it. They both felt it steal their breath, narrowing their focus. In that moment, it was all that mattered to them.

It came from behind them, away from the house. It was only a short burst, quickly muffled.

Addison's heart entered his throat. Duke's legs were already moving.

The cry had come from the village hall.

There was no time for backup. Usually, breaching the door to a potential kidnapping was a job for the firearms unit. But they couldn't wait. By the time they would have been locked and loaded, they'd be calling for the coroner, not the custody suite.

Addison jumped the small fence into the thick garden that hugged the hall like a gothic Christmas garland. Evergreen ferns were splintered by the bare branches of dead trees, all of it strangled by poison ivy. Behind him, Duke entered to the sound of metal crashing against the concrete footpath. Two wire-framed cages hit the floor and burst into a cacophony of shrill squawks and frantic feathers. A blizzard of black and white buzzed within the small cages.

Magpies.

It had been the first link Addison had seen, and now it confirmed it all. Not that it made him feel any easier. The only doubt it removed was whether they were following the right lead, whether they were heading towards the right man. And now that everything suggested that they were, nothing told them what type of man they were about to meet.

Fear set in.

Blood boiled beneath his skin. His heart raced, clouding his judgement and narrowing his sight. Addison knew he was in trouble. The chemical cocktail was in his bloodstream, making him more primal than primed. He needed to be sharp, to keep his wits about him. No doubt... a young girl's life depended on it.

A young girl who was now in the care of a killer.

An old door was all that separated them. The single stained-glass windowpane blocked their view of the inside. A small light flickered from within, burning the waxy glass into a shade of blood-orange.

Duke's boot took the door clean off the hinges.

The room went dark.

A soft scent of smoke dusted the air.

The daylight from outside did little to help, braving only a few yards in front of them.

Sound only entered from the outside. Nothing could be heard coming from within. The stillness shook them, chilling their bones and pulling at their skin.

'Hello...' Duke listened as his voice bounced off walls at least twenty feet away. The echoes began to fade into the darkness when he spoke again. 'Quentin... we need to talk. We want to help you.'

He took a few steps into the dark until he was completely out of sight from Addison. Silence greeted him.

Addison followed, but used the wall as a guide. His hands scuttled like a spider across the brickwork, desperately searching for a switch. Instead, he found a heavy steel lever, pressed flush against the wall. It looked like something out of Frankenstein's laboratory.

'Duke...' Addison whispered. He got no reply. 'Duke...'

Still nothing.

Addison pulled the lever. It punched the wall with a flat thud.

Clunk.

Clunk.

Clunk.

Lights began to come to life. Huge industrial-sized lamps hung overhead, staining the room with a strained light.

Focusing, a part of Addison wished he was still in the dark. Upon the wall, staring back at him, were the frozen faces of stolen children. A single row of death masks looked back with cold, closed eyes. Eyes he had seen before, all of them once filled with joy and life.

Elizabeth, Amber, Joseph...

They all stared back at him. Familiar faces and a few more that he recognised from the early missing person's case files. He counted at least twelve sets of eyes, all closed. It was then that he could sense a set of open eyes upon his back.

Turning, he saw Duke stood ten feet in front of him. He was motionless, facing the small stage that filled the front of the room. They were both now members of the audience, both passive witnesses to the set of horror laid out before them. An audience of two, both praying that the scene didn't play out the way they imagined.

Each of them prayed for a twist.

But the play had begun, and this appeared to be the final act.

The scene was set.

It was the scene from the photograph they had found in Benjamin Farrow's property. The same one that had been hand-fed to Mitchell Mason as he lay dying in his home. Children, all at play. Some reading, some dancing, one swinging from a makeshift swing.

Joseph.

Addison had never seen anything like this before. The models looked lifelike, all frozen at points of motion, all showing signs of life. For the briefest of moments, he thought he had found them all, all safe, all alive and well, ready to be taken home to those that loved them. Until he looked closer. Until he could see the rough stitching across the skin, the cold stone eyes, the signs of decay.

They were all dead. Apart from the one girl stood centre-stage with a knife to her throat.

No doubt, the giant stood behind her was Quentin Harvey.

'Who are you? What are you doing here? Are you both cops?'

The giant spoke with frustration in his voice. He looked confused, disorientated. He pointed the knife towards them both as he spoke, before quickly returning it to the girl's neck.

'I saw you both... you went to my house. Why were you looking in there? There's nothing worth seeing in there.' His voice rumbled as if the words passed through rocks boiling in the pit of his stomach.

It suddenly occurred to Addison that Quentin wasn't ashamed of what he'd done. Instead, there was a sense of pride to it, a sense of show-and-tell. Clearly, what now rattled him was the fact that they'd interrupted him, that his display wasn't yet ready to be seen. It was incomplete. That's where the frustration sat, simmering beneath the skin, irritating his plans. This wasn't to be his great reveal. They had spoilt it for him. His moment had been tarnished, taken away from him.

And now he was pissed.

'This isn't what it looks like,' Quentin's huge hand was vibrating with rage. 'None of you would understand its meaning.'

'Quentin... we know what you've been through. We've seen the reports.' Duke spoke sincerely. His arms were held wide open.

'You know nothing!' The words hit the walls like a cannonball. 'You've never wanted to know. None of you would listen to any of us. We tried to tell you, but we caused more problems than we were worth. You left us for dead, wishing we'd just disappear. Believe me, we tried. But life has a way of haunting you, digging up the past and burying you in the whole it leaves behind. But I was sick of hiding what happened to us. That's why I did all this.'

He waved the knife as if to present his masterpiece, before returning it to the young girl's trembling throat. This time he pressed a little harder. Addison could see the small trickle of blood leaving the freshly cut skin. The girl was crying, but her mouth was muffled. Heavy duct-tape had been wrapped around the lower part of her face.

'Quentin...' Duke remained calm, although sweat was beginning to dapple his pale bald head. 'You don't want to hurt Christine. You're scaring her. She's got nothing to do with this.'

'She has EVERYTHING to do with this!'

He raised his arm as if he was ready to slice her head clean off.

'These children, *they* escaped. They were free. For a while at least. It would never have lasted. Life lets everybody down. Before long, it kills the child within, and gives birth to a shadow of who you were. They wouldn't know true freedom, just the loss of their peace and their innocence.' He started to bang his fist against his head. 'That's why I save them, I keep them where they're safe. I don't kill the children... I preserve them. It's adults that don't belong here. They hurt me. They hurt us. But you are right... I'm not looking to hurt her...' He seemed to relax. 'I'm setting her free.'

That's when he cut her throat.

Pushing her body from the stage, she hit the cold ground in front of him.

Addison ran to her whilst Quentin stood over them watching. Reaching Christine, Addison pulled the tape from her face. A small sock had been stuffed into her mouth. She took a lungful of air as Addison removed the sock, her hands instinctively gripping her throat, locked in panic and fear. Her trembling fingers were coloured a dark shade of red. Addison pulled her hands away briefly; he needed to see how bad the wound was.

But there was nothing. Nothing more than a small nick from where the blade had been pressed against her skin. Her palms were clean. All the blood was on the outside of her hands.

Drip.

Drip.

Drip.

Blood began to speckle her face.

Looking up, Addison could see the source. Stood over them both, Quentin hung his left hand out, blood pouring from the wrist.

'I don't butcher my work.' Quentin laughed hysterically. His fist was clenched, the cut was deep and ragged, the flow of blood unrelenting. 'I wouldn't destroy something as delicate as her. She's so pretty. She was set to be my finest piece. Then, we could have all been together, forever.'

'Put the knife down.' Duke was more forceful this time. It was only his own safety he needed to worry about now. Addison stood guard between the giant and the girl. All that stood between Quentin and Duke was the knife he was quite clearly prepared to use.

'I said... put... the knife... down.'

'Why?' Quentin turned his attention to Duke. 'So that you can *take care* of me? Don't worry officer... I can take care of myself. It's all the other children out there that you need to be concerned about. The quiet ones, the ones who won't talk about the monsters that visit them at night. That's why we take them... us... the children. We do it to protect them. So, officer... back... the fuck... off.'

'You need help. We must stop this. You and I both know that. We can't allow you to carry on, Quentin. We *will* stop this. Nobody else needs to get hurt.'

The giant smiled. He mimicked Duke's last words.

'*Nobody else needs to get hurt.*'

He then added his own.

'Apart from you!'

Quentin threw the knife with such force that it put Duke down the instant the blade hit him.

'No!' Addison's scream hit every wall.

The young girl was still getting her breath, her body frozen by shock. He couldn't leave her, but his best friend lay dying only a few feet away. A small pool of blood had already begun to deepen around his body.

'You said *us*.' Addison stood, holding Christine's hand. He wanted Quentin's attention. He needed to distract him so that he could get closer to Duke. 'Just then... you also said *we*. Who are you working with? Who's doing all this?'

He took three sidesteps closer to his friend.

'The forgotten. The ones that were meant to disappear.' Quentin's frame seemed to have doubled in size. His arms were as long as his legs, and his thick neck pulsated beneath the face of a man crying with pure anguish. His features were broken, distorted to the point that they looked painful.

'Who are you referring to?' Addison was now only a yard away from Duke. He could see that his body was still, his breathing beginning to shallow out.

'I can see what you're doing. I'm not that stupid!' Quentin picked up a tiny cardboard box. 'They used to call me Magpie. Using codewords and nicknames – that's how they kept it all a secret. And that's what we were to them, dirty little secrets, all of us.'

Addison was kneeling next to Duke, pressing his fingers under his jaw. The pulse that beat back at him was slowing down.

'I didn't want it to end this way.' Quentin was walking amongst his cast, stroking their cold skin as he passed.

'It doesn't have to.' Addison fixed his eyes on the giant. Blood was still pouring from his arm. 'Come with us... tell us what you know, and we can make this all go away.'

'That's exactly what they wanted. For it to all to go *away*.'

He was panting now. His huge hands planted against the side of his head. 'I was their Magpie... their little thief, but it was them that took everything from me. *Everything*. I was just taking it all back. Until you came along. I'm sorry, but I can't tolerate what threatens my work. I'm afraid you can't leave, ever. You're now a part of this.'

Quentin opened the box and removed a small piece of wood. It looked tiny between his thick fingers. He scratched the head of the wood against the side of the box and a small flame flickered at the end.

'What the hell!' Addison pulled at Duke's arm but he was unresponsive. Christine clung to his other arm, tucking her face into his jacket to block out the horror that played out in front of her.

'You're now a part of all of this. Part of the story, part of the scene, part of the secret. A secret... never to be told!!'

That's when Addison could smell it.
Petrol.
Pools of it shimmered under the huge lights like an exploded rainbow.
Then Quentin dropped the match.

Chapter 50

Addison wasn't sure what hit him first, the heat from the flames or the full force of Quentin's shoulder bursting into his gut.

The giant's momentum had carried them across the room, pinning Addison to the wall. Christine had been dislocated from his arm on impact. She lay face down, motionless next to Duke's body.

Flames licked at the walls, thick bales of smoke pumped soot towards the ceiling, choking out the light. Wood crackled and splintered upon the stage, as skin melted upon the faces of the frozen children.

The heat was intense, clawing out every drop of air left in Addison's lungs. Quentin stumbled back. He looked dazed, dark red liquid filled a small dent on his brow where his head had hit the wall like a sledgehammer. Thick hot blood continued to pour from his severed wrist.

Addison seized his opportunity. His hand met with a loose brick, and with one swift motion, the brick met with Quentin's temple.

But he just stood there. Rocking from one foot to the other, until he was completely steady.

Addison threw his next punch but it came to a sudden stop as Quentin caught the fist in the palm of his huge hand. Addison could feel his knees buckle as Quentin's free hand landed like an axe against his back. Pain shot down his spine, splintering his senses. But he wasn't on the floor for long.

Quentin took hold of Addison with both hands, lifting him from under his arms. Addison swung in vain, hitting the giant in the face, but with little force. It served only to frustrate him further. He brought Addison to his feet, taking hold of him by the throat.

For a second Addison was airborne, until he was slammed down against the thick surface of Quentin's worktop. Agony stretched through every aching limb. The adrenaline coursing through his veins did little to quieten the pain. He could feel the hulk's hands tighten around his throat. He could feel the heat closing in around him, the smoke darkening the corners of his eyes.

He had taken his last breath.

Quentin's face contorted into a sharp smile as he watched the face unfold in front of him. He watched the man panic as the air left his pinched throat, his lips turning blue as the light began to drain from his eyes. This was his favourite part. This was where they revealed their true selves. His victim was about to blossom.

The bloom before the doom.

Quentin's thick lips stretched out revealing the shattered teeth within. Blood caked his gums, staining his flapping tongue. He pressed a little harder, already the blood vessels were bursting within the whites of the man's eyes. Both of his small weak hands gripped at Quentin's fingers, but there was no removing them now. They were fixed in place, forged by excitement and anticipation.

The reveal was coming.

But pain came first.

A pain that released his hands. A pain that left him, only to return... again.

And again.

And again.

Addison could feel the air flow into his lungs. He could feel strength returning to his limbs, as his eyes adjusted and began to focus.

A huge figure flailed above him, his silhouette spiralling within the smoke. His screams following every pop of punctured flesh.

It was only brief, but it was enough to allow Addison to take advantage. Pulling himself from the worktop, he took to his feet.

Then the screaming stopped, followed swiftly by a gloomy thud. That's when Addison saw her. Christine's body had been chucked against the wall, her hand still gripping a knife covered in thick warm blood. Beside her, Quentin staggered to his feet. His shirt was torn at the back, stab wounds sat within every gap of shredded fabric. Blood flowed from his skin.

Addison had to take his chance. Pushing with all he had, he dug his shoulder into Quentin's gut, lunging forward towards the bench. The side of it struck the small of his back, flipping him onto the worktop. Quentin was dazed, his head hitting the table like a dense lump of clay. The giant was stunned. But it wouldn't last.

Acting fast, Addison used the heavy leather straps that sat at each corner of the counter to bind Quentin to the desk. He couldn't risk leaving him unrestrained whilst he checked on Christine and Duke. The straps were enough to bind his wrists, but his legs were too thick to tie down. It wasn't ideal, but it had to do.

Sprinting through the smoke, Addison followed the wall until he found the young girl. She was awake; bruised but breathing. Without pausing, he scooped her up into his arms and made for the door. Spirals of smoke began to thicken above them. Windows smashed under the pressure, as the air grew heavy within the intense heat.

The dot of light that pierced the smoke opened up as they drew closer to the door. Until they were finally through.

The air outside cut through his throat like sharpened ice. The sunlight blinded him, the gentle breeze did little to cool his skin. But it was the briefest of respites. He couldn't afford to rest. Instead, he lay the girl down, handed her his phone and told her to call for help.

Within seconds, Addison was back inside the fiery belly of the beast. To his right, the stage was alight, pieces of the set crumbled into the flames, fuelling its hunger, forcing the fierce fire to swallow the children one by one.

First it took Amber, then Joseph, and finally as the flames felt their way through the stage, they swallowed the girl ghost that had haunted them all. Elizabeth Silver was truly gone.

Beneath it all lay Duke. He hadn't moved since Addison had last seen him.

It wasn't long before he was with him again.

'Duke!' Addison slapped his face. 'Come on… don't quit on me yet!'

No response.

Addison checked his wounds. The knife had been removed, no doubt by Christine. Now, it lay hidden amongst the smoke, only a few feet away from the giant.

'Duke… I need you with me. Come on!' Addison shook at his shoulders, before checking for a pulse.

Got it.

It was only faint, but it was there. Feeling the smoke closing in, Addison took a deep breath and passed it through Duke's open mouth. His friend's chest rose slowly before deflating. He went to offer a second breath, but the look of pure confusion on Duke's face suggested it wasn't necessary.

'Is this how you treat everyone you take to the theatre?' Duke's laugh was halted by him spluttering for breath. 'Hellfire! What happened here?'

He sat up, looking around him. The room was a mixture of black and orange, twisted together, hand in hand, dancing towards the crumbling ceiling. Duke looked bemused. He wasn't yet aware of the wound that ran clean through his left shoulder.

'We need to get out of here.' Addison pulled Duke to his feet, keeping his head down, safe from the smoke that strangled the air above them.

'What about the girl?'

'She's safe.'

'And Quentin?' Duke looked around him. There was no sign of the man.

'He's been taken care of.' Addison pulled at Duke's arm, but he was met with resistance.

'Addison, we can't just leave him here. What if he escapes? We can't take that risk. We've got to take him in.'

Addison knew he was right.

'Okay. This way.'

Duke followed Addison through the small hall where the seats had once sat, towards the back of the room, just to the side of the doorway. The fire continued to rage all around them, climbing up the bricks and biting at the roof above.

'Jesus Christ!' Duke could only just make out the workbench through the flames. Plumes of smoke hung like a curtain either side, slowly drawing in. 'Is that Quentin? We need to get him out of there.'

'It's not that simple,' Addison grimaced.

Right on cue, the giant kicked into action. His legs thrashed wildly, as his arms remained bound to the bench. His screams curdled under the weight of the smoke.

'He needs our help.' Duke turned towards where Quentin was trapped.

'He'll kill us.' Addison took hold of Duke's arm.

'We can't just leave him here!'

'Hold on.' Addison saw something flicker on the floor. He bent down and picked it up. 'We'll have a better chance with this.' He showed Duke the knife. A flash of recognition crossed his face as he looked from the blade to his own shoulder. Addison couldn't afford to let Duke concentrate on his wound. 'No time to explain all that. Look, I'll cut him free and we'll both drag him outside. But if he goes for us... I will put him down.'

'Agreed.' Duke slowly put his finger through the hole in his shoulder until realising it wasn't going to stop. He stood for a second, staring at the blood on his index finger.

'Ready?' Addison shook him to his senses.

'Ready.'

It was too late.

Huge sections of the ceiling began to rain down. Slabs of concrete, splintered by wooden beams blocked their path. They couldn't reach him, and even if they had, they would have all been trapped together.

'Holy shit!' Duke tried to find a way through, but it was impossible. Behind the shutter of concrete, they could hear Quentin screaming. Not for help. Screams of pure torment.

'We have to leave.' Addison pulled on Duke's sleeve. This time he followed.

Sprinting towards the doorway, the walls began to tighten. Bricks collapsed on one another, folding under the pressure of the fire. Flames licked at both their feet as they continued to run. Reaching the doorway, Addison paused and pushed Duke through first. He turned to take one last look behind him, but all was gone. The hall, the children, their killer. All lost to the flames.

*

Behind the fallen rooftop, Quentin lay strapped to his bench. His end was sealed, seared into the fabric of his fate by the flames that had once tried to claim him as a child. Maybe he was never meant to have escaped. Maybe their secret was better left untold.

He turned and faced the row of faces, once frozen in time, now altered by fire. One by one they had begun to melt and crumble. None of them were saved. None of them were free.

A tear ran down his face until the flames turned it to steam upon his skin. His secret was safe. The fire was now upon him. His past was devoured in flame.

He would never know peace.

Chapter 51

He felt the loss.

They weren't family, not by blood anyway, but they were as close as you could come to it. Like shadows in the darkness, they blended into the world around them, inseparable from one another, joined by a shared devotion: to feel free.

The news of their death almost destroyed him. He had seen on the TV reports how the remains had been found in the fire at the old village hall. He'd never been to the place, he couldn't even point it out on a map, but a part of him had perished there.

The police had found more than one body, the yellow newsreel stretched like a tightened noose around the neck of the screen, slowly revealing the names of all those lost, strangling the breath from everyone that recognised them. One name in particular stood out.

Elizabeth Silver.

The ghost child that had haunted his dreams.

His obsession with her had stretched long before her disappearance. He had cared about the girl before anybody else had, before all the fuss and frenzy, before the media mourned the loss of a stranger.

From the moment she was taken she was lost. He realised that now, as her name crawled across the screen, she was truly gone.

Her killer had been named before. The man that had been judged to have taken her had shared the same space as him for just over a year. But it wasn't the name that the reporters were using today. The picture wasn't the face he had become accustomed to seeing.

Seth could feel his pulse racing at the image of the man's face. The sense of loss stabbed at his heart with every beat, hitting deeper and deeper each and every time. Water had filled his eyes, but had not yet broken upon his face, as he stared unblinkingly at the TV screen.

He stared at the man's face.

He felt the loss. Their games would never be played again. The secrets that they shared were all but whispers in the wind. Memories hit his head like bullets, exploding into scenes of them at play, together scheming and forgetting the world around them.

Then he blinked, and the sight of the man on the screen blurred. Tears streamed down his broken face, zig-zagging through the scars of his skin, with some pooling within the split that ripped his upper lip apart.

According to the report, Quentin Harvey was the man behind the abductions. The police were not looking for any more suspects. The families of the victims had been notified.

The details were scant, but enough to whet the appetite of the masses. They were now scurrying for more sustenance, hungry for the details in a feigned attempt at interest and appal, when all they really wished to do was have their own misdoings lost within the vacuum caused by someone else's horror. What was deviant came to define the righteous by separation alone.

That's why he was separate.

He was deviant, unable to adhere to the usual socially accepted responses to tragedy. His life had been torn to pieces by other people, and all he was expected to feel was sadness and pain. It wasn't right to be vengeful. It wasn't right to seek answers from those that had rolled a grenade into your life just to enjoy the brief rapture of chaos. No energy was put towards piecing his life together. Those that were meant to care only stood by whilst society expected them to. Once that was done, the shards of his life that were too sharp to handle had been swept under the carpet like broken glass. But the fragments still cut at his feet as he tried to move forward. Each chip tripped him up, splintering his soul until it grew septic and all that poured into his mind were thoughts of retribution.

That's when the plan found its way into the poison. They were all in on it. They all supported what was to be done.

Memories would be saved, restored and preserved for celebration and not remorse.

That's why they had done what they had done.

Him.

His friends.

His family.

Chapter 52

Beverly Silver had seen the news.

There was nothing new about it. The police had called a few hours before to inform her, but she already knew. She had always known that her little girl was gone.

What she didn't know was who had taken her.

The family liaison officer had advised her that with Benjamin Farrow's case being up for review, the recent revelations would no doubt result in his release.

The two officers who had remained at her house, however, were in some disagreement over that fact.

'I still think there are questions unanswered.' Duke paced around the front room. His injured shoulder had been stapled, stitched and glued together, and he had re-dressed the wound on doctor's orders, but he had completely ignored the rest period advised.

'I don't think this is the best place to be having this discussion.' Addison spoke in a hushed whisper that almost whistled through his gritted teeth. He could hear his hostess turning the kettle on in the kitchen. He leaned around the door to check on her. She was stood by the sink, hands planted on the counter, head facing towards the back garden. The soft breeze that brushed through the light bushes outside served only to show just how still the woman was.

Addison admired how Beverly always looked 'ready'. He'd never seen her looking anything but her best, as if at any moment her family would be turning up to take her out for the day. Her blond hair was brushed, worn in the way you would imagine a vicar's wife would choose, and her make-up was clean and precise. She presented herself to the world in the exact same way that she conducted herself. Elegant, pure and wholesome.

It was her eyes that let her down.

The strength, the togetherness, that she wished to show was denied by the utter loss that dulled her once bright blue eyes. And though she fought to defy what now defined her, her loneliness – like a single part of a jigsaw puzzle – only presented the pieces that were missing in her life.

'Duke,' said Addison. 'Right now, we need to be looking out for her.' He flicked his head towards the kitchen.

'I always was.' Duke sank as he spoke. His tone was of someone on the brink of defeat.

'Don't sound so down.' Addison went to pat his friend on the shoulder before realising his error. His hand hovered awkwardly as he spoke. 'We got some sort of closure for her at least. I know it's shitty, but it's something. Somewhere to start from...'

'Somewhere to start from?' Duke had a freshly lit fire in his belly. 'Have you ever played the lottery and forgotten to check your numbers, say for a few days maybe? Chances are you know you haven't won. Your life hasn't miraculously changed for the better overnight, all the things that ache and ail you haven't disappeared. Money is still an issue. Bills need to be paid, compromises between the life you live and the one you want have to be made on a daily basis. You haven't won. You *know* you haven't won, but for a moment – before your loss is confirmed – it's the existence of possibility that gives you hope. For people like Beverly, possibility is a painkiller. Closure doesn't always offer peace... it cuts off the one thing that's keeping you alive.'

'But surely you gave her that when you sent Farrow down the steps.'

'We gave her the man responsible... or so we thought. We didn't give Beverly her daughter back, and neither did Farrow.'

'Maybe he never could.' Beverly's voice seemed to drop the temperature in the room. She placed a single cup of tea on the side. Elizabeth's face was printed on the front of it. 'I think you both should leave.'

'I'm sorry,' Addison mumbled as he left the room like a scolded schoolboy.

Duke remained. His expression was from one friend to another. A friend that had let the other down. He dropped his head for a second, before taking hold of Beverly's hand.

'If you must know, I agree with you.' Beverly's voice made Duke look her in the eye. 'There are questions left unanswered.'

'I'll get the answers you deserve.'

Duke meant it.

Outside, Addison had already started the car. Sports news played out from the radio, a welcome break from the endless regurgitation of what the press thought had happened at the village hall. They mentioned the fire, and those lost in it, but nothing to do with the models and masks Quentin Harvey had made. Those details had been spared and saved only for the investigators. No doubt they would leak eventually, but for now the inane debate around a high-profile footballer's transfer saga was better than the half-baked crime theories from the countless ring-a-rhetoric of so-called subject matter experts that plumped out the other channels.

No doubt Harvey would be described as a loner, odd to all that knew him, with causal links bolted onto him like various power cables, all charged with creating a monster, and earthed into some disparate, deviant pastime that none of us could possibly share. The message to all was – 'don't worry people, this one was different, you're safe'.

The fact was, Harvey's past, though traumatic and terrible, was not unique to him. Many had suffered the same fate but had somehow managed to stray from the path that had caused a victim of such violent crime to choose to become something equal, if not even worse than his tormentors.

Maybe that was it. Maybe the only way you can remove those that cause you fear is to become something that they fear completely. Own what controls you. Reclaim what had been taken.

Addison couldn't work it out.

Why had he taken the children? Why not just kill those that had hurt you? Addison couldn't condone either act, but at least he could rationalise revenge.

Addison couldn't shake it off. The radio report had moved onto discussing the player's wage demands, and whether he should force a move away from his club who had 'only' offered him £100,000 a week. The absurd nature of the footballing world seemed to exist on a different plane to that where Addison existed. Keeping an eye on that world offered him some form of escape from the one that closed him in. The policing world was his planet. He didn't know much else, and wouldn't have the faintest idea of what to do if he had to start all over again.

He thought of Beverly, how she had found herself at that point in her life. The point where hope had gone, replaced by the blunt agony that often accompanies the cold truth. Hope held colour and light. But the truth she now owned muted whatever soothing sounds hope had created, completely parking the life she had once shared with her daughter Elizabeth. Her truth showed no future, just frozen memories to keep her warm at night.

Duke entered the car with a sense of urgency.

'We need to head back to the station. I've got a few enquiries that I need to make.'

Addison paused to get a measure on his friend. He wasn't sure if he was ready to accept the truth they knew. His skin looked sticky and pallid.

'Are you all right?' Addison kept the gear in neutral.

'What? Yeah, I'm fine.'

'Duke... we got our man. You did what you set out to do.'

'Did I?' He shifted in his seat.

'Yes. Quentin Harvey has been stopped. You did that. Who knows how many other parents have had their lives kept just as they are because of you. They'll never know what it feels like to have their child taken from them. You should be proud of what you've been part of.'

'What? Sending an innocent man to prison, is that something I should be proud of? Quentin Harvey said *us*, when talking about what he was doing... he said *us*. What if there's more of them?'

'Harvey was insane.' Addison could see where this was going. His friend had been under a lot of stress, a stress that could cloud the judgement and create a bias that blinds all possibilities apart from the first one to be accepted. 'Duke, his medical reports suggested split personalities, I read somewhere that he was suspected of being bipolar and possibly suffered from MPD... multiple personality disorder. When you were recovering in hospital, I called some of the shrinks that looked after him. Apparently, Harvey would talk about himself in three parts. Everything he did was split into three different personalities... three separate traits that when put together were capable of doing what he did. He acted like a slave to these personas, as if they led him blindly through all the abuse he suffered when he was young.'

'What about the photo of them together?' Duke's frustration had begun to steam up the windows. 'He had a photograph of himself as a child with Farrow... they have a connection.'

'Along with several hundred other children that passed through those doors. For all we know, Harvey got lucky when he took Elizabeth: her link to Farrow gave him the perfect scapegoat, whether intended or otherwise.'

'Did we ever check out any of the other children from the home? You said that when you visited the site, where the abuse was likely to have taken place – in the basement, was it? – there were several names on the wall. Do you remember?'

Addison dug his notebook from his back pocket. It took him a few seconds to trace the date back.

'Here it is.' He took a second to read his own scribbled writing. 'Yeah, you're right. Checking the historic complaints against the care home, it seemed that the children were abused in the cellar. Piper and I think we found the cellar, though it gave her the creeps so I went in alone. On the wall, a few names had been scratched into the brick... Francis, William, Quentin, Jacob, Benjamin. I made a note here saying that the names William and Jacob had a line dug through them.'

'And?' Duke opened his palms up and shrugged.

'And what?'

'And... was there any work done around these names?'

'Duke, I didn't want to tell you this at the time... but I've found no record of a Jacob or a William at the care home. It's likely these are the two people that Harvey referred to during his therapy sessions. Maybe he scratched them out himself... because they weren't real? One therapist said that Harvey would talk about them, and how they died. He said they'd been stolen from them. That the people running the place had taken them away, and they never returned.'

'Christ.' Duke threw his head back. 'And what about the other name... Francis?'

'I have a registration date, but little else. Every chance it's the little guy in the photo with Farrow and Harvey. Some reports say they were friends but not entirely friendly. If anything, Francis was closer to Farrow than Harvey. The name appears more in Farrow's files than Quentin Harvey's. Apart from that photo... the kid... Quentin... was on his own.'

'Well, that's that then.' Duke's shoulders dipped. He slumped into his seat. 'Take me back to the office. I still need to make a couple of calls.'

He turned the volume up on the radio, before looking out of the window.

The message was clear. Duke had heard enough.

Chapter 53

His meeting with Russel Alderman had been as productive as it was uncomfortable. Hopefully it would be the last time he'd ever have to deal with the greaseball solicitor. Naturally, the man who overindulged in every aspect of his self-centred, slimy existence, had the audacity to claim some form of credit for the police investigation into Quentin Harvey.

The revelations of the case had been a godsend for Benjamin Farrow's review. The evidence that was never there was now in plain sight. Evidence that pointed directly to another man, a man witnessed by police to have constructed a twisted scene with the bodies of several abducted children, a man who had confessed to the police before dying in front of them. A man that Benjamin had known but hadn't seen for some time.

Association alone was not strong enough to keep Benjamin in the frame. The case would have had to be airtight against him to keep Russell Alderman from screaming for his client's release.

By all accounts, he was soon to be a free man. And, if Alderman & Co were granted license to exploit the injustice suffered, Benjamin Farrow was to become a very wealthy man as well.

But the thought of fresh air was enough for now. The freedom to walk for as long as his legs could carry him was worth more than any financial settlement. There was no compensation for time. It was the one thing that you could spend, but never buy. And Benjamin Farrow would never have sold the time he had lost to the Elizabeth Silver case. Not for all the wealth in the world.

All he dreamed of was heading to a place where nobody knew who he was, where his face was not known, where his name was not tied to that of a murdered child. Her face would never leave his mind. She would still be able to creep into his dreams and steal the peace that sleep promised. He knew her memory would never let him rest. He would never forget that face. All he wanted was for people not to see it when they saw him.

His meeting with the prison psychiatrist was a more relaxed affair than any of his previous meetings. Monica Dawkins had crossed both an ethical and a professional line, possibly even criminal, when she first had sex with Benjamin. It was a line that they had crossed so often that the boundaries were smudged into nothing but a blur. What was clear, to one of them at least, was that this was to be the last time that they met.

'I can't say how happy I am for you.' She held onto the tips of his fingers as he turned for the door. She was in a worse state of undress than him, with her blouse missing a button, revealing the floral bra she had only just put back on. She had worn hold-ups on purpose, having seen his eyes focus on them during one of their first meetings. She tugged at his fingers, hoping he'd turn around for one last kiss. His blond hair had been cut short, making him look older, manlier. He was no longer the broken boy in an adult shell that she had first examined. There was a strength in him, a stability that came from a life that was on a firm footing. There was no uncertainty left. He was the good man she had hoped he was. The good man that she had stopped herself from loving every time that they had met.

'We can't see each other again.' Benjamin's voice was fired towards the back of the door. 'Thank you for all that you've done for me. You'll never know how valuable you are to me.'

His fingers left hers as he left the room. Sinking into her expensive leather chair, she cancelled her remaining appointments and reached for the bottle of wine she had hidden under her desk. She didn't surface for the rest of the day, before signing herself off for the week.

The next week had moved at a speed that he hadn't been used to for some time. As if set to fast-forward, his days, filled with various messages from his solicitors and orders from the guards, had gathered at a pace that only suggested one thing… the end was near. Like the last few days of summer, or the final moments of a holiday, days passed quicker when there were few left to buffer your time spent in that one place.

His meeting with the prison warden had been a brief, polite, but cold process. There were no apologies, no emotion, just information surrounding his imminent release. Benjamin could count on one hand the amount of times he had seen the warden, and he had no intentions of the amount ever breaking onto his second. Tall, weathered but polished like a long-serving military boot, the warden's advice was nothing more than a generic offering, heard by countless children from near enough everyone in their lives.

'Stay out of trouble.'

A handshake was neither offered nor expected.

But Benjamin's exit from the office was enjoyed by all.

As he was led back to his cell, for what was to be his last night in earth's very own anus, Benjamin saw his surroundings in a different light. The violence that orbited his world had never come crashing in, no matter how many times Jenkins and his crew threatened to boil over. They'd attacked him often, but they had never beaten him. And now, they never would. Since their leader had been silenced, their threat did little more than simmer in the background, culminating in nothing more than bitter glances, not unlike a spurned ex-partner, who hates you as much as they're obsessed with you. Their hatred of him was addictive. It gave them meaning: a purpose, a reason to ignore the animals that they were and only see the cage they shared as being too small for them both to occupy. Well, they'd have room for one more after tonight. Finally, Benjamin was to be set free.

All he had left to do was say goodbye to the one man who had stood by him the whole time.

Seth was sat on the edge of his bed, his knees jittering as he bounced gently on the balls of his feet. The sleeves of his sweater were pulled up over his hands, as he rested his sunken chin on them. The man looked sad, lost. Whatever dark place his mind had dragged him to, Benjamin's entrance snapped him back into the room.

'Is this a good time?' Benjamin pretended to knock at the open door. Seeing his friend nod and usher him inside with a whip of his hand, Benjamin checked the corridor before closing the door behind him.

The noise from outside was replaced by a thick silence that hummed from wall to wall.

'Are you okay?' Benjamin stood over Seth, whose eyes remained fixed to the floor. 'Aren't you happy for me?'

'I heard the news.' Seth's voice was muffled by his sleeve. 'As long as it's what you deserve.'

'What!' Benjamin spat the words out as if they'd cause him to vomit if he'd swallowed them.

'Well…' Seth continued to bounce as he spoke. 'It just seems to me that you're more gleeful than angry. I'd have thought, if I'd been caged for something that I didn't do, I'd be more angry than happy.'

'Anger can only get you so far.'

'It got me here.' Seth's voice rattled behind his broken teeth.

'And is this what you deserve?' Benjamin didn't mean to sound sarcastic, but his friend's attitude was beginning to piss him off.

'I'll get that soon enough. All I require is an ending. Hopefully, one I deserve. Things are better that way. If left unpunished, guilt only hurts those touched by it. It haunts the innocent alone.'

'Let me tell you something about hurt... about guilt... and what people deserve.' Benjamin's throat sounded full, strained by pain. 'My mother was raped when she was fourteen years old. Did she deserve that? They don't know who by, he didn't leave any evidence. Just me. My mother was too young, too broken to take care of me, and she was made to feel guilty, to feel dirty and wrong for giving me up. She hadn't planned to become pregnant. They say she wanted to be a teacher... to help people. Did she deserve to have that taken from her? For some reason, everybody she knew felt that she did. They all felt that she had in some way asked for it, that she must have encouraged her attacker somehow. But nobody would ask for that. All that she asked was for at least one life not to be ruined by what had happened. They say she left a note when she killed herself. It was the same note that she'd left in my pocket when she dropped me off at the care home. Did I deserve that? For years, I hated her. What she did to me made me angry. It made me feel like I wasn't enough to save her. But when "they" started to visit me at night, when they made us do things to them... that's when I realised. She was trying to save me. Beasts existed. They prey on the vulnerable and the weak. My mother was trying to hide me from the monsters, not feed me to them. There's no way she would have known, and, in some way, I'm glad she never lived to learn it. Say what you want about my mother giving me up, at least she was willing to have me in the first place. Not like anyone else. At least she tried to keep me safe. So, when they started to do the things they did to me... did she deserve that? Did my mother's memory deserve that?'

'They say you knew him...' Seth's voice remained cold. 'The one whose time you've been serving.'

'I did.' Benjamin appeared puzzled.

'The man who died in the fire. Was he a friend of yours?'

'He was. A good friend in fact.' Benjamin's eyes glazed over, as if washed by a distant memory. 'It's no surprise that I served his time... we suffered the same fate. His name was Quentin Harvey. He knew me as Benjamin Randal. Not that they used our names when they called for us.'

'They?'

'The men that abused us.' Benjamin's eyes remained focused on the past. 'They used codenames... I seem to remember Quentin's was Magpie, on account of him being quite good at stealing things. They called another good friend of mine Sunshine.'

'And yours?' Seth wanted to keep him where he was. Often the truth was trapped in the past.

'Moonlight,' he sighed. 'They called me Moonlight. They told me I had that name because whenever I saw it... the light of the moon... that's when they would be coming for me. Every night I'd lay awake, twitching at every sound, flinching from every shadow that shifted. Did I deserve that?'

'No,' Seth whispered. 'No child deserves that.'

'Apparently, we did. That's how they made us feel, as if we had caused the pain because we were the only ones feeling it. The men... they took great delight in doing what they did to us. Some of us spoke up... but then they disappeared. Huge fires always took place outside immediately after you saw them last, and just before you never saw them again. Often, we could smell the flesh cooking, the stench of hair burning. They said they were preparing breakfast, but we were never served a hot meal. Sometimes, I wish they had killed me. Instead, they obliterated my childhood, they wiped it out completely. That's what bonded us.'

'You and him? The man from the fire... Quentin?'

'Yes... and others. All of us had our childhoods taken away. Innocence was removed and replaced only with the realisation that fear was justified. There were monsters beneath the bed. The shadows did move, each holding within them creatures that would crush your soul. We lost our youth and almost our minds. One night, they started their final fire. They chained us to the walls of the cellar and left us to die. But we managed to escape. It was this trauma that kept us together, uniting us in a bond stronger than anything else. We were separate souls stapled together through a shared agony and torment. We used the pain to patch what was left of us back up, to cover the cracks in our minds. Looking back, I'd say the cracks were far wider, and deeper, than we could have ever imagined. With our lives in shreds, parts of our stories became entwined, stitched so tightly that the bond became unbreakable, locking the agony inside. We all changed that day. We may not have died, but what was born from the fire was something many would say deserved killing. We began to share darkened dreams, plans of escape and revenge. Pain was as much our poison as it was our lifeblood. It made us hate those that were gifted all the things that life had denied us. We grew to despise those who had what we all deserved. That's why we took Elizabeth. She wasn't the first, but she was the start of a game we created.'

'What did you say?' Seth's heart landed on his tongue.

'Elizabeth... she had it all. She had a future that all of us were promised, but not all of us received. But we knew it would let her down. Childhood was our true face. Once we are older, we all wear masks to protect us from reality. Life is torture, savoured only by the few who tread everyone else into the dirt. Dreams are squashed, memories embittered by the incessant trudge towards a lonely grave. All of us look behind us, be it for the brighter times, or to simply check that the monsters of our past are out of sight.'

'She had a family.' Seth's words vibrated from the shock he was feeling.

'Fuck them,' Benjamin snarled, almost imploring his friend to believe him. 'They didn't know her. She only served to remind them of the time they had lost, the time that all adults have lost. She distracted them from the horror of growing old. She was a blood transfusion, a shot in the arm, a fleeting remedy that they would one day outgrow and discard. They used her. The families that took these children, they all used them. So, we took them back.'

'For what purpose? For what use?'

'To save them... to preserve them. We'd freeze them in a time when all remained in front, and nothing lurked behind. They were free.' A smile creased the corners of his face. 'We all wear masks, and so should you. I have many; most of them made for survival. I didn't expect to be caught so soon when we took Elizabeth from her home, but at least the plan was set. I'm not sure why Quentin took so long to take the next one, but you must admit, his timing was perfect. He didn't see how I killed Elizabeth, the way I slid the stiletto blade under her jaw as I choked her with my spare hand. But I did educate him... although from what I hear he just throttled the rest with his huge hands. At least I was more delicate, more considerate. I was gentle when I let Elizabeth reveal herself to me. She was beautiful. For some reason, Quentin couldn't watch her die, but he really missed out. Sadly, now he'll miss out on all the rest. My friend's sacrifice has allowed me to wear the mask of an innocent man, I believe I deserve that. Although, I think I'll let the dust settle before I restart our game.'

Seth had sat still as Benjamin spoke. But now that the room was met by silence, Seth began to stir. Now he was standing, much straighter than Benjamin had ever seen him stand, his posture held more purpose than design. His voice, though split by his cut tongue, carried a clarity that Benjamin had not heard from his friend before.

'It is strange that you talk of masks,' said Seth. 'You say that you now wear one of an innocent man, but to me, that suggests that beneath it all you know that you are truly guilty. Masks are not the man beneath them. Often our true faces are tailored by what manifests from within. Our true face can be contorted by the vile bile that pulses through our veins. But not always. Sometimes, we must wear what lies beneath the surface to show it exists. Sometimes, the pain is hidden, lurking underneath the ordinary. Constant cries of torment, shrill voices that haunt the mind, reside deep beneath the skin. These screams split your mind into tiny pieces, but always fail to rip through the flesh. The surface can suggest calm, defying the tireless tides that rage beneath. So, what lies beneath *must* be revealed. All of this...' Seth pointed to his broken features: his blind eye; the smashed teeth; the scar that cut through his face and broke his lips into four lumps of folded flesh, 'I did all this to myself. This was my mask.'

Benjamin began to back away. His back met with the closed cell door. Seth's voice remained steady.

'My torment was hidden. And although my face was associated with tragedy, it never truly represented what I felt. Ironically, aligning my appearance to my anguish provided me a degree of anonymity. But I craved this, I no longer needed those around me to know who I was... or what I was about to do. My invisibility would protect those who sat beside me within the frames of our family portraits. Some would get the distance they deserved from the actions I would have to take. Others, they would get the answers they craved.'

He stepped closer.

'What are you talking about?'

'It was quite apt that they called you Moonlight. You see, it was the darkness that stole my shadow. The one thing that was always with me, stitched tightly to my side, forever reminding me that sunlight surrounded us both, that was stolen from me. I lost myself when I lost my shadow. The man I was before was gone. So, I needed to be someone else. I called myself Seth, it was a cover beneath which I could cloak all of my sins to come. Many of them mortal, one of them deadly. My wrath is wrapped by revenge. Unlike you, I'll serve my sentence gladly. I'll get what I deserve. And, so will she.'

Seth slid the sharpened shank from under his sleeve and punched it into Benjamin's side. Blood poured from the wound, cloaking his hand completely.

'Like I said,' Seth pulled Benjamin in close enough that his words burned his ear. 'I called myself Seth. But my wife called me Steven... and Elizabeth Silver... she called me Dad.'

That was when the blade struck the side of Benjamin's neck. The blood continued to decorate Seth's shaking hand as the life left Benjamin's eyes. The mask slipped. Shock changed to anger, and then quickly to sadness and torment.

The last look he gave, the one that revealed the true man inside, was one of complete fear.

Chapter 54

Her voice was gentle.

'It's done. We were right.'

She hung up the phone.

He didn't say anything.

The sense of relief was nothing compared to the sense of regret. Regret that such drastic means had to be taken to achieve the truth.

Beverly Silver had already lost a daughter, and now her husband's fate was also sealed. Duke hadn't been keen on the plan from the start, but when the doubts surrounding Benjamin Farrow's guilt began to creep in, he knew that he needed to act, he needed to know – if only for a moment – that they had achieved justice for Elizabeth. Duke knew that one day his condition would take a hold on him, he knew it would wipe his mind like a scratched record, removing key parts, and breaking up the sequence so that it never played out the way it was meant to. Recent memories would be misted over, there'd be no clarity to his thoughts, no room for persuasion, just thoughts fixed in time, locked within a mind slowly closing in on itself.

That's why he needed to know. He already believed it, but in this case the truth served him better. Belief always required hope and faith, two things he had lost some time ago. But the truth was fixed, and he was desperate to lock that in. The truth bought his mind a sense of peace. Belief, like his mind, could be lost. But the truth, now known to all, would never be forgotten or challenged again.

Part of him felt guilty. The thought of whether he could have done anything differently the first time around tortured him. Maybe, if he had found something concrete, a piece of evidence that was beyond any doubt, then the Silvers would not have had to pull their world apart in a bid to get the truth.

Beverly assured Duke that Steven had died the day Elizabeth was taken, that the man she knew had disappeared with their daughter, leaving just a shell behind. It was Steven who had come up with the plan. He wanted Duke to find a series of unsolved crimes, none that had a victim in need of closure, but various thefts and break-ins that had been filed pending any new evidence. Once found, all that was left to do was for Steven to be caught committing a similar crime. With the help of his old combat knife, a bottle of acid and enough rum to put the navy to sleep, Steven had already taken care of his transformation. All that was left to do was catch Steven... now Seth... in the act.

Steven's DNA was never on record, so the custody suite accepted the identity he provided. Followed by a few falsified address checks, and Seth now had a criminal record. Armed with the crime details of the previous thefts, Seth confessed to all during interview. It was only a short period on remand before he was sentenced to two months in prison. Once inside, Seth had to escalate his behaviour until he was considered too dangerous for release. By the time he shared the same cell-space as Benjamin Farrow, Seth was one of the most feared men on the inside.

The Tasking Team office was awash with mixed emotion. Excitement shared the same space as sympathy. Duke hadn't had to tell his crew that Benjamin Farrow had been killed, the bastard's face filled half of every news bulletin on the TV. All that Duke's team knew was that the man had been murdered, seemingly killed in a frenzied attack by a fellow cellmate. What the press didn't know was that his killer, having completed the act, had walked directly to the warden's office and confessed to his crime – although he refused to offer any motive. Duke and Seth had agreed that only they and Beverly would know the truth. It was the best way of protecting Beverly from the plot.

'Can you fucking believe all this?'

Geoff Talbot was already on his third black coffee of the morning. His wide eyes were fighting against his furrowed brow.

'I just pray for all the lost souls. So much pain in the world today.' Maggie McAndrew was pawing at some well-worn rosary beads. She held her hand out for Geoff to take, but he looked at it as if she had offered him up a plate of week-old roadkill.

At the sight of Duke entering the room, Darren Hoggit ran nervously to prop open the already open door.

'Hi Duke, can I get you anything... tea, coffee... something from the café maybe?'

'Get your nose out of my arse, Hoggit. There aren't any secrets buried up there.' Duke was forced to brush past the man who was half blocking the doorway. 'Anyway, we already know you've been titillating some local widower with your war stories, so I'm afraid you'll have to find some other way of lubricating those old joints for your nightly knee-trembler. Maybe offer her some of that whiskey you seemed to have cleaned your teeth with this morning.'

Geoff laughed loudly as Hoggit melted into the background.

'Where's young Addison?' Duke looked around the small office. 'This was meant to be that cool part that you see in the movies where the top cop insults the audience's intelligence by summarising the whole case near the end of the film. I can't do it without my little ride-along, he's the most confused out of the lot of you.'

Right on cue, Addison entered the room. He was holding a bunch of papers in his hand.

'What's all that? It better be important, you're kind of spoiling my moment here.' Duke opened his arms wide with an exaggerated shrug.

'Trust me... it is.' Addison walked into Duke's office. There was only room for two people in the room, and Duke got the message. He followed Addison inside and closed the door.

'Are you all right?' Duke spoke first.

'Are you?' Addison fixed his stare on Duke. He paused, letting the question hang for a second, allowing it to gain weight and pressure.

'What have you got there?' Duke nodded to the papers now perched on the side of his table.

'This could be big...' Addison handed the documents to Duke. 'Remember Norris Draper?'

'Of course, he's the dead guy who used to run Precious Moments with the equally dead Mitchell Mason.' Duke spoke with little emotion for the men.

'How's the investigation into their deaths looking?' Addison rocked on his feet from toes to heel.

'Last I heard, Draper's was put down to unsuspicious circumstances, although the fact Mason was murdered only a couple of days later did make them reconsider whether any links were to be made. From what DCI Wilson tells me, given the link with Quentin Harvey – with Mason being force-fed the same photo that Harvey used to create the setting for his depraved display – they're looking to close the case off with Harvey being considered the culprit. There's nothing else out there to suggest otherwise.'

'Maybe not...' Addison nodded to the papers in Duke's hands. 'What you're holding there is part of Norris Draper's last Will and Testament. It seems that, in the event of his death, he had instructed his solicitors to send those documents to the police. They initially landed at his former care home, who called me directly. Given that we were the last officers to visit him, they thought it was something for us.'

'And?' It was clear Duke wanted to hear the highlights rather than read the whole thing.

'In that document, Norris Draper not only admits to his involvement in the child abuse that took place at Precious Moments, he also incriminates Mitchell Mason, and offers an entire list of every man who used their "*services*". Most of them are dead... but those that are alive climbed quite high on the public ladder.'

'Well, it would appear they're set for quite the fall.' Duke folded the documents. 'We need to take this to DCI Wilson. This is her investigation.'

'No problem, let me just run the rest of my checks before we do. I need to check that they don't cross over into the Elizabeth Silver case. The guys on this list are powerful, and I'm sure their tentacles could reach into the courtroom if they needed to. I just want to make sure they had nothing to do with Benjamin Farrow's conviction. So, I'd rather spot any outside influence first before leaving it to another department to discover. At least then, we'll know what type of fight we're in before the first punch lands. You can't counter what you can't see coming, and I want to blindside these guys.'

'Do *you* think there's a crossover?' Duke watched his friend. 'Any hint of "outside influence", as you called it?'

'I doubt it. On first impression, these slimeballs sit more in the cause than the symptoms of what Quentin Harvey became. They did the damage, and they certainly didn't highlight it. But I have to make sure that they didn't hold any influence over the investigation on Benjamin Farrow. Just for my peace of mind.'

Duke knew they hadn't. Nobody had. True, mistakes were made... but they were honest ones, ones which caused evidence to be removed from the case rather than it be planted into it. Evidence which Duke now knew pointed to the right man.

Duke and Addison took a walk through the town. Claymore's streets were mostly still during the day, except for the three parts that divided a day's work. The morning commute had already lumbered passed, and the rush home was for many still some five hours away. Right now, the working day was at its hump, and Duke and Addison enjoyed being part of the audience to the activity that came with lunchtime.

Dozens of workers burst from their offices to descend onto the various high-street sandwich stalls and coffee-houses. Even the pubs swelled with fully functioning alcoholics and easily excited office workers looking to sample the daily specials.

But Duke and Addison weren't looking to eat. The fresh air was enough for them. Eventually their strolling feet took them to the top of the mount, to the spot where it had all begun. Addison dragged his finger across the metal map that gave a historic view of the landscape which framed the sunken horizon. His fingertip paused on the scratch that sat where you would have once found Elizabeth Silver, at peace, with her family. He looked out towards the house. It looked like the rest of them, but it didn't feel the same. Not to Addison. All the others were anonymous, the grief they held – if any – was housed within their walls, shielded from the eyes of the outside world. But the Silver residence was an open house when it came to the pain that it had suffered. It was in part a public house, used for many to dine out upon when talking to friends of their previous visits to the house where the infamous girl-ghost once lived. The house was no longer a home. Family made a house a home, not a woman left alone with nothing but loss to keep her company.

'Poor Beverly. I can't imagine what she's going through right now.' Duke broke the silence. He could see where Addison was looking. His finger still sat upon the scratched piece of metal. Duke was sat on the bench. He patted the space to his side as an invite for Addison to join him.

Addison sat down. Both men stared out in front, silent but for the soundtrack of the wind and a scattering of birds that chirped from the nearby woodlands.

'Who's Seth Abbott?' Addison kept his eyes forwards as he spoke.

'Who?' Duke shifted a little in his seat.

'He was the man that killed Benjamin Farrow. Seems to me, he had a reason to do what he did. He must have had some cause, some form of justification. After all, why would he kill an innocent man?'

'Maybe he was jealous that Farrow was escaping.' The wording made Duke feel uneasy. It reminded him of the twisted rationale used by Quentin Harvey when he took the children who had escaped the care system.

'Escaped?' Addison's tone was one of feigned confusion. 'Do innocent men *escape*? The allusive, yes... but not the innocent. This was justice, wasn't it?'

The words hung in the air.

Does Addison know?

'Seth Abbott. I did some digging. Not much of a past really... in fact, he seems to surface just after Elizabeth disappears. You know, when Beverly was left all alone. Then Seth Abbott appears... in all his gory glory. Are you trying to tell me that a guy that fierce wouldn't have come to our attention before? Unless there was a cause, a method to all the madness. And the name... Seth Abbott. It means *Appointed* and *Father* in Hebrew. Strange really, how a man once accused of stealing an adopted child is killed by the *Appointed Father.*'

'Since when did you know Hebrew?'

'Google's a wonderful tool, Duke.'

'Other search engines are available,' he said with a hint of a smile.

'As are names. Even Jewish ones; ones that a Jewish man, maybe a very angry Jewish man, would know the true meaning of. I don't know. Maybe it's just one huge bizarre – if not slightly loose – coincidence. Although, you said it yourself, you don't believe in coincidence, right?'

'I wouldn't know. Do I look like I speak Hebrew? Why would I know how a man gets his name?'

'Because you made it for him. You made the first arrest. It was you that made him a criminal.'

Duke felt the sharp pang of adrenaline in his heart.

Addison could feel his friend's unease.

'Duke,' he looked towards him. 'What are you not telling me?'

Epilogue

The wine had flowed freely all night.

She was glad that he had invited her around. What had started off as a thinly veiled work-related meeting – with Addison asking her to consider helping him expose some historic child abusers – soon turned into an impromptu dinner, countless drinks, and some of the best sex they had ever enjoyed as a couple.

As always, she was happy that he'd called. She was growing to like him more than she had hoped. Initially he was useful, but then he had become rather endearing. She admired his intensity; all the passion he had thrown into this case. But the conclusion of the investigation meant that there was no longer any call for such enthusiasm and focus. His charm was no longer playing second fiddle to his work ethic. His demeanour had relaxed, and she was already finding herself becoming bored by it.

Charm was an act, no matter how many dimensions it had, and that was something she knew only too well.

Checking he was still asleep, she left his naked body entwined with the bedsheets that they had both recently thrashed around in. His flat was only small, so she made sure she caused little noise as she crept into the kitchen. There, she opened her laptop and logged on. The blue light of the screen lit the counter, but wasn't strong enough to reach every corner of the room. She sat for a moment within this electric blue mist, as she waited for all her systems to load up. Closing various windows warning her of suspected malware, she eventually clicked open her homepage and keyed in the first name on the list.

The list of suspects Addison had stupidly showed her had been left out upon the kitchen counter. She'd made sure of that. Once she knew where it was, she covered it with her laptop bag before throwing all of her energy into seducing her man. It was the oldest distraction in the book. And now she had what she needed.

With a single click, the search tool brought back a whole host of possible matches, all linked to countless articles and social media platforms. She decided to start with images.

Streams of profile pictures and published photographs plucked from various news articles filled the screen.

Her eyes began to scan them.

It didn't take long.

She recognised him instantly.

It was a face she had seen within the shadows, a somewhat younger likeness at the time compared to the weathered, well-fatted face that now looked back at her. Nevertheless, it was undeniably him.

She had remembered all of their faces: all of their voices, their smells, the heat of their breath, the feel of their fingers.

She'd buried none of it.

Instead, she had carved them into hulking stones, each of which served to prop up her collapsing mind.

Each stone had a name, under which a list of sins was etched. They would serve as headstones to the graves she was already digging.

No, she hadn't buried any of her pain.

It was them that she planned to bury.

She had already killed the one that they called Mason. She hadn't planned to kill him so soon, but when Addison had made the mistake of tipping her off on where to find Mason, she knew that she had to act quickly.

And now, with only good intent in his heart, Addison had handed her the whole list of sinners.

Packing up her laptop, she got dressed, making sure to fold the list inside of her coat. Addison mentioned that this was the only copy, so she reckoned she had quite a head start on anyone coming after her.

The room was completely dark but for the small sliver of light that crept in as she pulled open the front door just enough for her to slip through. She took care to close it quietly behind her.

It was her last subtle act.

Having recently lost two of her closest childhood friends, she had very little left to lose, and subtlety was no longer required.

She would complete their game.

Addison had known her as Piper, but her abusers had called her Little Miss Sunshine, or just Sunshine for short.

And her true friends, the family that she had forged through their shared torment, her brothers Benjamin and Quentin, they knew who she really was.

They had stood by her throughout her childhood. And they had stood by her within the photograph that she had fed to Mason as she slit his throat.

They were her brothers.

They called her Francis.

She had started it all.

ND - #0255 - 270225 - C0 - 234/156/20 - PB - 9781780915548 - Gloss Lamination